PENNY JORDAN
A
COLLECTION

Penny Jordan Born in Preston, Lancashire, Penny Jordan now lives with her husband in a beautiful fourteenth-century house in rural Cheshire. Hers is a success almost as breathtaking as the exploits of the characters she so skilfully and knowingly portrays. Penny has been writing for over ten years and now has over seventy novels to her name including the phenomenally successful *Power Play* and *Silver*. With over thirty million copies of her books in print and translations into seventeen languages, she has firmly established herself as a leading authoress of extraordinary scope.

CONTENTS:

Shadow Marriage

Man-Hater

Passionate Protection

SHADOW MARRIAGE

BY
PENNY JORDAN

WORLDWIDE BOOKS
LONDON • SYDNEY • TORONTO

First published in Great Britain in 1984
Reprinted in Great Britain in 1992
by Worldwide Books, Eton House,
18-24 Paradise Road, Richmond, Surrey TW9 1SR

© Penny Jordan 1984

ISBN 0 373 58587 X

99-9205

Made and printed in Great Britain

CHAPTER ONE

'SARAH?'

She recognised the voice of her agent immediately, and her fingers tensed on the receiver in response to its jovial tone, hope feathering fingers of tension along her spine.

'Good news,' Carew told her buoyantly, 'and not ad-work this time, before you ask. It's a film part, and a good one. Want to hear more?'

The teasing enquiry reminded her that she was twenty-three and not eighteen, and long past the stage of dry-mouthed excitement over any part.

'It depends,' she responded cautiously. Her voice was warmly husky; extraordinarily sexy, was how one director had once described it, but Sarah had made it clear to Carew before she became one of his clients that she had no intention of accepting parts that emphasised or relied on her sexuality— in any way. And she had stuck to her statement rigidly, even though it had often meant that she had been forced, on more than one occasion, to take other jobs to pay her rent—working in shops and offices, glad of the odd well paid commercial which came her way.

'It's a beaut,' Carew assured her, and although she could not see his face she could picture it well enough, and the jumbled chaos that passed for his office.

'You'll love it,' he continued. 'I'm having the

script sent round to you right away. We've got a meeting with the director tomorrow. Lunch at the Savoy. You're one lucky female, Sarah. The part was as good as cast, and then Guy Holland happened to see that ad you did for the shampoo people. You'll be flattered to know that he rang me at home last night. It's only by chance that he's over here at all. A large part of the filming is going to take place in Spain. He's a stickler for authenticity, and he was only in London overnight, so . . .'

'Carew, tell me more about the film,' Sarah cut in quickly. She knew Guy Holland's reputation— who didn't in the film world?—and there was only one other director that she could think of who possessed an equivalent aura; whose name provoked the same powerful charisma.

'Oh, it's about Richard the First,' Carew told her obligingly, 'and before you ask, it's no mere costume piece. According to Guy the screenplay is one of the best he's ever seen, and it's been written by an amateur, someone who has guarded his identity so closely that no one seems to know exactly who he is. Anyway,' he seemed to collect his thoughts with an effort, as though he realised how tense and impatient she was growing, 'it seems the long and short of it is that Guy wants you to play Joanna—Richard's sister. The part's a gem, Sarah. I've only glanced through the screenplay, but what I've read is enough to convince me that Guy isn't exaggerating when he says he's got half a dozen top actresses going down on their knees for it.'

'But his budget is limited, and so he's got to make do with me,' she cut in drily.

'No way. Like·I told you, Guy is a stickler for accuracy, and according to him your colouring is exactly right for Joanna. The first thing he wanted to know was if your hair was natural.'

Sarah pulled a wry face into the receiver. Her hair was a particularly distinctive red-gold, and she had the pale Celtic skin to go with it—unfashionably pale really, her eyes a deep smoky grey, bordering on lavender whenever her emotions were intensely aroused.

'The second thing he wanted to know was how long it was. It's just as well you didn't agree to have it cut for that ad. Apparently whoever plays Joanna must have long hair.'

Sarah grinned to herself as she listened to him. At the time he had been all for her having her hair cut as the shampoo company had wished, but she had been with Carew long enough to accept that at bottom his clients' interests were paramount.

'Excited?' he questioned.

'I might be—when I've read the part.'

She didn't say any more, but hc interpreted her remark easily.

'It's perfectly all right—there aren't any sex scenes. At least, not for you. I've already checked that out. The script should be with you within the hour. Give me a ring when you've read it, won't you?'

As she replaced the receiver Sarah tried not to give in to the insidious tug of excitement spiralling through her. A film part as juicy as this one promised to be was a gift she had long ago made up her mind she would never receive. For one thing, she liked living and working in London, which was hardly the Mecca of the film world. For another, her insistence on parts without any sexual overtones automatically narrowed her field considerably. She knew quite well that Carew was curious about her rigid refusal, his instinct telling him that there was more to it than a natural disinclination to use her body to further her career. After all, she had joined him straight from her part in the highly acclaimed film of Shakespeare's life in which she had played the wanton Mistress Mary Fitton of Gawsworth— Shakespeare's 'Dark Lady'.

For that part she had received rave reviews. She had put her heart and soul into it, immersing herself completely in it, so much so that afterwards she had wondered if she hadn't been infected with some of Mary's wantonness herself. Certainly that would explain why she had . . .

The heavy clatter of something falling through her letter box dragged her thoughts away from the past, and she hurried into the small hall, picking up the heavy package, and retreating with it to the comfort of her sitting room.

Her flat might only be small, but Sarah had an inborn flair for colour and tranquillity—something she had inherited from her parents, no doubt. Her father had been an acclaimed interior designer, and her mother his assistant. The one shred of comfort she had been able to salvage from the destruction of her life after they had been killed in a plane crash had been that they had gone together.

She had only just entered drama school when it happened; a late entrant, having decided at the last minute not to go on to university, but to try her hand as an actress instead.

She had only been nineteen when she was offered the part of Mary Fitton. Shakespeare had been played by Dale Hammond, an actor whose star was very much in the ascendant. Unlike her, Dale had gone on to international fame, and a smile plucked at Sarah's lips as she remembered several instances of his Puckish sense of humour. They had got on well together, so well that she had found no embarrassment in their intensely emotional and sensual scenes together, unlike those she had had to play with Benedict de l'Isle, the actor who was playing the Earl of Southampton, her other lover, and reputedly Shakespeare's as well!

As she unwrapped the package, she shivered, suddenly cold, unwilling to remember the desire that had flamed between the two of them; a desire which had left its mark on the film, highlighting the emotional drama they played out as Southampton and Mary Fitton. Dale had been her friend, and in consequence of their friendship she had been able to relax while they played their love scenes, but with Benedict there had been no relaxation possible. And that was why . . .

The script slipped from her fingers, landing on the polished wooden floor with a thud, bringing her sharply back from the past. Schooling her thoughts, Sarah bent and picked it up, flicking through the opening pages and then going back to read them more slowly as the typed words enthralled her imagination.

Two hours later, when she put aside the final page, her thoughts were still coloured by all that

she had read. For that brief span of time she had
been living in the twelfth century, totally absorbed
by the lives of the characters she had been reading
about; Richard, third son of Henry II and his
estranged wife Eleanor of Aquitaine; adored by his
mother and hated by his father. Richard, who
would one day be king. Sarah shivered in sudden
reaction, trying to visualise the man who had
written so sensitively and deeply about a man who,
she realised for the first time, had been an
intensely tortured individual, torn between duty
and desire, unable to fulfil one without destroying
the other. She didn't have enough knowledge
about the Plantagenet era to know how factual or
otherwise the script was, but she remembered
enough to sense that it had been carefully
researched, and that in depicting Richard as a man
tormented by his intense love for another knight,
the writer had leaned towards the truth rather than
inventing the relationship simply for effect. Having
read the script, it was dizzyingly heady to know
that Guy Holland wanted her for Joanna. The part
wasn't a large one, but then none of the female
parts were. The only other ones of any magnitude
were Eleanor, Richard's mother, and Berengaria,
his wife.

Unlike earlier thirties films about Richard, this
one was not concerned primarily with the Third
Crusade, which she was surprised to see had
occupied a relatively short span of Richard's life.
What did amaze her was the discovery that he had
first gone to war as a teenager, defying, and
eventually defeating, his father. But it was her part
as Joanna she must concentrate on. She had three

major scenes—the first when Richard accompanied her through Spain on her way to her first husband, the aged William of Sicily, a man who was fifty to her seventeen; the second when Richard came to Sicily with his army en route for the Crusade and rescued her from her unscrupulous brother-in-law, Tancred, following the death of William, and the third when she renounced the man she loved—one of Richard's knights—before agreeing to marry Raymond of Toulouse, her second husband.

Carew hadn't exaggerated when he described the part as 'meaty', and Sarah hurried to the phone, quickly dialling his number.

Heather, his assistant, recognised her voice straightaway and put her through.

'Umm, that voice—it's like being drowned in melted honey!' Carew told her extravagantly. 'Guy will find it a bonus he hadn't expected. Well, you've read it, I take it? What do you think?'

'You know what I think,' Sarah managed in a husky whisper. 'Oh, Carew . . .'

Stupidly tears filled her eyes and she had to shake them away. She had fought so hard to tell herself that it didn't matter that her career had never been the success she had wanted, that she had hardly dared to let herself hope that she might get a part like this. Now she no longer doubted that Guy Holland hadn't been boasting when he claimed that half a dozen Hollywood greats were clamouring for it, and she could only bless the perverseness that made him such a stickler for detail that he wanted a genuine long-haired redhead for his Joanna.

'Well, don't forget there's still tomorrow,'

Carew cautioned her, quickly soothing her leaping fears by adding, 'Not that you've anything to worry about. Once Guy sees you . . .'

'Who's playing Richard?' Sara wanted to know.

'An old friend of yours.' He paused expectantly, and Sarah felt her blood run cold. 'Dale Hammond,' Carew told her, obviously disappointed by her lack of response. 'Apparently Guy has certain reservations about him, but his colouring is right, and there's no denying that he has the experience for the part. Guy is very anxious that Richard should be played sympathetically, and yet remain very much the male animal.'

The part would be extremely challenging and taxing, Sarah could see that, and in her mind's eye she collated Dale's roles since his *Shakespeare*. He had the experience for the role, he also had the slightly malicious sense of humour that had come across so well in his *Shakespeare*, and which was evident in some ways in *Richard*, but he would need intense depth and breadth for the role, if he was to be played as she sensed the playwright had intended him to be. As she hung up, promising Carew that she would not forget their lunch date, she frowned thoughtfully, curious about the writer of the film, experiencing something which was almost a comradeship with him, so caught up in the spell of his words that it was almost as though her senses knew him.

She spent the morning in her local library, and emerged with her arms piled high with reference books, with barely an hour to spare before her lunch date.

She dressed quickly; a dove-grey silk dress with undertones of lavender to darken her eyes, leaving her skin free of make-up apart from a slick of colour along her lips, braiding her hair and twisting it into a coronet on top of her head.

The effect was startling, and she smiled a trifle wryly at her haunting reflection. Guy Holland was no fool. He would realise instantly that she was trying to portray his 'Joanna'. Whether she had succeeded or not she had yet to discover.

She arrived exactly on the dot of one and was shown to a secluded table in the cocktail bar. Carew's eyes widened as he saw her and he struggled to his feet, a small, rotund man, with a shock of untidy fair hair and owlish brown eyes. His companion uncoiled himself from his chair far more elegantly, one lean, tanned hand extended to grip hers, his eyes coolly appreciative as they studied her, and was studied in return.

His first question wasn't what she had expected at all. His glance lingered on her hand as his own was withdrawn, and she had to fight against a deeply instinctive desire to wrench off the plain gold ring adorning her left hand.

'You're married?'

'I ... I'm divorced,' she managed curtly, frowning as Carew rushed into what she considered to be unnecessary explanations. 'Sarah was married briefly to Benedict de l'Isle.'

'Really?' Darkly silvered eyebrows rose speculatively. 'I know Ben quite well. I hadn't realised he'd been married.'

'I'm sure he wants to forget it as much as I do,' Sarah told him, glaring at Carew. What on earth had he said anything for? He knew she abhorred all mention of her brief and all too disastrous marriage to Benedict de l'Isle. A marriage that had been over almost before it had begun. A marriage entered into through ignorance and folly on her part and reluctance and guilt on Benedict's. How much reluctance she had discovered on the night of their wedding. Thank God Dale had been there to help her. Without him . . .

'You've read the script. What do you think of it?' Guy asked her, resuming his seat.

'It's marvellous.' Her eyes glowed with conviction. 'The whole thing's so powerfully compulsive that I feel I almost know the writer. He makes you feel what's written; experience Richard's anguish, and understand all that he must endure. I . . .' She broke off, feeling flustered as she realised Guy was watching her speculatively. 'I'm sorry,' she apologised awkwardly. 'You must be used to this reaction by now.'

'I'm certainly used to hearing the script praised,' he agreed, 'but you're the first person I've come across to mention the actual writer with such emotion. Normally any emotion is reserved for the box office receipts, or star prestige,' he added with dry cynicism. 'You feel you could handle the part?' He watched her carefully as he spoke, and Sarah sensed that his question was in some way a test.

'I hope so. Joanna grows from a child to a woman during the course of the film. She falls in love with Richard's squire as a child, but gives herself to him as a woman, knowing the price she must pay for her love is marriage to Raymond of Toulouse.'

'I hear you flatly refuse to play any heavy sex scenes,' Guy intervened, suddenly changing the subject. 'Why?'

Sarah shrugged, her palms damp, fear cramping through her although she fought to control it. 'Perhaps because I feel true sensuality is more effective for being implied than actually witnessed.'

'Umm. I suspect the two actors who are to play Richard and his lover heartily feel the same thing. Unfortunately, as far as they are concerned the script calls for some decidedly physical scenes.'

'Oh, but in the context of the script they're . . .' She broke off, flushed and confused, as Guy Holland turned to her.

'Go on,' he prompted, 'they're what?'

'Almost hauntingly emotional,' she responded hesitantly, unable to find the words to convey the terrible sadness that had gripped her when she read the script.

'Let's just hope the censors see it that way,' Guy told her with another flash of dry humour.

They were shown into the restaurant and were halfway through their meal before he put Sarah out of her misery and confirmed that she had got the part.

'You won't be an entirely popular choice,' he warned her, 'but as far as I'm concerned, you're the right one.' He went on to discuss other members of the cast. Berengaria was to be played by a well known film star whose smoulderingly sensual nature was at such odds with Berengaria's naïve innocence that Sarah could only hope that she was an excellent actress.

'She wasn't my choice,' Guy told her, startling her by reading her thoughts, 'but let's just say she comes with the script, and I wanted it badly enough to agree.'

Sarah caught her breath. Did that mean that Gina Frey knew who had written the screenplay and was romantically involved with him?

It was a question she sensed would not be answered even if she asked, so instead she opened a discussion about filming sequence and dates and discovered that most of the filming was to be done in Spain, where there were enough castles, desert and empty spaces for them to be able to recreate the feel of the twelfth century.

After lunch they returned to Carew's office to finalise details and sign contracts, promising that she would be in Spain for the end of the month.

'After all,' she commented to Carew when Guy had gone, 'what's to stop me?'

'You'd better go out and buy yourself a ton of sunscreen,' Carew warned her. 'Guy won't be too happy if your skin gets burned, and you'll be filming all through the summer. I wonder why he wanted to know about your marriage?' he added, eyeing her thoughtfully. Although he was basically a kind-hearted man, on occasions it irked him that Sarah was so resolute about not discussing her brief marriage. After all, Benedict de l'Isle was of sufficient importance in the film world for his name to carry weight; Sarah could have used it. When she had first come to him he had read up on her press-cuttings, and it had been from them and not from her that he had learned of their affair while they were playing opposite one another in *Shakespeare*; she as Mary Fitton and he as Southampton, the man who ultimately destroyed her. They had been married at the end of the filming; there had been a party for all the cast, and then, within a week, it was all over. To quote Benedict de l'Isle, as many of the papers had done with evident glee, his new wife, like Mistress Fitton, had been unable to choose between her two lovers and in the end had chosen wrongly. He eyed Sarah obliquely. If de l'Isle had been speaking the truth, did that mean that she and Dale had been lovers, and if so . . .

Anxious to get back to her library books and her research, Sarah was oblivious to his thoughts. This part was a gift from the gods in more senses than one. Another twelve months without a decent part and who knows, she might have been on the verge of abandoning her career. But she *had* got the part, and she fully intended to leave her stamp on it; to *be* the Princess Joanna, spoiled darling of the greatest house in Christendom until the woman accepted what the child could not; that princesses were but pawns, bought and sold to bind allegiances.

CHAPTER TWO

THERE would be a car waiting for her at the airport, Guy had promised, and Sarah looked dazedly for it as she emerged from the terminal building, and into the slumbrous heat of the Spanish night.

Because it was the height of the tourist season, she had had some problems getting a flight and, in the end, had had to fly in on a late evening one. She was a relative newcomer to the cast, and she knew from what Guy had told her that some studio filming had already taken place, mainly the earlier scenes involving Richard as a youth and some of his clashes with his father. Telling herself that it was only natural that she should feel nervous, she searched the row of stationary cars, wondering which one was waiting for *her*.

'Sarah! Sweetling!'

Even if she hadn't recognised the tall, broad-shouldered man striding towards her, she would have recognised the endearment he had picked up when they filmed *Shakespeare*, and his name left her lips on a pleased cry as she hurried towards him.

'Dale, put me down!' she protested as he swung her up into his arms, kissing her theatrically, adding with a grin, 'I'm honoured, aren't I, dear brother? Being collected by my liege lord himself, and the most prominent member of the cast.'

'And I haven't come alone,' Dale told her,

18

moving slightly aside so that Sarah could see the man standing behind him. Tall with brown hair, he smiled warmly at her, his brown eyes faintly amused by Dale's obvious 'play-acting'. 'Meet your lover-to-be,' Dale told her, adding, 'Paul, come over here and be introduced to Sarah.'

As they shook hands, Sarah found herself warming to Paul with a sense of relief, here was no Ben to disturb her hardwon peace of mind; less exuberant than Dale, there was nevertheless something very attractive and reassuring about him. Within seconds they were chatting away almost like old friends, and it wasn't until she saw Dale frowning that Sarah felt a tiny shiver of apprehension dance along her skin. 'Dale, is something wrong?' she asked hesitantly. It wasn't exactly unheard-of for petty quarrels and jealousies to develop in the tightly knit community involved in the making of any film, but the Dale she remembered had always been able to smile and shrug off these small unpleasantnesses. And yet, old friends though they were, it was practically unheard-of for a principal member of the cast to come and pick up a rather minor one. It was almost as though Dale had taken the opportunity to do so quite deliberately. Paul, too, looked rather grave, and as Sarah glanced from one face to the other, Paul suggested tactfully, 'I'll put the luggage in the car.'

'I came to pick you up because I wanted to have a word with you, Sarah,' Dale told her. 'Well, more to warn you really . . .'

'Warn me?' Sarah could feel tension coiling along her spine.

'Umm, Paul insisted on coming with me, which was rather a nuisance. Judging by the looks he was giving you I shouldn't be at all surprised if he wants to extend your relationship beyond the confines of a working one. What do you think of him?'

Sarah tried not to feel too exasperated. 'We've only just met,' she protested. 'He seems very pleasant, but I'm not in the market for personal relationships—you know that, Dale.'

'Umm, just checking.' But the smile he gave her was understanding and friendly. 'Look, Paul will be back in a second, and I'd better tell you before he comes. We've got a new director . . .' He paused and Sarah felt her heartstrings jerk and tighten indefinably with tension.

'I thought Guy was going to direct, himself?' she protested shakily.

'So he was,' Dale agreed bitterly, 'and if I'd known any different, I wouldn't have taken the damned part, but it seems something went wrong on his last film, and he's having to re-shoot several scenes. The backers demanded it, and because everything was set up here, and any delay now would mean waiting until next summer, we've got ourselves a new director.' He glanced at her as Paul closed the car boot and started walking towards them.

'It's Ben, Sarah,' he told her quickly, his hand going to her arm as he saw her sway slightly. 'Look, I know what a shock this must be to you, that's why I wanted to be the first to tell you. Knowing that bastard, he'd just let you walk right into him without any preparation at all. You must have done quite well out of him when the divorce went through.' He gave her an oblique look. 'I mean, by that time he'd have been working in America; he went there right after *Shakespeare* finished, didn't he?'

Sarah made no response—she wasn't capable of doing so. Ben directing *Richard*—she couldn't believe it! She didn't want to believe it. Paul came to join them, and if he found anything strange in her pale face and strained features, he was too polite to say so, simply opening the front passenger door of the car for her when she reached it, and helping her with her seat-belt, causing Dale to raise an eyebrow and comment that he obviously believed in working himself into the right mood for a part. 'Not that you'll find Sarah a walk-over,' he added, grinning at Sarah encouragingly. 'She knows all about the dangers of getting involved with her leading men, don't you, sweetling?'

Sarah knew that Dale was only teasing her, but she wished he had been a little more reticent when she saw the way Paul looked at her. 'Some of them have caused problems,' she agreed lightly.

'And in case you think she means me, Sarah and I have always had a very special relationship, haven't we?' Dale chipped in.

They had in many ways, and Sarah grinned back at him, trying to banish from her mind the knowledge that soon she was going to come face to face with Ben, Ben whose acting ability in *Shakespeare* had been so greatly acclaimed, but who had gone on to find equal fame in directing and producing. She could vouch personally for his acting ability; she had had first-hand personal experience of it. She smiled rather bitterly to herself. God, how naïve she had been! Dale had been a good friend to her then. If it hadn't been for him she would never have known the truth; never known how cruelly Ben had deceived her. She had thought he loved her as she loved him while all she had really been to him was the fulfilment of a bet. Even now to think about what had happened brought her flesh out in goose-bumps, shivering with distaste and despair. Dale, frantic when he learned that Ben had married her, had told her the truth, wanting to protect her; Ben with whom she was so crazily and deeply in love had married her for no other reason than simply to win a bet. It had started in complete innocence, on Dale's part at least. When the three of them started to film *Shakespeare*, Dale had bet Ben a thousand pounds that he would be the first one to get her into bed, and Ben had accepted the wager. When he had told her of his own part in what had happened Dale had had the grace to be very shamefaced, but he had not known her then; she had just been another very pretty girl and the bet had been made half in jest, but already there had been a certain competitiveness between himself and Ben; Dale being the more acclaimed and well-known actor of the two, and Ben had obviously determined that this time he was going to be the winner.

Sarah had had no idea about the bet between her two fellow actors; no idea of what was intended, and while from the very first she had been wary of Dale's outrageously flirtatious

manner and had kept him at bay, she had had no
defences against her own feelings for Benedict,
falling in love with him almost at first sight,
allowing herself to become so bemused by him and
their roles that she had permitted him to make
love to her, and she had thought when she had
refused to allow him to make their relationship
public that his proposal of marriage stemmed from
his desire and love for her, not realising that he
simply saw it as the only way he could force Dale to
acknowledge that he was the winner of their bet.

Dale had been enjoying a brief break away from
the set when it happened and only returned the
day they were married by special licence, less than
a week after Ben had made love to her. Dale had
got slightly drunk at the post-wedding party given
by the cast, and he had followed up to her hotel
room when she went to get changed, to tell her the
truth. Sarah had still been in tears when they
heard Ben outside the door, and it had been then
that Dale had whispered to her that they would
turn the tables on him, taking her in his arms and
wrenching unfastened the front of her dress so that
Ben had discovered them together locked in what
appeared to be an intensely passionate embrace,
Dale's cool comment that he had after all lost, as
Sarah preferred him, driving Benedict from the
room and ultimately from her life. She could still
vividly remember the climax to their wedding party
when Ben very obviously drunk, had announced to
the assembled cast that she and Dale were lovers.

She thought guiltily about Dale's comment on
their divorce. She always described herself as
'divorced', but the plain facts of the matter were

that she was still, legally at least, married to Ben. They had been married in England, where the law had been and still was that only an uncontested divorce could be obtained after three years. Where both parties were not in agreement the waiting period was five years, and it was still only three and a half years since they had been married. Why Ben refused to give her a divorce she had no idea, unless it was because he feared she might make some sort of financial claim on him. Either that, or he simply wanted to punish her. But she wasn't the guilty party. She had married him because she was deeply in love with him and had believed he felt the same way about her. Their love scenes together had possessed an intensity, a luminosity which had far transcended even the most gifted acting, or so she had believed, and driven half mad by her love for him and the constant exposure to the sensuality imposed on them by their roles, she had abandoned all her dearly held beliefs—and herself—to him.

The screech of the car brakes jerked her back to the present. Dale had always been an aggressive driver and in that regard he didn't seem to have changed.

'I've just been telling Sarah about our new director,' he commented to Paul. 'Unlike me,' he added for Sarah's benefit, 'Paul likes our new director. Of course he isn't the only one. Gina, my sweetly innocent Berengaria, had made her preferences in that quarter very well known. Of course Ben's playing it cool—he can hardly do otherwise since Gina's lover is one of our most influential backers. He's having quite a hard time of it trying to keep Gina at bay without offending her, but then he always was adept at double-dealing. Still, you're going to come as quite a shock to him.'

From the back seat Paul interrupted gently, 'A very pleasant one, I'm sure, Sarah. It's just that there's been a change on the continuity side as well, and the girl who replaced Ellen, our first continuity girl, must have forgotten to take Rachel Ware's name out and insert yours in the casting list.'

Sarah's heart sank even further. She hadn't realised that someone else had actually been cast for the part ahead of her. 'Come on, Dale,' Paul protested. 'You're frightening the life out of Sarah! Ben won't eat you,' he told her. 'Oh, he's demanding all right—knows exactly what he wants from the cast and makes sure he gets it, but . . .'

'Sarah knows all about Ben, Paul,' Dale interrupted, his eyes leaving the road for a second as he turned his head to frown at the man in the back seat. 'We both worked with him on *Shakespeare*. You'll have to forgive Paul's ignorance,' he added to Sarah. 'He's come rather late to the acting scene. He was training to be a chartered accountant when he suddenly got the bug.'

'I qualified, too,' Paul put in with a disarming grin. 'I had a girl-friend who was a model, and she got me some ad work, which is how I got started.'

'Yes, he's the original chocolate-box hero,' Dale retorted.

So Paul didn't know about her marriage to Ben; of course it was over three years ago and had happened in England, and Sarah couldn't help hoping that the rest of the cast were similarly ignorant. It wasn't going to be easy working with him, especially not with the eyes of the rest of the cast monitoring their responses to one another.

'Is it much further?' Sarah queried, trying to ease the crick in her neck. They seemed to have been speeding through the dark, apparently empty countryside, for half a lifetime, and on top of her flight, the journey was beginning to take its toll on her.

'Only another ten miles or so,' Paul comforted her from the back.

'If Guy wasn't such a fanatic for realism we could have shot most of these scenes in the Californian desert and used the studios for everything else,' Dale chimed in rather bitterly.

Telling herself that it was only natural that Dale should sound a little disgruntled, after all Hollywood was home to him now and he must have grown accustomed to all the luxuries it offered, Sarah wondered what he would say if she confided to him how thrilled she was that they *were* filming on location.

'Well, here we are,' Dale announced fifteen minutes later as he pulled off the main road and they bumped down a dusty, narrow track.

Ahead of them a collection of lights shone from the windows of large trailers, and the guard on duty at the makeshift 'gate' grinned a welcome to Dale, eyeing Sarah with a flat curiosity that made her raise her eyebrows a little. 'He obviously thinks I'm someone you've picked up for the evening,' she commented to Dale as he parked his car outside a darkened trailer and Paul got out, having wished them both goodnight,

'*And* he's probably envying me,' Dale retorted with a grin, coming round to open her door. 'By the way,' he added casually, 'one of the problems we have here is that we're a little short on accommodation at the moment. Will you slap my face, sweetling, if I suggest you share with me for tonight? There's a separate bedroom, and rather than rouse half the outfit . . .'

Hiding her surprise, Sarah nodded her agreement. A glance at her watch showed her that it was after one in the morning, and her body ached for sleep. She knew Dale well enough to know that she could trust him, and although she had half expected to have to share a trailer—accommodation always being notoriously problematical on location—she had reckoned on sharing with one of the other girls.

'You were to have shared with Gina,' Dale explained to her as he extracted a key from his pocket and unlocked the metal door, flicking on the light as he did so, and allowing Sarah to step past him into the illuminated interior, 'but our dear Garia kicked up a fuss. It seems that sharing with someone would not be convenient—unless of course that someone happens to be our director. However, Ben isn't playing—at least not publicly. With all the other problems he's got on his hands, I don't suppose he's any too keen to upset one of our backers. He's going to have a hard time of it, trying to appease both Gina and her lover. He could, of course, always bow out and let someone else take over, but his last film wasn't exactly a box-office winner and . . .'

'Oh, but surely,' Sarah broke in impulsively,

without thinking, 'it got the Best Film Award,
and . . .'

'It might have got the Award, sweetling,' Dale
told her dryly, 'but if you want my opinion, Ben
over-stepped himself, spending so much on
making it, and that money won't be easily
recouped. Would you like a drink before I show
you to your room, madam?' he parodied, laughing
at her, as he changed the subject and indicated one
of the three doors leading off the narrow corridor
which ran from the living area in which they were
standing, and down past a small but very highly
sophisticated kitchen.

'If you don't mind, I think I'll go straight to
bed,' Sarah told him, suddenly conscious of the
hectic day behind her, fulfilling the last of her ad
commitments, and the long journey to their
destination. 'Are you sure you don't mind putting
me up for tonight, Dale, I could . . .'

Was there a touch of impatience in the frown
lining his forehead? Dale was probably tired, too,
and she was fussing unnecessarily, Sarah told
herself when he assured her that he didn't.

'Come on, you can have this room. I'll say this
for Guy,' he added as he pushed open the door,
'these trailers are well equipped, even down to air-
conditioning. He even had a temporary pool
installed on the site. Not that we get much chance
to use it with dear old Ben in charge. He's a real
slavedriver!' He slanted Sarah a sideways glance,
and her scalp prickled with sensitive awareness.
There had always been keen competition between
the two men, but now she sensed that this had
changed, deepened in some way, and this suspicion

was confirmed when Dale said slowly, 'He's changed since we filmed *Shakespeare* together, Sarah, and much as I hate to say it, he's a sore loser. Don't worry about it, though,' he told her, his expression lightening, 'Uncle Dale's here to protect you.'

Was the air-conditioning the sole reason she was shivering? Sarah wondered half an hour later as she prepared for bed in the small but luxurious 'room' Dale had given her. It was senseless unpacking until she discovered where she was to stay, so, having showered in Dale's minute but compact bathroom, she pulled on the nightdress she had extracted from one of her cases and climbed into bed.

It was silly to feel so apprehensive simply because she was working with Ben again. He would want to forget the past as much as she did. Hadn't he said when he stormed out of their room on the night of the party that he never wanted to set eyes on her again? So why hadn't he agreed to their divorce? Perhaps Dale was right and he was worried that she might make a huge financial claim on him—after all, he was now a very successful and presumably wealthy man. Her face tightened in disgust. He had indeed changed if he thought she would take a single penny from him. All she wanted was her freedom.

She sighed, remembering how she had fretted over the difficulty in getting a divorce. Her solicitor had been patient, but clearly a little at a loss.

'Is there someone else you want to marry?' he had enquired, and when Sarah shook her head had looked both thoughtful and perplexed, pointing

out that the waiting period was meant to give
couples a chance to see if they could not bury their
differences and make a go of their marriages. A
tight fist seemed to grip her heart, squeezing it
until the pain was almost more than she could
endure. What was the matter? Sarah asked herself
bitterly. Surely she had learned long ago the folly
of loving Ben? Hadn't his treatment of her then—
seducing her and then marrying her simply to get
one up on Dale—killed all she had ever felt for
him? So why did she feel this nerve-clenching sense
of apprehension, and yes, anticipation at the
thought of seeing him?

Too tired to find an answer to the riddle, she fell
into an exhausted sleep.

The unfamiliar noises of the site woke her, and
Sarah opened her eyes slowly, sitting upright when
she remembered where she was. She glanced at her
watch. Just gone seven, and already, if the sounds
she could hear were any indication, the day's work
was well under way.

Showering quickly, she returned to her room to
pull on a checked cotton shirt and some ancient
jeans, brushing her hair quickly and securing it off
her face with a band. The first thing she had to do
was to find Ben's assistant, report in to him or her
and find out when she would be needed for
filming.

Fortunately the weeks in between learning that
she had got the part and her arrival in Spain had
given her enough time to learn her lines, although
she was fully prepared to find that some of them
might have been changed in the interim. Would

the mysterious author of the film script be in evidence? It wasn't entirely unheard-of for writers to want to be present when their work was filmed, and since apparently the writer had also done the film script it was perfectly feasible that he would be on site. Sarah's stomach tightened in a small thrill of anticipation and, chiding herself for being too impressionable, she quickly packed up her things and straightened the bed. It was almost as though she had a crush on the man—and without knowing the first thing about him! But that wasn't true, she admitted thoughtfully. She *did* know about him. It was impossible to read the script and not be aware that he was a man of considerable compassion; of deeply felt but perhaps sometimes hidden emotions; a man to whom loyalty and self-respect meant far more than the indulgence in momentary pleasure.

There was no sign of Dale when she emerged from her room, and not knowing whether he was still asleep or already working, Sarah found the coffee percolator and filled it almost automatically, unable to resist the temptation to open the door and enjoy the lazy warmth of the morning as she waited for it to be ready. Later on the heat might be oppressive, especially if she was working, but right now it was just perfect, the tender fingers of morning sunshine warming the bare skin of her throat and arms, making her want to bask like a lazy cat. She closed her eyes languorously, opening them again quickly as a shadow blotted out the warmth of the sun, some sixth sense alerting her, awareness prickling dangerously over her skin as her muscles tightened and she saw that the object that had come between herself and the sun was none other than her husband, Benedict de l'Isle, director and producer and the Most Important Man under God on the site.

He saw her at the same moment as she saw him, halting almost mid-stride, a look, almost of shock, rippling across features that looked as though they had been hewn from stone. If Dale was. the archetype of fair-headed good looks, his face open and sunny, then Ben was his direct opposite, Lucifer fallen to earth with his darkly bitter features, his hair as black as night, and his profile that of a man to whom the weaknesses of others were unknown. Eyes the colour of jade assessed her ruthlessly, stripping away the veneer of sophistication she had gathered over the years, and with it the barrier of her clothes, so that Sarah felt as though she stood before him as she had done on the set for *Shakespeare*, naked, and vulnerable. And then she remembered that Dale had told her Ben didn't know she was among the cast. That gave her enough courage to lift her head and match him stare for stare. Her heart hammered violently against the confines of her flesh. She had forgotten how tall he was. She was five eight and even with the advantage of the steps she still had to look up to him. The surprise, if indeed there had been any, was gone, and had been replaced by the same icy contempt she remembered from another confrontation. It was really amazing how green eyes could be so cold, she thought, shivering a little as she realised the interested stares they were attracting from the small crowd that seemed to have gathered almost instinctively, drawn by the scent of blood no doubt, she thought bitterly. Well, if Ben thought he was going to take this part away from her! Her eyes smouldered darkly. She needed it far too much to give it up tamely, and she had her contract . . .

With a little start she realised that already she was on the defensive, feeling too vulnerable, too aware of the power of the man watching her.

She shivered again as Ben's mouth curled tauntingly, stepping backwards and instantly grateful for the warm support of Dale's arm, as it curved round her. She hadn't realised he was there, Paul at his side, and the brief glance she gave him showed that she was tremulously glad of his presence.

'Morning, Ben,' he drawled affably. 'Come to say hello to your ex-wife?'

Sarah saw Paul's eyes widen, but barely had time to register her protest of Dale's unwise comment, her swiftly indrawn breath checked as Ben's face darkened, his eyes and mouth hard with contempt. What on earth had possessed Dale to challenge him like that? Paul too looked to be concerned and slightly shocked. Obviously he had meant well, but Sarah shivered, wishing he had kept quiet.

'My ex-wife?' Ben murmured softly, cruelty glinting in the smile he gave Sarah as he reached them, grasping her hand, and uncurling fingers almost numb with shock as he jerked her forward so that she practically fell into his arms.

'You mean to say you haven't told him, darling?'

The words were murmured against her ear,

shivering across Her skin, Ben's hold tightening round her until she could barely breathe. Almost as though she were standing outside herself Sarah witnessed the small tableau—Dale, standing in the doorway of the trailer, wary, and questioning, his eyes searching her face as he tested it for reaction. Ben and herself locked in an embrace which made her frighteningly aware of the muscled power of his body, her back and legs warmed by the male flesh of his body, the contrast of his darkly tanned forearm resting alongside the pale fragility of hers, his fingers curling possessively round her wrist, holding it just before the curve of her breasts, so that he couldn't help but be aware of the hurried thud of her heart.

'Told me what?' Dale demanded at length with just enough edge under the light voice he used for Sarah to know that he was taken off guard.

'Why, simply that she isn't and never has been my "ex",' Ben drawled lightly, the concerted but very audible gasp that went up from their 'audience' reminding Sarah that he always had been a first-rate actor, able to draw every last ounce of emotion out of any scene.

'You could have told Dale our little secret, darling,' Ben murmured behind her. She felt him bend his head, and then the warm brush of his mouth against her skin, just below her ear, making her shiver in shocked response. 'I know I said I didn't want it made public just yet, but since I took this job especially to be near you, I think we've rather given ourselves away, don't you?'

Sarah was too numb to speak. She couldn't bring herself to look at Dale. How could she deny

Ben's assertion that she was still his wife, when in effect it was perfectly true? But as for the rest of his statement! She tugged away from him, her eyes already darkening with anger, and thought she had caught him off guard as she found herself free, but her freedom only extended to the length of time it took Ben to turn her in his arms, so that her breasts were crushed against the thin silk of his shirt, her nostrils full of the male scent of him, the grainy texture of his skin, and the hard pressure of his body as he held her against him.

'For those of you who don't know,' he drawled, raising his voice so that it reached the crowd of onlookers, now much larger than it had originally been and every one of them unashamedly listening, 'Sarah and I have been separated for the past few years, but now we're back together again, and my only regret is that on this occasion I won't be playing her lover   at least not in public!'

There was a wave of goodnatured laughter, only Dale and Sarah not joining in. She couldn't believe this, Sarah thought dazedly. Why had he done it? And then as she heard him saying coolly, 'I didn't realise you were arriving last night, darling. You should have let me know. Never mind, you're here now. I'll get someone to move your things to my trailer. Thanks for looking after her, Dale. It's almost like old times,' she knew. He wasn't going to have it said a second time that his wife had a lover who wasn't her husband. But why not simply divorce her? He didn't want her. He had made that more than plain enough; had told her to go to Dale. She could still remember the cruelty of his words when he had done so. All she had ever been to him had been the winning of a bet!

The crowd was slowly beginning to drift away. Break-ups and reconciliations were common enough in their industry not to cause too much comment, although it would have seriously undermined Ben's authority had it been thought that his estranged wife was having an affair with another member of the cast.

'Let me go!' Sarah demanded tersely, not even bothering to conceal the shaken anger she was feeling. Dale was still watching them and came down the steps, frowning as he approached them.

'Look, Sarah, if . . .'

'Leave it, Dale,' Ben cut in in clipped accents. 'Like I said, I'll have someone move Sarah's things to my trailer. You're supposed to be filming in half an hour, aren't you?' he added, flicking a glance at his watch. 'They'll be waiting for you in Make-up.'

Faced with what was tantamount to an order, Dale had little alternative but to go, and Sarah watched him leave, anger and anguish mingled in her eyes as Ben retained his hold on her until Dale was swallowed up in the dust and heat of the morning.

'Well now,' he drawled when Dale had gone, 'are you going to tell me what you were doing spending the night in his trailer, or can I guess?'

'You *can*,' Sarah spat back, 'but if you judge Dale and me by your own standards, then you wouldn't come within a mile of the truth! And speaking of motives, Ben, why did you announce that we were reconciled?'

'We've got to work together, Sarah. I want to

make a success of this film, and I'm not having the cast and crew more interested in gossiping about us than in doing a first-rate job.'

'But no one need even have known that we were married,' Sarah bit out. 'I . . .'

'I quite agree,' Ben cut in tersely, 'and who have we to thank for the fact that they do know?'

For a moment Sarah looked at him blankly, then she remembered Dale announcing her as Ben's 'ex-wife'. 'Dale didn't mean anything,' she said uncomfortably. 'You know what he's like.'

'Probably better than you,' came the crisply derisive response, 'but the damage is done now, Sarah. I've got enough problems on my hands already without you and Dale stirring up more. I'd feel much happier if you weren't here to add to them, but failing that, it will make life that little bit easier for me to have you under my eye, where I can see you. And, Sarah . . .' She turned to look at him, dry-mouthed with apprehension at the tone of his voice. 'Any attempt on your part to resume your affair with Dale, and I'll get myself another Joanna, contract or no contract, understand?'

Just for a second she toyed with the idea of telling him what he could do with his part, but she needed it too much; needed and wanted it. Ever since she had read the script she had known how much she wanted to be in the film. Not just because it was destined to be an out-and-out success, but because something about the way it was written, the development of the characters, struck a sympathetic chord deep inside her.

'I don't want to share a trailer with you,' she heard herself saying childishly, knowing that they both knew that she had given in. 'I . . .'

'I'm not exactly thrilled about it myself,' Ben agreed curtly, 'but needs must, and anyway, we've nowhere else to put you.'

'Because Gina insists on having a trailer to herself. Why don't you simply share with her, and let me have your trailer?' Sarah suggested sweetly. 'That way you'll be keeping both your main actresses happy.'

'Dale *has* been busy, hasn't he?' was Ben's only comment, but Sarah hadn't missed the way his eyes narrowed, nor the dark flush running along the high cheekbones. Somehow her comment had got to him, which in itself was worthy of further investigation. Was he not as immune to Gina as he pretended? 'Well, just try to remember that this time you're playing brother and sister, and not lovers. And if you want to blame someone because you're having to share with me, then blame Dale— after all, he's the one who announced that we were married.' He glanced at his watch again. 'I'm due on set in ten minutes. You'll find my trailer on the far side of the camp. It's on its own—a brown and cream monstrosity, you can't miss it. By the way,' he added, halting her and pinning her where she stood with the icy intentness of his scrutiny, 'how come you changed the time of your flight? I had fully intended to come and collect you myself.'

'You had? But . . .'

Two facts hit her simultaneously. One was that Dale had been wrong and that Ben had known she was to play Joanna. The other was that someone had obviously misled him over her flight, because she had certainly not altered it.

'But?' he encouraged, still watching her. 'But you and Dale decided it would create more of an impact if you were seen with him? Nice try, Sarah, but this time you've been out-manoeuvred.'

'Because you lied about us being reconciled,' Sarah said bitterly, ignoring the accusation he had tossed at her. 'Reconciled!' She laughed acidly. 'You never even wanted to marry me in the first place—you . . .'

'But I did,' Ben cut in grimly, 'and having done so, I'm having to pay for my mistake—just like you—and be warned, Sarah, this time I'm not going to allow you and Dale to make a laughing-stock out of me!'

He was gone before she could retort, striding through the heat and dust-hazed morning, the rigid line of his disappearing back reminding Sarah of the hard pressure of his body against hers. In Dale she had seen few changes if any to mark the intervening years; in Ben she saw many. As Southampton he had won acclaim for his acting ability, and had been more of a heart-throb than Dale, his darkly macho good looks causing more of an impact on the audience. He had been just thirty when they met. Now he was thirty-three, going on thirty-four, and like something cast in iron, he had hardened rather than mellowed. Oh, he was still good-looking—Sarah closed her eyes, quivering in recognition of the sexual appeal that nothing could destroy, and she hadn't been immune to it. Held prisoner in his arms, it had been fatally easy to remember how it had been between them, and even if there had not been the love she believed at the time, there had still been the passion and desire. If she closed her eyes she could still feel the echoes of it now, tongues of flame licking through her veins, the weak wanting in the pit of her stomach; the need to touch and taste the male flesh against her own. She opened her eyes, half dizzy from the emotions she fought to control, telling herself that it was the sunshine that made her feel so weak and disorientated. She glanced around her and sighed, wishing with all her heart that Guy Holland was still directing the film. Just for a moment she contemplated breaking her contract, and then her fighting instinct came to the fore. Ben probably expected her to run from him like a frightened rabbit—just as Mary Fitton had run from Southampton—well, she would show him! Before she could change her mind she swung round on her heel and headed in the direction Ben had pointed out to her.

Before she got to Ben's trailer, Sarah found the trailers which were being used as the administrative offices for the unit. One of the four girls working there, a plump, cheerful brunette, produced a work schedule, adding by way of warning, 'Of course it changes from day to day—you know what it's like—but we'll be pinning a fresh one up here every morning, and of course if you're in any doubt, you're lucky, you can always check with the boss at night!' Her ready smile robbed the words of any offence, and when Sarah smiled back the girl gave a relieved grin and extended a small capable hand. 'I haven't introduced myself, by the way. I'm Lois and the others are Anne, Helen and Sue, respectively. Thank goodness you're human. After all the tantrums we've had from Madame

Gina we were getting a bit worried about you, especially after this morning's surprise. We had no idea the boss was married, much less to one of our leading ladies.'

'We've been separated for some time,' Sarah told her, unwilling to discuss her relationship with Ben and yet unwilling to offend by seeming aloof.

'We all envy you like mad,' Lois confided with another grin, 'and my, oh my, won't our Gina be surprised! She got him earmarked as her private property, and he must be relieved that she'll have to back down a little now that you've arrived. Anything going on between the two of them was bound to cause unpleasant repercussions if it ever got back to the ears of her boy-friend. He's one of our backers,' she added by way of clarification, and Sarah didn't tell her that Dale had already informed her of this relationship. 'Guy fought damned hard to get the money for this film, and we're all relieved that Ben agreed to take over from him. It's hard enough getting money out of backers these days to produce a film, without having to contend with a director who's a yes-man and cuts corners and costs at every turn.'

Sarah could see that the other girl thought highly of Ben, which she knew from past experience was an accolade in itself. The crew were notorious for being 'anti' directors, and if a director did command their respect one could be sure that it had been hard won.

Half an hour later, having accepted the cup of coffee Lois offered, Sarah opened the door of Ben's trailer. Slightly larger than Dale's, it was on its own away from the others. Privileges of power,

Sarah thought wryly, wondering why Ben had opted for seclusion. So that Gina could visit him unnoticed? She told herself she was being stupid, especially in view of all that she had been told, and anyway, why should it concern her if Gina and Ben had an affair?

Unlike Dale's, the living area of the trailer was cluttered with mounds of paper. A typewriter sat uncovered on the table, and Sarah glanced curiously at it. The administration unit was fully equipped with all manner of electronic marvels, including a word processor, and she couldn't understand why Ben should need a machine in his own living accommodation. Shrugging her shoulders, she investigated the doors leading off the corridor. One opened on to a kitchen very like Dale's, only larger, with a breakfast bar in it. Next to it was a bathroom, and guessing that Ben would choose the bedroom nearest to it, Sarah pushed open the other door, into what was patently the unused bedroom.

Most of her luggage was still in Dale's car, and since she couldn't unpack she might as well make herself some belated breakfast and then explore the set. A swift glance at the schedule Lois had given her confirmed that she would not be needed until towards the end of the week, but she noticed that she had a wardrobe consultation first thing in the morning, and doubtless there would be many other things to fill in her time.

Half an hour later, having breakfasted on toast and coffee, and cleaned up after herself, she decided it was time to make her tour of the site, and familiarise herself with what was going to be her home for the next two or three months.

CHAPTER THREE

THE film company must have several million dollars tied up in the location site alone, Sarah decided, pausing to marvel at the swimming pool which had been dug in the sand and formed from some sort of plasticised liner. At one end a bar had been erected, complete with a 'coconut matting' roof and realistically weathered tables and chairs. To one side of it was a partially open restaurant where she guessed most of the crew and cast would take their meals, although it was possible to be entirely self-sufficient by using the freezer and fridge built into the trailer kitchens. A dozen or so people were seated outside the bar, the men drinking beer and the girls a mixture of the former and lemonade, reminding Sarah that the Spanish climate was a hot one and that she would be wise to protect her complexion from it. She did not need to be told how important it was not to let her skin burn—apart from the undoubted pain of doing so it could have a disastrous effect on any film shot out of sequence—she could hardly appear pale-skinned at the beginning of a scene, and then bright pink halfway through it.

She ought to have bought herself a sunhat before leaving England, but there had been so much to do she had forgotten it. She did have plenty of sunscreen, thanks to Carew, but she would need a hat if she was not to suffer from

sunstroke. It wasn't even midday yet and the heat
was almost suffocating. She glanced longingly at
the pool, and then reminded herself that she was
here to work, not play. She would go and watch
the shooting, she decided on impulse. She had
never seen Ben direct and it would be as well to
discover what type of method he adopted—
whether it was of the 'stick' or 'carrot' variety. It
was a well known maxim in Hollywood circles that
the better the director the more his cast loathed
him. Suppressing a shiver, Sarah wound her way
through the seemingly haphazard arrangement of
trailers back to the administration centre.

'You want to know where they're filming? Sure,'
Lois agreed laconically. 'Why not come with me?
I've got to take some stuff out for the boss. We'll
take one of the buggies.' She glanced at Sarah's
uncovered head. 'Go ahead and tell me if I'm
stepping out of line, but shouldn't you be wearing
a hat, your being a redhead an' all?'

'I would if I'd had the sense to buy one in
London,' Sarah agreed ruefully. 'First thing
tomorrow I must find someone to take me to the
nearest town so that I can buy one. Will anyone be
going in?'

Lois shook her head regretfully. 'I doubt it.
There's nothing in the can for sending off. We've
been having problems with one of the cameras, but
it's okay now and the boss said only yesterday that
he didn't want anyone sneaking off to town—
we've got too much lost time to catch up on. I
expect he'll make allowances for you, though,' she
told Sarah with a sideways grin. 'He won't want
one of his leading ladies to go down with

sunstroke—nor his wife to suffer from a headache!'
She laughed when she saw Sarah's expression.
'Honey, you're going to have to toughen up some
if you're going to survive on location. You haven't
done much film work, I guess?' she hazarded
sympathetically. 'Some of the guys don't mince
their words. You should have heard them this
morning when they found out about you! Word is
that you must be some lady to have been able to
tie the boss down. I guess it's not exactly news to
you that the fact that he's one very virile man
hasn't gone unnoticed in Tinsel Town.'

Sarah smiled and said nothing. Of course she
hadn't expected Ben to live the life of a monk
when they separated, so why this curious pang of
something that could almost be called pain, slicing
through her body, cutting through her defences
and leaving her aching and vulnerable to the
white-hot pangs of jealousy ripping through her?

Lois led the way to a beach buggy parked not
far away. 'The film crew have commandeered most
of the jeeps,' she explained briefly, 'but these little
guys are far better than any car in the rough.'

'What are they filming today?' Sarah asked,
trying to remember what she had seen on the
schedule. Hadn't it been some part of the Crusade;
just before Richard ordered the execution of his
Muslim hostages?

When she questioned Lois, the other girl agreed.
'Originally the boss hoped to have it in the can by
last week, but with the camera out of action . . .
There's an old castle out here that we're using as
part of the set. At the moment it's standing in for
the walls of Acre.'

Sarah knew from the script that in reprisal for refusing to release his Christian prisoners and to pay the ransom demanded of him, Richard had punished the Muslim leader Salah-ed-Din by putting to the sword the Muslim prisoners the Christian forces had taken when they captured Acre. For a Christian knight it was a barbaric act, especially when he had made his wife and sister witness it, but then Richard had been reputed to have a temper to match his red-gold hair, and Salah-ed-Din's refusal to accede to his demands must have infuriated him, but Sarah knew that the script, while faithfully following actual events, had allowed a little fiction to creep in along with the death of one of the fictional characters, Richard's lover, the knight Philip, who had left Richard on Cyprus to join the Knights Templar, a celibate fighting order, in order to do penance for their sin. This knight had been captured by a band of ferocious warriors known as 'Assassins', a title derived from the fact that they ate the hashish drug. From her own careful research, Sarah knew that it was quite true that the stronghold of the Knights Templar had been attacked by the Assassins and that many had been killed in the hills surrounding the citadel.

She also knew that this scene now to be shot was the culmination of Richard's relationship with his lover. Salah-ed-Din, unwilling to pay the ransom Richard demanded for the return of his prisoners, had instead offered to Richard the life of his lover. Richard had refused, and at the appointed time when Salah-ed-Din should have sent his ransom to the Christian camp, instead he had sent a dying man, his body tied to one of the creamy pale Arabian horses so greatly valued by the Moors, blood pouring from the wound in his side.

Declining to accompany Lois when she went across to Ben, Sarah attached herself to a group of extras just off set. The ancient castle was decrepit enough to have an air of authenticity, its walls half crumbling into the dusty sand, the sun glittering hotly on the pale stone.

A line of brightly striped pavilions had been erected at the base of the walls; the tents of the Christian army. Some distance away were another group of tents, this time representing those of the Muslim forces, and it was in a mock-up of one of these that the filming was taking place.

The actor playing the Muslim leader sat impassive and cross-legged before a small brazier, white-robed and impressive, half a dozen ferociously warlike attendants at his back.

Seated opposite him on a small stool, arms folded across his chest, sat Dale, and Sarah caught her breath at the change in him. Make-up and period clothes had transformed him into exactly what she had visualised Richard to be. Contact lenses had changed his grey eyes to steely blue, and watching him, Sarah found it hard to believe that he *wasn't* Richard in the flesh, her vivid imagination instantly transporting her back in time to the twelfth century, her senses instantly responsive to the scene being played out before her.

Salah-ed-Din was speaking, his voice even and devoid of all expression, his smile cruelly mocking, as he murmured softly, 'It is indeed regrettable, Lord Richard, that we have not as yet been able to collect the full sum of the ransom you demand.' He shrugged fatalistically. 'We are a poor people, and have to squeeze the money out like water from the desert.'

'With a ruby on your finger the size of a pigeon's egg?' Richard mocked. 'You know my terms. If the hostages and the money are not paid over within the month, the garrison of Acre shall be put to the sword.'

The Muslim leader laughed softly. 'Ah, Richard. Always so sure; so frank! But I think this time I shall be the victor. Why should I pay you good money when there are other ways? The Chief of the Assassins has lately sent me a gift. I would show it to you,' He clapped his hands and Sarah found she was holding her breath, her throat and chest hurting even though she knew what was coming.

'Is it true that the French King leaves us?' the Muslim enquired as his bodyguard disappeared.

'You are behind the times,' Richard responded. 'He has already gone.'

There was some commotion beyond the tent, and Sarah gritted her teeth, one half of her knowing that she was being stupid because none of what she was seeing was real, the other half totally caught up in what was happening.

'Ah, here is my gift,' the Muslim leader exclaimed in gentle satisfaction as his men reappeared, carrying what on first sight appeared to be a bundle of rags. 'Bring it here so that the Lord King may view it better,' Salah-ed-Din commanded softly.

Instantly obedient, his bodyguards tumbled the bundle on to the floor. A man lay there, his pale skin heavily bruised, blood staining the palms of his hands, his breathing shallow, the dark hair disordered and the white tunic bearing the Cross of the Knights of Malta dusty and torn.

'Lift his head.'

Sarah glanced at Richard. He was totally absorbed in the man before him, dark colour running up under his ruddy skin, fingers biting into the palms of his hands.

'The Assassins were curious to witness the method by which the prophet you call Jesus died,' Salah-ed-Din told Richard softly. 'Fortunately I managed to curb their enthusiasm before it went too far.'

The camera panned on to the bloodstained palms, the torn surplice with the slit along the side, thickly encrusted with blood, and Sarah shivered despite the heat of the afternoon.

'He will not know you, Lord Richard.' The words came softly, tenderly almost. 'He has been given the drug hashish. Our physicians can save him. You have only to give the word. This man whom you so dearly love—you hold his life in your palm. I will give him to you instead of the ransom.'

'No!'

The word was ripped from Richard's throat, his face a tortured mask. Sarah discovered she was holding her breath again, this time her palms wet with sweat.

'No?' Salah-ed-Din questioned.

'No,' Richard repeated more firmly, with less

anguish. 'Were the terms of our treaty only one dinar and one prisoner, they could not be altered, nor would he wish me to do so.' He bent forward and touched the dark hair yearningly, wiping the blood from the cut lips before pressing his own against them in brief agony, and then turned to leave the tent, throwing curtly over his shoulder, 'You have fourteen days to find the ransom money.'

'Phew!' Behind her Sarah heard someone let out a pent-up breath. 'Gut-gripping stuff,' someone else agreed, and there was general laughter in the release from tension.

'Can it, Rick,' Sarah heard Ben saying coolly as he strolled up to Dale.

'Satisfied, oh master?' Sarah heard Dale demand caustically, adding, 'God, Ben, I'm not doing it again. I've already sweated blood over this scene!'

'And came up with a first-rate performance.' It was said so quietly Sarah barely caught it, trying to suppress her feeling of surprise at Ben's praise, although logically there was no reason why she should feel surprised. Ben was quite right, it had been a first-rate performance, the credit, she suspected, as much due to the director as to the cast. Dale was extremely proud of his rogue male image, and could surely only have been persuaded to accept the role because of the film's box office potential.

'I'm going to get cleaned up,' exclaimed the actor who was playing Richard's lover. Sarah recognised him from a tough spy series she had seen on television and suppressed a small smile as she heard him to say to Dale, 'I don't know about you, but the only way I'm able to play this is by telling myself you're a delectable female, dressed up in male clothing!'

General laughter greeted the comment, and the group round the set started to disperse.

'Want a ride back with me?'

Sarah jumped. She hadn't seen Dale approaching and was just about to reply when a shadow darkened her vision, Ben's fingers curling painfully round her upper arm.

'No need,' he informed Dale coolly. 'She's coming back with me, aren't you, darling?' Before Sarah could retreat he bent his head. Her lips parted on a startled cry of panic as his fingers snapped round her wrists, pinning them to her sides. With a callous lack of concern for her feelings, Ben's mouth closed over hers. Time swung back leaving Sarah dizzily suspended in space, a helpless groan smothered in her throat as his fingers left her wrist to circle it; stroking, caressing, his mouth leaving her lips to find the hidden susceptible spot behind her ear.

Her breathing ragged, Sarah tried to pull away, her voice slurred and unsteady as she begged him to let her go.

'Kiss me,' Ben ordered thickly against her throat, his fingers stroking along its vulnerable length, and Sarah knew with a sickening sense of unreality that he wouldn't let her go until she obeyed; and worse—that the reason for his command was to humiliate her in front of Dale. Closing her eyes, she tried to force her trembling lips to keep still, her body stiffly unyielding as she forced her mouth to brush Ben's fleetingly. His hand tightened in her hair, his fingers spread against the back of her head, forcing her mouth to remain in contact with his, his mocking, 'If that's the best you can do, you're no actress,' whispered against her skin and making her retort savagely, 'I loathe the feel of you so much I *can't* act!' invoking first a muttered curse, and then not the cruel embrace she had tensed herself against but instead, the sensual brush of his tongue over the outline of her closed lips, again and again until her senses stirred in spite of herself and her mouth parted on a husky moan,

'Say again that you loathe me—if you dare,' Ben murmured triumphantly, lifting his head to scrutinise her softly flushed face and betrayingly languorous eyes.

'What a pity Dale didn't stay to see how much you loathe me,' Ben taunted sardonically as he released her. 'Perhaps then he'd appreciate how I felt when I found the two of you together—you in his arms, not three days after you had promised yourself to me.'

'What are you doing, Ben?' Sarah demanded tiredly, pulling away from him, unaware of the defeated droop of her neck, or the brilliant disorder of her hair, cascading round her shoulders as she turned away from him. 'Keeping your hand in as an actor? Pity there's no appreciative audience. I'm tired,' she added wanly. 'I'd like to get back to the site. If you don't want to take me I'll go as I came, with Lois.'

'I'll take you,' Ben informed her grittily. 'Go and collect your hat and we'll leave.'

While Ben had been kissing her, stamping her

irrevocably as his property, Sarah thought bitterly, everyone else had moved tactfully away; the camera crew were dismantling their equipment, people making a general move towards packing up, and it was plain that filming was over for the day.

'Ben darling, how much longer are you going to be?'

'Gina, you'll have to find someone else to take you back, Sarah and I are going into town.'

Sarah turned and saw Gina Frey pouting sulkily at Ben, but it was on Sarah that her eyes rested, and the animosity in them was unmistakable.

'I thought town was barred to the cast and crew,' she said acidly.

'So it is, but you must allow me to bend the rules a little in my own favour. Sarah and I have only recently been reconciled.' Sarah wasn't aware that Ben had reached for her hand until he raised it to his lips, turning it palm upwards and touching the softly sensitive skin there with the tip of his tongue. It was impossible to stop the response rippling through her. That Gina was as aware of it as Ben, she couldn't doubt. The other woman's dark eyes narrowed and then flashed bitterly. 'I'm taking Sarah out to dinner.'

It was obvious to Sarah that Gina wanted to object, and equally plain that there was little she could say. However, Gina obviously wasn't easily thrown.

'R.J. will be phoning me later,' she purred felinely. 'He keeps asking how the filming's going. He's getting most anxious about his investment, poor darling.' Eyes narrowed, teeth gleaming against the red gloss of her lips, she eyed Ben triumphantly, her meaning quite plain! 'Play along with me or I'll cause trouble with one of the backers,' and Sarah waited tensely to see how Ben would respond.

'I think you'll find he's feeling much happier now,' Ben told her expressionlessly. 'I spoke to him this morning to tell him that the camera was fixed and that we should be able to make some progress. In fact, I've invited him out here so that he can see for himself how we spend our backers' money.'

A low hiss as she expelled her breath was Gina's only response before she turned and stormed angrily away.

'Phew!' Ben shook his head rather like a diver emerging from the surf, a wicked grin tugging at the corners of his mouth. Seen like that he looked years younger, but the familiar tug on her heartstrings warned Sarah that she would be a fool to forget what he really was. He had undermined her defences dangerously easily already. She mustn't let it happen again. 'Now, your hat, and then we'll be on our way. We're dining with some friends of mine.'

'We are?' Sarah stared at him. 'But you said nothing to me before! I can't go out to dinner dressed like this!' Infuriated with herself, she stared up at him. What she had intended to say was that she wouldn't go out to dinner with him full stop. 'And I don't have a hat,' she added petulantly. 'I forgot to buy one. I'll get one tomorrow.'

'Indeed you will,' Ben agreed grittily. 'You crazy

little fool, do you know what the temperature is out here?' He gestured around him, indicating the exposed and burning half-desert plain. 'And you with that pale Celtic skin and God alone knows how little resistance to the sun!'

'Don't worry, I covered myself liberally with sunscreen before I came out,' Sarah told him acidly. 'I'm not a complete fool, Ben, I do realise that you won't want me looking like a freshly boiled lobster.'

'Correct me if I'm wrong, but to the best of my knowledge they haven't as yet invented a sunscreen that can be applied to the head, right?' Ben demanded, teeth snapping together over the final word. 'Have you no sense, Sarah?' he demanded huskily, raking irate fingers through his hair. 'And as for not being suitably dressed for dinner,' he added, not waiting for an answer, 'that can soon be remedied. I could do with a shower myself, but I've had enough of Gina for one day without having to endure her company on the ride back to the site.'

'You really don't like her, do you?' Sarah asked, surprised into the question by his grim expression.

'She's a man-eater, and not even a subtle one at that. You know me, Sarah,' he mocked, watching her colour come and go as his eyes moved slowly over her jean-clad legs and upwards, resting momentarily on the soft thrust of her breasts against the cotton of her blouse. 'At heart I'm a hunter . . .'

'A hunter who enjoys maiming and wounding his prey,' Sarah agreed bitterly. 'Yes, I know you, Ben.'

'Then you'll know I mean what I say when I tell you that if you so much as let any member of the cast or crew even suspect that we're not the happily reunited lovers I've told them we are, then I'll make you sorry you were ever born!'

'Again?' Sarah drawled with fine irony, watching his face darken with the swift tide of colour running up under his skin, his fingers clenching as though he would dearly like to fasten them round her throat. 'How very boring!'

'Oh, I don't think you'll think so,' Ben assured her tautly. 'Hell can come in many different guises.'

And as she shivered under the impact of the implied threat Sarah cursed bitterly at the whim of fate that had brought them together again. She could, if she was completely impartial and logical, accept why Ben would not want the rest of the crew and cast to think she was having an affair with Dale; she could even by stretching that logic and impartiality to its fullest extent appreciate why he had taken the steps he had to make sure they would not, but this . . . this constant tormenting of her nerves; the subtle sexual pressure he was exerting; these were things she could not understand, and they unnerved her, completely undermining the self-confidence she had built up after their break-up.

'I think I'll just go over and check tomorrow's schedule,' Sarah announced as Ben unlocked the trailer door. 'I should be back by the time you've had your shower.'

'Make sure you are,' Ben warned her. 'Don't

make me come looking for you, Sarah.'

The bar by the pool was crowded, as was the restaurant. Lois called out a greeting as Sarah walked past. She was seated with some of the camera crew who acknowledged her as well. 'Nothing for you tomorrow apart from wardrobe,' Lois called to her, obviously anticipating where she was going. 'Want to join us?'

'I can't, I'm afraid. Ben's taking me out to dinner.' Sarah didn't realise how intimate the words sounded until they were uttered, but Lois, irrepressible as ever, joked:

'To judge from the way he was behaving this afternoon I thought you *were* his dinner, or was that just an appetiser?'

Her cheeks stinging with colour, Sarah made some inarticulate response. She knew that Lois meant well, but her comment had reminded her uncomfortably of how she hadn't been able to stop herself from responding to Ben's touch. She started to shake, memories rolling over her, swamping her.

'Sarah, are you all right? You're so pale. Aren't you feeling well?'

The concern in Dale's voice, the caring touch of his hand on her arm, were instantly soothing.

'It's nothing,' she assured him huskily, glad of his sudden appearance. 'I just felt slightly sick.'

'I'm not surprised, after that display Ben gave this afternoon. You know what it's all about, of course? He's using you to keep Gina at bay,' Dale told her before she could respond. 'He hopes that by producing a "wife", he'll be able to hold off

Gina and still keep R.J. as a backer. He always was a quick thinker, I'll give him that. Be careful, Sarah, that you don't get in deeper than you expect. If I know Ben he won't be averse to doing everything he can to make your "reconciliation" look viable.' His eyes dropped to her hand, which he was now holding lightly within his own. 'I'm no angel myself, but unlike Ben I like my sex sweetened with at least some emotion. He's a cold devil, Sarah. He always was.'

'You can't be trying to warn me that Ben might want to . . . to . . . make love to me,' she got out at last, trembling over the words, guiltily aware that the response of her body to them wasn't entirely one of revulsion.

'You'd better believe it,' Dale told her grimly. 'He wants you, Sarah, I saw it in his eyes this afternoon.'

'No . . . No, I'm sure you're wrong.' Why did her voice sound so breathless? 'I . . .'

'He wants you,' Dale pressed bitterly. 'He wants you because he thinks he'll be taking you away from me. He never was a good loser.'

With a small cry Sarah pulled away from him. Not now—dear God, not now! She didn't *want* to be reminded of the past; of the wager which had caused her so much pain; the pain that lived inside her still; eating at her, destroying her faith in men, her ability to give her love and herself to any man, still hurting from the wounds inflicted by Ben's duplicity and coldhearted seduction of her. He had blinded her with false words of love and even falser promises for the future, and like a fool she had believed him. Without being aware of it her feet had carried her back to the trailer. The sun was setting, a crimson ball of fire dying into clouds of purple and amber, and she paused to watch, an odd lump in her throat, reluctant to walk into the trailer and yet fearful of the consequences if she did not.

Her fingers were on the handle when it turned against her and the door was thrust open. Ben stood in the aperture, a towel knotted carelessly round his hips, moisture gleaming on his skin. Had his body always been so overpoweringly male? Sarah shuddered, unable to draw her eyes away, conscious of the trembling reaction in her stomach.

'I thought you were going to stand there all night. You always were one for putting off the evil moment, weren't you, Sarah? Remember how you didn't want to do that scene for *Shakespeare*? The one where I finally got to take you to bed?' he added cruelly, watching the colour run up under her skin with detached amusement. 'I suppose that's why you married me before deciding you wanted Dale. How long did he stay with you? What's the matter?' he asked softly. 'You're trembling like a virgin who's never seen a man before,' his mouth mocked her, 'and we both know you're not that, don't we, Sarah?' he said slowly, watching the hot colour consume her pale skin. 'Oh, come, surely it can't have been as memorable as all that? Not when you've got Dale to remember as well.'

'That's . . .' That's not true, she had been about to say, but those words could never be uttered. Better that he think her a wanton than a fool. 'That's a vile thing to say,' she finished weakly.

'So it was,' Ben agreed blandly, his expression changing as he added acidly, 'and an even viler thing to do, wouldn't you say? You'd better get changed,' he told her, changing the subject, like a predator suddenly tiring of tormenting its prey. 'The couple we're dining with are Spaniards—so you can err on the side of formality. And take a coat. My car is parked in the compound and they've been forecasting rain for the last couple of days. That's why it's so hot. Fortunately it won't affect the filming.'

'Ben . . .' Her voice sounded thick with tears even in her own ears, and she wanted to cringe beneath the look he gave her.

'Couldn't we . . . couldn't we call a truce for the duration of the film?' she pleaded weakly. She couldn't go on like this, fencing with him, unable to defend herself from his expert thrusts. Already she felt as though she were bleeding from a thousand tiny cuts.

'A truce?' Ben laughed harshly. 'Oh no, Sarah, that isn't what I have in mind at all. The bathroom's all yours,' he called over his shoulder as he went back inside. 'We could have shared it, but then you always were something of a prude. Perhaps Dale's managed to coax you out of it.'

A prude! Sarah felt as though he had stuck a knife straight into her heart. She had been shy and inexperienced, yes, but surely no man could describe the complete and utter abandonment she had experienced in Ben's arms as prudish?

'That's something you'll never find out,' she managed to throw at him as she followed him into the trailer, forgetting in her determination to retaliate that her words might be taken as a challenge.

She didn't relax until he was in his room, and all the time she was showering, despite the locked door between them, she felt strung up and on edge, her fingers clumsy as she donned fresh underwear, and pulled on a silk dress in her favourite shade of lavender grey. It was a hot, sultry night and she was careful to apply only the minimum of make-up. She saw Ben studying her when she emerged from her room and asked defensively, 'Is something wrong?'

'Not as far as I'm concerned, I'm just wondering how far your appearance is going to go to reinforcing our host's belief that all film actresses wear skin-tight dresses with slit skirts and have brass-blonde hair. He's rather old-fashioned,' he added lightly. 'You should have a lot in common. Tell me something that's always puzzled me, Sarah—how did you manage to salve your puritan conscience when you took Dale for your lover? Or did you love him so much conscience never came into it?'

'I ... I don't want to talk about it,' she managed desperately. 'The past is over, Ben. I don't want to remember any of it.'

'I bet you damn well don't! I wish to God I could forget as easily,' he snarled, frightening her with the rage she saw in his eyes as he threw open the door. The soft silk of his shirt sleeve brushed her bare arm as he stood back for her to pass, and instantly an electric awareness of him pulsed through her. It was no good, she thought dizzily, trying to regain control of her thudding pulses. Nothing had changed. She loved him still, foolishly, crazily in view of all that had happened, but quite, quite irrevocably.

CHAPTER FOUR

'YOUR friends live here?' Sarah stared aghast at the impressive villa with its private drive.

'I got to know them when I came out to do some preliminary work on ... on the locations. The family once owned the castle we're using for some of the shots. Now most of their wealth comes from sherry. There's no need to be nervous.'

'I'm not,' Sarah flashed back, angry that he had seen through her defences, conscious that she was lying and of a sense of trepidation about facing Ben's friends. 'Do they ... do they know you're bringing me with you? That we're married?' she questioned dry-mouthed. What had Ben told them about her?

'Yes, and yes, but you needn't worry that you'll be asked any awkward questions. I've simply told them that we'd had problems but that we've now reconciled them.'

'And later,' Sarah found herself asking tautly, 'when all this is over, what will you tell them then?'

'Does it matter? I'll think of something.' Ben was getting out of the car, coming round to her door and opening it for her, his hand touching her arm impersonally as he helped her out, and she found she was shivering despite the heat pressing down on her like a heavy blanket, her teeth almost chattering as she flung at him:

'Of course you will. You're good at that, aren't

you, Ben? Always quick to turn a situation to your own advantage.'

'Meaning what?' he demanded icily, gripping her arm and swinging her round to face him. Heavy cloud blanketed the stars and moon and it was impossible for her to see his face, but she could feel the tautly suppressed anger coming off his body.

'Meaning what, Sarah?' he reiterated harshly. 'Snide little innuendoes are one thing, aren't they? Actually being able to validate them is something else again.'

The scorn in his voice lashed at her pride. She *wouldn't* just stand there and let him tear her to pieces! 'Meaning that you've used me and our marriage to keep Gina at bay, just as you used me once before to . . .' She couldn't go on, her voice totally suspended, she could only shake her head weakly, unable to put into words how she had felt when Dale told her about their bet.

'Oh, I see!' She felt him take a step towards her and shrank back against the car instinctively, shuddering as the clouds parted momentarily and a silvered beam revealed his features to her quite distinctly. His eyes were hard and cold, his mouth grimly sardonic, contempt and mockery dominating his expression. 'You worked that out all by yourself, did you?'

'No!' Goaded, Sarah defended herself instantly. He wasn't going to accuse her of simply imagining things. 'Dale . . .'

'Ah yes, Dale,' Ben broke in dangerously, not giving her the chance to continue. 'I thought he'd figure somewhere in this. Dale told you I was

using you to keep Gina at bay, did he, Sarah? *Did*
he, Sarah?' he demanded savagely, his fingers
closing on her wrist so painfully that she cried out.

'You're hurting me!' she protested huskily,

'Not half as much as I'd like to,' was his brutal
retort. 'How it must gall Dale to know that I had
you first!'

The crudity of his comment and the savage
satisfaction in the way he voiced it held her silent
for a handful of seconds, all ability to respond
suspended by the ferocity of the pain invading her.

'Not half as much as it does me,' she told him
quietly, when she was able. 'Ben, I don't think
tonight's a good idea, I . . .'

'Too late,' he mocked her, 'we've been seen.' He
gestured towards the front door which was being
opened, and then he leaned forward suddenly,
capturing her lips, the pressure of his mouth hard
and sure, his head lifting almost immediately.
'There,' he drawled, stopping her as she opened
her handbag to reach for her lipstick. 'No, leave
it,' he ordered, taking the tube from her and
dropping it back into her bag, snapping it shut.

'But they'll know you've been kissing me,' Sarah
protested, not understanding.

'So they will,' Ben agreed laconically, 'which is
better than having them think I've been quarrelling
with you, wouldn't you agree?'

'And so you're playing Joanna?'

Sarah nodded her head. The Sarjoves were a
pleasant couple, Miguel Sarjoves a South American
by birth who had married Luisa when she was
visiting his country with her aunt. As Luisa had

had no brothers, and he himself was a younger son, he had returned to Spain with her, managing her share of the family sherry business. They had two daughters and a son, Luisa had told her over dinner, all of whom were away at school. Now they were seated in the handsome drawing room drinking coffee, and Luisa was questioning Sarah about her role in the film.

'It's a marvellous part,' Sarah enthused. 'I can't get over how lucky I am to have got it.'

'Oh, but surely,' Luisa began, glancing at Ben, 'as . . .'

'I didn't give Sarah the part,' Ben interrupted easily. 'Guy did that.'

'Yes, mainly because my colouring was so right,' Sarah informed her.

'We had no idea that Ben was married until he told us about you,' Luisa admitted. 'He stayed with us for several months and I thought at the time that there was something troubling him, some problem . . .'

'He was probably worrying about how much filming would have to be done on location and how much it was going to cost,' Sarah told her dryly, knowing quite well that whatever Ben had been worried about, it couldn't have been her.

Luisa was regarding her oddly, her eyes going to Ben's shuttered face and then back again. 'Oh, but I meant when he was . . .'

'Sarah, if you're ready, I think it's time we were making a move,' Ben interrupted lazily. 'Filming starts at six tomorrow—one of the battle scenes— and apart from the fact that the light will be better, even with modern techniques, chain mail still weighs heavy. There's a limit to the time one can expect the cast to wear it in this heat!'

The drive back to the site was accomplished without incident. Sarah's head had started to ache during the meal and she had put it down to the fact that she wasn't used to dining so late, plus the richness of the food and wine, and she had been glad that Ben had left her in peace.

The storm still had not broken, and the night was oppressive as she slid from the car, leaving Ben to lock it as she walked towards the trailer. He caught up with her just as she drew level with the pool area and it was obvious from the activity round the bar that some people were not too concerned with getting up early in the morning.

'Hey, boss, come and have a drink with us,' someone called out, but Ben shook his head, cupping Sarah's elbow, his refusal giving rise to several witticisms that brought a film of colour to Sarah's face.

They entered the trailer in silence, and Ben went straight to the living area and opened a cupboard, producing a bottle and a glass. Sarah frowned as she watched him pour some of the fiery spirit into the tumbler, wondering a little that he should want it after what they had eaten and drunk with their hosts.

'I think I'll go to bed, if you don't mind,' she heard herself saying, recognising the edge of tension in her voice.

'How polite we are!' Ben jeered as he picked up the glass. 'Pity you didn't ask me if I'd any objections before you took Dale for your lover.'

In the bathroom Sarah showered quickly, dreading the moment when she would have to emerge from its sanctuary dressed only in her nightdress and thin robe, but when she did Ben never raised his head from the paperwork spread out over the table. He had switched off all the lights apart from a powerful lamp which threw into relief the angled planes of his face, distorting them slightly so that Sarah could almost deceive herself that she saw vulnerability and pain etched against the darkness of his skin. He had always tanned easily. She remembered when they were filming *Shakespeare* there had been a particularly hot spell and he had been lazily amused by the contrast in the colour and texture of their bodies. When he had made love to her it had been almost as though his skin transferred the heat and molten power of the sun to hers, burning her more tender flesh with the contact. How magical that night had seemed! He had taken her out to dinner and throughout the meal all she could think of was how she had felt when he held her against him that day during the filming. He had glanced up and caught her eyes on the exposed vee of flesh at his throat, and with a sudden imprecation he had grasped her hand, reaction shivering across her skin as he muttered her name huskily.

After that she had only toyed with her meal. He had driven her back to her lodgings, turning to her in the darkness of his car, kissing her with a hunger that swept aside all her fears and reservations. She had played Mary Fitton for so long that her body had become pliantly responsive to his, responding instantly to the stroke of his

thumb over the tautness of her breast. When he
bent his head to its burgeoning arousal she had
had a momentary detached image of its darkness
against the paleness of her skin before the dark
floodtide of desire closed swirlingly over her. She
couldn't remember what Ben had said when he
finally released her, only the brief drive to his flat,
the silence thick with his unspoken intent. In his
bedroom she had trembled eagerly against him
when he touched her, wanting his total possession
of her with a need that pushed aside the barriers of
prudence and inexperience.

Afterwards he had been full of remorse, or so it
had seemed, teasing her a little over her panic that
others might guess they had been lovers, demanding to know if she was ashamed of their
relationship, but she hadn't been able to explain
her dread of the knowing eyes of the rest of the
cast, the laughter and comments that would
follow, not realising until later, when she saw the
first rushes, that she had already betrayed herself
and that her love for Ben was there for all to see in
the incandescence of their love scenes.

Of course, she hadn't realised then why he
wanted their affair to become public knowledge;
hadn't known a thing about his bet with Dale.
That had come after he had been forced to take
the almost unbelievable step of marrying her. 'Oh,
Ben's like that in pursuit of his goal,' Dale had
told her carelessly when she refused to accept that
he would go so far simply to win a wager. 'Singleminded isn't the word. Besides, making you fall in
love with him has a double advantage. One, he
gets to win the bet, and two, it comes across so

obviously on film, and gives his performance the edge over mine. You don't know him like I do, Sarah,' he had told her. 'We went through drama school together. I've seen him in action before.' And because she had doubted all along that Ben could actually love her, and because she knew Dale had no axe to grind, Sarah had been forced to accept that he was right.

She slept fitfully, missing the open window she always insisted on at home, but knowing that the heat outside would quickly negate the cooling effect of the air-conditioning if she did open one. Her headache grew progressively worse, nausea adding to her misery. There was a medicine cabinet in the bathroom, with luck with some aspirin in it, and she swung her feet out of the bed, surprised to discover that she was shivering with cold, despite the clammy stickiness of her skin. When she opened the door, the brief staccato noise of the typewriter startled her. It was gone two in the morning; what was Ben doing typing, and why?

Whatever he was doing was totally engrossing; his head turned to one side away from her as he studied something beside him, her presence unnoticed as she crept into the bathroom. Without sleep to fog her brain she was unpleasantly aware that her 'symptoms' could easily be those of sunstroke, and she could only pray that it was only a mild dose and that she would be fully recovered by morning. Just as soon as she had seen Wardrobe she *must* get herself a hat!

Unwilling to draw Ben's attention to herself, she

resisted the desire to switch on the bathroom light
and instead felt her way towards the medicine
cupboard, her eyes adjusting themselves to the
lack of light enough for her to get it open. There
were several bottles inside, any of which might
contain what she wanted. Giving an exasperated
sigh as much at her own folly as anything else, she
reached for one, intending to hold it up to the light
of the window, but somehow it slipped from her
fingers, crashing down into the basin below,
showering her with fragments of glass as it
splintered, and leaving her transfixed with shock.

She heard Ben curse fluently, the trailer
illuminated with light as he moved, switching
lights on, thrusting open the bathroom door to
stare at her in mingled anger and scorn.

'I had a headache . . . I saw you were working
and didn't want to disturb you . . .' Heavens, she
sounded like a terrified child, Sarah thought
mentally, suddenly intensely conscious of the fact
that his silk shirt was open almost to the waist,
exposing tanned flesh, darkened by a fine covering
of hair. Instantly she was aware of her body's
response; the provocative firming of her breasts,
imperfectly concealed by her thin cotton nightdress, and she made to take a step forward,
desperate to escape the close confines of the small
room, dominated by Ben's masculinity and her
reaction to it, even the air so thick with tension
that she could barely breathe.

'Sarah, no!' The whiplash command cut through
her thoughts. She paused, heard Ben swear, and
the next moment he was crunching through the
broken glass to swing her into his arms.

'What's the matter with you?' he demanded furiously. 'Do you want to cut your feet to ribbons?'

She had completely forgotten the broken glass and shuddered violently as she looked down at it.

'You're cold!'

To her surprise there was concern in his voice. Still holding her in his arms, he carried her through into the living area, barely half a dozen strides in all, but more than enough to make her uncomfortably aware of the suppleness and strength of sinews and bone covered by skin that gleamed like oiled silk. Before he put her down Ben steadied himself against the door, the movement catching her off guard and making her clutch at his shirt, the skin beneath it vibrantly warm and slightly damp with the perspiration she could see clinging to the pores of his face. Was it really so warm? She shivered convulsively as he put her down, unaware of the material of her nightdress tightening across her breasts until she realised that Ben was looking at her, his body slightly tensed. From being cold Sarah suddenly felt as though she were consumed by a burning heat. It seared her skin, drying out her mouth, her breathing suddenly forced and uneven. She touched her tongue to her dry lips, wanting to break the silence that stretched between them taut as fine wire and yet at the same time strangely unwilling to break the spell it wove.

Like someone in a dream she saw Ben's hand come up, slowly, as though he were moving through water, his thumb brushing the erect peak of her nipple, his eyes darkening to onyx as he bent over her, tugging at the ribbons securing the bodice of her nightdress, his fingers unbelievably gentle as they cupped the swollen flesh he had exposed.

He made a brief sound, swiftly checked as Sarah's gaze flew to his face, familiar and yet oddly unfamiliar as he looked down at her, an expression in his eyes that made her catch her breath quiveringly, panting slightly as he bent his head and slowly touched his lips to the place where his thumb had lingered.

Pain and pleasure seared through her together as Sarah closed her eyes, not knowing which of them had made the faint sound of satisfaction, oblivious to everything but a compelling desire to weave her fingers into the fine black silk of Ben's hair and hold him against her breast. She moved towards him, jarring her arm against the table, and the impact filled the small space with alien sounds. Ben's brilliant unfocused gaze left her body, his features hardening as they swept her face and she was thrust from him.

'Go back to bed, Sarah,' he told her hardily. 'I'm in no mood tonight to play stand-in for Dale.'

It shattered her mood instantaneously, and it wasn't until she was on her feet that she remembered the shattered glass in the bathroom, and the aspirin she still hadn't got. Well, Ben could clear up the broken glass, she told herself, childishly, and as for the aspirin—after what had just happened she doubted if a whole bottleful would be sufficient to make her sleep. Her body trembled with nervous tension, every nerve ending still raw with the ache Ben's touch had evoked, and she knew shamingly that if he were to come to her now she would be dangerously close to begging him to make love to her. However, she wasn't entirely a fool—not nowadays—and she didn't waste time delving into the reasons behind Ben's actions. They had been pure reflex, an entirely impersonal reaction of any male who suddenly became aware that he was holding a half-naked female in his arms.

She supposed it was only to be expected that she should wake up heavy-eyed, with her head throbbing and her stomach still queasy, Sarah decided as she crawled out of bed, reaching for her robe. A glance at her watch showed that it was just after eight. Fortunately her wardrobe call wasn't until ten, and at least she would have the trailer to herself.

There was no sign of any broken glass in the bathroom. Ben had made some attempt to tidy away his papers in the living area, although one had drifted down on to the floor. She bent to pick it up automatically, glancing at the typewritten page, her brows drawing together in a frown as she read it. It was obviously a page of typescript, but just as obviously it had nothing to do with their present film. Perhaps Ben was already looking for his next film, that wouldn't be entirely unheard-of, but there were several mistakes in the typing, and what she was holding was a carbon copy rather than an original, the typescript looking as though it could belong to Ben's rather battered manual machine. Telling herself that she was becoming dangerously obsessive about him, Sarah placed the paper on the table and set about making herself a cup of coffee. The thought of food made her feel faintly ill, and she noticed as she glanced through the window that the sky was unpleasantly sullen, the sun shining brassily down on the hard-baked earth.

By nine-thirty she had re-read her lines and was ready for her wardrobe appointment. Afterwards she would seek out Lois or one of the other girls and find out where she could best get transport to take her into town. Today she must get a hat. She was nearly sure that her headache and nausea were the result of too much exposure to the sun, and today, if anything, it was even hotter.

The wardrobe mistress, Linda Dawes, was a slim blonde girl with a businesslike manner, who measured Sarah quickly and then complimented her on the factuality of her data sheet. 'You wouldn't believe the number of actresses, and actors come to that, who tell us they're inches thinner than they actually are, and we're supposed to make their costumes! I must be lucky this time out, both you and Eva Martell who's playing Eleanor measure out exactly right. She's got an appointment this morning too, which means I'll probably be able to finish early enough to have a dip in the pool. Stifling outside, isn't it?'

Sarah agreed. 'And I've got to find something to drive into town later. I have to get a hat,' she explained. 'Unless you've got something?'

Linda shook her head. 'Sorry, I haven't, but I can lend you my car. It's not exactly in the first flush of youth.' She looked doubtfully at Sarah, but she was too grateful for the offer to reject it.

'It's an old Mini, I'll give you the keys later. It's parked in the compound and you can't miss it. It's bright yellow.'

As she worked Sarah discovered that Linda was English like herself, but that she had worked in Hollywood for several years. 'There's so much more scope over there,' she told Sarah. 'We've designed these costumes to complement your colouring,' she explained, as she produced several silky tunics in rich greens and blues. 'Nothing too subtle—they simply didn't have the means of dyeing them, although we can go to town a bit more later in the film—once you're married to William of Sicily. Messina was an international port and it's feasible that silks and fabrics from the East would find their way there. In particular I thought you ought to wear something gauzy and provocative for your meeting with de Courcy, when he comes to tell you that Richard has managed to secure your dowry. You loved him as a girl, now you're a widow—a woman—and you want him to be aware of the fact. You married as you had to—a man of fifty, impotent and gross, and now you feel you've earned the right to love, and you do still love him, and since you are a queen and he is merely a knight you have to show him that love.'

'By dressing in Eastern silks?' Sarah teased, but she could tell that Linda was completely absorbed in her job.

'What do you think of the script?' Linda asked her, her mouth half full of pins as she slipped the first of the costumes over Sarah's head.

'It's fantastic. I only wish there was a chance of

meeting the author. I thought he might be here— on site—you know they sometimes are.'

'Umm.' Linda frowned, studying the fall of the fabric. 'You know it's rumoured that . . .' She broke off as the trailer door opened and a tall elegant woman in her late forties entered, apologising as she saw Sarah. 'I'm sorry, I know I'm a little early.'

'We're nearly through,' Linda assured her. 'Like you, Sarah was strictly accurate with her measurements—thank God. Do you two know one another, Eva?' she asked the older woman.

'Only slightly,' Eva Martell replied, smiling at Sarah. 'We worked together briefly on *Shakespeare*, I don't know if you remember?'

'Yes, I do,' Sarah confirmed warmly. The older woman had had a small part, sandwiched in between other work in America, but Sarah could still remember how kind she had been to a raw young girl fresh out of drama school.

'And now you and Ben are back together. I'm glad. He went through a bad time after you left him, and of course Dale's gloating didn't help, but they say that's Dale all over. He's always been jealous of Ben. Of course he's a first-rate actor, but he doesn't have Ben's talent for diversification. Even when they were at drama school together it was obvious that Ben would never simply be content to act.'

It was plain to Sarah that nothing she could say could correct the older woman's erroneous impressions, and she wondered a little cynically what Eva's response would be were she to tell her the true facts surrounding her relationship with and marriage to Ben. Dale jealous of Ben! Why, it was ridiculous. Dale had known right from the start that all she felt for him was brotherly affection, an affection which she knew he returned—witness the way he had allowed her to use him to protect her pride, letting Ben think they were lovers.

'Hey, don't forget these,' Linda called after her as she finished dressing and walked towards the trailer door. 'My car keys,' she explained when Sarah looked blank. 'You wanted to go into town?'

Thanking her for reminding her, Sarah said goodbye to Eva and left the trailer.

If anything the heat had intensified. The short walk from Linda's trailer to Ben's was enough to make her feel sick and shaky, her head tender to the harsh brilliance of the sun. Once inside, she gulped thankfully at the cool air, nauseated by the thought of lunch and settling instead for some fresh orange juice she found in the fridge. She must come to some arrangement with Ben over the cost of her keep. The fridge and freezer were well stocked and she suspected he probably ordered food weekly from the stores. She would check at the shop later in the day when she replaced the juice she had drunk—and she had better get some aspirins. She was glad there was no one to see the way her face flamed painfully as she remembered the way Ben had watched and touched her, almost as though he hadn't been able to stop himself. She was being stupid, she chided herself, allowing her imagination to colour reality with her own desires. Never at any time, apart from the night they had made love, had Ben given any indication of not being wholly in control of his reactions, and even that night had been a sham; a deliberate intent to seduce her. For making love to her she could forgive him, but for allowing her to believe that he had done so in love, she could not. Quickly rinsing her glass, she found her handbag, checked that she had money and traveller's cheques, and before the weight of her thoughts became too much for her, left the trailer.

Linda had been right when she described her car as 'ancient', Sarah reflected, as the small vehicle ploughed through the dust of the main road, but at least with such a variety of odd sounds and rattles to choose from, she wasn't going to worry about a particular one.

It took longer to reach the small town she had passed through with Dale than she expected, but then she had been travelling in the luxury of Dale's expensive sports car. A small smile tugged at her lips. Dale had always had a little-boy need for the trappings of fame; unlike Ben who she remembered had driven an ordinary saloon car when they were filming *Shakespeare*, although she had to admit the BMW he had been driving the previous evening had been considerably more luxurious.

CHAPTER FIVE

PARKING her car under the shade of one of the trees in the town's small, dusty square, Sarah climbed out and looked uncertainly around her. The square was empty and quiet—too quiet, she realised, noticing the shuttered and silent appearance of the buildings bordering it, and then it struck her! She was in Spain, not England, and it was siesta time! The headache which had been plaguing her all morning returned, the agonising throbbing in her temples increasing as she tried to think. It was barely gone lunchtime, which meant that it could be several hours before the shops reopened. What should she do? She couldn't even see a café where she could sit and wait. This was no holiday town geared to the odd ways of *turistas*, she probably wouldn't even be able to *find* a hat when the shops did open, she reflected forlornly, wishing she had given a little more thought to her mission before setting out. There wasn't even a chemist's shop open where she might have been able to buy something to relieve her headache and nausea.

She shivered suddenly. How silent the square was, the air oppressive, the sultry glare of the sun almost menacing. As she glanced at the horizon she saw the thick pall of cloud, presaging the storm Ben had mentioned. She had no alternative but to return to the site. At least if there was a storm, she comforted herself, it would negate the risk of her suffering from fresh sunstroke. She recollected that there had been a shop selling sunhats at the airport, and if the worst came to the worst she could always go there tomorrow; she wasn't needed for filming for another day. Trying to uplift her depressed spirits by this reasoning, she headed back to the car. Nothing seemed to have gone right since she arrived in Spain, and she had been so looking forward to it; so excited when she saw Dale waiting for her outside the airport building. Dale . . . she bit her lip as she got into the car. How sweet and understanding he was! Never once had he taken her to task for lying to him about her divorce. She frowned a little, wondering why he had *not* mentioned it, especially as he must have found it embarrassing to learn the truth from Ben rather than from her. How Ben must have gloated to be able to throw that 'ex-wife' back in his face! She frowned, her hands stilling, the scene coming unbidden to the surface of her mind in a series of sharply clear pictures. Dale, tossing the casual words at Ben. Ben, grim-faced, relentless, Dale, smiling mockingly, *Dale* . . . gloating?

Sarah shied away from the image. How ridiculous she was being! Dale had had nothing to gloat about, the words had simply slipped from his tongue accidentally; meant at worst as a lightly teasing comment. She was letting her foolish love for Ben play on her imagination, she thought shakily as she started the car. Dale was the one who had protected her from Ben's treachery, upholding her pride . . .

She realised as she drove out of the square that

the sun had stopped shining and that the clouds no longer lay massed along the horizon, but instead were threateningly overhead, heavy and ominous. If anything the heat seemed to have increased; not a pleasant heat, but a damply oppressive one, her hands sticky where they clung to the steering-wheel, perspiration beading her temples, her head swimming with pain and nausea.

She heard the thunder as she left the town, the muted rumble in the distance making her automatically increase her speed. She was not particularly frightened of thunderstorms, but this one promised to be extraordinarily spectacular and the effects of the compressed electric energy were making themselves felt on her body. Her skin seemed to burn one minute and then turn to ice the next, her head throbbing agonisingly as she tried to concentrate on her driving. She had only gone half a dozen miles when she felt the small car begin to lose acceleration. Thinking that the loss of power was her own fault, she pressed instinctively on the accelerator, realising with apprehension that the car wasn't responding.

She knew next to nothing about the mechanics of engines, and when the Mini finally coughed to a standstill, for several seconds she could do nothing but sit still in stunned disbelief. What on earth was she going to do? The most sensible course of action open to her was to return to the town. She couldn't remember seeing a garage, but surely there must be one? And a telephone. She would have to phone the site to let them know what had happened to her, although she doubted that she would be missed until Ben returned to the trailer in the evening. But getting back to the town meant a walk of six miles. It was a daunting thought, especially as the first large drops of rain were already beginning to fall, darkening the road surface, and splattering noisily on the car's metal roof.

Perhaps if she simply sat where she was? But she couldn't help remembering that she had seen no traffic on the road during her outward journey. As she had realised when she was in the town, it was siesta-time, and besides, she wasn't altogether sure it would be wise to simply hang around waiting for some knight of the road to offer her a lift.

Rather reluctantly she opened the car door and eased herself out. She hadn't brought a coat, and before she had gone much more than a hundred yards, she was soaked by the heavy rain. The thunder was nearer now, sheet lightning splitting open the clouds, and it was still so oppressively hot! She wouldn't have been entirely surprised to have seen steam coming off her clothes! Struck by a fit of giggles, she suddenly realised that she was feeling quite lightheaded, almost as though her feet weren't touching the ground. It was an extraordinary sensation, and one that sent alarm bells ringing in that part of her brain that still held on to common sense. She was beginning to feel quite dizzy and faint, and she moistened her suddenly dry mouth, telling herself that she simply could not faint, here in the middle of the road during a thunderstorm. Her eyes felt oddly heavy, her legs suddenly dangerously wobbly. The road seemed to shimmer and shiver around her. The sound of a car, at first a distant hum, grew louder, and she started to shiver. Dared she risk trying to stop it? The decision was taken out of her hands when she realised it was coming towards her, travelling in the opposite direction from the town, a powerful maroon blur, which took up a good three-quarters of the narrow road, the front wheel hitting a pothole and sending a wave of water cascading over her jeans and thin tee-shirt. Drenched and furious, Sarah wasn't aware that the car had stopped until she heard the faint slam of its door, followed by purposeful footsteps. She turned, her eyes widening in disbelief as she saw her husband coming towards her through the rain, black hair plastered wetly to his skull, the formal suit he was wearing turning him into an imposing stranger. But he *was* a stranger, she thought vaguely as he drew level with her and started to speak, his briefly furious questions reaching her through a barrier of protective fog, the only thing penetrating it his savage exclamation of anger as the drumming in her ears reached crescendo proportions and she slid helplessly to the ground.

When she came round she was sitting in his car. They were motionless on the side of the road, Ben's face decidedly grim as she opened her eyes and found him watching her.

'What the hell's going on?' he demanded bitingly. No words of comfort, no enquiries as to her state of health! Stifling the tears threatening to flow, Sarah tried to sit upright, shivering as she felt the clammy touch of her soaking clothes. 'Well? I'm waiting?'

He could wait until hell froze over as far as she was concerned, Sarah decided crossly, and then seeing the look on his face changed her mind and said quickly, 'I wanted to get myself a hat. Linda, from Costumes, offered to lend me her Mini, but it broke down. I was just walking back to find a garage.'

'You went to buy a hat in the middle of the siesta period? In a town where the women cover their heads with shawls, if they use anything? Have you run completely mad?'

Quivering with anger and humiliation, Sarah turned her head. She *would not* cry, she told herself, biting so hard on her bottom lip that she could taste her blood. She had started to shiver, suddenly desperately cold, unaware of how pale and fragile she looked, her eyes smudged pools of violet in the pallor of her face.

'You were five miles away from the town. Have you any idea of the condition you'd have been in if I hadn't come along when I did?'

Ben was seething, and although in some ways she could understand why her foolishness was infuriating him, she hated knowing that his concern was for the film and the effects any illness of hers might have upon it, rather than for her herself.

'How lucky for me then that you did,' she finally managed in a shakily defiant voice.

'I had to go into Seville. I wanted to send off the rushes from yesterday for myself, and I had some other business to attend to. As you so rightly say, luckily for you. What's the matter?' Ben asked sharply as she shivered again. 'You're not ill, are you?'

If he thought she was ill, he might take her part

away from her, and besides, she wasn't really, Sarah thought hazily. She was just suffering from too much exposure to the sun, or was it too much exposure to Ben that made her feel so weak and trembly?

'I'm wet and cold,' she managed, trying to sound cool and in control. 'I've also got the most dreadful headache.' She saw his mouth compress and realised that she had been unwise, when he gritted, 'You're suffering from heat-stroke, you little fool, and by the looks of it you're trying to compound it by contracting pneumonia as well! You'd better get those wet things off. Here, you can wear this,' he told her carelessly, removing his jacket. 'Once we get going the heater will soon warm the car, but it won't dry out those soaking jeans.'

Even though she knew he was right, she felt a curious reluctance to do as he said. He had seen her in far less than her bra and briefs, she reminded herself as her fingers fumbled with her zip—and as recently as last night. She knew he didn't care a damn about her, and yet she felt ridiculously shy at the thought of removing her clothes.

'Come on, Sarah,' he demanded impatiently. 'I have seen it all before, you know.'

The contempt in his voice opened a still raw wound, reminding her of the look in his eyes, and the—as she had foolishly thought it—reverence in his voice, that night when he had made her his. But that had all been nothing more than a hateful sham.

Averting her head, she slid off her jeans, her

fingers trembling as she tried to tug them free. At her side Ben made a small, explosive sound of impatience, the telling noise jerking her head up so that she could see the tautly implacable line of his jaw. 'Oh, for God's sake,' he muttered, a man goaded beyond the limits of his endurance. 'What are you—a child? Here, let me.' Before she could stop him his brown fingers curled round her ankle and then tugged remorselessly at the heavy, clinging denim. 'And now this,' he continued curtly when her jeans had been tossed into the back seat, and it was useless for her to protest that her tee-shirt was something she could manage quite adequately without his help. The heavy rain had soaked right through the thin fabric and through the soft silk of the bra she was wearing underneath, plastering it to the curves of her breasts, fuller now that she was a woman rather than a girl. For a few brief seconds as he tugged her tee shirt free of her arms, Ben's gaze rested on those curves, and to her utter chagrin and humiliation, Sarah felt them swell and firm, her reaction clearly visible in the burgeoning outline of her nipples against the now taut fabric of her bra. Colour washed her skin in a hot tide, her hands shaking as she shrank back into her seat, pulling on Ben's jacket, expecting with every tension-filled second that passed to hear him making some mocking comment. When he didn't, she risked a glance upwards, feeling happier now that she had the protection of his jacket concealing her body. To her surprise he was staring rigidly out of the window, his skin drawn tightly against the harsh bones of his face, his flesh white where he had compressed his mouth.

'Ready?'

He must have felt her move rather than seen her, because he hadn't so much as spared her a glance. When she gave a rather croaky 'yes', he started the engine, the sound not quite enough to drown out a fresh clap of thunder.

Neither of them spoke, but the silence wasn't an easy one. Sarah felt on edge with the tension of it, the comfort of Ben's jacket fast turning to torture. The fine wool smelled faintly of his cologne, and being wrapped in it was heartbreakingly like being wrapped in Ben's arms, especially when she closed her eyes. At least her headache seemed to have subsided, she thought numbly as they turned off the road and bumped down the track leading to the site.

'I must tell Linda about her car,' she mumbled as Ben drove past the compound and parked outside his trailer.

'Leave it,' he told her curtly. 'I'll see to it. There's a garage in the town—I'll get them to send someone out to it.'

Sarah reached for the door handle, biting back a startled gasp as Ben moved across her, and told her to wait. She closed her eyes as he slid out of the car and came round to her door, opening it quickly and bending to take her in his arms. She started to protest, but he silenced her with a frown, opening the trailer door and carrying her inside, and into her room.

'Stay there,' he commanded briefly as he turned back to the door. 'How are you feeling now?' he asked over his shoulder. 'Faint? Sick?'

'Not as bad as I did,' Sarah responded. 'My head still aches, but that's all.' Even as she spoke she started to shiver, not knowing whether it was reaction to being in Ben's arms or the chilly atmosphere of the trailer. She was reaching up to turn off her air-conditioning unit when Ben came back. He had taken off his shirt and trousers which had got soaked in the short journey from the car to the trailer, and was wearing a towelling robe. Sarah felt her heart pound, her breath catching in her throat as he stood over her frowning. His hair was tousled as though he had been drying it.

'Here, take these,' he instructed her, handing her two capsules. 'I'll get you a glass of water to go with them.'

When he came back she was still shivering. Her whole body felt chilled and she longed for a hot bath, followed by a long sleep. She took the glass he proffered, puzzled but not alarmed when he sat down on the edge of her bed. When she had drunk the water he took the glass from her and picked up a towel. 'Turn round,' he told her coolly. When she looked hesitant, he told her coldly, 'I'm going to dry your hair for you, not rape you. Although it wouldn't be rape, would it, Sarah?' She felt her skin burn at the mocking cynicism she heard in his voice, glad that she had her back to him and that he couldn't see her face.

It was oddly soothing having him rub her hair, his movements brisk but gentle, and she felt as though she could sit there all day—no, not sit there, but lie in his arms, she admitted on a sudden rush of knowledge, her body aching with a sense of rejection as he got up.

When he left without a word she thought he wasn't coming back, but she had just removed his jacket, unable to stop herself from pressing her face against its warmth, when he returned, a fresh towel in his hand, his eyes unreadable as she dropped the jacket as though it had been live coals. Had he seen? He couldn't have done, otherwise surely he would have made some biting comment?

It wasn't until he sat down beside her and calmly unfastened her bra, that Sarah realised he intended to stay. She opened her mouth to protest and found she was being enveloped in a thick, fluffy towel, Ben's hands hard and firm as they rubbed warmth into her chilled skin.

'Ben, I can manage,' she stammered, terrified that he would guess the effect his ministrations were having on her foolishly responsive body, but all he did was raise his eyebrows and comment scathingly:

'Sure you can—the way you were "managing" this afternoon, no doubt. Sit still, Sarah,' he told her, adding drawlingly, 'Who knows? Perhaps you might enjoy it?'

The trouble was *she* did know—that she would! And the knowledge was humiliating. Terrified that he would realise too, she forced herself to keep absolutely still, fighting down the weakly melting tide of desire running hotly through her body when his hand accidentally touched her breast.

'For God's sake relax,' Ben told her. 'What is it? The storm?'

The storm? Sarah had practically forgotten about it, until a particularly loud clap of thunder outside made her jump nervously. No, it was a storm of a different kind she feared—the storm of emotion Ben was arousing by touching her.

'Sarah?' She heard him curse as she stiffened. Simultaneously lightning illuminated the room and she saw her reflection in the mirror, her face white and tense, then Ben was pulling her back against him until her back curved against his chest, his arms locking round her.

'You really are scared, aren't you?' He turned her in his arms, searching her face, and Sarah couldn't deny it. She wasn't just scared; she was petrified. Petrified that if he continued to hold her the way he was doing she would betray herself completely. She hadn't forgotten how a younger Sarah and fought to conceal from him his ultimate victory; that not only had he seduced her body, he had also seduced her heart and mind, and she didn't want him to know it now, either. 'Come on, relax,' Ben told her. 'There's nothing to be afraid of.'

Oh, but there was, Sarah thought yearningly as he pulled her head down against his shoulder. Her body curved into the protection of his, one arm holding her against him while his free hand stroked soothingly over her back. At least it was meant to be soothing, she was sure, only its effect on her was very different. Feelings she had fought to suppress ever since she had seen him boiled up inside her. The shoulder she was pillowed against was hard and warm. The towelling robe had fallen open, revealing his skin sleekly brown over his collarbone. Quite what came over her afterwards Sarah wasn't sure, she only knew that she was impelled by some force greater than her will to touch her lips to that warm flesh, and then merely touching it with her lips wasn't enough. Her fingertips traced the shape of it, her lips following their course, and she was drowning in a wealth of sensations; the smooth satiny feel of Ben's skin and the underlying hard bone; the salt maleness she could taste beneath her mouth; the heady scent of it; her need of him so compulsive that she was barely aware of his curse as he started to jerk away from her, changing his mind and instead, lowering his head until his tongue found the sensitive cord in her neck, his hands pushing aside her towel to explore and possess the curves beneath.

Outside the storm raged, but it was nothing to the feelings raging inside her, Sarah thought weakly as she let Ben lay her on the bed, her hands going eagerly to his body when he joined her, pushing the robe off his shoulders, her pulses thudding when he shrugged it off completely.

A pulse beat tensely against his jaw and she reached upwards, kissing the spot, feeling his hands tighten on her body, her lips moving slowly over his throat, feeling the clenched tension of his skin as he swallowed, muttering something she couldn't decipher, before grasping her shoulders, her protest muffled beneath the hot possession of his mouth as it took hers in a kiss that had none of the sophistication she remembered from earlier kisses, but echoed the savage demand she could feel exploding inside her and went on until they were both out of breath, their hearts thudding in heavy unison, until Ben raised his head and looked at her, his thumb probing the full softness of her lip where she had bitten it earlier.

'Did I do that?'

The look in his eyes made her shake with need. She shook her head, in denial. 'No, it was . . .'

'Don't say it, Sarah,' he warned her, his voice suddenly bitter. 'God, you must have been desperate! Does Dale know the effect storms have on you? A potent stimulant, obviously. Was it he who taught you so well, Sarah? For a moment there you almost had me going out of my mind! But then that was the idea, wasn't it? Just like old times,' he added sardonically. 'Well, if that's the way you want it . . .' Before she could utter a word he bent his head, his tongue teasing the outline of her lips, but Sarah could sense the difference. Whatever it was that had burned between them before was gone. She felt sick and miserable, disgusted by her own lack of will power, hating the coldly assessing way Ben's eyes slid over her body, his hand cupping her breast.

'No!' She pulled sharply away from him, reaching for her towel and pulling it protectively around her.

'Ben, why are you doing this?' she demanded huskily. Why was he tormenting her?

'You really need to ask?' His eyes were cruel. 'You're a very desirable woman, Sarah, and I still want you. You know that, and knowing it, it's up to you to tell me "no". If you don't, you can be sure that sooner or later I'm going to think you're saying "yes", and I don't think Dale's going to like that. You surprise me, you know,' he added, as he stretched out a lazy hand for his robe, totally unconcerned about his nudity. 'I know Dale likes to play the field, but I always thought of you as the type of woman who wants her man all to herself. You and Dale didn't stay together long after you left me, and yet here you are, back in his arms . . .'

A denial trembled on her lips and was instantly silenced. His admission that he wanted her had stunned her and she knew that she wasn't strong enough to resist him if made love to her. Believing that Dale was still her lover might keep him at bay. It would also salve her pride, and so she kept silent.

CHAPTER SIX

'No, Gina, you must look more cowed. Remember Richard is your *beau idéal*, and now you're married to him. And yet you don't know him; you're inclined to be in awe of him.' Ben shouted the directions from where he was standing several feet away from the small group standing by the city walls.

They were filming the execution of the garrison of Acre. Sarah was standing next to Gina, wondering tiredly how many more times they would have to go through the scene. In point of fact the female parts in this scene were very small. All that was required of the three of them, herself as Joanna, Gina Frey as Berengaria, Richard's bride, and Eva as his mother Eleanor, was for them to look on with emotions which would mirror their differing personalities. However, Gina had other ideas, and Sarah could see that Ben was fast losing patience with her. The other woman was miscast, and she was making not the slightest effort to *be* Berengaria, as far as Sarah could see.

'Gina!' Ben was on the point of losing his temper; even Gina looked slightly apprehensive. 'Either you play Berengaria, or you leave this cast,' he grated at her. 'And don't threaten me with R.J. If this goes on much longer, you'll have cost him more money than the rest of the cast put together—and so I shall tell him!'

This time when they went through the scene

Gina was perfect; her distress when the camera homed in on her face, after having witnessed the savagery of her husband's command, sufficiently eloquent for Ben to call tiredly, 'That's it—can it.'

'You'd think she'd realise by now that Ben simply isn't interested in her,' Eva murmured to Sarah as they both went to sit in the shade. The storm had passed leaving the air clearer, but it was still hot, and Sarah wasn't going to be foolish enough to get heatstroke again. Not after what had happened last time! How close she had come to betraying her feelings to Ben!

'I think she took fright when Ben told her he'd get rid of her,' Sarah agreed. She felt hot and tired, her body aching with the effort of standing still for so many takes; funny how standing still was more exhausting than moving about.

'Umm—well, of course he's got a tremendous amount tied up in this film, so it's no wonder he wants it all to be exactly right.'

'As director he does have a lot of responsibility,' Sarah assented.

'Oh, but . . .' Eva looked at her, then changed her mind. Sarah didn't press her to continue, but she couldn't help wondering what she had been about to say. Could Ben have money tied up in the film? It wouldn't be totally unusual. He was coming towards them, and despite the gruelling heat and the problems of the morning he looked enviably cool and in control. He flopped down beside them, idly picking up Sarah's hand and holding it loosely between his own. For effect? She longed to pull away, but Eva was talking and would surely have noticed.

'It's coming along very well, Ben,' she said warmly. 'Don't you think so?'

'Umm, we're not doing too badly.' He was noncommittal, his mind obviously on other things, and when Eva excused herself saying that she felt her make-up was in need of attention Sarah wondered if she had left them alone deliberately. Although the crew and cast were all friendly, Sarah often found herself isolated with Ben, almost as though they *were* lovers ... Her face burned at the implication of her thoughts. 'Not getting too hot again, are you?' Ben queried sharply, adding, 'Stay there, I've got something for you.' He disappeared and returned ten minutes or so later, walking from the direction of the vehicles they had used to get the equipment and themselves out to the castle. 'Here.' He tossed a paper package at her, and as she caught it, Sarah frowned. What on earth was it? 'Open it, it won't bite,' he told her lazily, dropping down beside her again. 'I got it yesterday, I had to go to Seville.'

'Again?' That was twice in as many days.

'It's the nearest place I can telephone the States from. Aren't you going to open it?'

She did so reluctantly, amazement mirrored in her eyes as she pulled away the paper to reveal a pretty soft green straw hat, with a brim large enough to shade her face. 'Just see that you wear it,' was Ben's only comment as he watched her try it on, his eyes on Dale, who was lounging by the side of the canteen, ripping the metal tag off a canned drink. Sarah, following the direction of his gaze, frowned. Dale was behaving rather oddly towards her; effusively affectionate one moment and then critically resentful the next. She couldn't blame him for being a little annoyed with her—after all, she had deceived him about her divorce, but the deception hadn't been deliberate, and she missed the companionship they had previously shared. Only this morning he had made a lunge towards her, grabbing her and kissing her, ignoring her breathless protest and causing Ben to frown at them. He had released her with exaggerated care too, Sarah remembered, making some comment about forgetting that she was now 'Ben's property'.

'You might try having a word with Dale about his drinking,' Ben's voice broke in upon her thoughts. 'He's going a bit over the top.'

'I expect he's worried about his part.' Sarah was quick to defend him. 'It can't be easy for him, playing Richard, it's a very demanding role.'

'You think it would have been better to take the easy way out and make some sort of hero out of a legend?' Ben taunted. 'Do you find the script's portrayal of him . . . unacceptable?'

'Because of his lover, do you mean?' Sarah responded frankly. 'No, I don't, but it's typical of you that you should think I might do, Ben. If you want my honest opinion, I think the script deserves half a dozen Oscars. I'd love to meet the writer. I can't remember when I last read anything that showed such a depth of compassion and comprehension. Logically the most one ought to be able to feel for Richard is perhaps pity, but instead when I read the script I found myself actually wishing there was some way there could be a happy ending.'

'With Berengaria?' Ben mocked, his mouth twisting.

'No.' Sarah shook her head. 'With Philip,' she corrected him firmly. 'That's how powerfully the script is written.'

'Because it makes the unacceptable acceptable?' Ben mocked, but he was watching her closely, and Sarah was angry enough to say flatly:

'No, because it shows him as a human being, with virtues and failings, just like any other, and because it has the compassion not to condemn him for them, and I wouldn't like to think myself any less capable of compassion than the man who wrote it—but then I don't suppose that's something you'd be able to understand, Ben,' she said bitterly. 'Compassion doesn't have any place in your life, does it?' Without another word she got up and walked away from him, but even though she had not intended to do so, something made her pause and turn round. He was watching her, and the sunlight dancing on the ground must have played tricks on her eyes because, for a second, he looked almost bereft.

Having lost time at the beginning of the filming, Ben seemed determined to make up for it. He had a gift for directing that enabled him to get the best out of his cast, Sarah was forced to acknowledge, watching him work, one day, waiting for her cue to join some of the male actors, Richard's knights, who were supposedly enjoying an afternoon's hawking.

They were filming her journey through France en route for Spain and her first husband, and shortly she would be joining the others on set, having left her women to hawk with the men. Beneath her the pretty mare she was riding pivoted and tossed her head, and Sarah smoothed her neck automatically, hoping that she would be able to play the scene to Ben's satisfaction. As the rebellious, turbulent teenage Joanna, very much attracted to one of Richard's knights, she had disobeyed her brother's orders that she was to remain with her women and had followed the men on her horse. The script called for her to gallop madly towards Alain de Courcy, losing her veil and the snood constraining her hair as she did so, arriving at his side, flushed and breathless, her hair all in disarray, eagerly showing her feelings for him in her expression, while Paul Howell, the actor playing Alain, had to grasp her bridle in concern and then lean towards her and kiss her.

Her eyes on the group of riders, Sarah watched as Paul detached himself from the others and bent to examine his horse's hoof. This was her cue, and the small mare responded immediately to her touch. She had always enjoyed riding, having learned as a schoolgirl, and it was undeniably pleasant to feel the coolness of a breeze against her face. Blotting out everything but the fact that she *was* Joanna Plantagenet, Sarah disposed of her veil, checking an inward sigh of relief as the snood obediently came away with it, her hair whipping against her face, her eyes lighting up as she saw Alain riding grimly towards her.

'My lady, forgive me, that was not well done of me, I . . .'

'There is no need to apologise, Sir Knight,'

Sarah responded, her lines coming unbidden, hurt rejection glimmering in her eyes as she concentrated on the emotions Joanna would have experienced at being rejected by the man she loved, after their first kiss.

They played the scene to the end without hitch, or interruption from Ben, who only came striding towards them when it was over.

'Ben, I'm not sure about that bit where I kiss her,' Paul commented worriedly. 'My horse moved. Do you want to shoot it again?'

'No.' His voice was terse, his mouth curtly uncompromising as he bit out the word. Paul looked slightly puzzled, but didn't say anything, and Sarah stifled her own surprise. She had been sure that Ben would want them to do the scene again. He had made Dale run through a scene three times the previous day, for an equally small flaw, but perhaps he was worrying about costs, she reflected, as she dismounted and handed the reins of her horse over to the waiting boy. After all, Dale's part was the major role, and yet Ben had been so particular about every aspect of the film. She was still looking puzzled when she saw Eva coming towards her, proffering a cold drink. Ben had gone to talk to the technicians, and Eva asked sympathetically:

'Something wrong?'

'Not really, I was just wondering why Ben didn't want us to re-do that scene.'

'Perhaps he just doesn't like seeing his wife in the arms of another man,' Eva offered with a smile. 'He *is* human, you know,' she added gently, 'and you have only recently been reconciled. I know externally he always seems a cool customer, but we both know that's just a veneer. Dale's the shallow one of the two, for all his much vaunted male macho image.'

There was talk of a party on the final night before they flew to America for the studio filming, which was to include her own love scene, and those scenes which took place before Richard's departure for the Crusade. Sarah wasn't particularly keen to go. There was a limit to how long she could keep up the role of dutiful wife. Although Ben had made no further attempt to touch her and she had been careful to make sure she gave him no excuse for doing so, his words still burned in her mind. She knew she couldn't allow him to make love to her without betraying her real feelings, and anyway, she didn't want only his physical desire. Most nights she heard him typing long after she had gone to bed. She had no idea what he was doing and guessed that he would not tell her even if she were to ask.

She refused the invitation to the party and then discovered that Ben had business in Seville and would not be back until late anyway. He made no suggestion that she accompany him, and although Dale tried to coax her to change her mind, she refused. Trying to be Joanna had taken more out of her than she had anticipated, and combined with the strain of living side by side with Ben, and yet trying to appear indifferent to him, was beginning to tell.

'Oh, come on, sweetling,' Dale protested when she refused. They were standing by his trailer, and he opened the door. 'Come inside and we'll have a drink and talk it over. I'm sure I can persuade you to change your mind.' He gave her a winning smile, but Sarah still shook her head.

'Really I'd rather not, Dale,' she told him firmly. 'I'm whacked.'

'Poor darling!' His voice was caressing and she couldn't avoid the arm he slid round her or the light pressure of his lips as they brushed hers. More exasperated than annoyed, she pushed him away, startled to discover Ben standing less than three yards away, watching them.

'Oh dear,' Dale drawled, 'all is discovered!'

It should have been funny, and she was sure Dale had meant it to be, but somehow it wasn't. Ben looked more contemptuous than amused, and Sarah found to her dismay that she felt sick and shaky, anxiety clawing at her stomach. Without uttering a word, Ben walked away, leaving Dale to pull a far from repentant face. 'He's only being dog-in-the-manger,' he told Sarah easily. 'We both know that. Unless, of course, I was right, and he's made good his old bet? Ben's the type who would believe better late than never, and like I told you, sweetling, he'd do it, just to give himself the pleasure of thinking he'd come between us.'

Her stomach churning unpleasantly, Sarah shook her head. 'You're wrong, Dale,' she announced with more firmness than she felt. 'I know you warned me to be on my guard before, but Ben doesn't ... hasn't ...' She struggled for words, and Dale relaxed.

'That's okay, then,' he said softly. 'I don't want him hurting my favourite girl—not a second time!'

Sarah could still hear the noise of the party when she prepared for bed. On the pretext of needing to read through her lines again she had stayed up until gone twelve, hoping that Ben might return, but he still wasn't back, and even if he had been she didn't quite know what she had hoped for.

At first when she heard the urgent knocking on the trailer door, she thought it was Ben, but when she opened it, it was Paul who stood there, his face creased in anxious concern.

'Sarah, can I have a word with Ben?'

'He isn't here,' she told him slowly. 'He's still in Seville. Can I help?'

'I don't know. It's Dale. He insisted on going into town after the party had finished. I went with him—he wasn't fit to drive, although he threatened that he would, and now . . .'

'He's drunk?' Sarah ventured.

'And how! He's still in the car, and I thought Ben might be able to . . .'

'If you can bring the car up here and we can get him into the trailer, I might be able to get some black coffee into him,' Sarah suggested, 'and then between us we could get him back to his own trailer to sleep it off.'

'Would you?' Paul looked relieved. 'I'll go and get him.'

By the time she heard the car Sarah had the coffee ready. It took the two of them to get Dale into the trailer, and once in he dropped senselessly on to the bunk-like settee, at first refusing all their efforts to get him to drink the coffee.

'We're never going to sober him up. I shouldn't

have involved you in this,' Paul muttered grimly. 'And what makes it worse is that I'm sure he's only doing it to spite Ben. Ben told him to cool his drinking and this is his way of getting back at him. He knows quite well the film's gone too far now for Ben to replace him, and if he starts delaying things now, making Ben waste time while he gets him sobered up, the backers are going to come down hard on Ben.'

He made it sound almost as though Dale hated Ben, Sarah thought. And she was just turning this thought over in her mind, when Paul gave a cry of pain as Dale moved, jerkily, and the mug of boiling hot coffee tipped over his wrist and hand, soaking through his jeans.

'You go and get changed,' Sarah told him as she mopped up the mess. 'Dale seems to be coming out of it now. I'll try and get some coffee into him while you're gone.'

'Thanks. I'll be as quick as I can.'

'Come on, Dale, drink this.' Paul had been gone for just over ten minutes, and Dale mumbled something unintelligible as Sarah held the mug to his mouth. At least he was sitting upright now, she thought tiredly. With any luck, by the time Paul returned, Dale would be able to make it to his own trailer under his own steam.

'Don't look at me like that, sweetling,' Dale remonstrated in slurred tones. 'Just because I had a good time! You're getting almost as bad as that husband of yours. Where is he, by the way?' he asked, looking round the trailer. 'Not gone off and left you, has he? Poor Sarah, we'll have to do something about that, won't we?'

'Dale, stop it!' Sarah protested as he put his arm round her, leaning drunkenly against her, his lips moving along her jaw. For someone who was drunk he showed surprising strength and determination, and Sarah grasped him crossly, trying to push him away. He didn't realise what he was doing, of course. He couldn't.

'Lovely Sarah,' he muttered thickly as she tried to move him, pressing his mouth against her throat. If she couldn't move him then she would have to move herself, Sarah decided despairingly, not realising as she pulled away that he was half lying on her robe. There was a brief tearing sound as she moved, but the words of protest she was about to utter were lost as the trailer door suddenly opened and she saw Ben looking down at them.

The look on his face beggared words, and Sarah felt herself flushing crimson with guilt as she realised that he had completely misinterpreted the scene.

'Couldn't he even wait to get you to bed?' Ben snarled at last. Adding grimly, 'I warned you, Sarah!'

'But Ben . . .' He's drunk, she had been about to say, but Dale suddenly lifted his head and looked at them, the smile he gave Ben bringing a dark tide of anger to the latter's face. Sarah shrank back as Ben reached for Dale, half dragging and half lifting him out of his seat.

'Ben, please, you don't understand,' Sarah protested, reading murder in the hot fury of his eyes.

'Be quiet!' he gritted at her. 'I'll deal with you

later.' Almost throwing Dale out of the trailer, he turned and followed him, while Sarah held her breath, praying that Paul would return in time for them to explain.

'I know you're burning to thump me, Ben,' she heard Dale say, suddenly far more sober than he had been in the trailer, 'but if you break my jaw, you'll only delay completion of the film. Never mind,' he mocked, and Sarah shivered at his foolhardiness, 'third time lucky!'

How could he remind Ben of the first time he had found them together in compromising circumstances? The look on her husband's face had shown all too clearly that his anger had exploded out of control, and Sarah was shivering when she heard him return.

'Dale might have got off scot-free,' she heard him saying suavely somewhere above her as he closed the door, 'but you're not going to! I'll have to think of a punishment that won't show; won't spoil that pale skin and delay filming, won't I, my dear wife?' He almost snarled the last words, and Sarah shrank from him as he reached down and with one violent movement ripped both what was left of her robe and the fine lawn nightgown she was wearing beneath it.

'Ben, please!' she begged in a last-ditch attempt to deflect the violence of his rage, but it wasn't any use, his hands were already on her body, and Sarah shivered as he swung her up into his arms and carried her the few yards to his bedroom. In contrast to the untidiness of the area where he worked in the trailer, everything was immaculately neat, the bed made and the room somehow impersonal. She

wasn't going to fight against him, she decided
resignedly; she would only lose, and anyway she had
a sickening suspicion that that was exactly what he
wanted her to do, and that the demons that rode him
would enjoy punishing her folly if she did, but a
deep-seated feminine instinct that wouldn't be
denied made her cringe instinctively from him when
he dropped her callously on the bed and then turned
to take off his clothes, his eyes glittering savagely as
he subjected her pale body to a slow and insulting
inspection that left her flushed and humiliated,
wishing she could match him look for look. But
somehow her glance skidded uncertainly from
broad male shoulders, downwards to the hard
flatness of his belly, registering somewhere along the
way that his tan extended to every inch of his body,
and wondering with a swift stab of jealousy if he
sunbathed alone, or if someone had been with him,
and if so, if he had turned to her in the drowsy heat of
a Californian afternoon, and they had made love.

'Frightened?' He purred the word with all the
deceptive softness of a jungle cat before demolish-
ing its prey. 'No need to be, I'm only taking what's
rightfully mine.'

'There's now a law that forbids a man to rape
his wife—just in case you didn't know,' Sarah
warned him, wishing her voice didn't sound quite
so breathless, but her words seemed to have no
effect upon him at all, he simply walked round the
bed still watching her, studying her, and she had to
fight against her need to protect herself from the
narrowed and mocking assessment of his gaze by
reaching for some form of cover.

'Shy?' The mocking jibe stung, and she gasped a

protest as Ben suddenly sat down beside her, reaching for her hands, and uncurling the fingers she hadn't realised were digging into the softness of the duvet. 'There's really no need to be,' Ben drawled softly. 'After all, the entire film-going world has seen you like this at one time or another, if only briefly.'

There had been a scene similar to this in *Shakespeare*, Sarah remembered, and how she had hated filming it, but it had been very brief and she hadn't been completely nude, and then Ben had been tender and understanding, helping her through what was for her a formidable ordeal. 'And Dale, of course,' Ben added, not quite as softly, moving slightly so that he was lying beside her, his head supported by his hand as he continued to study her. In spite of her fear, Sarah felt an immediate response. Her mind was a frantic ball of fear, tensed inside her skull, but her body . . . 'But tonight you're going to forget him.

'Don't say a word,' he warned her, when she opened her mouth to protest, and then his mouth was hard and angry on hers, deliberately punishing and inflicting hurt. She struggled against him, but his hands slid from her shoulders to her waist, digging into the vulnerable flesh.

Her struggles brought her into closer contact with his body, her breasts pressed against his chest, the friction of his hair-roughened flesh against their sensitive tips instantly arousing. Anger and despair burned through her, mingling with her love and need; she hated him for what he was trying to do to her; for all that he had already done to her; and yet she still loved him; yearned for him to love her with a matching intensity.

When Ben released her mouth it was throbbing from the violence of his kiss, his eyes brilliantly green as he looked down into her face. 'What's the matter?' he mocked. 'Too scared to fight?'

Something seemed to explode inside her, and her body tensed under the force of the emotion burning through her, her hand lifting to claw at the arrogantly mocking face.

Just for a moment she thought she glimpsed satisfaction in Ben's eyes as his fingers closed on her wrist, forcing her arm down to her side, his mouth on hers demanding a bitter tribute from the vanquished to the victor. A red mist seemed to dance before her eyes, a savage, choking feeling racing through her veins, her body tensing against the hard presence of Ben's hand cupping her breast, the hand he had released forming a small fist to hammer unavailingly at the breadth of his shoulders, while all the time the molten anger kept on growing and changing, so gradually that she didn't realise that anger had given way to an equally fierce passion, her body responding to Ben's with an intensity which surely betrayed her in a hundred ways. But when she looked into his face, there was no recognition of his victory there, the normally acutely perceptive green eyes hazed by a desire which she recognised was as strong as her own.

'Sarah.' He muttered her name thickly, as though he was barely aware of having done so, his hand tangling in her hair, tugging back her head, exposing the vulnerable column of her throat.

When his mouth moved over it she thought she would die of the explosive pleasure shooting through her body, and realised with passion-distorted haziness that he was as much in the grip of desire as she was herself; rationality suspended as their bodies took over from their minds. A tiny detached corner of hers registered that he was breathing harshly, his forehead damp as it rested against her skin, a dark flush colouring his skin, his hands trembling faintly against her body as his mouth burned compulsively against her skin, the savage teeth of anger softened by their mutual passion.

When his mouth left her throat she was shivering, shaking with something she no longer wanted to pretend was fear, the pressure of her fingers digging into the hardness of his back indicative not of anger, but of need, an inner instinct telling her that no matter what had motivated Ben originally, it, and his habitual cool control, were both suspended. Dimly she realised how much she had yearned to see him like this, as much a victim of need as she was herself, something she had always thought missing when he made love to her in the past. Even when he had finally possessed her she had been conscious of a holding back; a fine control.

'Sarah, touch me. Want me!' The words shivered across her skin, muttered against it, his gaze burning feverishly into her as he looked the length of her body, his eyes darkening in acknowledged arousal as his hands cupped her breasts witnessing the evidence of how he had affected her, her body unashamedly arching invitingly as he lowered his head and touched first one and then the other swollen nipple with his lips and then again with his tongue. Desire ran like quicksilver from the heat of his mouth on her body to every nerve ending, her nails biting deep in mute ecstasy against his skin. Through the melting pleasure his touch was giving her Sarah felt him tense, mutter something against her skin, and then possess the swollen fullness of one breast, sucking it with a compulsive hunger, which she knew once would have shocked her, but now only awoke a corresponding hunger within her to touch him, driving her to press her body closer to his in an aching frenzy of need, her hands moving hungrily over the satin smoothness of his skin, exploring the male shape of him as she had never done before, marvelling at the variety of sensations relayed to her as her fingertips moved over his body, and finding a deeply intense pleasure in Ben's shuddering response to her exploration; his hoarsely muttered insistence that she touch him with her mouth as well as with her hands, and her own eagerness to comply.

The climax was as frenetic as all that had gone before, Sarah aching for the complete fulfilment of Ben's possession long minutes before it was accomplished, when she sensed he denied them both to intensify their eventual mutual pleasure. But his control was obviously greater than hers, her need only briefly appeased by the hard urgency of his body against hers, whispered pleas mingled with the kisses she pressed against his skin, her tongue delighting in the faintly salt taste of him as it moved along his throat, her body registering the

tense response of his muscles to her touch with a
shivering delight that when communicated to him
dissolved the last barrier of his control, his hands
and mouth suddenly urgent in their demands, her
cries of pleasure lost beneath his kiss, both of them
abandoning themselves to the shuddering crescendo of pleasure.

Afterwards, lying limp and exhausted in his
arms, Sarah could barely comprehend what had
happened; how punishment had turned to pleasure,
anger igniting a passion which had burned with
unanticipated ferocity. She glanced at Ben. He was
lying with his eyes closed, but they opened as
though he sensed her look. Quite what she had
expected him to say, she wasn't sure, but when he
turned to her and said perfectly evenly and
mockingly, '*Now* tell me about Dale,' the fragile
illusion that they had shared something rare and
precious shattered into a thousand irreparable
fragments. Half a dozen retorts sprang to her lips,
only to be discarded. He had tricked her again.
What she had thought of as shared passion had
obviously all been a sham. In a daze of pain she
heard him adding insultingly, 'I'll say one thing for
him, though, he's taught you to be a woman,
Sarah, and a very passionate one. Perhaps it's a
pity after all that you don't have any major love
scene in *Richard*. You're wasting a very excellent
talent, my dear. You could make a fortune from
appearing in . . .'

She hit him before he could continue, the
imprint of her hand leaving a white and then red
mark against his face. Tears threatened, and
without waiting to see his reaction she fled,

terrified with every thudding heartbeat that he would pursue. Only when she had been lying in her own bed for half an hour did she realise that he wouldn't, and only then did she acknowledge that her punishment was perhaps that he had not.

What they had shared in making love had opened her eyes to many things she had not previously known; among them her own deeply passionate nature. Ben had made love to her to punish her, but even knowing that she hadn't been able to stop herself responding. Thank God they were leaving Spain in the morning, she thought achingly. She could not endure to live in such close confines with Ben any longer. He must surely have guessed how she felt about him. He hadn't taunted her with it yet, but no doubt he would. And it wasn't until she was on the point of sleep that she remembered Dale, and the original cause of Ben's anger.

'Well, that's that,' Lois exclaimed. 'Everything packed up and ready to go. I must admit I'm looking forward to getting back. My boy-friend works for a local radio station,' she explained, 'and being away on location without him is hell!'

Sarah had gone to see her to find out what arrangements had been made for her journey to Hollywood. She had learned that seats had been booked on flights for all the cast and crew. 'Although of course Gina is returning with R.J., in his private plane.' She pulled a face and grimaced. 'Poor guy, he's quite sweet, I don't think he honestly deserves her—she's such a bitch.'

R.J. had arrived the previous evening, just in

time to join the party, but because Sarah hadn't gone she hadn't seen him until the morning when he had arrived to discuss the film with Ben.

Sarah had been making coffee when Ben brought him in, and after being introduced, she had made herself scarce, realising that they wanted to talk privately. In fact she was only too glad not to have to face Ben alone. She had woken hating herself for what had happened between them, not knowing how on earth she was going to endure the mocking comments she was sure must be on the edge of his tongue.

'Sarah!'

She flushed wildly and turned, hearing Ben's voice, relieved to find that R.J. was still with him.

'R.J.'s offered us both a ride back in his private jet, and I've accepted. It will give you a few hours to get settled into the house before we get on with the rest of the filming.'

'The house?' Sarah eyed him uncertainly, and was rewarded with a briefly impatient frown.

'Yes, my house, on Malibu beach. I prefer to live there, and it isn't too far to the studio, or the location where we'll do the rest of the filming.'

'But . . .' but I don't want to stay with you, had been the words trembling on her lips, but she sensed that to utter them would bring down fresh censure on her head, and she felt too tired and drained to argue. Of course Ben would want this fiction of a marriage to continue until after he had completed work on the film. But how long would that be? How much longer could she endure? At least one small blessing was that in a house there would be more opportunity to avoid one another.

Last night, for instance, she had lain sleepless listening to the sound of him breathing, knowing that only a thin wall separated them. A thin wall . . . and a wide gulf embattled with contempt and deceit on Ben's side, and disillusionment and despair on hers, she decided tiredly.

CHAPTER SEVEN

How bare everything looked with the equipment half dismantled, Sarah thought, studying the activity going on all around her. Later, when they had all gone, the hire company would come to remove the trailers and then there would be nothing left to even show that they had been there; at least not outwardly. Rather like her relationship with Ben, she thought tiredly. Outwardly it might never have happened, but inwardly ... She stiffened slightly as she saw the object of her thoughts approaching, her muscles as tense as an angry cat's, ready to scratch rather than purr.

'I thought you finished packing half an hour ago,' was his opening comment, but Sarah didn't miss the way his eyes hardened over her closed and withdrawn expression, or the tautly controlled anger which seemed to emanate from him as he stood watching her, his body tautly lean, the action of sliding his hands into the pockets of his jeans drawing attention to the powerful strength of his thighs and their wholly male structure. Deeply flushed, she looked away, trying to control breathing suddenly as laboured as though she had been running.

'Sarah!' Her head snapped up as she heard someone call her name. Paul came loping towards her, his dark hair damp, a bronze sheen on his deeply tanned skin. By anyone else's standards he

was undoubtedly a very handsome man, Sarah
acknowledged, forcing a smile, but he didn't
possess one tenth of the sensual magnetism of the
man standing next to her.

'I just wanted to thank you for helping out last
night,' Paul began as he drew level with them. 'I
did start to come back when I'd dealt with my
arm, but when I got to Dale's trailer I saw he was
in it, and comparatively sober as well.' He turned
to Ben and grimaced. 'He gave us both a hard
time, Ben, and Sarah was a real good Samaritan,
offering to help me with him when I came to the
trailer looking for you.' With another smile he
sauntered off, leaving Sarah alone with Ben in a
silence that seemed fraught with unspoken undercurrents.

'What was all that about?' Ben's voice was
perfectly even, but nevertheless Sarah shivered as
much as if the temperature had suddenly dropped
by ten degrees.

'Sarah!' His tone warned her that he was getting
impatient. 'Tell me,' he demanded.

'You heard Paul,' she returned, trying to match
his cool dryness of tone. 'He knocked on the
trailer door some time after twelve last night. At
first I thought it was you. He explained that Dale
had . . . had been into town,' she hesitated a little
over the words, not wanting to betray to him
Dale's recklessness, but realised her small subterfuge had been in vain when Ben's mouth twisted
and he said sardonically:

'Had got himself so drunk that Paul had to
bring him back half insensible, is that what you
mean?'

'He ... he had been drinking,' Sarah agreed, trying to avoid the question. 'Paul wanted to try and ... sober him up. He'd come to you for help, and I ...'

'And you naturally leapt into the breach,' Ben sneered. 'But that still doesn't explain how I came to find you in his arms, does it? Or do you want him so much that you don't mind being mauled by someone in his condition?'

'It wasn't like that!'

'No? Then tell me what it was like?' Suddenly he seemed to have moved much too close to her, his fingers curling round her arm, and Sarah had the impression that if he could he'd like to shake the truth out of her.

'I made him some coffee, but as we were trying to get him to drink it, it spilled over Paul and he had to go and change and see to his arm. When he had gone, Dale ...'

'I think I can guess for myself what Dale did when he was alone with you,' Ben interrupted, his voice suddenly as dangerous as broken glass. 'Did it never occur to you that for a man in his supposed state he sobered up quickly enough when I appeared?'

It *had* struck her that Dale had made a remarkably swift recovery, and although she wasn't going to say as much to Ben, her expression gave her away, and he drawled sardonically, 'And taking that a step further, might it just be possible that Dale manoeuvred Paul deliberately, using him to ...'

'To be alone with me?' Sarah demanded, her temper suddenly rising. Why did everyone try to blacken Dale? 'If Dale wants to be alone with me, he doesn't need to resort to subterfuge.'

'Not unless he wants me to be a witness to it,' Ben agreed, watching the emotions chase one another across her face.

'But why . . . why should he want to do that?' Just for a moment Sarah felt as though she teetered on the edge of some breathtaking discovery; something so important and monumental that her mind reeled with the power of it, but no sooner had she grasped the possibility than it eluded her, and Ben's face, grimly closed and hard with anger, mocked the vulnerability of her thoughts.

'Leave it, Sarah,' he advised her grittily. 'You've just overplayed your hand.' He released her and walked away without a backward glance; leaving her smouldering with fresh anger. There hadn't been so much as an apology for last night; for wrongly accusing her, for . . . making love to her. Her heart thudded in suddenly accelerated confusion. Had she expected him to apologise? To tell her that he had made love to her out of desire and want, rather than anger? But there *had* been desire, she protested fiercely, and not just on her part.

'Just as soon as we take off I'll have the steward bring you a drink.'

They were in the cabin of R.J.'s private jet, and Sarah was still staring wonderingly around her, marvelling at the luxury of it. Gina was lying back in her own seat, eyes closed, her expression one of bored petulance, rejecting every attempt on the part of her lover to placate her.

Sarah had half expected her to insist on sitting with Ben, but it was evident that much as she wanted Ben, she wasn't prepared to risk losing her rich lover to get him, and Sarah could well imagine how that would gall a man of Ben's temperament. He would never stand for coming second—in any woman's affections.

Their take-off was smooth, the steward moving swiftly to dispense drinks. Sarah asked for something long and cold, and settled back in her seat to drink it. Ben was sitting next to her, and even without looking at him she was conscious of his proximity, wave after wave of heat suffusing her body as she recognised the intensity of her own desire to touch and be touched by him. She jerked her thoughts away from Ben painfully, to hear R.J. saying, 'I've got a little surprise for you, Ben—instead of the traditional film, we're going to watch the rushes. This husband of yours is in a class of his own,' R.J. told Sarah whimsically. 'Unlike every other director I know, he won't watch the rushes daily. He prefers to wait.'

'Because I like to see each piece of film cold,' Ben told him. 'When a scene's been freshly filmed my own reaction to it's still clouded by whatever I felt when it was done. I prefer to see it without the rose-tinted lenses.'

'Darling, you're too fussy,' Gina pouted. 'And so very strict!' She glanced at her lover. 'You wouldn't believe how nasty he's been to me!'

If the words held a suggestion of threat R.J. obviously didn't hear it. Instead, much to Sarah's surprise, he beamed. 'That's what I like to hear,' he told Ben, clapping him on the back, 'someone else being careful with my money.'

'Not just yours, darling,' Gina protested, flashing Ben a distinctly provocative look. 'Ben's invested in the film, too. Some day he's going to be nearly as rich as you.'

Once again the financier didn't rise to the bait, instead calling over the steward and murmuring some instructions. Within seconds the cabin was darkened, the screen seeming to appear like magic from the ceiling, and Sarah found that she was holding her breath as she watched.

'Well, darling, what do you think?' Gina lit a cigarette, as light once again flooded the cabin, leaning back in her seat in a pose Sarah thought was probably deliberately provocative, showing off the lines of her body in her thin silk suit.

'It's taking shape,' was Ben's only response, and yet Sarah had been sure that he was pleased, sensing it more from his silence and stillness as they watched the rushes than from any verbal comment he had made.

Her own scenes she had scrutinised carefully, holding her breath as she watched the one with Paul when he kissed her. The small flaw had been carefully edited out, and she frowned, wondering who had noticed, and how the studio had known to take it out.

Some time during the afternoon the effects of her sleepless night and the long flight overtook her. Through the waves of sleep engulfing her Sarah had a hazy impression of Ben bending over her, and the armrest between them being removed, his arm securing her against the length of his body, but it was just her imagination, she told herself. Ben had no desire at all to hold her in his arms.

She woke to a sensation of warmth and languorous happiness, opening her eyes slowly as she stretched, suddenly aware that she was pillowed against Ben's side, her head resting just below his shoulder, her body turned into his. His arm was round her, his hand curving possessively just below the swell of her breast. She moved slightly and felt the pressure of his arm tighten, a muttered protest alerting her to the fact that he was still asleep. On the other side of the cabin she could see the motionless figure of Gina, and raised herself slowly, taking care not to disturb Ben, as she looked down into his sleeping face, unprotected and vulnerable, its harshness softened by the thick sweep of his dark lashes, wondering a little at the acute weakening well of protective love the sight of him stirred within her. Even the hard lines of his mouth seemed softer, the full underlip denoting the intensity of his passion.

He stirred and opened his eyes, still glazed with sleep, his 'Sarah! Darling!' stirred her senses in much the same way that his expelled breath stirred the tendrils of hair at her temples, her defences unprepared for the warm pressure of his hand as it slid into her hair, propelling her against him, her mouth parting instinctively to the slow movement of his lips against hers, Ben's eyes closing again as his tongue gently explored the shape of her mouth, so slowly and seductively that it was like drowning in honey.

'Hey, come on, you two lovebirds! Time for breakfast!'

R.J.'s voice interrupted them, and Ben's eyes opened and hardened as they took in her flushed cheeks and slightly swollen mouth. 'What a pity Dale can't be the one to interrupt *us* now,' he whispered as he released her. 'Do you think he'd be disillusioned?'

His look and the tone of his voice reminded her of everything that she would rather forget.

'Dale knows I'm an actress, Ben,' she retorted, sounding braver than she felt. 'He knows I can always pretend that the man holding me in his arms is the one I really want.'

'Is that so? Then perhaps I ought to have had a tape beside me the other night.' His voice was ugly now, and she flinched from the acidity of it. 'It was my name you called, Sarah, me who you begged to make love to you? Remember?'

She was thankful that the sudden arrival of the steward meant that she needn't reply. He had come to take their order for breakfast, and she numbly asked him simply for a cup of coffee. shuddering as Ben drawled that he was hungry enough for a full breakfast. Her stomach was churning so much she doubted she could even drink her coffee, but their exchange patently hadn't affected Ben in the slightest. But then when had she ever touched his emotions? If he had cared in the slightest about her he would never have tried to make good his bet!

'Welcome to America.' Ben's tone was sardonic rather than welcoming, and Sarah fought to control the clenching muscles of her stomach as the hot sunshine of the Californian morning hit her. Thanks to R.J. they were whisked through Immigration in next to no time—Sarah had been a little startled to discover that Ben had retained his U.K. citizenship and was forced to go through Immigration with her. His work as a film director surely meant that he would spend the rest of his life in and around Hollywood, and she had never heard him say anything that might prove him to be inordinately proud of being British. But then she knew so little about him, she reflected miserably.

'This way.' A cool touch on her arm directed her to a line of waiting cars, and Ben came to rest beside a sleekly elegant black limousine. The chauffeur greeted him with a smile, glancing curiously at Sarah. 'My wife,' Ben informed him as he opened the door for her, then slid inside the cool welcome of the car.

'Which do you want, Mr de l'Isle,' the chauffeur asked him, 'the studio or your home?'

'Home, please, Ray,' Ben replied easily. 'Sarah will want to get settled in, but you can tell Andy I'll be in this afternoon. Ray drives for the studio, not for me,' Ben explained to Sarah as he settled back beside her. 'I've got a meeting there this afternoon. Try not to miss me too much, although I should be back for dinner.'

The mockery in his glance reminded Sarah, if she was in any need of a reminder, that the comment was for the benefit of their driver rather than for her, and she forced her glance away from the dark power of Ben's features and tried to study the scene outside the car. The highway they were travelling along was far wider than anything she had experienced before, packed with glittering pieces of metal. The ultimate consumer society, she found herself thinking as she studied the billboards and the obvious affluence surrounding her.

'We won't go into Hollywood,' Ben told her. 'Plenty of time for you to see that later. We'll take the coast road, Ray,' he told the driver, 'it should be quieter.'

The beauty of the countryside caught Sarah's breath, the tantalising glimpses she had of the ocean making her long for Ray to stop the car so that she could see more, and then the road was sweeping past luxurious and well-tended houses, dropping closer to the coast until it ran parallel to the beach, giving Sarah her first sight of what Ben told her drawlingly were 'beach houses'. Where on earth had she got the idea that they were simple dwellings constructed out of timber and built mainly on stilts? These houses were magnificent, breath-catching, their views only to be guessed at.

'I'll have to drop you there,' Ray announced suddenly, turning to grin at Ben. 'I daren't risk this along that apology you call a road.'

'Don't worry about it. We can use the Range Rover to go the rest of the way.'

'Do you want me to pick you up later?'

Ben shook his head. 'No need. I'll drive myself in.' He opened his door and slid out as Ray came round to help Sarah. The first thing that struck her was the dazing heat; the second the sudden sensation of disorientation. Ray was helping Ben with the cases, and then suddenly he was backing the car, turning it, and leaving them completely alone on what appeared to be a deserted stretch of road.

'This way,' Ben touched her arm, and Sarah withdrew from his touch as though it stung, barely aware of the grimly sardonic twist to his features. 'What's the matter?' he drawled as he led the way tõ a concrete building Sarah vaguely realised must be a garage. 'Hoping we'd be close enough to Hollywood for you to see lover-boy pretty regularly?' He shook his head. 'I don't mix with that crowd, Sarah. It's pretty remote down here. In fact this track . . .' he indicated the dust grooves in the tussocky sand, 'leads only to my house, so if it's company you want, you'll have to rely on mine.'

He opened the garage door and disappeared inside. She heard an engine fire and stood well back as a Range Rover appeared. 'Come on, get in.' Ben opened the door and leaned down, half lifting and half pulling her in, before completing his reversing manoeuvre. Before he closed the garage with some electronic device she caught a glimpse of a dark, expensive-looking saloon car, and then he was turning, facing down the narrow rutted track.

'You obviously like isolation.' Her voice sounded dry and cracked, edged with tension and pain.

Ben shrugged. 'I certainly prefer no company to the wrong company.' He turned to study her. 'Unlike you. How many men have there been in your life as well as Dale, Sarah? What sort of relationship is it you have with him, anyway? He isn't exactly the faithful type. What is it? An open affair, each of you free to do your own thing when the other isn't around?'

'There hasn't been anyone,' Sarah retorted hotly, just managing to catch back the words 'apart from you', shuddering to think of the effect of such a damning admission.

'You know, you say that emotively enough for it to be true.' He studied her again. 'But haven't you forgotten something? Or rather should I say "someone",' he added pointedly, and she flushed as she realised he was referring to himself. 'They say a woman never forgets her first lover, and I was the first, wasn't I, Sarah?'

Her voice seemed to have locked in her throat, her vocal chords incapable of uttering a sound. 'I . . . I don't want to talk about it,' she managed huskily at last.

'Because you hate yourself so much?' he taunted, but beneath the taunting Sarah sensed a deep seam of anger, tightly held under control, and it frightened her, making her glad when the Range Rover suddenly came to a halt at the entrance to a small bay.

'This beach is strictly private,' Ben told her as he climbed lithely out. She heard him coming alongside her, and panicked, thrusting open her door, half stumbling in her anxiety to get out before he could touch her. Her haste was her undoing, and she felt her feet slip from beneath her, her breath arrested as she heard Ben curse, hard hands grasping her waist, his body cushioning her from the fall as she was pressed along the hard length of it.

For a moment it seemed that time stood still,

her heart thudding painfully against her ribs, her
eyes for once on a level with Ben's, hers wide and
startled, his dark and unfathomable, then he started
to lower her to the ground, still holding her against
his body, his head lowering with her descent, his
arms suddenly clamping bruisingly round her. She
knew long before his mouth touched hers that he
was going to kiss her. Dry-mouthed and shaking,
she could only stare up at him, her voice an
inarticulate murmur as his head blotted out the
sunlight and hot delight burned through her. She felt
light, almost boneless in his arms, closing her mind
to reason and letting her hands slide up and into the
thickness of his hair. His body tensed and then he
was kissing her with hungry insistence, tasting the
warm sweetness of her soft lips, making her open her
mouth to him, her body drenched in such a fierce
thrust of pleasure that she murmured his name
involuntarily against his lips. Instantly she was
thrust away from him, contemptuous eyes raking
her trembling form.

'Tell me again that when I hold you you pretend
I'm Dale?' he murmured tauntingly. 'You might be
able to persuade your heart and mind to reject me,
Sarah, but your body feels differently,' and as
though to emphasise the validity of his claim his
hand moved slowly over her, stroking upwards
over the curve of her hip and the narrowness of
her waist coming to rest against the aching curve
of her breast, his thumb stretching the fine fabric
of her blouse until the betraying arousal of her
nipple was plainly visible through the thin cloth.
With a smile of triumph Ben let her go, returning
to the Range Rover to remove their cases.

Following him round to the back, as they turned
a corner, Sarah caught her first glimpse of his
house. The land rose sharply, sheltering the small
bay, and halfway up it on what appeared to be a
plateau was Ben's house. Steps led up to it, and
the hillside had been planted with a variety of
ground-hugging plants, many of which were in
bloom. Two tall cypresses guarded the tall grilled
gate at the top of the steps. Sarah was out of
breath from climbing them, but Ben, who had
their cases, seemed unaffected by the climb. She
stood aside as he unlocked the gate, and studied
the stone wall which ran in either direction away
from it.

'It keeps out unwanted visitors,' Ben drawled,
following her glance. 'I like my privacy.'

As she stepped through the gate, Sarah couldn't
repress a small gasp of delight. She was in a
courtyard-style garden, flagged and sunny, a
fountain tinkling melodically somewhere unseen,
the corners shadowed with trees, green and restful.
In front of her patio doors opened out on to the
courtyard, and looking up Sarah saw another
flight of steps leading up to what was obviously
one of the bedrooms, ending on an attractive
balcony. The balcony boasted a table and chairs. 'I
like to breakfast there,' Ben told her, glancing
upwards, then taking her arm and leading her
through another archway into what she supposed
must be the garden proper with neatly tended
lawns, and roses which sprawled lavishly against
the stone walls.

The house itself was long and low, apparently
built in an 'E' shape, to take advantage of the lie

of the land and get the maximum views, Ben told her when she remarked on it, hurrying her along so that she had barely time to glimpse into the rooms through the windows they passed. The middle section of the 'E' was a huge garden room, and Sarah was still gazing at this when they rounded the corner and she saw the graceful lines of the pool and its surrounding patio. Then they were past it and turning to walk down the side of the house to what she had thought to be the back but was, she realised, the front, complete with curling drive. Puzzled, she stared at it, wondering why Ben hadn't driven straight up, and humour touched his mouth as he watched and read her mind. 'It looks very impressive, but it doesn't go anywhere,' he explained at last. 'This house was built for a would-be millionaire who went broke before it was finished. The minute I saw it I knew it was exactly what I wanted. Californians are rather fonder of driving than they are of walking.'

'So you bought it to preserve your solitude?'

As a busy director, Sarah couldn't feel that he would have much time alone, but she didn't comment, but followed him into an oval hall from which a white staircase curved graciously upwards. The hall floor was tiled in marble, the walls a soft shimmering green. As she looked she heard footsteps and a plump Mexican woman appeared, beaming at Ben, then looking at Sarah.

'Margarita, this is my wife. Sarah, meet Margarita, my housekeeper. Between them she and Ramón, her husband, look after my home.'

Margarita grinned. 'Your wife, huh?' she announced with an American twang. 'Perhaps

there won't be so many nights spent working in
your study now, eh?'

Ben shook his head, and murmured something
in Spanish to which the other woman replied,
laughing and looking sideways at Sarah. 'I'll go
and fix you both something to eat,' she told them.
'Ramón is collecting the groceries. He'll attend to
the bags when he gets back.'

'What was she laughing about?' Sarah
demanded, hot-cheeked, when Margarita had
disappeared. She had always been sensitive about
being laughed at, especially when she didn't know
why.

'The fact that I've told her we'll be having
separate rooms. I do tend to work a lot at night,
and I told her I didn't want to disturb you.'

'To which she replied?' Sarah demanded, not
knowing whether to be glad or disappointed
about what he had just said.

'Merely that as my woman you'd rather be
disturbed than left to lie in a cold bed. Her words,
not mine,' he added with a dismissive shrug. 'I
could have told her that you've got your love to
keep you warm, but somehow I don't think she'd
have understood.'

They ate in silence, in an attractive room
overlooking the gardens, Sarah barely able to do
more than toy with the delicious cold soup
Margarita had served. Ben had showered and
changed before coming down to lunch, and his
hair was still damp, his body tautly muscular in
the thin lightweight grey suit he was wearing. To
eat he had discarded his jacket and the silk of his
shirt clung lovingly to his body, her awareness of

him so intense that she was oblivious to everything else. It took a real effort of will to drag her eyes away from him and concentrate on her meal, and she didn't realise how tense she had become until Ben pushed back his chair, the scraping sound rasping along her raw nerves.

'I'm going to the studio. You look tired,' he added curtly. 'Try and have a sleep—you're filming in the morning.'

'When will you be back?' Her voice was stilted and she bit her lip, vexed at her folly, when he raised an eyebrow, his eyes glinting mockingly.

'How very wifely you sound! I'll have to respond in like manner, won't I?' And then he was bending over her, her nostrils suddenly full of the arousing scents of his body, his damp hair brushing against her cheek as his fingers captured her jaw and his mouth touched hers, lightly tormenting, making her long to reach up and hold his mouth against her, her body aching for him to want her. 'In answer to your question,' he murmured when he released her lips, 'I don't know, but don't wait dinner—and don't wait up, unless of course you're prepared to take the consequences.'

He was gone before Sarah could speak, leaving her bemused and shaken. What had his last words meant? That he still wanted her? If she did wait up for him would he take her in his arms and carry her up that curving flight of stairs, and then make love to her as her feverish body ached for him to make love? But for how long would a purely physical act satisfy her starving senses? Oh, initially perhaps it would suffice, but later, when her heart ached to hear words of love; when her soul cried out for more communication than that offered by his body, how would she feel then?

In the end there was no decision to make. She went upstairs, intending merely to lie down for half an hour, but it was dark when she eventually awoke from a deep sleep to discover that someone had thrown a cover over her naked body and that the clock beside her bed showed just gone two.

Beside her was the towel in which she had wrapped herself after her shower. She remembered walking into her room and sitting down on the bed, intending to dry her hair. She must have fallen asleep then. No doubt Margarita had found her when she came to ask what she wanted for dinner. Had Ben returned? The house was in silence. Or was it? Sarah frowned and slid out of bed, opening her door, her ears straining for the familiar sound, her face relaxing when she heard it. Somewhere Ben was typing; she recognised the rattling staccato sound. What on earth was he working on so late into the night? Reminding herself that he was hardly likely to tell her, she set the alarm and climbed back into bed.

When the alarm went off at four she was glad of her extra hours of sleep. Showering quickly, drying herself and putting on fresh underwear, she set to work on her hair, the hair-dryer drowning out the click of her bedroom door, her first intimation that she wasn't alone coming when she glanced in the mirror and saw Ben standing behind her, carrying a tray.

'Breakfast,' he told her, putting it down on a small table. 'Sleep all right?'

She didn't know why, but the look on his face made her colour deeply, wishing she was wearing more than just her brief silk bra and matching French knickers.

'Very well,' she assured him, fighting for composure. He had stopped looking at her face and his eyes had dropped to her body, studying it with a cool thoroughness that disordered every pulse. 'I fell asleep straight after my shower . . .'

'I know.'

The laconic statement brought her head round, her eyes widening as they met his.

'I came up to see if you were all right when I got in,' he told her, answering her unspoken question. 'Margarita was concerned because you never turned up for dinner. You were deeply asleep, wrapped in a damp towel.'

She flushed to the roots of her hair, remembering how she had woken up, knowing that Ben must have seen her like that, must indeed have been the author of her being like that.

'You're blushing.' He stood up and leaned back against the door, indolently at ease, the action emphasising the taut muscles of his thighs. 'Why? You can't be ashamed of your body—it's very beautiful.'

'I'm not. It's just that, like anyone else, I don't like the thought of anyone . . . anyone . . .'

'Seeing it? What a contradiction you are!' He moved, his green gaze marking her sudden flinch. 'You're perfectly safe,' he drawled with almost insulting boredom. 'I might have said your body was beautiful, but that doesn't mean I'm stricken by a lust to possess it.' He glanced at his watch.

'Can you be ready in half an hour?'

Nodding, Sarah turned her attention back to the mirror and her hair, trying to blot out the disturbance caused by his appearance. Today they were filming her meeting with Alain de Courcy; her first since her marriage, and he had come to tell her that Richard had managed to regain her dowry from her brother-in-law Tancred and that she was free to leave the castle where Tancred had virtually imprisoned her and join Richard, who was en route for the Crusade.

'Ben?'

He stopped by the door and watched her. 'Last night I heard you typing. Surely you have a secretary who could do that sort of work?'

'Such wifely concern? Or was Margarita right and you're finding your bed cold and lonely? Save your concern for Dale, Sarah,' he told her harshly. 'Unless he pulls himself together he's going to need it!'

They reached the studio just after half past five. Sarah went straight to Wardrobe, immersing herself in her role as she was dressed in the thin gauzy silks of her costume, her hair hidden beneath the misty draperies of her veil.

She was a woman who had been married against her will to a man she loathed; a man she could not even respect; whose vices and affairs were notorious; a man whose death should have freed her to return to her family had it not been for the machinations of his half-brother who had refused to allow her to return home and who had, moreover, stolen her dowry. But now her brother had arrived, and Richard's fiery Plantagenet temperament would no more accept Tancred's cupidity than did her own, and she lived hourly in expectation of seeing her brother . . . her favourite brother . . .

Silk cushions were strewn over the set, incense burning aromatically, her servants and women dressed in brilliantly hued silks, the colours all chosen to complement and emphasise her own shimmering silvered green. Offset she saw Ben nod to the cameras and her mouth went dry with tension. She was Joanna, supposedly, and yet she felt nothing, her senses too magnetised by the man watching her. How would she feel if this was her and she had suddenly discovered she had another chance of happiness with Ben? She took a deep breath, no longer afraid. A shrill clarion of trumpets announced the arrival of Richard's envoy and she turned, smiling regally, regality giving way to disbelief and then joy as Paul strode towards her, causing muted panic and a flurry of silks among her attendants.

'All right, that's it.' From the set Sarah watched Ben massage the back of his neck, and behind him someone said laconically, 'You heard the man— can it.'

'Sarah, that was marvellous!' Eva praised warmly. 'Wasn't it, Ben?' She hadn't realised Ben was at her side, and shivered a little, wondering how he had moved so silently without her noticing it, when he was constantly in her thoughts.

'Sarah always was a good actress,' he agreed, but in a voice more underlined with contempt than praise, and she had to bite back the impulse to

throw in his face that only by pretending *he* was
Paul had she been able to invest it with emotion
and desire.

It had been like that with *Shakespeare*. She
hadn't needed to pretend when they did their love
scene; everything had been all too real.

'You were super, sweetling!'

Why had she never noticed before how insincere
Dale could be? She moved slightly as he put his arm
round her. 'What's the matter? Oh, I get it. I'm still
not forgiven for the other night, is that it?' Out of the
corner of her eye Sarah saw Ben's face tighten and
then he moved away, his glance scathing as it ripped
through her defences. 'How about having dinner
with me so that I can apologise in style?' He was
talking like someone out of his own films, Sarah
thought in detached contempt, unable to understand
why, suddenly, she should see him like this. Had *he*
changed, or had she?

'No, thanks, Dale. I'm whacked.'

'Are you?' His eyes were glittering as they
moved over her face, and just for a second it was
like coming face to face with a stranger. Fear ran
icily along her spine, and she had wondered why
she had never noticed before the vain egotism
underlying the charming exterior. 'Or are you
hoping to catch a bigger fish? You're still in love
with him, aren't you, Sarah? That's why you never
told me you were still married. You're wasting
your time,' he told her brutally. 'He might want
you, but he'll never be able to bring himself to take
you knowing you are my leavings.' He said it with
such a savage satisfaction that for a moment Sarah
was breathless.

'You hate him.' She said it wonderingly, more concerned with her own discovery than his admission of it, startled when Dale responded thickly:

'Damn you, yes! *I* should have been the one who got rave reviews for *Shakespeare*, but I didn't—and why? Because some stupid, big-eyed kid had to go and fall for him and turn him into one of the screen's hottest lovers. I could have killed you for that, Sarah!' He stormed away before she could protest, leaving her feeling as though the world had suddenly turned oddly on its axis. Why had she never realised before the depth of his jealousy of Ben? That he might be jealous had simply never crossed her mind. She had trusted him . . . And he had protected her when Ben . . . Unable to bear the pressure of her thoughts, she went to get dressed, frowning when she discovered she could not find her ring. She had taken off her wedding ring for the filming, and now she stared round, wondering where it could have gone. It didn't have sufficient commercial value for anyone to steal it, but to her its sentimental value was beyond worth. Losing it was like admitting that her marriage was a sham, a deep rending pain that made her draw in her breath on a sharply protesting 'No!'

She spent half an hour looking for it before conceding that it was irrevocably lost, and when she emerged from her dressing room she found Ben waiting for her outside.

'Nice piece of work today, Sarah.' She opened her mouth, startled, as Dale suddenly appeared, nothing about his voice or mien indicative of their last encounter. 'You should give her something a bit more meaty, Ben; a love scene, she's always been extra good at those.'

'We're trying to piece together a realistic reconstruction of the facts, not film soft porn,' Ben interceded cuttingly.

Sarah started to shiver, her voice tight with fear as she protested huskily, 'I don't do explicit love scenes, my agent has instructions to refuse any scripts that include them—I loathe them!' Her voice was so vehement that neither of the two men listening could doubt that she meant what she was saying.

Dale spoke first, his smile openly triumphant as he said to Ben, 'That puts you and me in a league all of our own, doesn't it?' Adding to Sarah, 'Don't forget, sweetling, the offer for tonight still stands.'

Half an hour later she saw him leaving with Gina Frey, and wondered at her own malice when she decided they were well suited to one another.

'Jealous?' She didn't have to turn her head to know that Ben was taunting her. 'You should know him well enough by now to know that if he can't have you he'll soon find someone else—but remember, Sarah, as long as we're preserving this fiction of our reconciliation, I won't have you going to him.'

Sarah ignored him, knowing it would do her no good to protest her lack of interest in Dale. She was still suffering from the shock of discovering another man behind the mask he had always worn for her; still trying to assess where her instincts and intuitions had failed her, allowing her to be deceived into thinking that his concern had all been for her. Oh, he had protected her from Ben, but only for his own ends, only because of his own jealousy. She shivered suddenly, wondering how much of that jealousy sprang from the fact that Ben had won their bet. At the time, Dale had professed disgust and shame that it had ever been initiated, but how much of that disgust and shame had been real, and how much the actor's skilled camouflage of real feelings?

'Tired?' It was the nearest thing to concern she had ever heard in Ben's voice and she had to blink fiercely against weak tears.

'A little,' she agreed. 'I suppose I'm still suffering from jet-lag.'

'No filming tomorrow, you'll be able to get some rest. It's Sunday,' Ben reminded her dryly, seeing her surprised expression. 'The rest of the cast and crew would probably lynch me if I suggested anything else!'

CHAPTER EIGHT

'MORE coffee? Waffles?'

Sighing her satisfaction, Sarah shook her head. She had never imagined it would be possible for her to feel so lazy. It was eleven o'clock, and she was only just having her breakfast. The sun glinted invitingly on the pool beyond the patio, and yet, she acknowledged, if she did swim, it would probably be in the ocean. She smiled at her own absurdity. She had never totally got over the childhood feeling that no holiday was complete without sea and sand, and since today was virtually a holiday, and she had both on her doorstep, so to speak, she felt almost duty bound to take advantage of them. She sipped her coffee, frowning as she noticed the naked look of her left hand. She had woken a couple of times during the night missing the weight of her wedding ring, or was what she had been missing the totally foolish but now admitted feeling she had always had, that as long as she had worn Ben's ring they were still linked?

'You going sunbathing?' Margarita enquired when she came out to clear the table, glancing speculatively at Sarah's pale skin.

Sarah shook her head. 'I don't tan,' she told her with a smile, 'but I probably will go down to the beach and swim. Is the water safe?'

'Sure, but why not use the pool?' Margarita queried.

'Oh, no reason.' Somehow Sarah felt reluctant

to explain her childish desire to swim in the sea; perhaps walk along the sand dodging the waves and investigate any hopeful-looking rock pools. As a child, how she had hoped against hope to see a fish! She had always been attracted by water, she acknowledged, drawn to it in a way she suspected most children were. And why not? The human body was largely comprised of it; the oceans of the world still possessed an aura of mystery, and terrifying power, the elemental ebb and flow of their tide echoing the beat of human life.

'Have you seen ... my husband?' Sarah ventured, wondering if Ben had gone out.

Margarita shrugged. 'Sure. He had his breakfast about seven and then he disappeared into his study. I wouldn't disturb him if I were you. He's probably writing.'

Writing? Guessing that Margarita meant that Ben was working, and still not sure enough of the sometimes confusing American usage of familiar English words, Sarah thanked her for her breakfast and went back to her room to change out of her skirt and blouse into a bikini, taking care to smother her skin in sunscreen and let it sink in before she pulled a towelling all-in-one shorts-suit over it. If she did swim she would have to be careful not to lie too long on the beach afterwards. The salt water would undoubtedly wash away the protective barrier of the cream and she had no desire to burn. As she picked up her towel her eyes were caught by the sun-hat Ben had bought her in Spain. Her fingers trembling, she picked it up. Was she really so badly affected that merely to *touch* something he had given her made her like this, her stomach churning and her body weak with need?

The beach on closer inspection proved even more delightful than she had supposed. The ocean had originally formed it by wearing away the softer rock and now the small beach was protected by two arms of harder granite stretching out into the Pacific ensuring strict privacy. As she had walked down through the close-planted shrubs and flowers, their varying scents had been wafted to her, the heat-laden air redolent with their mingled perfumes, bees humming lazily and clumsily from plant to plant.

On the shore the sea had receded, leaving a band of pristine wet sand, and Sarah walked along it, turning to view her own footprints, wondering angrily at the sense of desolation and loneliness that suddenly swept her, catching her breath on a gasp as she saw the silver sparkle of sea spray, and the upward curve of an arm, followed by the dark shape of Ben's head, his hair wetly plastered to his skull, the powerful crawl that propelled him through the water revealing the tautly brown skin of his back and shoulder, reminding her of her suspicion that he sunbathed nude. He had seen her, and was treading water as he found his depth, wading strongly ashore, her eyes riveted to his body, watching the play of muscles beneath his skin, the taut power of his shoulders as he lifted his hands to push back his hair and wipe the moisture from his face. He was watching her too, and suddenly she started to tremble, helplessly transfixed as he came on. His body was beautifully proportioned, not distorted with over-developed muscles, his skin gleaming beneath the hot caress of the sun, the salt water following the arrowing course of the newly slicked body hair disappearing into the water which lapped just below his navel.

Like someone trapped in a dream Sarah watched him come on, emerging from the water like some mythical god, or so it seemed to her bemused brain, her eyes following his progress, noting the tautly sleek and tanned skin which sheathed his muscles and the total difference of his male shape when compared mentally to hers, his obvious indifference to his nudity.

Suddenly the dream spell broke, the pounding of the surf echoed by the heavy thud of her own heart; panic; a primeval sense of fear, and a desperate need to escape the intimacy of the secluded cove ran through her body like fire, disregarding the sharp sound of her name on Ben's lips she started to run, blindly, not knowing why she was running or where, propelled by some nameless instinct; some frisson of awareness triggered off by the sight of Ben. She could hear him behind her; she could almost feel the heat of his breath against her skin, but still she ran, her feet entangled in the gritty silk of the sand, the impact of Ben's arms reaching out to imprison her, driving out her gasped breath, her body falling helplessly on to the sand, taking Ben's with it, only his quick twist saving her from taking his full weight, her body jarred nevertheless by the suddenness of her fall.

'Why did you run?'

Ben's voice seemed to reach her from far away, her whole body trembling with nervous reaction.

Her lips felt dry, and she licked them, tasting the salt, feeling the hectic pound of her heart, trying to move surreptitiously away, feeling Ben's fingers bite into her waist as she did.

She started to struggle, impelled to do so as much by her own treacherous need as by the desire she could see glinting from Ben's eyes, darkening as he resisted her struggles, pinning her to the sand beneath him and securing her there with the weight of his thigh, his chest barely moving while her breath was coming in short jerky gasps, her eyes dilating in sudden shock at the intimate contact of his body. His thigh was roughened by dark hairs, rubbing harshly against the softness of her as she arched desperately to try and throw him off, their eyes locked in a bitter duel, until her sudden desperate movement drew his to the upward thrust of her breasts in their thin covering of cotton. Both of them went still. Sarah could almost feel the insidious beat of her own pulses, her stillness that of the captured, Ben's that of the captor, each infused with subtle innuendo.

It was possible for a man and woman to know of their attraction for one another without so much as a word, if one knew how to read their body signals, or so Sarah had read, and she wondered if Ben could read in hers, all that she was trying so desperately to hide. She should never have run from him, because to do so had surely incited the desire she could feel beating up alongside his anger. It was there in the burning fixity of his glance as it rested on her breasts; in the taut power of his thigh pressing her into the sand. He shifted slightly, balancing himself as he reached deftly behind her, unsnapping the plastic fastening of her bikini top, the sudden shift in his weight revealing his arousal and desire, not a word spoken as he rolled over, taking her with him, her body imprisoned against his, her bikini top sliding away as he tugged it until her nipples brushed against his chest, their involuntary response increasing his arousal, his hands moving down her body, following the line of her spine, the rounded curves of her bottom, holding her until every inch of her was aware of his desire, kissing her, sliding the hot potency of his mouth along her skin, teasing and tormenting, until she was ready to give him anything, if only he would appease the throbbing ache consuming her.

When his fingers tugged at the tiny bows securing her bikini briefs she was far beyond any rational protest. The brief scrap of cotton had long since become an intolerable barrier between them, and when he tugged it, muttering his pleasure into her throat, her body shivered violently in response.

'It feels so good,' he muttered thickly, 'to have all of you against me.' Sarah felt him moving, rolling her down on to her side, her eyes opening to the emerald brilliance of his as he held her a little away from him, studying the pale silk of her skin, now dusted with sand, starting at her toes, which curled protestingly into the sand under his intimate exploration, then moving upwards until her body quivered helplessly beneath a rising tide of desire. He touched his lips to her breasts, first one and then the other, as though unable to resist bestowing the brief caress, his throat beaded with perspiration, the skin tightening on a convulsive

swallow as he lifted his head and slid his hands
into her hair, his lips just touching hers and then
lifting, returning time and time again in the briefly
unsatisfying kisses that had her aching for so much
more, her head moving protestingly from side to
side each time her mouth was tormented, her
fingers catching in the black silk of his hair as
restraint was abandoned and she clung to him,
murmuring her protest against his skin, exulting in
the fierce tension of his body as her hands touched
it, his mouth opening over hers with hotly
demanding urgency. Spiralling waves of pleasure
thudded through her, culminating in a desire so
intense it seemed impossible to endure. Every time
he touched her she wanted him more, and now her
body wasn't prepared to be denied any more.

When he released her mouth Ben was breathing
as hard as if he had been running, his chest rising
and falling with the effort of it, his head tipped
back, and his eyes closed, his hands sliding
possessively to cover her breasts, his body
shuddering as his thumbs investigated their
aroused fullness, his touch making her arch
hungrily against him, her hands moving down to
his waist, impelled by her aching urgency to move
lower until he tensed and muttered, pushing her
back on the sand, his hands exploring every inch
of her, knowing just how and where to stroke and
caress her, slowly driving her far beyond the point
where she was conscious of anything other than
his mastery of her body and his knowledge of all
its secrets. Her fingertips grazed the tender skin of
his stomach, making him shudder wrenchingly,
holding her off so that she could see the dully

hectic colour reddening his cheek bones, and the
febrile glitter of his eyes, his whole body tense as
she touched her lips to the skin so recently
explored by her fingers, her insides turning weak
with molten delight at the discovery of his own
vulnerability; the hoarse cry he wasn't quite able
to suppress as her lips moved lower; the biting
strength in the arms that suddenly gripped and
lifted her. Her body clenched in fierce pleasure as
his mouth dropped to her breasts, exploring the
deep cleft between them, until with a thick
exclamation his fingers curved possessively around
their swollen fullness, his lips moving provocatively
from one to the other until his body was hard and
thrusting against her, and he was holding her so
tightly that she could feel the erotic drag of his
teeth against her skin, their breathing mutually
laboured and uneven.

The shrill sound that cut across it stiffened
Sarah into stunned shock. Dimly she was aware of
Ben swearing as he rolled away, his voice thick
and unsteady as he told her, 'Telephone, and if I
don't go and answer it soon, someone's going to
come down here looking for me, and there's no
way I want anyone else to see you looking like
that.' His eyes skimmed the shape of her body,
watching the delicate flush of colour staining her
skin as Sarah became aware of her betraying
arousal, and then to her surprise Ben reached for
her and kissed her hard although unsatisfyingly on
the mouth. 'That's just to remind you that we've
got unfinished business for later.' He stood up,
reaching for her towel, saying with a grin, 'I'm not
particularly prudish, but I don't think it would be

wise to bump into Margarita in my present state!'
and laughed as she coloured richly and started
scrambling into her own clothes.

By the time she was dressed he was already at
the top of the steps. She made no haste to hurry
after him. If he had a phone call there was not
much point, and as she made her way slowly up
the steps, her body still languorous with pleasure,
she shivered in anticipation of the promise implicit
in his last words. Did they mean he had forgiven
her? Or simply that his desire for her was so great
that it overruled everything else?

'It was Gina inviting us over,' Ben told her,
coming out on to the patio as she crossed it. 'She's
having a barbecue, and little though I want to go I
feel on this occasion it might be . . . politic . . .'

Because he resented what might happen if they
remained alone? Did that mean he was already
regretting his words on the beach? Since she didn't
feel able to ask him, Sarah simply inclined her
head, hoping her voice sounded indifferently
steady as she said evenly, 'In that case I'd better go
and get changed. What sort of thing ought I to
wear?'

'Ordinarily I'd say jeans and a tee-shirt, but
knowing Gina she'll be doing things in style —
probably with Pucci silks!'

They weren't something Sarah possessed, but
she did have some silk trousers with a matching
jacket, in a pale cream. She had bought them in a
sale, getting them because they were such a small
size, and had been lucky enough to buy with them
a cream camisole top embroidered in rich pinks
and lilacs. The suit looked good on her, she knew,

her hair floating on her shoulders, her feet bare in strappy kid sandals, her make-up deliberately brief, knowing that she would find it next to impossible to keep it on in the heat. As a precaution she picked up her bikini and rolled it up in a towelling robe. There might be swimming, and if there was she didn't want to be obliged to borrow anything of Gina's, so instinctive and deeply felt was her dislike of the other woman.

Ben's silent appreciation when she descended the stairs brought faint colour to her skin, and her chin lifted warily, until she realised he was smiling.

'I've just realised how often you do that,' he commented thoughtfully, watching her with narrowed eyes. 'Every time you feel threatened in the slightest way, your chin lifts.'

'Perhaps because someone once told me you should take all life's blows on it,' Sarah joked, wishing he was less perceptive. She wasn't ready yet to have him know every last intimate thing about her, able to judge her moods and feelings. Today he had unbent towards her, but she wasn't sure how long that would last; or ir indeed he really meant it. She wasn't naïve enough to believe that simply because a man desired her it meant happy ever after, but at least it was a step in the right direction, a more optimistic inner voice crowed. And they were married. Who knew what the future might hold?

She spent the drive to Gina's indulging in the most satisfying of daydreams, her mouth curved in a softly tender smile, unaware of the looks Ben darted her when his attention wasn't on the road.

'Here we are.' She came down to earth with a

bump as he turned the car into Gina's drive. Unlike Ben's house Gina's wasn't secluded, but one of many along what was all the same a most exclusive and elegant road.

A crowd of people, including some faces she recognised, were gathered round the pool, the majority of the women dressed as Ben had predicted in expensive couture play-clothes. Accepting a drink from one of the waiters, Sarah studied her surroundings. They were everything she had imagined Hollywood to be—and dreaded—expensive, soulless and somehow a fitting background for a woman like Gina. But it would never suit her; she wanted a home; not necessarily as large as Ben's, but a home nevertheless where she could bring up a family. A giant hand squeezed her heart. Children. Ben's children—God, how she ached to bear them! The primitiveness of her own response amazed her. She had always known that she liked children, but never that she would feel this earthy sensual need to have her body ripen with a man's seed, his child growing within her.

'Ah, darling, there you are.' Sarah was ignored as Gina swept Ben up into the crowd surrounding her. Not wanting to seem clinging, she turned back to study the view, wondering if Gina shared the house with her lover, or owned it in her own right.

'Sarah!' She hadn't heard Dale approach and she didn't smile. 'You're angry.' His voice held wry self-remorse. 'I suppose I deserve it. Look, could you try and forget what I said at the studio? My only excuse is that I'm off my head with jealousy. I always did envy Ben you, but never as much as I do now. Will you forgive me, Sarah?'

She didn't want to, but to do so was easier than prolonging the interview. 'We ought to talk,' he added softly, grasping her hand. 'Come on, we'll go inside.' She couldn't release his grip of her fingers and short of making a scene there was little she could do. He seemed to know exactly where he was going, although Sarah was dismayed to be dragged into a ground floor bedroom, its windows open to the pool area.

'Sweetling, I'm so sorry.' Dale's voice was huskily urgent. 'Can't we kiss and make up?' His hands grasping her upper arms, his mouth probing the unyielding line of hers as Sarah fought silently against his kiss, angry enough to want to tear herself out of his arms, but unwilling to provoke a further scene by doing so.

'Oh, darling, I'm sure you can't have seen them come in here. It's a bedroom!'

Sarah froze in panic as she heard Gina's voice outside, her footsteps accompanied by a heavier masculine tread. The door was pushed open, her scream of fright silenced as Dale thrust her down on the bed, and turned quickly, his face expressing the full gamut of guilt and defiance as he stared upwards towards Ben.

Sarah wanted to cover her eyes, to die quickly and painlessly, but the look in Ben's eyes promised that she would do neither. She sat up, words of explanation tumbling from her lips, but Dale beat her to it, perfidious, jealous Dale who was even now holding out a shiny gold ring, his voice sorrowful, belying the mocking cruelty in his eyes as he handed it to her. 'You'd better take this, sweetling. You left it in my shower.'

Sarah felt as though she were taking part in a horrendous play. Ben, Dale and Gina were all watching her with varying expressions, Dale's triumphantly cruel, Gina's all spite and malice, and Ben's—dear God, how could she endure the look in Ben's eyes! It stripped her of all her defences, laid her wide open to the searing contempt of his bitter glance. It was pointless trying to defend herself and so she didn't bother, but struggled to sit up, wondering numbly what was going to happen.

'Come on, Ben, you've always known the score.' That was Dale, letting his triumph show, only Ben wasn't to know why he was triumphant. He assumed it was because she and Dale were lovers.

'Perhaps I've been listening to another tune.' That was Ben, his voice flat and almost defeated, hardening slowly as he added, harshly, 'It seems you have a natural propensity for bedroom scenes, Sarah, and as a director I'd be a fool if I didn't make use of such a God-given talent. Seeing that you haven't been at any pains to hide your ... affair from the eyes of the world, you won't have any objection to my changing some of your final love scene, making it a little more explicit. That's what you recommended, wasn't it, Dale? And if he doesn't mind then why the hell should I?' Ben finished thickly. 'Let's see you display your natural aptitude between the sheets where it does any actress the most good—up on the screen!'

'No!' What should have been a shout was a husky croak of denial, and horror flitted darkly over her features as she stared up at the silent trio. 'You can't do that, Ben,' she husked defiantly.

'You can't just change the script like that! You'll need to get the permission of the writer, and then there's the re-writing of the script, and the backers . . .'

'The backers wanted a hot love scene in the film all along,' Ben told her ruthlessly. 'They'll be over the moon—and don't even think of trying to break your contract, or the studio will break you.' Sarah knew his threat was all too real, and shuddered in real anguish. She couldn't play a heavy love scene. She *couldn't*! She struggled upwards, panting, clutching at straws, repeating shakily, 'You can't do it, Ben. You'll never get the writer's permission, the script is perfect as it is, he won't let you butcher it simply to torment me . . .'

Gina's jeering laughter filled the silence. 'You little fool,' she scoffed, 'who do you think wrote it? Hasn't he even told you that much? Well, go on, darling,' she urged Ben triumphantly, 'tell your stupid little wife exactly who is the writer she so blatantly hero-worships, and exactly why you can alter the script if you wish.' Without giving Ben a chance to respond, she turned on Sarah, her eyes glittering with dislike. 'Ben wrote the film,' she told her. 'Everyone connected with the film knew that. All but you. Some re-conciliation! Ben obviously didn't have much faith in it succeeding. I suppose he didn't tell you because he didn't want you filing a hefty claim for alimony. Your husband's an extremely wealthy man, and he can do just what he likes with this film, sweetie—and with you. He owns fifty per cent of the studio!'

Sarah lay limply on the bed, her eyes burning

with horror and pain, pleading with Ben to deny
Gina's assertions.

'It's true?' Her voice was a broken whisper, her
pride irreparably broken as two painful tears
welled up in her eyes and ran unchecked down her
face, her body feeling as though it had been
physically beaten, real sickness tasting sour in her
mouth. Ben was that man whom she had secretly so
much admired; Ben had written that hauntingly
emotive script, Ben who had never shown her an
ounce of the compassion he had given so liberally
to his characters.

'Come on, Sarah, we're going home.' Strangely
enough, of the trio he was the only one who
evinced no signs of triumph, his hands cool and
firm on her body as he pulled her upright.

'Home?' Sarah spat the word hysterically. 'You
honestly expect me to go back with you after this?'

'You'd better believe it.' His voice was coldly
emphatic, and Gina shivered sensually, cooing,
'Darling, you sound so masculine! Such a turn-on
to find a really strong man!'

Strong! He was made of ... of ... ice, Sarah
thought bitterly. 'I'm not coming with you.'

'Oh yes, you are.' He bent swiftly and scooped
her up into his arms, shouldering his way past
Dale and out of the door. They emerged from the
side at a side entrance close to where the cars were
parked, and Ben dumped her unceremoniously in
his.

'I haven't come this far with the film to have it
all ruined now by you. You're not pulling out
now, Sarah,' he warned her. 'I've got too much at
stake.'

'Then don't make me do this love scene—I can't, Ben!' God, how she hated herself for pleading, her mind writhed in torment, but anything was better than having to endure such an ordeal.

He paused, turning to her, his eyes merciless in their scrutiny. 'Why is it you hate them so much? It doesn't matter,' he told her curtly before she could reply. 'Perhaps the fact that you do is revenge enough. You think it strange that I should feel a need for revenge?' His mouth curled disdainfully. 'It is a little theatrical, I agree, but sometimes all of us need to seek pride's appeasement, and for what you've done to mine I could cheerfully consign you to the fires of hell itself. So you will do this scene, is that understood?'

Numbly Sarah sat in the seat, still unable to take it all in. *Ben* had written the script! That explained the typewriter and the constant use he made of it. Obviously he was now working on something else. Frantically she contemplated running away, letting Carew sort out her breaking of the contract when she got home, but Ben had her passport. She was trapped, trapped like a gazelle beneath the lion's paw, and her mind circled crazily in terror trying to find a way out.

CHAPTER NINE

IT was unthinkable that Sarah could sleep. Her first wild impulse on returning to the house was to ring Carew and beg him to find some way of releasing her from her contract; she no longer even cared that it would mean that she lost the role of a lifetime. She could not. She *would* not play out an explicit love scene, watched and bullied by Ben. Fear made her brain a tight ball of pain inside her skull. Ben had assessed her horrified response to the threat of such a love scene with a bitter triumph that warned her that he would do his utmost to exact retribution from her, drop by excruciating drop. There would be no compassion; no kindness shown to her. He probably wouldn't even allow them to have a closed set. Lifting her hot face from her pillow, she listened, catching the faint sound of someone typing, her heart thudding painfully against her chest wall. Ben was working. Re-writing her love scene? She wanted to go down and beg him to reconsider, explain to him that . . .

That she loved him and had done all along; that Dale had never been her lover, no matter how much he might have tried to make it look otherwise? Even if she were given a written guarantee that by doing so Ben would believe her she didn't have the courage to admit her feelings to him. She would be shown none of the compassion that came across so strongly in the film.

Two long and wearisome days crawled by when she never saw Ben, but heard the constant rattle of the typewriter keys through the closed study door. Filming had been suspended, and although Paul had telephoned and offered to take her out, Sarah had refused. 'I believe Ben is writing us a steamy love scene,' Paul commented before he hung up. 'I must say I'm surprised. From the way he looked at me when I kissed you, I thought he was tempted to cut the romance between us out altogether!' When Paul rang off, Sarah leaned back against the wall, replacing the receiver with fingers that shook so badly she had to use both hands, her teeth biting deep into her lower lip as she fought not to make a sound. She heard Margarita walk into the hall and was aware of the concerned look she gave her, but only in a vague way as though a clear plastic bubble separated her from the rest of mankind, and that only her pain was real.

On the third morning after Ben had found her in Gina's bedroom with Dale, Sarah was walking along the beach. She came down to it a good deal, drawn by the solitude and the hypnotic pounding of the surf against the sand, the sound vaguely comforting. Almost she was tempted to simply walk into the ocean until it wasn't possible to walk any more; to give herself up to its dark enchantment and allow it to steal away her breath and her life, but the same small flame of courage which had refused to allow her to deny her love for Ben kept her eyes fixed firmly on the horizon rather than the seductive drag of the tide, as she forced herself to remember time and time again how Ben had made love to her on this very beach;

how she had given herself up to him, and how she had even begun to hope that somehow they might find a way to ... to love one another, she admitted, her face a bitter mask of pain for her naïve folly.

When she heard Ben calling her from the top of the steps her first impulse was to run. But to where? Trying to suppress the nervous agitation churning her stomach, she started to climb the steps, her feet dragging. At the top Ben was waiting for her, leaning back against the wall, the breeze flattening the thin silk shirt he was wearing to the hard breadth of his chest, tight, dark jeans outlining the masculine thrust of his thighs.

'Not contemplating drowning yourself, I trust?' he mocked as she reached him. 'You won't escape me that way, Sarah,' he added savagely. 'I'd fight like ten demons to keep you in this world, on this side of the hereafter ...'

'So that you can torment and punish me?' Sarah managed, shivering in helpless response. 'What kind of man are you, Ben?' she choked unsteadily. 'What kind of pleasure do you get from doing this to me?'

'A kind you wouldn't begin to understand,' he assured her brutally. 'You're far too shallow. Now, I've finished the alterations. I want you to come and read them.' She looked up and instantly felt sick when she saw the green glitter of his eyes beneath the downcast black lashes. Outwardly he was completely calm, but underneath ... Sarah shuddered. His body seemed to emanate an intensity of anger that curled tight fingers of tension along her spine, her eyes unable to resist the magnetic pull of his as she found herself allowing him to propel her back into the house, and through the hall where he paused by the telephone and demanded suddenly, 'Who telephoned you this morning? Dale?'

'As a matter of fact it was Paul.' She tried to sound aloof and disdainful, her voice coolly clear. 'He's heard that you're changing our love scene.'

'And he objects?' Ben's mouth curled. 'Don't try that one on me, Sarah. He'll be thanking his lucky stars. A scene like the one we did on *Shakespeare* could make him the hottest box office property around, especially when it's played with you ... I know what it did for my career.'

He was goading her deliberately, baiting her and waiting for her response. He wanted her to lose her temper, Sarah could sense that, and because she could she deliberately refused to let her mind comprehend his insults, simply pinning a blank look on her face and waiting for him to open the study door.

'You can keep your cool now,' Ben murmured as he bent to turn the handle, 'but how long for? I saw your face when I told you I was altering the love scene—remember?'

'I'm not stupid, Ben,' Sarah retorted evenly. 'I know you're doing this to hurt me. What I don't understand is why.'

'You know why well enough——' Ben argued tersely, '—finding you like that with Dale . . .'

Sarah felt as though she were gripped in some painfully numbing cold. Had she ever known this man to whom she was married? He would destroy her—there was no other word to describe what he planned—and he would do it simply to salve his wounded pride.

'Sit down.' Ben thrust her down into a chair, without waiting for her response, then went over to the typewriter and riffling through some papers while Sarah looked around and tried to steady her pounding heart. The room was utilitarian rather than glamorous, one wall bookshelved and stacked with books, the room furnished with two desks and half a dozen or so filing cabinets.

'Here.' Ben passed her a sheaf of typewritten pages. 'You'll have to excuse my typing errors,' he added mockingly, 'but I'm sure you'll get the drift.'

Slowly, hardly daring to let her eyes rest on the paper, Sarah glanced down. At first the typing danced illegibly before her eyes, and she realised to her horror that her eyes were full of tears. It was several seconds before she could blink them away sufficiently to enable her to read, her knuckles white with the effort of keeping her hands steady as she did.

She had barely read one page when she let the papers fall, her face white with pain and disbelief.

'I can't do this, Ben,' she told him defiantly, every muscle tensed to back up her refusal. 'I can't . . .'

'Oh, come on, Sarah,' he drawled smoothly, bending to gather the scattered sheets and re-stacking them. 'What's all the fuss about? All you have to do is simply go to your lover and beg him to make love to you. Where is the difficulty in that? Dale tells me it's something you're very good at,' he added with insulting ease, giving her a smile that made her skin crawl. 'Now come on, read the rest.'

There was no way she was going to be allowed to escape. Slowly and bitterly she read on, her body growing a little colder and emptier with each line as she saw the explicit detail Ben had written into the script.

If she was simply reading the passage in a book she might find it powerfully erotic; she might even identify herself with Joanna, but to actually act out what Ben had written!

'We start shooting tomorrow,' he added blandly, watching her face for signs of betrayal. 'For this one I think we'll have a rehearsal. Full cast and crew, I want to get the feel of their reaction . . .'

Glancing into his face, Sarah allowed her lips to close over any plea for a closed set. He would love her to beg, and then to refuse her, she thought bitterly—well, from somewhere she would find the courage and the will-power to go through with this scene, and no matter what it cost her she would not betray to him by so much as a quiver what she was really feeling.

'Umm, I think that's okay.' Linda paused before studying Sarah's costume. The entire set seemed to quiver with anticipation over the filming of the love scene, a subtle tension infusing cast and crew alike. Sarah was wearing the boy's garments she had borrowed from Richard's page to enable her to walk through the camp unnoticed on her way to see her lover, Richard just having told her that she was to marry Raymond of Toulouse.

Beyond her line of vision Sarah knew Props

were preparing the set; the mock-up of her lover's pavilion. Initially the scene was to be played as before, only instead of immediately recognising her despite her page's disguise, this time Paul was to mistake her for a page and to command her to assist him bathe. This part of the scene she could probably endure, but she was dreading what would follow; her plea to her lover to make love to her and then their abandoned lovemaking which would follow.

'Sarah, are you ready?'

Ben! Sarah closed her eyes. He wouldn't stop hounding her. Sometimes she thought he had a Machiavellian talent for discovering her weak spots, pounding mercilessly at them until . . . Until what? Until she was totally destroyed? Shivering slightly, she walked slowly towards the set, forcing herself to exclude everything but her role. If she could just do that she might have a chance.

'Now, remember,' Ben instructed when she reached him, 'this is your only chance to be with your lover; what happens now must last a lifetime; you're a woman, not a child, initially you are the more powerful of the two. And Paul,' he continued, beckoning the actor over, 'at first you simply follow Sarah's lead. You love her, but you're Richard's knight and you know of his plans for her, but you're also a man, and she's a woman you've loved and desired and now she's in your bed, yet part of you resents her for coming to you. I want this love scene to have the raw explosive impact Richard's do not. There must be an element of conflict in it as well as ultimately love. Okay?'

Willing herself to close her mind to everything else, Sarah took her place, waiting for the cue that had her lifting back the flap of the pavilion and walking inside. Paul's non-recognition of her, his curt instruction to help him undress and bathe, all went well. She even managed the bit she had been dreading, where she had to unfasten and remove her tunic before begging Paul to make love to her with tolerable aplomb, although her fingers trembled as she reached for her tunic, her self-control suddenly faltering, and panic clawing at her spine until Paul realised what was happening and ignored the script's instructions that he was to wait until she was fully undressed before touching her, and instead picked her up as she stood shivering and carried her across to the bed.

'Cut!' Ben's voice sliced through the silence. 'That isn't how I want it played, Sarah . . .'

Sarah knew Paul must have felt her tense, her eyes wide and unseeing like a hunted animal, fingers curled into her palms. No one else could see her face because Paul's body hid her head, and after a quick concerned look at her he called back, 'Ben, it's only a rehearsal, we can put it right when we actually film.'

No cold voice came to argue against him, and Sarah felt her tense body relax slightly, aware of and grateful for Paul's concern as he leaned closer and asked her, 'Sarah, are you all right? Do you want me to get Ben?'

'No!' Her voice held sharp terror, and again Paul frowned, but Ben had already given the signal for them to continue. Twice Paul had to remind her of her lines and Sarah knew she had never given a worse or less convincing performance in her life. Had she been playing a terrified virgin about to be ravished by her captor her responses would have been first-class, but for a deeply sensual woman in the arms of the man she was supposed to love, they were appalling.

'Look, Ben, this just isn't working,' Paul said calmly, when Ben had ordered them to stop for the umpteenth time. 'We're all on edge. Sarah's a bundle of nerves, and I must admit I feel as awkward as hell trying to make love to her with her husband looking on. I know it's all part of an actor's work, but this time, it's just not working. Why don't you close the set, and perhaps it would be better if you stood in for me,' he suggested, shocking Sarah into sick immobility. 'After all, from the back we're much the same, both dark-haired, and they could always edit the rest later.'

Ben had joined them on the set, his eyes boring mercilessly into hers as Sarah tried not to let him see how she felt. 'Would you prefer that, Sarah?' he asked softly.

Her shudder betrayed her, and she knew she should not have let him witness it. It was bad enough enduring this with Paul whom she liked and that was all, but to endure it with Ben, who set her body on fire every time he came near her . . . She couldn't do it. But Ben intended to make her do it, she had read that much in his eyes, and there was absolutely nothing she could do to stop him.

She sat shivering while the set was cleared, pretending to read her lines, but in reality trying to will herself into a state of mind that would enable her to get through the scene.

'We'll film it this time,' Ben told the camera crew tersely. 'We've wasted enough time on it already.'

Although he and Paul were much of a height, Ben was broader, which meant that the chain mail was that much harder to remove, Sarah thought inconsequentially as she struggled to remove it, willing herself not to think of the body underneath. Above her Ben was speaking Paul's lines, which would later be dubbed, his eyes mirroring the anger he was supposed to feel after learning from Richard of Joanna's marriage. Undressing Paul had not produced the same trembling anguish she was experiencing now, Sarah acknowledged, her mind beating out the words, 'You're not Sarah, you're Joanna,' the refrain thudding feverishly inside her skull as she tried to enact them.

When it came to the part where she had to allow her hands to linger on Ben's body he had no need to manufacture his biting anger, Sarah thought distantly, all the breath shaken out of her as he grasped her tunic, soaking it, exclaiming, 'God's blood, boy, do you dare to caress me as though you were a woman?'

This was the cue for Sarah to reveal herself, and Ben had made sure that she had to do so in both senses of the word. A painful tattoo of resentment thudded inside her head and she managed to unfasten and remove her hose and tunic as per the script, not daring to look into Ben's face to see how he was reacting as she released her hair and let it swirl round her shoulders in a protective cloak.

'Joanna!'

Ben was still a first-rate actor, a tiny portion of her brain recorded as he stood up and stepped towards her, the word softened with surprise and then hardened with anger.

'By what miracle does the Queen of Sicily deign to honour the tent of a mere knight? Or have you come that I might congratulate you on another marriage? This time my lady is more fortunate. Raymond of Toulouse is neither old nor impotent, and it is well known that my lady comes from a lusty family.'

He waited, knowing that she must come to him, touch him, and, her face pinched with tension, Sarah did, not knowing or caring if she spoke her lines right or wrong, only emerging from the shadowy corners, deep within her mind, where she had hidden when she was on the bed, pinned there by Ben's superior weight, an anger burning up in him which seemed more real than assumed, fires burning deep within her body as his hands stroked over her skin.

Everything that she had feared about this scene rose up inside her to mock her, only her reactions were a thousand times worse than she had expected, because it wasn't Paul who held her, Paul with whom she must re-live the agony of remembrance, but *Ben*; Ben who had taught her body the meaning of love, who had taken her beyond shyness and selfconsciousness to a plane where nothing mattered other than him, and who had drawn from her the performance that had briefly made them both famous, and he was going to do the same thing again; deceiving her body with his touch, until her desire for him overruled the cautions of her mind.

His mouth burned against her skin, his gritted, 'And does my lady find my performance satisfactory? Perhaps her husband will give me some fine lands for it!' barely touching her consciousness, although the biting tone reached deep down inside her, touching her where she could still be hurt, the lash of his scorn drawing tears of blood. Her body tensed against him, she struggled to recall her lines, vaguely aware of him touching locked muscles, stroking them into acquiescence and acceptance of his touch and weight, the storm of his anger dying away to be replaced by gentleness and then desire. And it was the gentleness that finally betrayed her. It was no use telling her aching body that it was all false; that Ben was simply playing a part, because she was already softening in response, and not just softening, but responding, Sarah recognised in mounting horror, her mind desperately trying to withstand the seduction of his touch. And then she knew!

Ben intended her to respond to him; he wanted this final humiliation, and he wouldn't stop until he got it. Balked of humiliating her by forcing her to go through the love scene in public with Paul, he had sensed her reaction to him and was playing on it, using her vulnerability as a weapon against her, slowly breaking down her resistance, until she was a trembling, aching bundle of need lying weightless in his arms, feeling the slow scorch of his mouth and hands against her skin before the final tide of desire rushed over her and she clung helplessly, opening her eyes at his command to let him see down into the far reaches of her soul. For a moment something seemed to glimmer in his eyes, but then it was gone and he was speaking Paul's lines, jolting her into awareness of how much she had betrayed, and some part of her that was still functioning made her responses, but her voice was a whisper devoid of tone of depth; dead like the rest of her, her body merely a physically functioning shell inside which she had quietly and totally withdrawn.

Somehow she was back in Wardrobe, and Linda and her assistants were helping her to change, Linda's worried glances something she was aware of but too numb to question.

Outside Paul was waiting for her, dressed in a tee-shirt and jeans, frowning as he touched her icy hand. 'Ben's waiting for the rushes. How about a drink and then we'll go and see them.'

'No!' The denial burst inside her like a small volcano, but the sound emerging from her throat was quiet and without vehemence. 'I don't want to see them.'

'Sarah . . .'

'Please, Paul, I don't want to talk about it.' Suddenly she was unutterably tired. All she wanted to do was sleep, and never ever have to wake.

'That was some performance, according to the camera crew.' Dale's sneering voice raised the hairs at the back of her scalp, but she ignored him. 'But then Ben always did know how to get a response out of you, and we both know why.'

'Do we?' Somehow she managed to face him.

'Sure we do. You love him.' His eyes narrowed. 'Do you still love him—after what he's done to you today?'

'I'm no longer capable of loving anyone,' she told him emotionlessly. 'Not loving, nor hating.'

'Liar!' Dale mocked her tauntingly. 'You still love him, Sarah, and you always will.'

Dale was right, Sarah acknowledged tiredly. It seemed she had no pride and no matter what Ben did to her, nothing could kill her love. He had given instructions that no one was to leave the set in case they had to re-shoot, and Sarah sat alone in the canteen, toying with a cold cup of coffee, knowing that she simply could not go through the scene again.

She knew Ben had walked in even without lifting her head by the ripple of speculation running swiftly round the room.

'Paul, Sarah, we're doing the scene again. If you'd both get ready.'

Sarah lifted her head, her eyes dark with fear and pain, noticing vaguely that Ben's hair was untidy as though he had raked angry fingers through it and that his mouth was circled by a taut white line which presaged a savage outburst of anger.

'I won't do it!' Was that really her own voice, so strained and husky? Most of the crew and cast had left the restaurant, drifting back to the set, only Gina and Dale lingering, watching.

'Sarah . . .' That was Paul, and Sarah recognised the note of concern and warning.

'Poor Sarah!' That was Dale, his voice dripping pseudo-sympathy with every malice-tipped word.

'Of course you know why she hates doing love scenes so much, don't you, Ben? It's because the poor thing's so desperately in love with you. That wasn't acting when we filmed *Shakespeare*, and . . .'

Sarah couldn't listen to any more. She turned and ran, her feet skimming the floor, Ben's voice sharply calling her name failing to halt her, only adding to her panic. Ben's car stood in the lot and she slid into it, reaching for the ignition key, shivering as she saw Ben emerge from the canteen and search for her, his head turning sharply as he heard the engine fire. Dale was behind him and Sarah saw him put his hand on Ben's arm, and Ben start to shake it off, before stopping. No doubt Dale was telling him everything. It was his revenge on her because she had dared to prefer Ben, but she no longer cared. Ben knew she loved him, knew of her stupidity, and she felt more naked than she had done when she stood before him on the set and felt him scrutinise her body.

The car had automatic transmission and Sarah had travelled the road to the studio often enough to know the way. She couldn't stay in America any longer now, if Ben wanted to re-film the scene he would have to find another actress. The un-alleviated stress of being so close to him was driving her out of her mind—almost literally, she thought grimly. Any more of this agonising torment and tension and she could well end up in a mental hospital.

She realised she had reached the house and stopping the car jumped out. Her passport, she thought feverishly, she needed her passport. It was

Margarita and Ramón's day off and the house was silent, but not locked. She went straight to Ben's study, opening drawers, searching through them, panic making her clumsy, every movement impelled by a growing sense of urgency. Where was it? Did Ben have a secret safe? Could he have left it at the studio? No, it must be here somewhere . . . She renewed her assault upon the desk drawers.

'Sarah . . .!'

She stiffened. Ben had followed her. She could hear his footsteps in the hall, measured and firm. Her heart thudded suffocatingly, the study was suddenly too confining.

'Sarah, where are you?' She heard him move to the door, watching the handle depress with a horrified fascination before realising she could escape through the patio. The glass door jammed and she tugged at it frenziedly, hearing Ben enter the room behind her, his swift curse bitten off as he saw her. For a second neither of them moved and then Ben glanced at his desk, his jaw clenching in anger as he took a step towards her.

The patio door moved smoothly under her fingers and Sarah was running, her heart thudding frantically against her ribs, knowing Ben wasn't far behind her, careless of which direction she ran in, until Ben's voice made her tense and swing round, trying to get her bearings, shocked to discover that he was less than a yard away; close enough almost to reach out his hand and . . .

'No!' The vehement denial was choked out of her throat and she stepped back instinctively in the same moment that Ben moved, his harsh, 'Sarah, for God's sake, the pool!' ringing numbly in her ears as she slipped and fell backwards through space and then down, down into the embrace of the life-stealing water.

CHAPTER TEN

'YOU crazy little fool, didn't you hear me shout?' They were standing by the poolside, Sarah shivering and shaking with reaction and shock, dimly aware that Ben had followed her into the pool and dragged her out, his chest rising and falling heavily with the effort of doing so, his hands warm against the cold skin of her waist, chilled by her shock and her soaking clothes.

'It's no good, Ben, I won't do that scene again.' Her voice was ragged with pain, her throat stinging from the water she had swallowed, her hands going up to his chest to push him away, her fingers curling tightly into her palms as he refused to release her, her small fists flailing impotently against his chest.

'Sarah darling, please don't!'

There in the warm huskiness of his voice; the quiet despair and pain underlying the softly spoken words was all she had longed to hear for so many barren years when they had been apart, and Sarah finally knew that her reason must have deserted her. Ben would never speak to her like that! Tears of exhaustion and defeat flooded her eyes. What was he trying to do to her now? Was this some new form of torture his Machiavellian brain had devised? She couldn't endure it!

'All right, all right, it's all true,' she moaned feverishly, 'I do love you—I always did. There was never anyone but you, even when Dale told me about your bet. I should have hated and despised you for that, but I couldn't.'

If she had expected him to deny it she had misjudged him. There was silence and then a pitying, 'Oh, Sarah!' and the pressure of his hands moved from her waist to her back, holding her against him, allowing her to draw strength from his body.

'I can't film that scene again, Ben . . .' Her voice started to rise hysterically. 'I can't . . . I can't!'

'Shush now, it's all right. Let's get you dry.' She was in his arms, her hair curling damply over his arm, her eyes closing as she felt the reassuring beat of his heart beneath her cheek, only surely it was slightly unsteady, perhaps because of her weight. Exhausted by her emotional storm, she was barely aware of being carried into Ben's room until he opened his bathroom door and slid her to her feet, the hands that had held her in his arms quickly stripping off her wet clothes, ignoring her feeble protests, his ministrations not stopping until she was wrapped in a thick fluffy towel. Picking her up again, Ben opened the door, carried her across to his bed and placed her on it, the concern she saw in his eyes making her heartbeats thud.

'Dale was never my lover.'

Now why had she told him that? Her face flamed. What possible interest could it be to Ben who had shared her bed? The downward flick of his lashes so that she could not see his eyes confirmed her thoughts, his slow, 'I know,' startling her into forgetting her despair long enough to stare up at him.

'You do? But . . .'

'Let me get these wet things off and then we'll talk.'

He was gone about five minutes, returning wearing a navy towelling robe, his legs and feet bare beneath the hem, his hair ruffled as though it had been towelled.

'Your hair is soaking,' he told her, reaching out a hand to touch it. 'I'll get a towel.'

He came back and sat on the bed behind her, rubbing briskly at her damp hair, much as though she were a child, then combing gently through its damp length, the gentle tug of the comb and the warm pressure of his hand on her shoulder causing fresh emotions to flare. Dear God, would she never be free of this? Sarah wondered helplessly. Would she always be as vulnerable to his touch as she was now, or would the years to come bring some measure of peace, of indifference? She could only pray that it might be so.

'I've decided to change your love scene with Paul back to its original form.'

He was still sitting behind her, and short of twisting round to look into his face, Sarah had no way of knowing how he felt. She knew she should have felt relief, but somehow she was incapable of feeling any emotion, only a vast, empty nothingness, through which she managed to murmur a dull, 'Thank you.'

'*You're* thanking *me*?' She was twisted round in his arms, her vulnerable emotions subjected to the fierce scrutiny of his glance, his fingers tightening almost painfully on her upper arms. 'Dear God, Sarah!' He leaned his forehead against hers, his eyes closed, the dark lashes lying like twin fans. 'Dear God, Sarah, how you shame me!' His eyes opened, his index finger tracing the shape of her lips, his forehead creasing in a frown as they trembled. 'You must believe me. If I'd had any idea how you felt, I'd never have forced you into that scene.'

'I swore I'd never do another one after *Shakespeare*,' Sarah told him huskily, feeling that his apology deserved some response. 'I knew then that what I was doing wasn't acting, and I hated it when my ... my performance was acclaimed. If it hadn't been with you ... but then you knew that, didn't you?' she asked dully. 'You'd guessed how I felt about you before Dale said anything, otherwise you'd never have known how much it would torture me to have to do that scene with you today.'

She couldn't look at him, although she heard the small explosive sound of the expletive started and then caught back as her chin was gripped and her face turned up to his. 'You thought that?' Ben sounded bitterly incredulous. 'You thought I was callously tormenting you?' He shook his head as though unable to believe what he had heard. 'No, Sarah, no! Never that. We'll re-film that scene as it was meant to be, and I promise you no one will ever see today's filming.'

'You saw it,' Sarah said bitterly. 'What will you do with it? Destroy it?'

The look she saw in his eyes made her shudder with sickness. 'You won't destroy it?' she whispered incredulously. 'You'll keep it. You'd do that to me, knowing . . .'

His hand curled round her jaw, forcing her face upwards. 'Knowing what, Sarah?' he asked softly. 'That all that you feel for me is irrevocably shown on that piece of film?'

Reaction jolted through her, her inarticulate protest as she fought against the prison of his arms lost against the thickness of his robe as she tried to break free, withdrawing like a child in pain when her hand inadvertently touched his skin.

'Would you like to see it?'

'No!' Her cry was pure terror, and she felt herself falling into blackness, falling, falling until there was nothing but a deep pit of terror.

Some time later she woke and was handed a glass, a smiling but firm uniformed nurse urging her to drink. The fear that her mind had actually gone and she was indeed in some institution began to haunt her, although she was dimly aware that the room she was in was one she recognised and the nurse had been concerned rather than constraining.

The next time she opened her eyes, the sun was shining. Her body felt strangely weightless beneath the bedclothes and when she turned her head there was a stranger standing beside the bed smiling at her encouragingly.

'Ah, so you're back with us. You're to be congratulated, my dear, on your recuperative powers.'

'Where . . .?' Where am I? she had been about to croak, but she knew where she was, recognising her surroundings. She was in Ben's room, in Ben's bed, although she didn't remember it filled with these exotic flowers.

'You've had a nasty shock to the system,' her dark-suited companion told her, 'but it's all over now.' He was studying her so calmly and professionally that Sarah knew intuitively what he was. 'You're—you're a doctor?' She moistened her dry lips. 'Did . . . did Ben . . .'

'Yes, to both questions,' he agreed, smiling. 'You've given us all a very bad scare, young lady,' he told her mock-severely, 'especially your husband. I did think at one time you would have to be removed to hospital, but Ben was most adamant. He didn't want you waking up to find yourself in strange surroundings.'

A dim memory of endless nightmares when she had pleaded not to be committed to a mental hospital, crying that she was not insane, pleated a frown across her forehead, as she wondered how Ben could have known of those night terrors.

'What—what exactly happened to me?' she asked huskily, trying to banish her strange languor. 'I remember falling in the pool.' She remembered more than that, but she didn't want to think about it, much less talk about it.

'As you say, you fell in the pool; a not entirely unusual occurrence and certainly not one which would normally provoke the type of blackout you later suffered, but the shock coupled with the strain your husband tells me you've been under made your reaction far more severe than was expected. You're quite recovered,' he assured her with a kind smile. 'My dear, you must accept that sometimes we humans drive our minds and bodies further than they are prepared to go, and when that happens they're apt to make their objections known. Yours merely chose a particularly forceful way of doing so. You'll still feel weak for quite some time,' he told her, straightening up from the bed. 'I've told your husband that you mustn't even think of working for at least six months, if indeed you ever return to acting.' He paused and looked sombre. 'My dear, I am only telling you what you must in your heart of hearts already know. Your temperament is not such that it can absorb the intense emotions you demand of it without some degree of pain. I should think very carefully about the future . . .'

In other words she might as well make up her mind that she would never be able to return to acting, Sarah thought bitterly when she was alone. She didn't need the doctor's carefully guarded conversation to tell her how close she had come to some sort of breakdown, not entirely brought on by the agony of her love scene; not if she was honest with herself. The strain of keeping her feelings from Ben had exacerbated the situation. She sighed, tensing as the door opened to admit the subject of her thoughts, his face unexpectedly grim. He seemed to have lost weight, his tan less golden than it had been, weariness lying at the back of the green glance that searched her, and then she realised, biting hard on her lip. No more acting for six months, the doctor had told her, which meant Ben would not be able to change the end of the film.

'Doctor Lazelles tells me you're much recovered.'
'Yes.' How awkward and stilted she sounded!

'I'm sorry to have been such a nuisance. But now ... Ben, we have to talk ...' She bowed her head, not knowing how much Doctor Lazelles had said to him.

'Later.' Why was his voice so harsh, the planes of his face sharply drawn and the skin stretched tight? 'This evening,' he amended huskily. 'After dinner.'

'I can get up?'

Her eagerness brought a brief smile to the corners of his mouth, but his negative headshake was firm. 'I'm afraid not, though ...' he was watching her carefully, '... though I could have dinner in here with you, I'm sure Doctor Lazelles wouldn't object to that, if that's what you want?'

Sarah's heart started to beat heavily, her mind trying hazily to grasp why the thought of their having dinner together in this room should be so much more intimate than sharing their meal in the dining room.

'Yes, yes, that would be ... nice,' she managed shakily, wondering wryly at her inadequate choice of words and then shrinking back against her pillows as Ben approached the bed.

'Sarah?' His voice questioned her withdrawal, his eyes darkening as they surveyed her flushed face and downcast lashes. 'I wasn't going to touch you,' he said grimly at last. 'I only wanted to ask if there was anything I could get you.'

He was gone before she was forced to contradict him and tell him that her withdrawal had been from herself and her own needs rather than any fear of him.

She slept, and woke to find Margarita in the room, pulling two chairs up to a small table she had set by the window. 'You're awake.' She smiled warmly at Sarah. 'And getting better. Now perhaps Ben will not spend all night working in his study, and sleeping there instead of here, in his room. He has been like a man demented. All these flowers . . .' She smiled again and shrugged. 'But then that is a man in love for you. Would you like any help?' Sarah shook her head, only realising when Margarita had gone that she did want a bath and that it might have been sensible to have Margarita on hand in view of the fact that she hadn't been out of bed for nearly a week. The truth of this suspicion was proved when she swung her feet to the floor and tried to take her first step, the floor coming up towards her at an alarming rate, although she didn't pass out, and she was just making another attempt when the door on to the balcony opened smoothly and Ben walked in, his mouth compressing when he saw what she was trying to do.

'I wanted a bath, and I never thought until Margarita had gone,' Sarah protested, reading the disapproval of his unspoken thoughts.

'I'll help you.'

Why did he insist on holding her like this when he must be able to guess what it did to her? Sarah wondered weakly as molten fire spread through her veins, her hands automatically clutching at Ben's shoulders as he bent to take her weight. Inside the bathroom he sat her on a chair as carefully as though she were made of brittle glass, quickly running her bath even though she protested that she could manage.

'I'll wait outside, but don't lock the door,' he

warned her as he stood up, 'and if you feel the slightest bit faint, just holler.'

The caress of the water against her skin felt like smooth silk. Her illness had drained her of energy and Sarah found it took twice as long to do everything as it had done. Consequently she had barely finished washing when the bathroom door burst open and Ben strode in, his face tight with anxiety, his body stilling as he turned and saw her just about to step out of the bath.

For one heart-wrenching moment Sarah could only stare at him, hot colour suddenly running up under her skin as she remembered her nudity, her breath caught in a gasp as Ben lifted her bodily out of the water, uncaring of her protests that she would soak his clothes, holding her pinned against him with one hand while the other reached for a towel that reached from her neck to her ankles as he strode into the bedroom with her.

While she had been in the bathroom dusk had fallen, an electric dinner waggon mute evidence that Margarita had been in with their meal. The rough movement of Ben's hands over her back, rubbing it dry, was unbearably erotic, her breasts rasped by the crisp body hair darkening his chest where his shirt had come undone. When he sat down, pulling her on to his knees, Sarah's skin flushed to think of his eyes resting on the aroused peaks of her breasts, but he barely glanced at her body as he secured the towel firmly round her, oblivious to his own damp shirt clinging slickly to his skin where her body had pressed against it.

'Ben, there's something I have to tell you.' She

felt him tense as she spoke, his eyes as green and wary as a big cat's.

'When Doctor Lazelles was here he said . . . He said I mustn't think of returning to filming for at least six months.' She couldn't look at him, knowing what her admission would mean.

'And you're worried about your career? You needn't be,' he said lightly. 'With my fifty per cent interest in the studio I'm sure I can get my wife some work . . .'

Sarah shook her head. 'No, you don't understand. I'm not sure if I'll ever act again, so I'm not concerned about future roles, but *Richard*, Ben, my . . . my love scene . . .' Her voice trembled and threatened to desert her. She couldn't bring herself to look at him and hoped he wouldn't see how much she was trembling.

'I told you not to worry about that, Sarah. It won't ever be shown, I promise you, and if I can't destroy it—well, you'll have to put that down to . . .'

'But you'll have to show it! Don't you see? If I can't work for six months you'll either have to re-film completely using someone else, or use that scene. You can't delay completion . . .'

'Who says I can't?' Ben drawled arrogantly, adding huskily, 'Sarah, if I thought it would atone for the pain I've caused you I'd cheerfully consign the whole damn film to the flames. Have you any conception what it did to me standing by that bed listening to you begging me to rescue you from a mental hospital? Dear God, and you thought *you* were going off your head! It's nothing to what I felt. And anyway, I wouldn't use that scene. I couldn't. When I saw the rushes and saw the look on your face when I made love to you, I knew there was no way I was going to share that with anyone else in the world, and I was only amazed that I hadn't seen it for myself at the time. My only excuse is that I was raw inside with hurting and jealousy. Wanting you ... loving you ... hating Dale, as I'd always hated him for taking you from me. You'll never know how many times in these last years I've nearly been on that plane to come and get you, only to tell myself that it wasn't fair to you; that you didn't love me, and that the only reason you'd married me was that I'd bullied you into it, and because I'd taken your virginity. Dale lied to you, Sarah,' he said slowly, 'there never was any bet. It's true that I meant to have you right from the first, but as my wife ... nothing else. Can you try and believe that?'

'You love me?' Sarah could hardly believe it. Beneath the protective towel she shivered convulsively, her eyes darkening in awed amazement.

'If you don't believe me I'll show you the film. It does more than merely show your feelings, Sarah. If a man's body can tell a woman that he aches and yearns for her, mine did.'

'But you were always so angry ... so ...'

'With myself for still loving you, for not being able to *stop* loving you. God, I damn nearly wanted to kill Paul simply for kissing you, and that was in the script!'

Sarah laughed huskily, remembering Eva's comment that he was jealous. Then she hadn't believed her, but now ...

'After *Richard* I'm not doing any more

directing,' Ben told her. 'I want to concentrate on writing, but we won't be paupers, I've still got my interest in the studio, or am I going ahead too fast? Will you stay with me, Sarah, live with me; love me; bear my children? You know, Dale made one big mistake,' he told her quietly. 'He thought because I'd made you do that scene that I no longer loved you, and so he told me everything. What he didn't realise was that I was punishing myself, forcing myself to endure watching you in someone else's arms, telling myself it was either kill or cure.'

'And then you had to take Paul's place.'

'And I saw in your face how much you dreaded the thought of me doing so and saw red . . .'

'Because I knew I wouldn't be able to resist you,' Sarah said dreamily.

'And does that still hold good now?' The teasing quality had gone from Ben's voice, his face strained and vulnerable. Sarah let her fingertips explore the newly sharpened angles, realising with a pang that they were there on her account.

'For God's sake, Sarah,' he muttered thickly, grasping her wrist and turning his mouth into her palm. 'Don't toy with me, even though I know I deserve it. You haven't answered my question. Do you still love me?'

'So much,' Sarah admitted shakily. 'So very, very much!'

The pressure of his lips was no longer that of a supplicant, but Sarah didn't object, not even when his hands pushed aside her towel to study the pale curves of her body, her movements deliberately teasing as she stretched provocatively beneath his glance, yawning against her hand, claiming that she felt tired.

'You're no actress, my lady,' Ben muttered thickly against her ear, 'and as your director I ought to beat you for that hopeless performance—as it is I think I shall merely have to punish you by accepting the invitation this . . .' and he ran his hands slowly over her body, '. . . has just proffered. Unless of course you've any objections?'

'None, unless it be your tardiness, my lord,' Sarah drawled languidly, matching his mood, watching the little flames of green burn within his eyes, boneless and sensual as a small cat as her skin luxuriated in his touch, her ears filled by the sound of his murmured love words, feeling her body quicken in sexual excitement, Margarita's dinner forgotten as the shadows of dusk gave way to darkness and she finally rested in the sanctuary of her husband's arms.

MAN-HATER

BY
PENNY JORDAN

WORLDWIDE BOOKS
LONDON • SYDNEY • TORONTO

CHAPTER ONE

SHE must be getting old, Kelly thought tiredly as she snapped off the office lights. Time was when she had worked well into the evening and had still left the office with her batteries fully charged and her brain working on overdrive, but that had been when she had first started the agency off. Now that it was successful she was missing the challenge of those early days.

She sighed as she pressed the button for the lift. Her offices were in a prestigious block owned by one of the major insurance companies—clients of hers. The publicity work she had done for them had been so successful that she had been able to negotiate a very reasonable rent for the premises.

One of the reasons she had had to work late was that she had spent the morning with her accountant going over the figures for the company's current trading year. Ian Carlisle had been full of praise and admiration. The company looked set to turn in a record profit. 'And with the sound capital base it's had right from the start, you're in a very good position, Kelly,' he had told her.

Ian worked for the firm who handled her grandfather's affairs. He had been the one to shock her with the astounding news of her grandfather's wealth, shortly after his death. To find herself an heiress at eighteen had come so totally out of the blue that it had taken her quite some time to come to terms with it. Kelly had never dreamed that the grandparents who had brought her up in the modest detached house just outside London had possessed such wealth, and with hindsight she doubted that even her grandmother had known of her husband's predilection for the Stock Market, nor his astounding success.

At first Kelly had been too overwhelmed by the money to cope with the responsibility of it. It was only later—after Colin—that she had become possessed by the need to make the money work, to prove that women could be just as successful and astute as men.

So why was it that she felt so depressed? By rights she ought to be celebrating the company's third birthday and its enviable success—not planning a lonely meal in her apartment followed by an early night after she had checked Sylvester's figures for the Harding contract.

That success often equalled loneliness was something she was only just beginning to realise; but that was what she wanted, wasn't it? Far better the hard-won fruits of success than the perils of emotional commitment—of relying on another human begin. Since Colin she had not relied on anyone other than herself—and that was the way she wanted it, she told herself firmly.

Outside, the streets were empty of the rush hour traffic. Success meant that one could not work a mere nine-to-five day—but it had been worth it, Kelly assured herself, barely giving her reflection more than the merest fleeting glance as she glimpsed her slender trench-coated figure in the store window. Kelly's was one of the most successful companies of its kind in the city, and Kelly herself had the reputation of being a genius where getting good publicity for her clients was concerned. Top-class advertising agencies vied with one another to work alongside her, and she knew without a trace of vanity that the company's success was solely due to her own hard work and flair.

So why, tonight of all nights, was she in this oddly introspective mood? Why on earth was she questioning the quality of her life? The cost of total commitment to her career? She had made the choice, no one had forced her. After Colin she could simply have continued as she had done before; she was a wealthy young woman with no need to work. A form of therapy, Ian had once called it, and she wasn't sure if he wasn't right. And it had worked. So why was she feeling so restless? She was twenty-six; wealthy in her own right; commercially successful. She was attractive, intelligent, and had a close if small circle of friends. What on earth had she to feel restless about?

By the time she reached her apartment she had managed to throw off her earlier mood, and she unlocked her door with a small sigh of relief.

The apartment had been carefully chosen and decorated to reflect the image of the agency. The walls and carpet of the large living-room merged in matching softly grey blues; two large settees covered in off-white silk facing one another across a glass and stained-wood coffee table that matched the décor exactly, as did the silk-covered cushions heaped artfully on the off-white settees, in colours ranging from soft blue-grey to a rich deep azure. Kelly had employed the same firm of interior designers for the apartment as she had done for the office, and the result was a classical, if somewhat cold perfection. The apartment, as always, was impeccable. Kelly was lucky enough to have a first-class cleaner who came every morning to restore the apartment to its pristine splendour. Normally she enjoyed the cool remoteness of the living room with its gracefully modern Italian furniture, its 'touch me not' air of impeccability, but tonight, for some reason, it repelled her, and she found herself thinking instead of the house in Hampstead she had shared with Colin; of the bliss that had been hers for those few short months she had spent planning the décor—a décor far removed from the elegance of her apartment.

What was past was past, she told herself firmly as she shrugged off her trench coat in her bedroom, hanging it up as she had been taught to do by her grandmother, who had been a stickler for tidiness. She remembered that Colin had mocked her for this habit—as he had done for so many things, only at the time she had been too blind to recognise the truth for what it was, and had thought he was simply teasing her.

The excellence of her plain navy pin-striped skirt and white silk blouse spoke for themselves. The silk clung treacherously to the curves of her breasts— too generous in Kelly's opinion, and in the early days of the company she had had to freeze off the admiring looks of more than one client. Personally she thought her figure too voluptuous. Her waist was too narrow for the fullness of her breasts, her legs too long. If she had to find one word to describe her figure, that word would be 'flambovant', Kelly acknowledged distastefully, and she always dressed in a style that minimised rather than maximised her curves. Her hair was long and dark, and she normally wore it in a neat chignon. She had always worn it long.

Her grandmother used to brush it for her every night, and once released from its constraining pins it had the texture and sheen of rich silk. She really ought to have it cut, she thought, slipping off her skirt and carefully returning it to its hanger, but wearing it up helped to add to her air of reserve, and this had been a useful weapon in establishing the company. Men never tended to take seriously women they were thinking of going to bed with rather than giving a business contract to, and Kelly had found out very quickly that her distant air, coupled with her formal clothes and severe hairstyle, helped to preserve the image she wished to maintain.

The day had tired her more than she had thought. She had little appetite and longed only to relax and go to bed, but first she had those figures to check. She always changed her clothes when she came home at night, never into the jeans and tops she had favoured in the days before Colin, but tonight for some reason something within her rebelled and instead of reaching for the plain dress she had been about to put on, Kelly found herself removing from her wardrobe a richly patterned silk kimono that one of her Japanese customers had sent her the previous Christmas.

The azure blue background enhanced the darkness of her skin and the sapphire depths of her eyes. Her skin was almost too pale—a result of not having had a holiday for too long, she thought ruefully as she tied the sash, and removed the light layer of make-up she had worn during the day, brushing her hair methodically before returning to the living room and curling up on the settee with the papers she had brought home with her.

She was deeply engrossed in the figures when her doorbell pealed. Frowning, she went across to the intercom in the hallway and asked crisply to know the name of her visitor.

'It's me, Kelly—Jeremy Benson.'

Kelly's heart sank as she heard the familiar and, to her ears, faintly unpleasant drawl of her best friend's husband's voice. She had never liked Jeremy in the days when he and Sue were merely engaged, and her dislike had grown into loathing in the years that followed. Sue and Jeremy had been married for six years, and Kelly doubted that Jeremy had remained faithful to her friend for even one of them.

Sue and Kelly had been at school together. Sue was the closest friend she had, but ever since Jeremy had made it plain that he was sexually attracted to her, Kelly had found that she saw less and less of her friend, apart from brief shopping trips together, fitted in on Sue's infrequent visits to London, when Jeremy could not accompany them.

That Jeremy knew how she felt about him, and still persisted in his blatant attempts to seduce her, infuriated Kelly all the more and only reinforced her opinion of men in general, which was that as far as the majority of them were concerned, despite Women's Lib, and the much vaunted equality beloved of the newspapers, women were still *things* as opposed to people with equal rights, and that it was simply enough for a man to *want* and try to take, without having the slightest regard for the feelings, or lack of them, of the object of his wanting.

For Sue's sake, she had not told Jeremy how much she despised him. He was a weak and vindictive man and over the years she had seen him gradually alienate Sue from all her old friends, so that she was entirely dependent on him emotionally, while he was free to pursue his flirtations and affairs. Sue never mentioned Jeremy's failings to her, and Kelly genuinely believed that she was not aware of his real personality. She loved him, as she was constantly telling Kelly, and Kelly dreaded what would happen to her friend if she ever discovered the truth. Had she not had first-hand experience of the devastating effect such a discovery could have on a woman in love?

'Come on, Kelly, don't keep me waiting down here all night! I've got a message for you from Sue.'

It was on the tip of Kelly's tongue to tell him to simply give her the message and go, but she knew that, if she did, Jeremy would consider that he had scored against her. Jeremy was well aware of her aversion to him and, far from putting him off, it only seemed to increase his desire for her. If she refused to let him come up to the apartment he would goad her at a later date of being afraid to be alone with him; twisting the facts until it appeared that she was afraid to be alone with him because she desired him! Kelly knew quite well how his mind worked.

Her mouth twisting bitterly, she told him to come up.

His eyes widened appreciatively as she let him in, and as he bent forward to kiss her cheek, Kelly kept her body rigidly away from him.

He merely looked amused.

'Still the same old frigid Kelly,' he mocked. 'What's the matter? Afraid of what might happen between us if you really let go? No need to be, old girl.'

His manner, as always, set Kelly's teeth on edge and she could feel her temper simmering just below boiling point as she poured him a drink and handed it to him before sitting down opposite him.

'Fantastic place you've got here,' Jeremy said appreciatively, glancing round the room. 'Sue hasn't the faintest idea about décor,' he added disparagingly, 'but then, of course, I suppose everything's possible if one has the money.'

Two thrusts with one blow, Kelly thought acidly. First the criticism of her friend, and then the reminder that *she* had the wealth to buy good taste.

'You said you had a message for me from Sue,' she reminded him frostily.

'Welcoming, aren't you?' Jeremy complained, adopting a hurt little boy air that irritated Kelly beyond bearing, although she knew it worked well with poor Sue. 'We haven't seen you in months and now you can't wait to get rid of me.'

'I've got some work to do.' She indicated the pile of papers beside her. 'What are you doing in town anyway?'

Jeremy was an accountant with his own practice in the New Forest, where they lived, and it was a constant bone of contention with him that Kelly wouldn't transfer her business to his practice.

'A business meeting,' he told her. 'And Sue suggested I call and see you. She wants to show off the new house and suggested you might like to come down for the weekend. She's feeling a bit low at the moment, with the baby and everything.'

Was it *Sue* who wanted to show off the new house they had just bought, or Jeremy? Kelly wondered acidly, but the last part of Jeremy's sentence reminded her that her friend had just lost a much wanted baby, and it smote her conscience that apart from a telephone call she had not spoken much to Sue since the tragic event.

'What's the matter?' Jeremy asked, watching her craftily. 'Don't you fancy the idea? Or is it that you fancy it too much? There's something about you, Kelly. It really turns me on; the high-powered woman image. Poor Sue can't really hold a candle to you. She's developing into a boring little *hausfrau*, I'm afraid, and all this fuss about the baby hasn't helped.'

God, he really was callous and unfeeling! Kelly fumed, longing to tell him that in her opinion Sue was worth ten of him—at least. Part of her longed to refuse the invitation to refute his smug comments, but she valued her friendship with Sue and was suddenly conscious of the fact that her friend probably needed her company badly right now. If she refused there was no telling how Jeremy might react. He was vain enough to poison Sue's mind against her in the same way he had done with Sue's other friends, and she could not retaliate by telling Sue the truth—especially not now when she was bound to be feeling particularly insecure.

'I'll come,' she announced briefly, 'but you really

must leave now, Jeremy. I have to finish these figures tonight . . .'

She got up as she spoke, expecting him to follow her, but instead he reached up, caressing her hip, his gaze blatantly sexual as he stared at her body. A shudder of revulsion coursed through her, as Kelly pushed him away, her face taut with anger.

'All right, I get the message, but there'll be other times, Kelly,' Jeremy warned her. 'No woman, even a woman like you, can live the life of a nun for ever. See you at the weekend,' he added mockingly as she opened the door for him.

When he had gone reaction caught up with her and Kelly sank down on to the settee, her face a tortured mask of hatred and pain. God, the arrogance of the male sex! She loathed Jeremy's touch, and yet he assumed he had the God-given right to touch her, just because *he* wanted to!

Men! She despised them all! Frigid, Jeremy called her. Well, he was probably right. Colin had said much the same. Colin! She closed her eyes, unable to stop the shudders trembling through her. Dear God, would she never be able to forget?

She had met him just after her grandfather's death. He had worked in the same office as Ian, as a trainee accountant. They had met when Ian told her about her unexpected inheritance. At first she had been so overcome by the unexpected news that she hadn't even been able to think properly, and it was Colin who came running after her in the street with the umbrella she had left behind.

That had been the beginning; a fairly innocuous start to the events which had had such a cataclysmic effect upon her whole life.

It had been several days later when she received
a telephone call from Colin at her office, asking her
to go out with him. She had been drawn to him at
first sight and had willingly accepted.

They went out for a meal and then on to a film.
Colin had driven her back to her grandparents'
house, where she still lived, in the old banger he
had recently bought. He had kissed her goodnight,
gently but determinedly, and her heart had sung
with joy.

Six weeks later they were engaged. On Colin's
advice she sold the house. He wanted them to have
a completely fresh start, he had told her, but she
had been startled when he took her to see the large
house in Hampstead he thought they should buy.
When Kelly protested that it was very expensive,
he had reminded her that she was a very wealthy
young woman and that anyway the house was an
investment for the future, adding that when he had
his own practice it would be useful for entertaining
clients. Kelly had agreed, although Ian demurred a
little when she told him of her plans, warning her
that she would have to sell some of her investments
to raise the capital.

Several hectic weeks followed. The house was
huge and needed certain structural alterations;
Colin was away on a course, and their meetings
were only infrequent, restricted to discussions
on progress with the house, and briefly snatched
kisses.

Kelly had an aunt who lived in the north of
England, in the Borders. She was Kelly's father's
aunt really, and quite elderly, and Kelly had promised to visit her. She talked it over with Colin and it

was arranged that she would go up for a few days before the wedding so that she could relax. 'You've been working so hard on the house, sweet,' Colin had told her, 'that you deserve a rest. I'll be away in Birmingham at our other office, anyway . . . Oh, before you leave,' he had added, 'I've got one or two papers for you to sign—nothing very important.'

She had signed them between kisses, wondering what it would be like to be really Colin's wife. Her grandmother had brought her up strictly and, a little to her surprise, Colin had made no attempt to press upon her any of the intimacies she had expected. Was he aware of how nervous she felt? she wondered as she travelled north.

Four days later she was back. She had enjoyed her stay with her aunt who, although well into her eighties, was hale and hearty. They had talked about Kelly's grandparents, and Kelly's father, who had been in the army and had been killed in Northern Ireland by a car bomb. Kelly's mother had been with him, and their orphaned daughter had been brought up by her grandparents. She had been four when her parents were killed and barely remembered them.

The wedding was to be a quiet one—a register office affair, although Kelly would have preferred to be married in church.

They weren't having a honeymoon—Colin had promised to take her away later when he had passed his final exams.

They returned to the house in Hampstead after a brief reception at a large London hotel.

Ian had been there and had kissed her cheek

gravely as he told her how lovely she looked.

They returned to the Hampstead house early in the evening. Dusk was just falling, and the drawing room looked pleasant and warm as Kelly snapped on the lamps. All at once she felt awkward and uncertain. Colin had gone upstairs, and she wondered whether she ought to go up too, or whether to wait to change out of her wedding suit until he came down. If only she had more experience! She dismissed the disloyal thought that Colin's manner was not very lover-like. Perhaps he felt as uncertain as she did herself, and she wished that their courtship had not been so brief and hurried.

'Bathroom's free if you want to get changed.'

She wheeled round, blushing a little as Colin walked in. He had changed into jeans and a sweater, and a tingle of excitement fired her blood as she looked at him.

'Colin . . .'

She paused uncertainly, willing him to take her in his arms and kiss her, to melt her doubts and fears with the warmth of his love, but instead he merely indicated the drinks tray on the table and asked if she wanted him to pour her one.

Shaking her head, Kelly went upstairs, telling herself that her let-down feeling was only nerves. Of course it was foolish to expect Colin to sweep her into his arms and make mad passionate love to her; modern people simply didn't behave like that.

She had just walked out of the bathroom when she heard the low hum of voices from downstairs. With no intention of eavesdropping she hesitated, wondering who on earth could have called on them tonight of all nights, when the drawing-room door was suddenly thrown open and she heard Colin saying angrily, 'Pat, I told you never to come here!'

'You also told me you loved me,' Kelly heard a feminine voice reply. 'You told me you loved me, and that this house was going to be ours—that you would have your own practice and . . .'

Frozen with horror and disbelief, Kelly crept to the edge of the stairs. Colin and his companion were completely oblivious to her presence.

'And so we will, darling,' she heard Colin murmur softly. 'Everything will work out all right.'

'But you didn't have to marry her, did you?' Kelly heard 'Pat' demanding angrily, 'God, Colin, how could you?'

'Simple,' she heard Colin saying with new cynicism, 'I just closed my eyes and thought of all that lovely money. Oh, come on, Pat,' he added, 'you don't think I actually want her? God, she's the most boring female I've ever known, a little brown mouse and frigid with it. She can't hold a candle to you, my sweet. The only way I can endure this marriage is by telling myself that it's for us, that . . .'

'But she's your wife!'

'Only for six months at the most. I've already got her to sign the documents deeding the house to me. Once I've persuaded her to give me the money to set up my practice I'll tell her the marriage is over.'

Kelly felt sick with shock and disbelief. It couldn't be true. But it was true! She only had to look over the banister to see her Colin, her husband, with another woman in his arms, kissing her with a hunger he had never shown her, to know how true it was. Nausea welled up inside her and she rushed back into the bathroom. The pair downstairs were oblivious to everything but one another and never even heard her.

Did Colin actually intend to make love to her? Kelly wondered sickly when the bitter spasms were over. And Pat, how did she feel about sharing her lover with another woman? How could *she* herself permit Colin to touch her knowing what she now did?

'Kelly? Darling, what are you doing up here?'

Kelly stared at Colin, wondering why she expected him to have changed.

He was still exactly as he had been before she discovered the truth; she was the one who had changed. She was no longer the foolish naïve child she had been then. Bitter fury welled up inside her.

'What do you want, Colin?' she challenged. 'My signature to some more papers, is that it?'

She saw the colour drain out of his face.

'Darling . . .' he blustered, 'I don't know . . .'

'I heard everything,' Kelly cut in coolly, marvelling at her own control. 'Everything, and if you think I'd allow you to so much as touch me now I . . .'

'Why, you sanctimonious little prude!' Colin snarled, slamming the door and walked towards her. 'Do you honestly believe I *wanted* to touch you? No way,' he told her cruelly. 'You've got nothing that appeals to me, Kelly. You can't hold a candle to Pat, you're frigid, or damn near, and . . .'

'I do have one thing you want—apparently . . .' Kelly interrupted acidly, hoping he wouldn't guess at the pain that tore at her insides. 'My money—

well, you won't get a penny of it, Colin. First thing tomorrow I'm having our marriage annulled!'

'Annulled?' He advanced to the bed, the cruelty in his eyes frightening her into rigid tension. 'No way,' he told her softly. 'I might not want you, Kelly, but I sure as hell want that money, and there's no way you're going to cheat me of it now. So you think you'll get an annulment, do you?' He laughed softly in his throat and terror stalked her as he stared down at her, slowly removing his sweater and then his jeans.

She wanted to run, but fear held her rooted to the spot, cowering on the bed, wishing she had the courage to get up and flee. The silk wrap she had put on after her bath was ripped from neck to hem in the degrading scene that followed, pain and fear locking Kelly's throat against the screams of terror building up there. Colin's hands bruised her body, just as his callous words had bruised her heart.

'Frigid bitch!' he swore at her, when her body clenched protestingly against him, hurt and frightened beyond any possible arousal, and he flung himself off the bed to stare furiously down at her.

'You're not a woman, you're an iceberg,' he taunted her as he pulled on his jeans. 'No one could make love to you—they'd freeze first!'

He was gone before she could speak, leaving her dry-eyed, her heart pounding with fear, her body aching with tension and the bruises and scratches Colin had inflicted upon it.

Frigid, frigid, frigid—the word danced jerkily through her mind as she lay there, unable to move, unable to cry, unable to properly comprehend. She heard the door slam as Colin left the house—going where—to Pat, who wasn't an iceberg, who wouldn't make him freeze? And then what? Would he come back and carry out his threat? Could she endure it if he did? Rape was an ugly word for an ugly deed, but that was what it would be if Colin consummated their marriage.

She was still lying there in the darkness when she heard the doorbell. She let it peal, until she realised that it wasn't going to stop. It had to be Colin, and she dressed slowly, hoping he would go away, but he didn't.

She unlocked the door, noticing that a false dawn was pearling the sky. She must have been lying there half-conscious for several hours, but it had seemed like only minutes since he left.

'Mrs Langton?' She peered up at the policeman standing on the doorstep. 'May I come in for a second?'

Somehow he had done and he was inside and asking where the kitchen was, saying something about a nice cup of tea. Kelly's numbed mind couldn't follow what he was saying, only that he was using a soothing tone, the sort one used on frightened animals—or children. Slowly, what he was saying sank it.

'Now, come and sit down,' he said gently, his own manner awkward and compassionate.

'He wouldn't have felt a thing,' he told her. 'Killed straight off . . .' He didn't add that his sergeant had said—and so he deserved to be, driving like a maniac on the wrong side of the road, with too much drink inside him.

Colin was dead! Why didn't she feel something?

Anything? She couldn't. All she felt was numb. She watched the young policeman with a curious sense of detachment. He seemed more concerned than her. He drunk the tea he had made quickly and asked her if she had any family.

She shook her head and heard herself saying clearly,. 'It's all right, I shall be perfectly all right. Please don't worry . . .'

'Rum do,' the constable told the sergeant at the station later. 'Didn't so much as turn a hair.'

'Takes all sorts,' the sergeant commented, 'and news like that takes 'em all in different ways. Don't worry about it too much, lad,' he comforted the younger man—it was only his second 'fatal' and it was always hard to have to be the one to break the news.

Alone in the huge Victorian house, Kelly's own emotion was one of thankfulness. Of relief. Her love for Colin had gone, destroyed by the discovery that he had simply been using her. Her body ached from his cruelty, and her mind felt blunted and bruised. All she wanted to do was sleep. But there was one thing she must never do, and that was that she must never again be foolish enough to allow any man to deceive her as Colin had done. She must remember always that she was rich, that she was undesirable apart from her money and that she must always, always be on her guard. Always . . .

'Always . . .' With a start, Kelly realised that she had said the word aloud. Grimacing, she shrugged. She had come a long way from the girl she had been at eighteen. She was, after all, eight years older, eight years wiser. She glanced down at her hand where Colin's rings still glittered.

She wore them as a reminder; just as she used her married name. Since Colin's death she had learned that she *was* attractive to men, but she had never stopped wondering cynically why, and she thought she knew the answer. Those who were married simply wanted a few brief hours of escapism and thought they could use her body to achieve it, and those who weren't wanted to secure their future through her wealth and weren't averse to making love to her if by doing so they could achieve that object. She despised them all with equal fervour.

'A man-hater,' one of them had once called her, but didn't she have good reason to be? And hadn't Jeremy just confirmed that she was right?

CHAPTER TWO

SHE worried about the weekend when she should have been thinking about her work. There had been something in Jeremy's manner which suggested that he might be contemplating forcing the issue. A visit to her bedroom uninvited, perhaps? It had happened before—albeit not with Jeremy. And if she refused the invitation, how would Sue feel? Sue who had lost her longed-for baby before it was even born?

Kelly fretted over the problem for most of the day and left the office feeling jaded and tense.

She was half-way down a tube escalator when the advertisement caught her eye: 'Need a companion? An escort?' it asked. 'Phone us—we can provide either, male or female—to accompany you to that special function which you simply can't attend alone.'

Was it genuine, or was she being naïve? What was the matter with her? she asked herself as she hurried on to the tube. Surely she wasn't considering hiring an escort? But why not? It would be one way of keeping Jeremy at bay; and without the complications taking any other escort with her might involve. She had many male acquaintances, but there wasn't one of them who wouldn't leap immediately to the wrong conclusion if she suggested they spend the weekend with her.

She toyed with the idea all evening, alternately

dismissing and re-assessing it. It was ridiculous, farcical, but wasn't it also the ideal solution? There was nothing to be lost in simply making enquiries.

She dug out a telephone directory and searched through it. The agency had a surprisingly good address, a fairly new office block that Kelly knew quite well. She had contemplated taking a suite in it herself until she had received the offer from the insurance company for her present offices. Chewing her lip, she contemplated her alternatives. She could either go alone to Sue's and risk being proved right about Jeremy's attentions, or she could try and avert any unpleasantness by making enquiries at the agency and, if everything went well, employing one of their staff to accompany her.

Simple! So why should she be so wary and full of doubt? Was it because the idea of actually paying someone to accompany her smacked of a lack of femininity and—even worse—an admission that she could only attract male attention by paying for it? What did it matter? No one other than herself and the agency need know. Her motives were quite legitimate, and surely it was worth sinking her pride if it meant saving Sue pain and herself possible embarrassment. She had nothing to lose by simply calling at the agency and enquiring, had she?

As luck would have it, she had an appointment that took her in the vicinity of the agency's offices. She emerged on to the pavement from the impressively externally-mirrored building that housed the latest addition to their client list, sufficiently buoyed up with the success of obtaining a new and prestigious client to pluck up the courage to cross the busy street and walk purposefully into the marble foyer of the building opposite. There was no commissionnaire in evidence, but a quick glance at the nameplates by the lift confirmed that the agency was on the third floor. Feeling considerably more nervous than she had done at her previous interview, Kelly waited for the lift, smoothing the skirt of her new Jaeger suit anxiously. The suit wasn't something she would normally have chosen. Maisie, her assistant, had persuaded her into it for the meeting this morning. In a rich amethyst velvet, the skirt fell in soft gathers from a neat waistband. The jacket was faintly mediaeval, with a cropped close-fitting collarless bodice and slim slightly puffed sleeves, quilted with gold thread.

She was wearing a new blouse with it, cream silk with a large collar worn outside the jacket, and an amethyst velvet ribbon tied in a bow at her throat.

Somehow the outfit made her look faintly vulnerable rather than efficient; it even seemed to rob her chignon of something of its normal formality. Wisps of hair had escaped to curl round her temples, and Kelly toyed nervously with her pearl earrings as she sent the lift to the third floor.

She saw the entrance to the agency the moment she stepped out of the lift. The door to the foyer was open and there was a man with his back to her bending over a desk.

He straightened up as she knocked and walked in, turning to study her with lazy appreciation. Much to her chagrin, Kelly felt herself flushing with anger as his glance slid potently over the length of her legs in the sheer amethyst stockings that matched her outfit, pausing almost thoughtfully before moving upwards, assessing the slenderness of her

waist encased in a broad suede belt, the full curves
of her breasts beneath the velvet jacket, coming to
rest with amused comprehension on her taut and
angrily flushed face.

'My apologies,' he drawled in a voice that, Kelly
told herself unpleasantly, sounded like all the
very worst television commercials, and was very
obviously less than sincere.

'Don't apologise if you don't mean it,' she snapped. 'Insulting me once was enough!'

'Oh? And how did I do that?' The husky voice
hadn't changed, but Kelly had the disconcerting
feeling that somehow she had angered him.

'By looking at me as though I were a piece of
merchandise you were considering buying. That
was your first insult,' Kelly told him scathingly.
'Your second was expecting me to be deceived by
your less-than-sincere apology.'

'Oh, I wasn't apologising for looking,' she was
told softly. 'What I was apologising for was embarrassing you.'

'Embarrassing me!' Kelly stared at him in fury.
Did he actually think she had been embarrassed by
his insulting scrutiny? 'You didn't embarrass me in
the slightest,' she told him coldly, 'you merely
annoyed me. How would men like it if women
stared at them as though . . .'

'As though they were pieces of merchandise they
were considering buying?' he quoted mockingly. 'I
don't know what brings you here, Miss . . .'

'Mrs Langdon,' Kelly supplied for him coldly,
watching his eyes narrow as he glanced at her left
hand as though seeking confirmation of her statement. 'I'm here for the very simple reason that I

wish to avail myself of the services of this agency,' she went on tautly. Now that she was here, confronting this arrogant specimen of manhood, she was beginning to have grave doubts about her intentions.

'The agency?' He glanced at the door, frowned, tapping thoughtfully on the desk, while he subjected her to a provokingly intense study. 'You mean the escort agency, I take it?'

'Is there any other?' Kelly snapped, her patience worn thin by his manner and his scrutiny. He was completely unlike the species of male she had grown accustomed to over the years; they, well primed as to her reputation and her wealth, were normally either obsequious or respectful; sometimes flirtatious, but never, never did they regard her with the cool disdain of this man, whose grey eyes seemed to take her apart muscle by muscle, assessing each and every part of her as he did so. His hair was dark and brushed the collar of his jacket—too long, she thought scornfully, but doubtless there were some woman who found him attractive. As far as she was concerned, he was far too chocolate-boxy to appeal; he looked like one of the actors one saw on television, driving lorries and eating bars of chocolate or performing death defying acts on skis to deliver them. Some of her contempt showed in the withering glance she gave him, determined not to let his manner overset her.

'Umm . . . you're attractive enough, I suppose,' he ventured calmly, 'but I scarcely think your manner is likely to win you friends or influence people. If you really want a job I would suggest that . . .'

'*I* want a job?' Kelly broke in furiously, two

hectic spots of colour burning in her previously pale face. 'I haven't come here for a job, I've come here for an escort!'

'An escort?' If he was as stunned as he had sounded, he covered it up very quickly. 'I see, and just what sort of escort do you require, Mrs Langdon?' he asked smoothly, sitting down in the leather chair behind the desk, and pulling open a drawer. 'You must understand that this is a highly reputable and respectable agency, we don't . . .'

Kelly's furious gasp reached him and he straight-ened up, staring coldly at her. 'You're a married woman,' he pointed out.

'I'm a widow,' Kelly contradicted him, 'and I want to see the manager.' She threw the last com-ment at him through gritted teeth.

'By all means,' he agreed suavely, 'but you'll have to come back next week. He's on holiday at the moment.'

Next week! That would be far too late!

'Look, suppose you tell me your requirements . . . Do you need an escort for some official func-tion?'

'Not exactly,' Kelly replied hesitantly, strangely reluctant to admit to this infuriating man exactly what she did want.

'I see. Well, perhaps if you were to tell me exactly what you do want . . .' He removed what looked like an application form from the desk and bent his head over it. His hair was thick and dark and possessed a glossy, healthy sheen, Kelly noticed absently. Why on earth had she come here? She longed to turn tail and run out, but simply didn't dare. His face was perfectly composed and polite, and yet Kelly had the suspicion that inwardly he was laughing at her. Well, let him laugh, she thought angrily, she didn't care what he thought.

Quickly she told him an edited version of her story.

'I see,' he said slowly, when she had finished. 'You wish to hire an escort to accompany you to a friend's home for the weekend. Your friend is married and you feel that a threesome might be awkward?'

That was what Kelly had told him, and she had no intention of saying any more.

'And you don't have any male friends who could accompany you?'

'Sue, my friend, is inclined to matchmake,' Kelly told him quickly, not without some truth. 'I thought it best if I took a complete stranger—to avoid complications later.'

'I see.' His expression told her quite plainly that he did not, but Kelly had no intention of enlightening him. However, several minutes later she realised that she had underestimated him when he said softly, 'This escort wouldn't be more of a bodyguard by any chance, would he?'

'Bodyguard?' Kelly looked at him sharply. 'Look, if you don't want my business, just say so.' She was beginning to lose her temper. Something about this man unleashed a powerful wave of antagonism she hadn't experienced in years. It must be something to do with the sexual magnetism that almost oozed from him—part of his stock in trade, she reminded herself scathingly, wondering what part he played in the agency.

'Not at all,' he responded smoothly, 'I was merely trying to discover exactly what you had in mind. You must appreciate that a legitimate agency such as ours sometimes receives enquiries it isn't equipped to handle.'

Kelly went brick red as the meaning of his carefully chosen words sank in.

'All I want is a male escort for the weekend,' she ground out with loathing. 'Nothing else!'

'Well, in that case, Mrs Langdon,' he continued with a briskness that belied his earlier words, 'if you will simply give me the details I'm sure we'll be able to sort out something.'

Coolly and concisely, Kelly told him. She thought she saw him hesitate when she gave him her address, and wondered cynically if he was mentally adding another nought to the bill she would be presented with. If so, he was in for a rude awakening.

'Will you require a car?' he said formally.

'I have my own,' Kelly told him shortly. 'Can you provide someone?'

She was filled with distaste for what she was doing, but she had come too far to back down now, and she faced him with dogged determination, trying to ignore the embarrassment and anger she was experiencing.

He studied her for a moment, then said slowly, 'How important is it to you that we do?'

It was on the tip of her tongue to tell him that it wasn't important at all, but somehow she found herself saying huskily instead, 'Very important.'

'Yes.' The grey eyes held hers intently. 'Yes, I

thought it must be. Now, what time do you want our man to be at your apartment?'

Quickly Kelly told him, only too glad to escape from the office ten minutes later, filling her lungs with steadily deep breaths as she stepped outside on to the pavement, only too glad to have the ordeal behind her. What was the matter with her? She had faced formidable Boards of Directors without flinching, and yet in front of that one man she had been reduced to a shivering, trembling wreck. Why?

For the rest of the day she found it difficult to concentrate. She had told Maisie that she intended to be away for the weekend.

'Take a couple of extra days off,' Maisie urged. 'You could do with the break. Go out and buy yourself a new dress.'

'I don't need one,' Kelly told her briefly, only somehow she found herself leaving the office earlier than usual, and as it just happened to be a late shopping night, she found herself wandering through the Knightsbridge stores; something that she hadn't done in ages.

She saw a dress that caught her eye on one of the racks. In crêpe satin by Calvin Klein, it was a deceptively simple wrap-round dress in a brilliant shade of pink.

Somehow she found herself in the changing room with it over her arm, discarding her velvet suit in order to try it on. The neckline plunged almost to the waist, the long tight sleeves hugging her arms in much the same way as the satin hugged her body, the fabric caught up in a knot just above the waist. It was hideously expensive and not the sort of thing she wore at all, and yet somehow she found herself buying it, even though she told herself that she was mad and it was simply not the sort of thing to wear for a quiet dinner in the country.

Sue rang her while she was still recovering from the shock of her spending spree.

'You are still coming, aren't you, Kelly?' she pleaded. 'I'm so looking forward to seeing you. I've been so miserable!'

Kelly could tell that tears weren't far away, and hastened to assure her friend that she would indeed be there.

'Jeremy will be glad to. I sometimes think lately that he finds my company very boring,' she heard Sue saying wistfully. 'Since the baby I've felt so down, and Jeremy always enjoyed the company of lovely women. I feel such a failure, Kelly . . . Here I am and I can't even produce a baby, and you . . . you have a fantastic career, the whole world at your feet . . .'

'Sue, you're not to think like that,' Kelly told her.

'I know—pathetic, aren't I? But I just can't help it. I feel so alone, Kelly, so frightened somehow. When do you plan to arrive?'

'Well, actually, it isn't just me,' Kelly told her hesitantly. 'Is it okay if I bring a friend?'

For a moment there was silence and then Sue asked excitedly, 'A man? Kelly darling, tell me all about him!'

Kelly laughed. 'Wait and see.' Well, she could hardly describe a man she hadn't yet met, could she?

Her information seemed to have had a dramatic

effect on Sue's mood, she bubbled and chattered in a way that reminded Kelly of a much younger Sue, and by the time she had rung off, Kelly was convinced that she had made the right decision, no matter what the cost to her own pride. She only hoped that the agency managed to produce someone presentable. She was a fool really, she ought to have asked to see a photograph and some background details, but she had been too flustered and angrily aware of her companion to do so.

Saturday morning came round all too quickly. The arrangement was that her 'escort' would present himself at her apartment on Saturday morning at nine o'clock. Kelly was dressed and packed by eight-thirty, her stomach fizzing with a nervous dread she hadn't experienced since . . . since Colin, really.

She inspected her reflection in the mirror once again. She was wearing her velvet suit, but this time her hair was caught back in a pretty gold-threaded velvet snood she had found in Liberty's and which added to the mediaeval effect of her outfit. It also had a softening effect of the severity of her hairstyle, and Kelly was frowning slightly over this when she heard her doorbell.

Picking up her case and bag and checking that she had her keys, she headed for the hall, opening the door and coming to a full stop, her mouth opening in a round 'Oh' of surprise as she recognised the man leaning indolently against the wall.

'You!'

He smiled as he took her case from her slackened grip and locked the door for her with the keys she had dropped in her agitation.

'What are you doing here?' Kelly demanded acidly, furious with herself for letting him take the initiative and treat her like a demented child.

'You wanted an "escort" for the weekend—here I am.' He shrugged casually and glanced at his watch, completely impervious to her anger. 'Shall we go? We'll make better time if we miss the morning traffic. The roads are practically empty at the moment. Are these your car keys?' He extracted them from the ring, handing her back her door keys with another smile, deftly pocketing the keys for her car as he motioned her towards the lift.

This couldn't be happening, Kelly thought dazedly. She wasn't used to men taking control of her life in this way, especially men like this one— men who cashed in on their physical attractions in order to make a living. The sheer discrimination of her own thoughts shocked her, but they couldn't be denied; somehow it was different for women to exploit their looks in order to make a living than it was for a man. Telling herself she was being ridiculous, she headed for the lift, wishing the agency had sent anyone but this man. She had disliked him almost at first sight that day in the agency's offices, and now she felt a resurgence of her dislike, hating the calm way he was taking over, robbing her of the control she always had of her own life.

When the lift stopped he stepped forward first, and Kelly seethed impotently, longing to push past him, but lacking the sheer brute strength, and sudden colour flooded her angry face as she realised he was simply ensuring that she wouldn't be caught in the lift doors. The expression in his eyes as she swept past him told her that he had guessed the direction of her thoughts, and she flushed again. The weekend had promised to be difficult enough as it was, now it threatened to be intolerable.

'Why didn't you send someone else?' she muttered through clenched teeth to him as they entered the underground car park. 'Or was the money too much of a temptation?' she asked nastily.

She couldn't see his face, but the fingers cupping her elbow tensed suddenly and his smooth, 'You find man's very natural desire to provide himself with a living contemptible? How odd. Or is it simply the means by which I earn mine?' silenced her. She had been betrayed by her own emotions into making a judgment that was completely biased, and he had underlined that fact.

'It seems to me,' he remarked pleasantly, as she headed for the silver-grey Mercedes convertible she had bought the previous year, 'that you have a chip on your shoulder where the male sex is concerned. I wonder why?'

'Then don't!' Kelly snapped. 'That's not what I'm paying you for.'

'You like reminding me of that fact, don't you?' he continued evenly. 'Does it help to cancel out the old wounds, Kelly, knowing that now you can make the male dance to your tune?'

His words shivered across her skin, too close to the truth for comfort, but she refused to acknowledge their accuracy, or the danger emanating from the man standing at her side. How could a man like this possibly be dangerous? He was simply someone whom she was using to prevent herself from being trapped in a potentially difficult situation.

But he had used her name with an easy familiarity that had shocked her; and not just shocked. Hearing it on his lips had started a curious yearning ache deep inside her that she could neither define nor analyse.

'I was the only suitable candidate the agency had available,' he told her coolly, as they came to a full stop by the car. 'If you wish to change your mind and cancel the contract—then go ahead.'

Damn him, Kelly thought bitterly, he knew quite well she couldn't.

'Very well,' he continued, taking her silence for consent. 'In that case perhaps I'd better introduce myself properly. I'm . . .' he hesitated momentarily, 'Jake Fielding.'

'Jake.'

Somehow she found herself taking the hand he offered, her fingers curling instinctively at the first touch of the vibrantly male flesh against them.

He must have noticed her recoil, and she saw the speculation in his eyes as he bent to unlock the car door—the passenger door, Kelly noticed, as he swung it open and waited.

She looked up at him.

'You don't expect me to let you drive?'

'Why not? I have a current driving licence, if that's what's worrying you. You look tense and overtired,' he added unkindly, 'I thought you might enjoy an opportunity to relax before meeting your friends. Obviously you aren't looking forward to the weekend . . .'

'How did you know that?'

He looked surprised by her vehemence and shrugged. 'It's obvious, if you didn't need to feel on the defensive in some way you wouldn't have felt it necessary to hire me.'

There was no way Kelly could argue against such logic, and somehow she found herself slipping into the passenger seat while Jake put their cases in the boot and then came round to join her.

Whatever else she could say about him, she had to admit he was immaculately dressed, she thought, watching him discard the Burberry he had been wearing and toss it casually into the back of her car.

The fine beige wool trousers and toning checked shirt were exactly what one would expect to find a top executive type wearing in the country, as was the cashmere sweater he was wearing over the shirt, and Kelly had to repress a strange pang of pain as he started the car. It seemed so wrong somehow that with all her success and wealth she had to pay someone to accompany her to Sue's. What had gone wrong with her life?

Nothing, she told herself stoutly as the engine fired. She had everything she wanted; everything. Love was a chimera, she knew that; it didn't exist. God, she only had to look around her at her friends!

The automatic seatbelt device proffered the belt and Kelly reached for it automatically, shocked by the tingling sensation of hard male fingers brushing her own as Jake performed the small service for her.

She looked unwillingly at his hands. Dark hairs curled disturbingly against the wafer-thin gold wristwatch he wore. A present from a grateful customer? she wondered nastily, hating herself for the thought, and hating even more the strange pain that accompanied it.

'All set?'

She nodded briefly, reminding herself that Jake was simply a means of protecting herself against Jeremy—nothing more.

As Jake had predicted, they were early enough to miss the morning traffic and once they were free of London the roads were clear enough for Kelly to be able to appreciate the beauty of a countryside slowly awakening to spring. She had driven down to Sue's before, but never along this route, which seemed to meander through small villages and open countryside and when she commented on this fact, Jake merely said that since they were driving to the New Forest the drive might just as well be as pleasant as possible. He praised the car and asked her how long she had had it, and yet there was no envy in the question; if anything, his tone was slightly amused and, nettled, Kelly responded coolly that she had bought it six months previously—as a birthday present.

She knew the moment the boastful words left her mouth that they were a mistake.

'You bought it for yourself?' The pity in his eyes made her long to cause him a corresponding pain, but caution prevailed. What did it matter what he thought? After this weekend she would never see him again, and yet even though she closed her eyes and feigned sleep she kept seeing over and over again the pity in his eyes.

'We'll soon be reaching the Forest.'

The quiet words were pitched low enough to

rouse her without waking her if she had been deeply asleep, and Kelly lifted her head, glancing through the window, entranced to see the massed bulk of the Forest ahead of them.

'Would you like to stop for lunch?'

'Sue is expecting us,' Kelly told him curtly. She didn't like the way he kept insisting on taking control. She was the one in control. Ever since Colin she had had a dread of anything else.

His shrug seemed to indicate that it meant little to him, and Kelly felt rather like a sulky child being humoured by a tolerant adult.

'Tell me a little more about your friends,' Jake instructed as the new spring greenery of the Forest closed round them. 'How long have they been married? Do they have any family? I'll have to know,' he added when he saw her expression. 'If they're to accept me as a genuine friend of yours they'll expect me to know something about them.'

Grudgingly admitting that he was right, Kelly explained about Sue's miscarriage and consequent depression.

'Umm, but that still doesn't explain why you felt the need for a male companion. It obviously isn't to boost your reputation with your friend or score off against her in some feminine way.' He reduced speed, and glanced thoughtfully at her with cool grey eyes. 'Something tells me there's something you're holding back.'

'I've told you all you need to know,' Kelly denied, uncomfortably aware of the assessing quality of his gaze and the hurried thudding of her own heart. She couldn't admit the shameful truth; that she was using him as a barrier to hide behind, because for all her much vaunted independence, there was no other way she could get it through Jeremy's thick skull that she was totally uninterested in him.

Sue and Jeremy had an attractive brick-built house not far from Ringwood. The Mercedes pulled up outside it shortly after one, and as Kelly climbed shakily out of the car, the front door opened and a plump, pretty blonde girl came rushing out, enveloping her in a warm hug.

'Kelly, love, you look fantastic!' Sue beamed up at her. Barely five foot two, her lack of inches was something Sue constantly bemoaned; that and her tendency to put on weight.

'And this . . .' she began appreciatively, glancing from Jake to Kelly.

'Jake,' Kelly introduced hurriedly. 'I hope you don't mind . . .' Her voice trailed away, high colour touching her cheekbones as Sue grinned delightedly, 'Mind? Kelly, you know me better than that. But why haven't you told me before? I know you must be someone special,' she confided to Jake, oblivious to Kelly's agitation and embarrassment. 'Kelly would never have brought you down here otherwise. I can't remember the last time I've ever known her spend a weekend with any of her . . . Ah, here's Jeremy,' she broke off as the front door opened again and Jeremy emerged.

'Darling, come and say hello to Kelly and Jake,' Sue smiled, and Kelly heard the note of uncertainty in her voice; heard it and shivered with apprehension when she saw the expression in Jeremy's eyes.

'Kelly.' He reached for her, his eyes hard. 'I

suppose I can't kiss you properly with your friend here looking on.' He contented himself with a light peck, but Kelly was conscious of Jake's interested scrutiny. He was too astute, she admitted uneasily, and there was something about the way he watched her that she found unnerving. Perhaps he was an out-of-work actor simply studying human reactions, and yet there was something in the look he gave her as Jeremy released her and turned to shake hands with him that told her his interest had been specific rather than general.

'Come on inside,' Sue encouraged. 'Lunch is ready—a cold buffet meal, that's all, but I'll take you upstairs to your room first.'

Their room! Kelly froze and heard Jeremy saying smoothly behind her, 'I've finally managed to persuade Sue to join the twentieth century and to realise that consenting adults don't want separate rooms.'

He had done it deliberately. Kelly could see it in his eyes. She wanted to protest; she felt like a trapped animal and knew that Jeremy was waiting for her to retract, and then, astoundingly, Jake was slipping an arm round her waist, drawing her back against his body. She could feel the even beat of his heart against her back, her body enveloped in a protective warmth that made her eyes sting with tears as he lowered his head and murmured against her hair, 'What delightfully tactful friends you have, my love! I confess I hate wandering about in the darkness looking for the appropriate bedroom door!'

CHAPTER THREE

LUNCH was a nightmare during which Jeremy alternately humiliated Sue with his deliberate cruelty to her and cross-questioned Jake with a condescension that made Kelly wince.

Jake himself seemed impervious to his host's insulting manner, parrying his questions with a calm ease that Kelly couldn't help admiring, almost against her will. Her heart was in her mouth when Jeremy asked Jake what he did for a living, but Jake didn't hesitate for a moment.

'This and that,' he murmured with an easy smile, and from Jeremy's scowl Kelly knew that he had gathered from Jake's careless comment that he was implying that he was wealthy enough not to have to work.

From then on the two men treated one another with cool hostility, and Kelly was glad to escape into the kitchen on the pretext of helping Sue with the washing up.

'That was a lovely lunch,' she complimented her friend. Privately, now that the initial glow of excitement occasioned by the arrival had gone, she thought her friend looked far too pale and listless.

'Do you think so?' Sue grimaced. 'I think Jeremy believes I should have made more of an effort, but we seem to be entertaining constantly at the moment.' She pulled a face. 'I feel so tired, Kelly,' she complained. 'I've tried to tell him, but he just doesn't understand—about anything.'

She gave a muffled sob, causing Kelly to put aside the teatowel and take her in her arms. Her private opinion that Jeremy was a creep and that her friend would be better off without him was something she couldn't voice, so instead she comforted her by saying slowly, 'You've had a bad time recently, Sue, you're bound to be feeling a bit under the weather. You need a decent rest.'

'That's what Dad says,' Sue agreed shakily, 'but Jeremy says it's impossible for us to get away at the moment. Dad has a villa in Corfu, he's offered to lend it to us for Easter, but Jeremy doesn't seem very keen.' Her face suddenly lit up. 'Kelly, I've had the most marvellous idea!'

Kelly's heart sank as she guessed the words trembling on Sue's lips, but it was too late to stop them, and to her consternation Jake walked into the kitchen, both hands full of empty plates, his eyebrows raised in query, as Sue burst out impulsively, 'Oh, and you too, of course, Jake, you must both come . . .'

'Come where?'

'I was just telling Kelly that my father has a villa in Corfu. He's offered to lend it to us for Easter— I'd love to get away, but Jeremy isn't keen. I was just asking Kelly if she'd come with me, but it would be fantastic if we could make up a foursome.' She pulled another wry face at Kelly and said frankly, 'In fact I think Jeremy would prefer a foursome.' Her eyes clouded as she admitted unhappily, 'He's grown so distant recently, Kelly, I sometimes think that perhaps . . .'

'The only thing you need to think about is getting well again,' Kelly headed her off, dreading hearing Sue put into words any doubts about her husband's fidelity.

'And you will come? Oh, please!' Sue begged, tears sparkling in her eyes. 'Both of you must come. I can still remember what it feels like to be so much in love that you can't bear to spend a moment apart, believe it or not. You must be a very special man, Jake,' she teased suddenly, blinking away the betraying tears. 'I never thought Kelly would allow herself to fall in love again after losing Colin so tragically, but the very fact that she's brought you down here proves me wrong, and I can't tell you how glad I am. He obviously wasn't the slightest bit deceived by that cool, efficient façade you hide behind, Kelly,' she teased her friend, but tears still glimmered in her eyes, and Kelly felt a pang of pain for her friend that overrode her own embarrassment. Poor Sue, losing her baby was something she was finding it hard to come to terms with, and Jeremy didn't help, she thought angrily. Couldn't he see how much Sue needed his care and reassurance, or did he simply not care?

'Kelly?'

'Er . . .'

'You haven't told Sue whether we'll be able to join her at Easter or not yet,' Jake reminded her.

Kelly flashed him an irate glance. Of course it was impossible that they could. He knew that. She bit her lip, unnerved by the look she saw in his eyes. This man was her paid companion, she reminded herself, and he had no right to be behaving in the way that he was. She bitterly resented his assumption of control, the smooth way in which he had pre-empted her right to dominate their relationship.

'I . . . I'm not sure if I can get away from the office, Sue,' she lied desperately. 'Can I let you know?'

She hated seeing the disappointment in her friend's face, but what could she do?

After lunch they went for a walk. The countryside around the house was lovely, but the walk was spoiled for Kelly by Jeremy's boorish manner towards his wife and his constant references to the financial status of the owners of the properties they passed. She stiffened at one point when Jake murmured softly against her hair, 'You and Benson ought to get on like a house on fire—you both believe that everything can be calculated in terms of money; the only difference between you is that you have it and he doesn't. I wonder why he didn't marry you?'

'Perhaps because he wasn't given the opportunity,' Kelly snapped. 'Anyway, I was engaged myself when Sue met Jeremy.'

'Ah yes, of course.' They had fallen a little way behind Sue and Jeremy, and Kelly hesitated, glancing up into the mocking face above her as she heard the question in the smooth, drawling voice. 'Colin! Sue mentioned a tragedy . . .' He saw her wince and said coolly, 'Believe me, I'm not prying or consumed by curiosity about your past, it's simply that I don't want to make any mistakes.'

'Very professional!' Kelly bit her lip when she saw his expression. It was useless telling herself that he had no right to be annoyed; she could tell that he was.

'Look,' he grated against her ear, grasping her arm and swinging her round to face him, his fingers bruising the soft flesh of her upper arm with their grip, 'I don't know when, where or why you started hating the male sex, nor am I in the slightest interested in your sexual hang-ups, okay? Now tell me about Colin.'

Kelly was too angry to reply. How dared he talk to her like that! she fumed. She would report him to his boss; why on earth had she been landed with him? She had wanted an 'escort' who would melt into the background, not this totally male creature who exuded male dominance and insisted on taking control.

'Well? Or do I ask Jeremy?' he threatened softly. 'Something tells me he'd be only too delighted to help me delve into your past.'

'Colin was my husband,' Kelly muttered, hating him more with every passing second. What on earth had happened to her much vaunted hauteur? Something about this man shattered all her defences; he was like a steamroller, she thought bitterly, either too hard or too dense to see he was trespassing where he wasn't wanted, and yet she had the unnerving impression that he knew exactly how much she resented his probing; his determination to lay bare wounds she desperately wanted to cover up.

'And?'

The gall of the man! She drew in her breath in indignation, stunned into silent shock as his mouth suddenly descended on hers, blotting out the spring sunshine. A kaleidoscope of colours whirled between her tightly closed eyes, her entire body rejecting the male power of him, her mind silently shrieking its bitter resentment. Every muscle in her body tensed within the circle of his arms, her lips a stubbornly tight line of denial, as the warmth of his probed their curves. She opened her eyes, damning him with corrosive hatred, willing him to release her from the humiliation of the subjugation.

'Take it easy,' he murmured the words against her mouth. 'Sue and Jeremy are watching. Unless you want them to think we're in the middle of a lovers' quarrel you'd better kiss me back.'

'Go to hell,' Kelly muttered back, wrenching herself out of his arms and hurrying down the path. Her whole body was bathed in a fine film of perspiration. She felt sick and shaken. She hadn't been held like that since . . . since Colin, her mind forced her to admit. It had been a shock, finding herself in his arms like that, knowing herself incapable of breaking free without his tacit permission, and the knowledge had been frightening.

'Everything okay?' Sue asked solicitously, when she caught up with them. 'You look pale.'

Jeremy glared furiously at her and said acidly, 'Well, well, so the ice has melted at last! I don't know how you've done it, old man,' he commented to Jake when he caught them up, flinging his arm casually but so firmly round Kelly's shoulders that she couldn't break free.

'Done what?' Jake asked, his eyes never leaving Kelly's pale face.

'Melted the ice maiden,' Jeremy said maliciously. 'We'd all begun to think she'd frozen so hard it would take a pickaxe to get through to her.'

'Jeremy!' Sue reproached, giving Kelly an embarrassed glance.

'Oh, it's all right, Sue,' Kelly retorted, forgetting Jake for a moment in the heat of her anger. 'I'm well aware that Jeremy thinks I'm frigid just because I don't jump in and out of bed with every man I meet.'

'See how fortunate you are,' Jeremy said nastily to Jake. 'Why, I'll just bet if it hadn't been for Colin, she'd still be a virgin; rich and innocent.'

She could feel Jake looking at her and knew that her cheeks were hot. How dared Jeremy talk about her like that! Her hands clenched in the pockets of her suede jacket. She knew why he was doing it, of course. He was trying to get back at her for bringing Jake with her, just as he had done when he suggested that Sue gave them a double room. Their room! She had forgotten about that. She worried at her bottom lip, and then told herself that she was being stupid. Jake was hardly likely to pounce on her simply because they were sharing a room. Even so . . . She glanced uncertainly at him, and was rewarded by a quick hug.

'Kelly can give her money away to charity if she likes,' she heard Jake drawl convincingly. 'As my wife, she'll be supported by me, and not the other way around.'

'Lucky Kelly,' Jeremy retorted. 'Well, if you're looking for a charity, darling, do look in our direction first. I wish I'd had the good sense to find myself a rich wife.' The look he gave Sue made Kelly long to demolish him with a few well-chosen phrases, but she had her friend to think of and so merely gave him an ice-cold glare.

Jake was an excellent actor, she had to give him that. That bit about supporting his wife had been truly inspired, and totally convincing. She watched him covertly. He looked convincing. He looked the type of man on whom a woman could depend totally and completely. What on earth was she thinking? He was probably an out-of-work actor, used to playing all manner of parts. She was *paying* him to appear convincing!

When they returned to the house, Kelly went upstairs to unpack. She had been hoping that Jake would accompany her, so that they could discuss the best way to save them both embarrassment in view of the fact that they would be sharing the room, but instead he remained downstairs talking to Sue, merely interrupting his conversation to smile warmly at her and say casually, 'Unpack for me too, will you, darling. Although, thank God, I won't be needing the pyjamas I packed after all.'

Sue grinned appreciatively. 'You're blushing, Kelly,' she teased. 'Now I really have seen everything!'

It didn't take Kelly long to unpack. She hadn't brought much with her, just the new dress she had bought to change into for dinner, plus a skirt and jumper to wear tomorrow, her underwear and a silk nightgown she had bought on impulse several months before. She eyed it doubtfully as she lifted the soft blue fabric from her case. There was nothing particularly indecent about it, but it was more frilly and feminine than the nightshirts she normally favoured, and now she wished she hadn't packed it.

When she went downstairs, she could hear Sue and Jake still talking.

'I'm so glad she's found someone like you,' she heard Sue saying, as she paused outside the door. 'She's had a hard time since Colin died. I'd begun to think she was too frightened to let herself care for anyone else. Of course, you'll know better than anyone else that behind that cool façade she's . . .'

Kelly pushed open the door, unable to bear listening to her friend saying any more. She couldn't look at Jake.

'Kelly . . . come and sit down next to Jake and I'll make us all a cup of tea. Jeremy's had to go out, but he won't be long. I've invited another couple to join us for dinner. One of Jeremy's clients. You'll like them . . .'

Kelly couldn't bear the tense silence that followed Sue's departure. 'I suppose you enjoyed hearing all that,' she began fiercely.

'Not enjoyed, precisely,' Jake responded. 'It was certainly enlightening.' His arm was stretched across the back of the settee, and he started to wind a loose frond of hair from her chignon round his finger.

'Don't do that!' Kelly hissed, jerking away and then gasping with pain as he refused to let her go. 'Don't touch me!'

'We're supposed to be lovers, remember,' he drawled laconically. 'Sue expects to come back and find us in each other's arms. Think back,' he taunted. 'Try remembering what it was like with Colin.'

Kelly couldn't stop herself. She went white, shaking with nausea as she did remember. Colin, wrenching her head round, pulling her hair, slapping her face. She wanted to be sick; to scream and cry as she hadn't done then; she was aware of the room starting to recede, of Jake's muttered imprecation, and then she *was* in his arms, struggling against their confines, hating the frighteningly male contact of his body—and yet in some strange way some part of her longed to simply acquiesce, to give in and rest her head against his shoulder, to draw comfort from the sheer solid maleness of him.

'Kelly!'

She was aware of the anxiety in Sue's voice as Jake responded for her. 'She isn't feeling too well, but it's nothing to worry about.'

'Darling, you must go upstairs and rest, can I get you anything?'

'I just felt faint,' Kelly assured her. 'Nothing much—I came out without breakfast and felt slightly carsick, but I'm all right now.'

'I think Sue's right, you ought to go upstairs and rest,' Jake cut in firmly. 'I'd come with you,' he added with a wicked twinkle, 'but somehow I don't think you'd get much sleep if I did.'

Sue grinned, enjoying her friend's embarrassment, but Kelly was glad to escape from the room; from Jake's too disturbing presence. Something about him frightened her; and yet what possible reason could she have for feeling so threatened?

In spite of her resolution she did fall asleep. Maisie was right, she thought drowsily, lying on the large double bed, she did need a rest. The thought of Corfu at Easter was tempting, but only if she and

Sue could go alone. She couldn't bear the thought of fending Jeremy off for an entire week.

The door opening woke her. She glanced up sleepily, her heart pounding with fear, as she saw Jeremy standing there, watching her knowingly.

'Nights too exhausting for you nowadays, are they?' he taunted. 'So the iceberg's finally thawed! You should have told me, Kelly, I'd have been only too happy to oblige. Who is this guy anyway? I've never heard you mention him before. If you'd wanted a lover you only had to tell me.' He was coming closer to the bed. Kelly knew she ought to get up, but her muscles were locked in remembered terror and dread, her eyes wild and haunted as she stared up at him.

'You're a very desirable woman, Kelly, in spite of that cold front that comes on so strong,' Jeremy continued. His eyes were on her breasts and Kelly felt her heart pound with terror as he reached out towards her.

'She's also *my* woman,' Jake's voice interrupted coldly from the open door.

Jeremy whirled round, glowering furiously. 'What the . . .'

'Sue's looking for you,' she heard Jake say contemptuously, 'so unless you particularly want to cause an unpleasant scene I suggest you leave— now.'

Kelly couldn't move; not even when the door had closed behind him.

'So that's what it's all about,' Jake commented quietly. 'Pity,' he added, his mouth thinning, 'I was just beginning to be intrigued by you, wondering what lay behind the mask, but it's all a ploy, isn't it,

Kelly; a façade behind which you can conceal your affair with your friend's husband? Have you no compunction about what you're doing?' he demanded angrily. 'Don't you think Sue's had a raw enough deal as it is? Can't you see what Benson is? Or don't you care?'

'You've got it all wrong,' Kelly choked, struggling to sit up.

'You think so?' One dark eyebrow rose cynically. 'It seems pretty obvious to me that the reason you needed an "escort" for this weekend was not so much to make up a foursome as to deceive your friend as to your real relationship with her husband.'

'No!'

'No? Then what?' he taunted.

'It was because of Jeremy, because I knew he . . . he wanted me,' she shuddered, 'that I wanted an escort. I couldn't disappoint Sue, as you say, she's been through too much, but I knew if I came here alone Jeremy would . . .'

'Try to make love to you?' Jake supplied, watching her with an intensity that was unnerving. 'And that was why you came to the agency?'

'Yes.'

'Umm.'

'You don't believe me?' Kelly was astounded to hear herself asking the question. What did it matter to her whether he believed her or not?

'Oh, on the contrary, I believe you completely,' he averred, 'but what does puzzle me is why a cool, controlled lady like you should act like a terrified innocent every time a man comes near her. You were petrified just then,' he reminded her, 'and I only have to come within a yard of you and you shrink away from me.'

'You're exaggerating,' Kelly lied nervously, sliding off the bed. There was a look in his eyes she didn't like. It was distinctly speculative, and more . . . much more, she acknowledged, shivering with a sensual awareness of all that the look he was giving her implied.

'Let's just put that to the test, shall we?' Jake murmured dulcetly.

'I don't know what sort of game you think you're playing,' Kelly gasped, 'but may I remind you that you happen to be in my employ, and that I could report you to the agency for this!'

'Go ahead,' he invited, mocking her. 'It might just be worth it.'

Before she could stop him he had reached her, ignoring her stiffening muscles as his arms went round her, one hand tracing the rigid line of her spine, while the other deftly removed the snood constraining her hair, his fingers sliding through the silken weight he had released.

'Stop this!' Kelly ordered. 'Stop it right now!'

She saw him frown, his eyes darkening suddenly as he exclaimed, 'You're frightened! I wonder why . . .'

'I'm not frightened,' Kelly denied, 'I'm just furiously angry. Who do you think you are? Just because you're a man you think you can assume whatever physical rights you choose to take—well, not with me, I . . .' Her eyes blazed their defiance up at him, her fists beating an angry tattoo against the impervious wall of his chest.

'I've just saved you from a fate worse than death,

remember?' he taunted. 'Don't I get a reward?'

'What do you want?' Kelly demanded nastily, 'a bonus?'

'Why, you . . .'

It was too late to tell herself that she had gone too far, much too late to evade the bruising pressure of his mouth on hers, stifling her protests, cutting off her breath, as he ground her lips back against her teeth, making her feel faint with fear and pain, only her eyes mirroring her shock and bitter resentment.

'Kelly!' Her bruised mouth was released, and she winced with pain when his thumb brushed softly against its swollen fullness. 'God, I . . .'

'You wanted to hurt me,' she stormed at him. 'Well, you did. Satisfied? Is your male ego flattered by the knowledge that you can hurt me physically? You men, you're all the same!' she raged half hysterically. 'You . . .'

'No!' The harsh denial cut through her furious ravings. 'No, Kelly, we're not all the same. I'm sorry I hurt you.' He bent his head and she flinched, watching his eyes narrow and harden in some purpose she couldn't guess at.

'You made me angry and I got angry back, but it wasn't a deliberate attempt to hurt you. Hasn't anyone ever told you that any man is bound to act like that when a woman freezes in his arms? Didn't Colin ever tell you that?'

She went milk-white, her eyes dark with pain, her fingers curling against his shoulder.

'Kelly?'

'I . . .' She gasped as his mouth brushed the parted softness of hers, but it was too late to reject him. Her defences were already far too weak and it seemed far easier simply to lie passively against him, and give in to the gentle motion of his mouth against hers; teasing, and tantalising with a touch as gentle as butterfly wings, the moist warmth of his mouth stroking over the outline of her lips, encouraging them to soften and part to cling helplessly to the hard warmth of his; her mind reeling, spinning with the impact of what was happening to her.

'Kelly, are you all right?'

She was dimly aware of Sue's voice outside the door, of Jake releasing her slowly, his eyes holding hers, daring her to deny that she hadn't responded to him; that she hadn't—she shivered with the knowledge—actually for one brief second physically wanted him.

'Kelly!'

She made a superhuman effort to regain control of her senses.

'We're coming, Sue,' she called back to her friend. 'I'm fine now.'

'Kelly . . .'

Jake was watching her, and she sensed that there was something that he wanted to say to her. Could he have guessed how long it was since she had been kissed like that? How many years her starved senses had been denied the sensual contact they had just enjoyed?

'I must go . . . I . . .'

'Kelly, what is it you're so frightened of?' he asked quietly.

'Nothing,' she lied tautly. 'I'm not frightened of anything . . . Now, will you let me go,' she hissed, pulling away from him and heading for the door.

Was she going completely out of her mind? Allowing him to kiss her like that? What on earth was happening to her? She had been told she was frigid for so long that she had come to believe it, she acknowledged as she opened the door. She had thought herself impervious to the kind of sexual arousal Jake had just subjected her to, but she wasn't, and the knowledge terrified her. It was like looking in a mirror and seeing a completely different reflection from the one she was accustomed to. Jake had kissed her—once—and her body ached with a need she was terrified to put a name to. Why? Why now? and why, oh, why with this man who saw and knew far too much about her already?

'So you're Kelly's friend?' Jennifer Gordon eyed Jake appreciatively. 'Lucky Kelly!'

'Exactly my sentiments,' Sue admitted with a laugh. At the other end of the table Jeremy shot his wife a thin-lipped smile and said nastily, 'Sorry, darling—you couldn't afford him, could she, Kelly?'

Jennifer Gordon's cold blue eyes sharpened speculatively, and Kelly longed to dash the contents of her wine glass in Jeremy's over-fed and pasty face.

'My feelings for Kelly have nothing to do with her wealth,' Jake cut in coldly, and if Kelly hadn't known better she could have sworn that that was real anger she saw in his eyes, real intent behind the pointed comment, real desire in the look he bestowed upon her as he lifted her hand and turned it palm upwards, towards his lips, his brief caress

where her pulse raced treacherously sending shimmering waves of reaction through her.

She wouldn't be sorry when the whole farce was
over, Kelly decided later, smiling politely as the
Gordons left. It was well after one, Jeremy was
obviously and unpleasantly drunk, and Sue had
borne his snide insults so bravely all evening that
Kelly could have wept for her. Sue was worth
twenty of her husband, Kelly fumed; how could she
simply sit there and allow him to insult her, the way
he had done?

Half an hour later she was on the point of going
upstairs when Jeremy staggered out into the hall.

'I wish you luck of her,' he muttered to Jake, who
was behind her. 'Frigid little bitch!'

Kelly was glad Sue hadn't been there to overhear
him, and her face was still flushed with anger when
she walked into the bedroom.

'I'm sorry about this,' she apologised in a stilted
fashion to Jake. 'Jeremy's idea of a joke.'

He recognised the bitterness in her voice and
glanced thoughtfully at her. 'Meaning that since he
never loses an opportunity of calling you "frigid"
he thinks he's punishing us both by telling Sue that
we wanted to sleep together? You've been behaving rather strangely for a liberated and experienced
lady.'

'Meaning what exactly?' Kelly demanded, suspecting that he was mocking her.

'Merely that I thought every woman knew these
days that feminine frigidity is a myth put about by
incompetent male lovers.'

His raised eyebrows invited her to comment and
when she didn't he mused thoughtfully, 'Personal-

ly, I'm still romantic enough to believe that sex—no
matter how excellent—lacks impact without the
intensity of mutual desire—mutual love.'

Kelly stared at him in surprise. These were the
last sentiments she had expected to hear him express.

'What's wrong? You know,' he added thoughtfully, 'there's something distinctly intriguing about
you, Kelly. On the one hand we have the cool
controlled career woman, who cuts emotion right
out of her life; on the other we have the grieving
widow who misses her husband so much that she
can't bear to let another man near her. Something
tells me the real Kelly is neither of those women.
You could represent an irresistible challenge to
some man, Kelly.'

'But not to you,' she parried dangerously, daring
him to contradict her.

'Oh, I don't know . . . But that's not what you
hired me for—or is it?' he asked softly. 'Is that what
you wanted, Kelly? A man to share your bed
without question or criticism; someone who you
could simply pay to disappear when you'd grown
bored with him . . .'

'That's a disgusting suggestion!' Kelly choked. 'If
I wanted someone to go to bed with, I wouldn't
have to resort to buying myself a man!'

'I wasn't suggesting you would,' Jake retorted
quietly. 'I was merely implying that your inadequacies might prompt you to do as men do in
similar circumstances—that is, you might prefer to
pay for your pleasure; treat your partner as an
object; a commodity who you could simply use and
discard . . .'

Kelly wasn't listening; she hadn't heard more than the first few words.

'What inadequacies?' she demanded shakily. 'What do you mean?'

Jake shrugged. 'You know damned well what I mean, Kelly. You freeze every time anyone comes near you—you've been married; you're not a child; I don't know what it is that makes it impossible for you to react normally to men, but it's definitely there.'

Kelly didn't dare to respond. Instead, she picked up her robe and bolted for the bathroom. Hateful creature! How dared he imply that she might feel inadequate! If she didn't like being mauled and pawed by all and sundry that was only because she was choosy. She despised men . . . and she had every right to. She had proved that a woman could be every bit as successful, every bit as ruthless and determined . . . But what about the cost of proving it? Slowly she stopped undressing, shivering slightly. The cost had been high, she acknowledged. She trusted no one; shared her life with no one; neither lover nor family. She was completely and absolutely alone, and she was tired of telling herself that she preferred it that way.

She was glad that she had the privacy of the bathroom, and that she could run the water to drown out the sound of her tears. Not that there was much sound; they flowed silently and steadily, as though they had been dammed up for far too long, until she was too exhausted to do more than shower briefly and get ready for bed.

When she opened the door, Jake was sitting in an armchair apparently engrossed in a book.

'Ah,' he explained when she walked in. 'Bath-room free? What's the plan for tomorrow?' he asked casually, picking up the pyjamas she had laid on the bed, and a towelling robe. 'What time do you plan to leave?'

'After lunch,' Kelly told him expressionlessly, wondering why she should feel so affected by the fact that he had barely glanced at her. That was what they had arranged before dinner, wasn't it? That since they had to share a room, they would do so in a civilised and unfussing manner. At least, she amended, that was what she had arranged. Jake had merely listened grimly in a silence which she remembered now had been fraught with an odd sort of tension.

She heard the bathroom door close behind him as she unpinned her hair and started to brush it methodically. She hoped that before he emerged she would be in bed and feigning sleep. Not that she had any fears that he might attempt to touch her; his comments about her inadequacies had more than banished those, and her face burned fiercely as she remembered the look which had accompanied them! How dared he pity her! How dared he!

CHAPTER FOUR

KELLY moved restlessly in her sleep, tormented by the ghosts who pursued her. Colin . . . mocking her. Colin . . . hurting her. She cried out, twisting desperately to escape the clutching hands she knew from experience could cause such pain, suddenly jerked from her nightmare as a light snapped on and a husky voice growled sleepily, 'For God's sake, what's going on?'

It took her several seconds to realise where she was, who the voice belonged to, by which time Jake too was fully awake, his face puzzled and concerned as he studied her.

'That was some nightmare,' he commented briefly. 'Are you all right?'

She wanted to say 'yes', but the word stuck in her throat. She sat up, shivering as she felt the chill night air striking her bare back and shoulders, unconscious of the terror trapped in her eyes as she glanced nervously round the room.

'Would you like a drink? A cup of tea?'

A cup of tea! Oh, how she yearned for one.

'I'll go down and make us one. You stay here.'

'Us.' How intimate the small word sounded! Kelly shivered when Jake left the room, without him it seemed alien and empty, her nightmares crowding back, dragging her back into the past. Why, tonight of all nights, did she have to re-live the horror of her wedding night? She had stopped dreaming about it years ago, but tonight for some reason the old nightmare had surfaced in all its shocking intensity. She could almost imagine she saw the bruises forming on her smooth flesh where Colin had punished her. She moaned softly, her eyes going blank, and she was shivering with reaction and terror when Jake came back, frowning as he put the mug of steaming tea on the table beside her, the bed depressing under his weight as he sat down.

'Want to tell me about it?' His hand stroked her hair back off her hot face.

'Your hair's lovely,' he told her unexpectedly. 'Like silk, and your skin's so pale.' His glance lingered appreciatively on the outline of her breasts beneath the flimsy fabric of her nightgown, his eyes narrowing as she flushed darkly.

'You don't have to say that,' she told him jerkily, trying to draw away, but his arm round her waist constrained her.

'What?' He was frowning again. 'What don't I have to say, Kelly?'

'You don't have to flatter me,' she retorted tightly.

'I wasn't flattering you.' His voice was pleasant but firm. 'Flattery implies that I was speaking with some ulterior motive. I was simply stating facts; that you have lovely skin and hair, which you do.'

With his free hand he touched the shining length of her hair, his thumb tracing the line of her shoulder. Delicious tremors of sensation slid over her skin, and Kelly shivered again.

'You're cold.'

Before she could protest, she was drawn against him, her skin flushing heatedly as she realised that the smooth warmth she could feel against her back was his naked chest; for he had not worn the jacket of the pyjamas she had put out for him.

'Don't panic.' She could hear the amusement in his voice as it brushed her ear. 'I'm simply doing the gentlemanly thing and helping you to keep warm while you drink your tea. Here.' He reached forward and handed her the mug, but Kelly had to hold it with both hands, she was trembling so much; and it wasn't just her hands, her whole body was trembling, trembling so much that she was spilling the tea, and then suddenly weak tears were sliding down her face, and she was shivering and crying alternately, unable to understand what was happening to her.

'Kelly, for God's sake!'

Jake didn't sound amused now, and he didn't sound angry either . . . He sounded . . . concerned. But why should he be concerned about her?

She felt his hands on her arms, turning her, holding her against the warmth of his chest, her face buried in the curve of his shoulder, his hands on her back, stroking, soothing, calming her over-wrought emotions, the murmurs of comfort she could hear above her head, the soothing sound of waves against a beach. She felt lulled and safe, warm and protected, and it came to her on a jolting tide of awareness that she didn't want to leave his arms. She wanted to stay there. She stilled, and lifted her head.

'Kelly!'

There was a raw note of warning in Jake's voice, and she realised for the first time that her breasts were pressed against the exposed flesh of his chest, their only covering the fine satin of her nightgown.

'Kelly.'

This time her name was a statement of intent, and although he gave her plenty of opportunity to do so, Kelly made no attempt to move away as he lowered his head, touching the stilled softness of her lips. Her eyes clung to his. This couldn't be happening, Kelly thought heatedly. She couldn't be in this bedroom, in bed with this stranger, letting him kiss her, wanting him to make love to her, but she was and she did, and she couldn't understand what was happening to her. Suddenly, she didn't want to understand, she simply wanted to touch and be touched, to be close to and part of another human being.

Her small choked cry was lost beneath the heated pressure of Jake's kiss, a potent, drugging kiss that blinded her to what shreds of reason she had left. Her arms crept round his neck, his smothered groan as the brief movement brought her breasts in closer contact with Jake's chest, activating a response inside her that urged her to press her body closer to his, to exult in the hurried throb of his heart as his hands moved to the neck of her nightgown, unfastening the small bows that fastened it, his eyes darkening as he held her gently away, pushing aside the fabric to expose the swollen peaks that had wantonly incited him to do just exactly that. Kelly couldn't believe her own behaviour. Her stomach muscles quivered in aching protest, not at what she was doing—no, what she ached for was Jake's possession; his desire and the knowledge that she was desirable and capable of arousing such a man.

'Aren't you going to take it off?' Her mouth was dry as she whispered the words, Jake's eyes darkening in acknowledging response as he murmured huskily, 'Just try and stop me.' And then he was pushing aside the blue satin, and she should have felt embarrassed about the way he was studying her body, but all she could do was to try and control the fierce tide of exultation that swept her as she saw the dark colour running up under his tan as he studied her, and then he was removing his pyjamas, and she closed her eyes, seeing for a moment Colin, but it was only for a moment, for Jake was nothing like Colin, and her eyes widened in appreciation of his muscular masculinity, her fingers touching the tanned skin with tentative hesitancy as she became lost in a voyage of tactile discovery.

'Kelly, Kelly, what are you trying to do to me?' Jake groaned, the sound muffled against her throat as his tongue stroked over the sensitive skin, his hands exploring her body with a much surer touch than hers had on him.

She gasped as he pushed her down against the pillows, one hand tangling in the silky length of her hair while the other cupped one pale breast.

'I've been wanting to do this ever since you walked into that damned office,' Jake muttered thickly against her skin, and then Kelly was incapable of thinking, of breathing almost as he lowered his head, his tongue stroking urgently against her nipple, her mind reeling with shock and excitement as he savoured the arousal of her flesh, teasing it until she was almost lightheaded with the pounding ache of desire in her body.

'Jake!' She moaned his name despairingly, touching the dark hair, gasping her shock aloud as his hand slid over her hip and stroked her stomach, the sensations he aroused inside her as he sucked her throbbing breast spiralling wildly out of control until she couldn't contain them any more and she was clutching anxiously at his shoulders, her body arching willing beneath him, eager for the pleasure he was giving her.

'So good,' Jake muttered thickly as his lips caressed her breast. 'I've wanted you like this from the first moment I saw you.' He sounded almost drugged, his voice roughened by a desire that Kelly felt too. His free hand slid down to her hips, holding her against him, his teeth nibbling seductively at her sensitised skin, his body unashamedly aroused, and incredibly she felt a heated response; a need that burned through her.

The nightmare which had originally woken her was completely forgotten—everything was forgotten apart from Jake and the sensations he was bringing to life in her passion-drugged body. She responded to his touch with a feverish intensity that drove out everything else. She didn't know what subtle chemistry there was between them that made her react to him in the way she did, she only knew that it was there. She moaned, every nerve-ending tingling erotically, her body crying out for his possession. His hand touched her thigh, his lips murmuring her name hoarsely against her skin, and she shivered suddenly as the memories stormed back, and it was not Jake touching her, but Colin.

Colin who called her name and violated her body, her emotions.

She tensed instinctively, dimly aware of Jake lifting his body from hers, watching her, his eyes dark and hard.

'Kelly? What the hell is this?' he demanded tersely. 'What sort of game do you think you're playing?'

'Don't touch me,' Kelly moaned softly. She was shivering, tears filling her eyes, the past sweeping her inexorably backwards in time, and she shuddered in revulsion remembering how it had been; how Colin had hurt her.

'Don't touch you? Don't worry, I won't,' Jake bit out grimly. 'There's only one excuse—one permissible explanation for what you've just done. If you were a virgin I might . . . just might be able to understand, but we both know you're not. So why?'

'Colin,' Kelly muttered sickly barely aware of what she was saying. 'You reminded me of Colin and . . .'

The oath that ripped from Jake's throat silenced her, and too late she realised he had misunderstood. He stood over her, pulling on his robe, his face like granite, as he reached for one of the blankets, wrenching it off the bed.

'I never play substitute,' he told her icily. 'Never, Kelly. Got that? Oh, there's no need to look at me like that,' he added silkily, 'I don't get my kicks from using force. You're sick, Kelly. You're looking for a man who's prepared to play a part, who's prepared to be "Colin", but I'm not that man. The next time I touch you, Kelly, it will be because you ask me. Me . . . not Colin, not anyone else. Me!'

He was angry, furiously, bitterly angry. How could she tell him that he was wrong; that it wasn't like that? That just for a moment she had remembered the brutality of Colin's lovemaking, and the memory had turned her from a warm, responsive woman into a terrified numbed child? And what about him? He had wanted her right from the start, he had said, but wasn't that just exactly the sort of polished line a man like him would use? How many lonely, defenceless women had hoped to find love in his arms? She shuddered again as realisation of what she had been about to do swept over her. She had wanted Jake with a physical compulsion totally outside her experience, and he had played on that, sensing her want, feeding it, but why? He was an attractive, experienced predatory male; he was also, she suspected, a poor one. The conclusions were obvious—so obvious that she couldn't understand why she herself hadn't drawn them before!

Only another hour and then they could leave, Kelly decided thankfully, glancing surreptitiously at her watch. The weekend had been a complete disaster in every way, and as for last night! She shuddered, unable to stop her memory from playing back for her a blow-by-blow repetition of the night's events. What on earth had possessed her? There could only be one word for it—lust! All the repressed desires of all those years since Colin, and she hated herself for what had happened. She would have preferred to pretend that it hadn't happened, but the aching throb of her swollen breasts reminded her all too uncomfortably that it had.

'Kelly, you haven't been listening to me,' Sue reproached. 'I was just saying to Jake that it would be lovely if you could both join me at Easter.'

'*I* might be able to, Sue,' Kelly told her, forcing herself to pay attention, 'but I'm afraid it's impossible as far as Jake is concerned, isn't it, darling?'

'Oh, I don't know.'

She glared furiously at Jake, wondering what on earth he thought he was doing.

'I dare say something could be arranged,' he said smoothly. 'It's time I had a break.'

'But you said you were far too busy,' Kelly improvised wildly.

'Mmm, perhaps I'm having second thoughts. It's certainly a tempting prospect: you, me, the sun and the sea.'

'Quite the romantic, isn't he?' Jeremy sneered. An animosity had developed between the two men, brought on, Kelly was sure, by Jeremy's fury because she had outmanoeuvred him by bringing Jake with her. That at least had been the right decision and made everything else worth while. Sue looked a good deal more cheerful this morning, and Kelly shuddered to think what might have happened if she hadn't had Jake to keep Jeremy at bay.

'Oh, please say you will,' Sue implored, 'and it needn't be too expensive. Daddy is letting us have the villa rent free.'

'Sounds terrific,' Jake responded with a smile.

No doubt it did to him, Kelly thought sourly, all her previous doubts re-surfacing. Why was he encouraging Sue? To make sure he got a free holiday? What had been behind his behaviour last night? Her heart started to thump uncomfortably. She was a rich woman and a lonely one. Only she knew how close she had come last night to giving in to the most basic impulse of all human beings; the need to be close to another of their own kind. But what if Jake had sensed her need? He was a man who quite patently had expensive tastes and equally obviously did not have the means to indulge them. His clothes were expensive; surely he couldn't afford them out of the wages he earned from the agency? If he was an actor he wasn't a very well-known one; perhaps he had grown tired of waiting for the big break of playing the polished escort to rich women. Perhaps he had decided it was time he cashed in on his undoubted attractions? Why should she find the thought so disturbing?

'So you will come?' Sue sounded excited and Kelly dragged her mind back to the present.

'Of course we will, won't we, darling?'

'We will what?' she asked Jake suspiciously. He hadn't touched her this morning—at least not physically—he undressed her mentally every time he looked at her, and she seethed with bitter indignation as she watched him doing so.

'We will join Sue at Easter? We could both do with the break.'

'You may do, but I . . .'

'You do too,' Jake said firmly. 'After all, I could hardly go without you.'

Too true, she thought ironically. How could he afford it?

'I'm not sure, Sue,' she began, suppressing a gasp of pain as Jake gripped her fingers painfully, warning her not to go on.

'What was all that for?' she demanded angrily

when they were alone. 'I don't have the slightest intention of going to Corfu with you and you know it!'

'Why not? Do you prefer to remain in England— with Jeremy?'

'Jeremy!' Funny, but she had almost forgotten him; forgotten the reason she had hired Jake in the first place.

'Yes, Jeremy,' Jake mocked. 'Sue's husband. Surely you haven't forgotten him already? If you stay behind, he's bound to jump to the conclusion that you've done so because of him.'

It was true, and Kelly couldn't deny it. If she remained in London Jeremy would invent some excuse to come and see her.

'I don't know what you're trying to achieve by this,' she told him angrily, 'unless it's a free holiday!'

She had expected him to be angry, but instead he merely laughed. 'That helps,' he admitted, 'but there are other considerations.'

'Such as the fact that you're getting tired of being a paid companion,' Kelly hazarded wildly. 'Well, if you think . . .'

'How would you know what I think?' he goaded softly. 'And, Kelly—' She turned to glare at him. 'Try backing out of this,' he said softly, 'and I'll see that Sue gets to know the truth about her husband.'

Kelly paled.

'You wouldn't!'

'Try me,' he advised grimly.

'You're despicable, do you know that?'

'Then that makes two of us, doesn't it?' he said quietly. 'Or doesn't what you did last night come into that class in your book? Never mind,' he told her grimly, 'it does in mine.'

'You don't understand . . .'

'Then tell me,' he invited levelly, but Kelly couldn't say a word; couldn't betray to him now, in the cold light of day, the fact that she had withdrawn through fear and remembered pain. Only a virgin, he had said, and she wasn't that . . . but he was wrong, she was! And she was beginning to think she was destined to remain so for the rest of her life. Last night she had wanted him, this morning she was bewildered by the emotions he aroused in her.

Easter was less than a month away. Sue talked excitedly all through lunch of the holiday, while Jeremy sulked.

'That's right,' he goaded Sue. 'Go off and leave me while you enjoy yourself.'

'Why don't you come with us?' Jake interposed smoothly. 'Surely you could manage a few days?'

'Oh yes, darling, do,' Sue breathed.

'I might,' Jeremy muttered.

Less than an hour later they were on their way back to London. Kelly hunched furiously in her seat as she seethed inwardly at the way in which Jake had manipulated her.

'Sulking?' he asked trenchantly as they neared London.

'You had no right to accept Sue's invitation. Why did you?'

'Oh, I have my reasons,' he told her lazily, 'and like I said, don't try backing out, Kelly,' he warned her, 'or you know what will happen.'

'What are you looking for? It can't just be a free holiday.'

'Not just,' he agreed, smiling mockingly at her. 'Don't worry, Kelly,' he drawled as he manoeuvred the powerful car into another lane, 'I'm not Jeremy, and I have no intention of forcing myself on you.'

No, but he wouldn't need to use force, Kelly admitted, shivering a little. Had he guessed how much he had aroused her? She was rich and she was vulnerable—too vulnerable, and she only wished she knew what was in his mind.

He stopped the car an hour later outside her block of apartments, getting out and retrieving her case.

'I'll park this and then see you up,' he told her easily, not giving her the opportunity to refuse.

He was back within minutes, his hand under her elbow, as he guided her towards the lift.

'I'm perfectly capable of managing on my own,' she told him stiffly.

'Ah, but I must do the job properly.'

He saw her to her door, turning the key in the lock for her.

'The bill,' she began hesitantly. Would they invoice her, or did she pay now, or . . .

'Leave it until we get back from Corfu,' Jake advised her carelessly. 'Still,' he added thoughtfully, 'I don't suppose there's any harm in my taking a little something on account.'

He bent his head, his lips brushing hers lightly, mocking her startled expression.

'Why did you do that?' Kelly demanded when he had finished. 'You said . . .'

'I know what I said,' he agreed hardly, 'but perhaps I've decided to give you a second chance. See you at Heathrow.'

He was gone before she could respond. What did he mean? she seethed, as she walked into her apartment. *He* had decided to give *her* a second chance? A second chance of what?

She returned to her office on Monday morning, fully determined to put a call through to the agency and cancel the trip to Corfu, but when she reached the office it was to find that she had to fly out to New York urgently to discuss a new contract. It was ten days before she was back. She tried the agency several times but without getting an answer, resolving that she would just have to keep on trying until she did get through.

CHAPTER FIVE

'OH, I'm so looking forward to getting away,' Sue murmured, easing off her shoes. 'Aren't you?'

She had rung up the previous day to tell Kelly that she was coming up to London to shop and they had arranged to have lunch together.

'Jeremy is coming with us after all,' Sue continued without waiting for an answer. 'Kelly . . .'

Kelly's heart sank. There was a note in Sue's voice that warned her of what was to come.

'Kelly, I know you'll think I'm being stupid,' Sue got out in a rush, 'but I'm so worried. Jeremy's been so . . . so different since I lost the baby.' She produced a watery smile. 'I'd even got to the stage of wondering if there was someone else!'

'Then you're a fool,' Kelly told her firmly, mentally adding to herself, Who would be stupid enough to want Jeremy?

'Look, love,' she told Sue. 'Things have been difficult for you both lately. I know how much it hurt you—losing the baby . . .'

'Jeremy too,' Sue broke in loyally. 'Oh, I know he doesn't show it much, but he was looking forward to being a father . . .'

Kelly didn't know what to say. To murmur that there would be other babies seemed so crass somehow.

'I'm sorry, I told myself I wasn't going to moan on to you. How's Jake?' Sue asked, determinedly changing the subject. 'I like him, Kelly. He's so right for you somehow.'

Kelly smiled noncommittally. She had already decided to tell Sue that her 'romance' with Jake was off. Then she was going to telephone the agency and cancel the arrangements for Corfu. So Jake thought he could blackmail her into providing him with a free holiday, did he? He was in for a big shock!

'Oh, here's Jeremy,' Sue exclaimed, her face breaking into a smile. 'He said he'd try to join us if he could.'

Jeremy greeted his wife, and Kelly tried to conceal her distaste as he turned to kiss her, making sure it was her cheek that received the moistly unpleasant touch of his lips and not her mouth.

Jeremy ordered fresh tea for himself and Sue excused herself to go to the ladies', leaving Kelly alone with Jeremy.

'All set for Corfu, then?' he asked, leering at her faintly. 'How's the great romance? Shouldn't have thought he was your type, Kelly. Doesn't exactly strike me as the faithful sort either. Never mind,' he told her with another leer, his hand finding its way to her knee, 'I'm always ready to make sure you don't get too lonely. You've only got to say the word.' He was eyeing her speculatively, and Kelly felt sickened by the expression in his eyes. Were all men like this? Lusting after every woman who caught their eye with no thought of loyalty or respect?

'Pity he's coming to Corfu with us,' Jeremy added, his eyes narrowing as he watched her. 'So the ice-lady isn't quite as cold as she pretended to be. How did he do it, Kelly?'

Kelly was thankful that Sue returned before she had to answer. Jeremy sickened her, but he was still Sue's husband. She gritted her teeth, knowing now that it would be impossible to cancel the coming holiday. Jeremy had invaded the privacy of her bedroom once already—she wouldn't put it past him to try again. She was going to have to find an opportunity to tell Sue that this time she and Jake wouldn't want to share a room, although quite how she was going to do that she didn't yet know.

Her vulnerability to Jake's practised charm was something that astounded and terrified her. It was a galling admission to make, but she knew that she couldn't trust herself to resist him if he tried to make love to her again. She couldn't analyse what had happened to her; perhaps sheer old-fashioned frustration was the simplest answer; she was twenty-six and had never had a lover, had never wanted one, until now. She had once thought that Colin's treatment of her had frozen all her natural responses for good, but she had been wrong. In spite of his charm, his pleasant manners, and his obvious physical attraction, something about Jake frightened her; or was it her own reaction to him which was so terrifying?

Heathrow was a seething cauldron of humanity. Kelly searched desperately for Sue's familiar face amongst the crowds milling everywhere, wishing she had not had to come straight from the office to the airport. She felt hot, tired and grubby, uncomfortably out of place among these people in their obvious holiday clothes. She was wearing a wool and linen mix suit severely tailored, and a toning high-necked silk blouse. The temperature had started to rise during the day; she had had problems getting a taxi, and her suitcase felt uncomfortably heavy.

A light touch on her shoulder had her whirling round, her eyes darkening in bitter recognition as she saw Jake standing there. Unlike her he was dressed for the flight, in jeans which clung smoothly to the intensely masculine shape of his body, and a checked shirt open at the neck to reveal the dark hair shadowing his chest. Her heart in her mouth, Kelly could only stare at him, shocked by her own response to the intense masculinity of him. Eyes narrowed, he watched her. Did he know what sort of effect he had on her? She felt herself flushing as foolishly as any schoolgirl and turned angrily to lift her suitcase.

'I'll take that.'

'I can manage.'

'Who would dare doubt it?' His eyes mocked her. 'But we are supposed to be lovers, remember? Sue and Jeremy are waiting in the bar.'

He lifted her suitcase effortlessly, matching his long stride to her shorter one, indicating the bar where Sue and Jeremy were waiting.

'I'll get this checked in for you,' he told her. 'Sue's given me the tickets.'

Sue had made all the arrangements and Kelly had sent her a cheque for their tickets. Her mouth compressed angrily at his assumption of control, her body bristling with resentment. What was it about him that affected her like this? Was it because he made her feel so vulnerable? So . . . feminine? Was that why she had hired him? Because somehow the fact that she was paying for his time gave her the upper hand, made her feel safer —evened out the differences between them? Was she afraid to give him any advantage over her? Was she afraid of him? She shivered, not liking the direction of her thoughts. Since Colin, she had deliberately kept any involvement with the opposite sex to a bare minimum; in fact her male friends were mostly older, well-married men; or younger less sexually aggressive ones . . .

'What would you like to drink?'

She hadn't heard him arrive and jumped slightly, her eyes widening as he placed his hand on her shoulder, bending towards her, capturing her parted lips and caressing them briefly.

'Mmm . . . nice,' he murmured as he released her. She could feel Sue and Jeremy watching them and flushed angrily. There had been no necessity for Jake to kiss her like that. It was already well established in their minds that they were lovers; there had been no need for him to underline it. Her lips tingled pleasurably, and she hated herself because she knew that when he kissed her she had felt an almost irresistible urge to touch him.

They went through the normal boarding formalities without any problems, and as the engines warmed up Kelly experienced her normal stomach-clenching fear. She had never been able to get over her dislike of flying and she knew her nails were digging into the arms of her seat, her eyes fixed rigidly on the back of the seat in front of her.

She closed her eyes, willing herself to keep calm, not to give in to the fear clenching her muscles.

'So you are human after all,' Jake murmured against her hair. He lifted her hand from the seat arm, clasping it warmly between his. She wanted to pull away, but the plane started to move and her nails curled protestingly into her palm.

'It's okay, we'll soon be up.' Jake spoke soothingly, transferring one arm round her trembling shoulders, her face buried in the curve of his chest, his free hand still clasping hers. Beneath her cheek his body felt solid and muscular. She was suddenly aware of the warm masculine smell of him, the reassuring thump of his heart; the comfort of his arm holding her, protecting her . . .

What on earth was she thinking? This was a man who made his living from making himself attractive to women. The plane lifted, and she moaned a small protest, closing her eyes and clutching instinctively at the open neck of his shirt. And then they were airborne, and the pounding of her heart had lessened. The stewardesses were moving about, the relieved chatter of the passengers filtering through the tense silence of take-off.

'All right?' Jake asked matter-of-factly, releasing her.

'Fine.' She knew she sounded abrupt, but she hated him seeing and knowing her weaknesses.

'You really hate it, don't you?' he drawled sardonically.

Kelly glanced at him suspiciously.

'Tell me something. Have you ever relied on anyone, Kelly; let your defences down; given them your trust? Or did you bury all the normal feminine responses with your husband?'

'For "feminine" read "weak and vulnerable", I suppose you mean?' Kelly stormed back.

Jake was shaking his head, his mouth wry. 'No, that's what you mean, Kelly. When I say "feminine", I mean a woman's instinctive and very flattering need to lean on a male shoulder occasionally. Don't you ever stop to think how emasculating your attitude is, what a turn-off it can be? I pity the poor male who's fool enough to fall for you, Kelly, you'd never give him a chance, would you? You'd never let him be a man . . . or a lover.'

Her face was darkly flushed. Kelly hated him for what he was saying, but wasn't it true?

'I don't want a man,' she managed thickly at last, 'or a lover.'

'Why? Because no one could compare with Colin?'

'You're just like all the rest,' Kelly hit out wildly. 'You want a woman to be subservient, to . . .'

'What I want a woman to be *is* a woman,' Jake corrected. 'A woman isn't a man, Kelly, and that means she is neither inferior nor superior; she is simply different, and I personally wouldn't want it any other way.'

No, because he knew how vulnerable her sex was to men like him, Kelly seethed, men who used their sexuality to beguile and deceive, just as Colin had once deceived her into believing he loved her. All he had loved was her money!

Her head started to thump and she searched in her bag for some aspirins. When Jake saw her produce them he summoned the stewardess and asked for some Perrier water, handing it to her.

'I could have asked for that myself if I wanted it,' she snapped childishly.

His mouth thinned. 'As I am sitting nearer the aisle I simply thought I'd save you the trouble. You know what the problem is with women like you, Kelly—women who want to boss the whole world—they daren't let themselves be women; so they spend all their time fighting to overcome their sexuality, fighting to make themselves asexual. Have you ever looked at yourself—properly, I mean?' he demanded thin-lipped. 'Those clothes, the way you wear your hair . . . everything laced up tight and repressed . . .'

'What are you trying to say?' Kelly whispered back furiously. 'I'm a business-woman and my clothes and hair reflect my life-style.'

'Exactly, you're a cool hard lady, Kelly, and you like letting the world know it. But don't expect me to toe the line.'

'You're paid to toe it—remember!'

She watched the grey eyes darken to flint.

'Of course,' he agreed sardonically. 'That's how you prefer your men, isn't it, Kelly? Bought and paid for—obedience guaranteed. It makes you feel good, doesn't it, reminding me of your wealth . . . Be careful, Kelly,' he warned her. 'The road you've taken leads only to loneliness.'

'Perhaps that's what I want,' she retorted in a clipped voice, but inside she felt like crying; crying like a lost and frightened child, only there wasn't much point, was there? She had learned a long time ago that when she cried there was no one there to dry her tears, and the only person she could rely on was herself.

She must have slept—the effect of the headache pills, because the next thing she knew was that Jake was shaking her gently, telling her that they were coming in to land. She opened her eyes, flushing selfconsciously as she realised that she was in his arms.

He smiled sardonically. 'Don't worry about it,' he told her. 'Even Homer nods, so they tell me. Personally I'd hate to be you, Kelly, terrified of giving in to even the slightest human instinct . . . but then each to his own.'

Was that how she struck others? Kelly wondered as they left the plane. She knew that she had a formidable reputation at work, but then she was head of the agency and she had worked hard to build it up. She had to keep on top of things, otherwise she would lose everything she had worked for . . . But what was 'everything'? It didn't take too much of an effort to remember back to the days when all she wanted from life was a home and family, love . . . she pushed the thought away. Love! She ought to have learned by now that the love she had once dreamed of simply didn't exist. She only had to look at her friends. How many of them were really happily married? But at least they had had the courage to try; to commit themselves to another human being, whereas she . . . They hadn't experienced what she had, she reminded herself bitterly, they hadn't . . .

'Kelly?'

She realised with a start that Sue was watching

her anxiously. 'Are you all right?' her friend asked. 'You look so pale.'

'A headache,' she responded briefly. 'There was a crisis at the office before I left.'

'Good old Kelly,' Jeremy jeered. 'Always reminding us what a big business-woman she is! You've got a winner there, Jake. If I were you I'd give up work and let Kelly keep you.'

'You might just have an idea there,' Jake responded lazily. 'There's something very sexy about successful women.'

'Ignore Jeremy,' Sue whispered as they waited for the men to collect the luggage. 'I don't know what's got into him lately.'

Kelly did. He was trying to needle her, trying to humiliate her in front of Jake. Little did he know!

Two hire cars were waiting for them at the airport. They had decided on two at Jake's suggestion so that they could go their separate ways if they wished, and now that Jeremy had elected to join the party, Kelly was glad. Things were bad enough without the added strain of keeping up the fiction of devoted 'lovers' in front of Jeremy.

Sue knew where the villa was, having stayed there before, so they left first, with Jake and Kelly following.

The sun was blindingly brilliant and Kelly blinked painfully as she searched in her bag for her glasses. Unlike her, Jake seemed completely unaffected by the heat. Sue had told them that it was a four-hour drive to the villa and, since the small car did not have air-conditioning, Kelly wished she had had the forethought to bring a change of clothes with her for travelling—she could easily have

changed on the plane and her silk blouse was
sticking uncomfortably to her skin, her thick skirt
oppressively hot.

Jake, on the other hand, looked perfectly comfortable and relaxed in his jeans and shirt, and
Kelly envied him.

They were driving through a small village when
he braked suddenly, stopping outside a small
general store. At first Kelly thought there was
something wrong with the car, but anxiety turned
to irritation when he calmly climbed out and sauntered across the road to the shop. It was the kind
that seemed to sell everything, judging by the
articles hanging up outside. Jake disappeared into
the dim interior, returning five minutes later with a
parcel which he tossed across to her as he climbed
in and restarted the engine. 'A present for you,' he
said casually.

'What is it?' Kelly asked suspiciously.

'Open it and see.'

Inside the bag was a pretty pink crinkle cotton
dress; a tiered affair with shoestring straps and a
scalloped hem.

'I'll stop the car when we reach a quiet bit of road
and you can put it on,' Jake told her, apparently
oblivious to her expression.

'Put it on? I don't want to put it on,' Kelly told
him angrily. 'I . . .' She broke off as the car
screeched to an abrupt halt and Jake turned to her,
sparks of anger glinting in his eyes.

'Look, we've got a three-and-a-half-hour drive in
front of us with the hottest part of the day coming
up. Any woman with the slightest bit of sense
would have realised that before she set off and

dressed appropriately as Sue did. Look at yourself! You're hot and you're uncomfortable . . . but if you want to go on suffering, that's okay by me. I simply thought you might feel cooler in that,' he picked up the cotton dress, 'than what you're wearing.'

He was right, of course, Kelly knew that, and she was behaving like a cross child. She was too hot, and she should have had the sense to know that it would be much hotter here than it was at home . . . She bit her lip, turning away so that he wouldn't see the glitter of tears in her eyes. What on earth was the matter with her?

'You're right,' she agreed huskily. 'I'm sorry.'

'It's relatively quiet here,' Jake said coldly. 'I'll get out and stretch my legs if you want to change. Don't worry about us getting lost. I've been to Corfu before and Sue's given me directions.'

So he'd visited Corfu before. Who with? Kelly wondered curiously. Another 'client'?

She wriggled out of the straight skirt, keeping an eye on his retreating back. He sat down on a rocky outcrop, the wind lifting the thick dark hair, the thin shirt stretched over the lean muscles of his back. Her fingers trembled over the buttons of her blouse. Oh, the bliss of taking it off! She frowned as she realised that the bra she was wearing would show under the strappy dress, and quickly took it off. Her skin looked pale against the warm pink cotton. Jake turned and seemed to be studying the car, and she fumbled with the straps in her nervousness, tying them in clumsy bows. Jake started to walk back and Kelly grimaced as she caught her hair in the hook of her blouse, pulling out a few pins. She glanced in the driving mirror, pulling a face when she saw how untidy she looked. Strands of hair hung down her back, her make-up was smudged and she felt sticky and grubby.

'Here, these might help.' Jake was opening the door, and handing her a pack of tissues. He seemed to think of everything, she thought wrathfully, dabbing at her sticky skin. The untidiness of her hair irritated her, and she pulled out the rest of the pins, rummaging in her handbag for her brush, dragging it ruthlessly through the tangled skeins of hair. She couldn't be bothered putting it up in a chignon again, but there was a rubber band in her bag and she used it to secure her hair off her face, quickly plaiting it, while Jake watched.

'What's the matter?' she demanded crossly, seeing the lazy amusement in his eyes. 'Surely you aren't going to tell me you haven't seen a woman brushing her hair before?'

'I was just marvelling at the transformation,' he told her drily, touching the long plait. 'You look about sixteen with this, although . . .' his eyes dropped to her body, and Kelly was suddenly conscious of the fact that her breasts were almost visible beneath the fine cotton and, worse, the effect his intent gaze was having upon her body.

'Feeling better now?' he asked, switching his gaze from her breasts to her hot face.

Grimly, Kelly nodded her head.

'You're going to have to do better than that, you know, if you're going to convince Benson that we're still lovers.'

The amused glance he gave her fired the anger that had been simmering inside her for so long.

'I didn't invite you to join me on this holiday,' she breathed bitterly. 'You blackmailed me into having you along. God alone knows why, although I think I'm beginning to guess!'

'You are?' The grey gaze narrowed on her face, watching her, making it difficult for her to breathe, hating the close confines of the car, hating the way he made her feel; the emotions his proximity forced to life inside her, emotions she did not want to feel.

'Enlighten me, then—let's see if you're right.'

He was still smiling, watching her with a lazy satisfaction that reminded her of a jungle cat toying with his prey, and fury boiled up inside her, the sheer pressure of her rage exploding through her normal caution.

'Well, let's just say if you're hoping I'm going to be a meal ticket for life for you, you're wrong, and forcing yourself on me for this holiday isn't going to change my mind! If you . . .'

'Stop right there!'

The ice-cold words cut through her tirade, and Kelly shivered nervously in the dangerous silence that followed.

'Let's get this straight. You think I'm after your money?'

'Well, aren't you?' Kelly challenged dangerously. 'You're obviously a man with expensive tastes.' She glanced disparagingly at his expensive Rollex watch, her eyes skittering away from him as she saw the molten anger banked down under the hard grey eyes.

'Lady, I feel sorry for you,' he grated, forcing her to look at him. 'You're really screwed up inside, aren't you? Is it because of what I am, or what you are, that you think you can buy me? Oh yes, you do think that,' he went on brutally before she could object. 'You must do. What is it, Kelly, can't you believe anyone would want you for your own sake? Well, I've got news for you,' he told her, his voice hard with contempt. 'There just isn't enough money in the world, never mind in your bank account, to make me want to marry you. I presume that *is* what all this is about?' He laughed harshly. 'My God, I don't think I'm really sitting here listening to this!'

Despite his sardonic manner, Kelly could sense the anger she had ignited within him, and it frightened her. He had no reason to feel angry, she reasoned. She had every right to think as she did . . . every reason . . .

'Then why did you insist on coming on holiday with us?' she demanded.

'Why?' He grimaced as though he had an unpleasant taste in his mouth. 'If I told you, you wouldn't believe me. If I had any sense I'd turn this car right round and get on the first plane back to the U.K.'

'Then why don't you?' Kelly challenged. 'I don't want you here.'

'You'd rather have dear Jeremy, is that what you're trying to tell me? If it wasn't for Sue I'd say the pair of you deserve one another, but she doesn't deserve to be hurt, and for her sake . . .'

For *Sue's* sake! Kelly felt as though someone had stuck a knife straight through her heart and was slowly, painfully turning it until she wanted to cry out with the agony it was causing her. What was the matter with her? What did this man matter to her?

By rights she ought to despise him, but he seemed to be the one who was full of contempt for her!

'What happened to make you so suspicious, Kelly?' Jake taunted as he set the car in motion again. 'Oh, I know you lost a husband; but people can only make allowances for so much . . .'

What would he say if she told him the reason she was so suspicious was Colin himself? She shuddered, wondering what was happening to her. She hadn't told anyone about Colin. Not anyone! Since the dreadful night of their wedding she hadn't allowed any man close enough to her to learn the truth, but Jake had got close to her . . . too close. Was that why she felt so antagonistic towards him? Did her antagonism really mask fear? Kelly wasn't a fool. If she was genuinely indifferent to Jake she simply wouldn't have the power to arouse the emotions in her that he did. She was frightened of him and she was frightened of herself, of her reactions to him. He had pushed open a door she had kept locked for too long, and her body still ached with the memory of how she had felt when he touched her.

Colour rushed to her cheeks as she remembered the abandoned way she had responded to his lovemaking. It had had an almost cataclysmic effect upon her, releasing the dammed-up springs of emotion, destroying for ever the myth that she was frigid.

The miles slipped by without Kelly being aware of them. She sat rigidly in her seat, conscious of Jake's tightly controlled anger; of the grim line of his mouth as they left the main road and began to drop through forested countryside, tantalising glimpses of the sea appearing here and there between the trees. Soon they were passing villas set amongst the trees, sugar almond colours, glimpsed through high walls.

They drew level with an open gateway, and Jake turned into it. Sue and Jeremy were just emerging from their hirc car, and Sue came hurrying towards them.

'You made it, then!'

'Your directions were fine,' Jake assured her, giving her a warm smile as he switched off the engine. Pain ached through Kelly, tears stinging her eyes. What was the matter with her? Surely she couldn't be jealous of Sue? Jake was simply someone she was employing to keep Jeremy away, that was all, and she had never been the possessive type even with Colin.

'Kelly, you look pale,' Sue commiserated. 'Are you okay?'

'Just a headache,' Kelly mumbled. 'I'll be fine.'

She felt limp and washed out beside Sue, who seemed to have taken on a new lease of life all of a sudden. Jake climbed out and came round to her side of the car, opening the door while Kelly was still fumbling with the catch. His fingers brushed the curve of her breast as he helped her out and she recoiled as though she had been stung. Her body actually seemed to burn where he had touched her. She saw the sardonic expression in his eyes, the hardness of his mouth, and trembled without knowing why. Jake seemed to have changed—or was it merely that she was seeing him properly for the first time? She had angered him by telling him that she thought he was interested in her money, but surely it was a perfectly natural assumption, in the circumstances?

'Come on, I'll show you to your room,' Sue told her. 'Luckily Dad has staff who come in from the village, so everything will be ready for us. There's quite a British community round here,' Sue went on. 'Business-men and so forth. Dad bought the villa when he retired—you'll like it.'

Kelly did. It was larger than she had imagined, and as she followed Sue through a large lounge, she glimpsed the oval shape of a swimming pool through the picture windows.

'There is a beach,' Sue told her, following her glance, 'but the ground is rocky, and it's quite a steep walk down. Here's your room.' She opened a door, and Kelly walked inside. The room was a good size, decorated in soft muted shades of coffee and peach, with a window overlooking the cliffside and the sea, which Kelly could just glimpse through the pines. Single beds, separated by a white cane table, and a couple of matching chairs were the only furniture in the room.

'Bathroom off there,' Sue went on, indicating one of a pair of doors. 'The other door is to the dressing room. Sorry about the single beds,' she added with a grin.

'Don't give it another thought.' Kelly hadn't realised Jake was behind them. 'Personally, I don't think there's anything cosier than sharing a single bed,' he drawled, looking at Kelly.

She knew she was blushing, but couldn't do anything about it. Why was it that those few words conjured up such a picture of intimacy that her whole body felt flushed with heat and excitement? She could picture all too easily how Jake might enjoy sharing a single bed; how his lean body would shape itself to that of his female companion, his arms holding her secure.

'I'll leave you to unpack. Dad said he'd arrange for a cold meal to be left for us—I'll just go and check.'

There was silence when Sue had gone. Kelly couldn't turn round for the life of her, even though she knew Jake was there. When he closed the door, the faint click sounded like a gunshot and she whirled round in shock.

'I would have thought this time you'd insist on separate rooms,' Jake told her cynically, his mouth wry.

'I would have done,' Kelly agreed tautly, 'but I didn't want to arouse Jeremy's suspicions.'

'Of course not. Although I should have thought someone like him would just suit you—he's married, so you needn't be frightened of him wanting your money, need you? So I'm to be your body-guard, am I?' he drawled, eyebrows lifting. 'Well, in that case, I'll have to make sure you get value for money, won't I? I don't want you feeling that you've been shortchanged, Kelly.'

'I don't know what you're so angry about,' Kelly told him.

'No?' His hard laugh held disbelief. 'You aren't that naïve, Kelly. Damn it all, you've handed me the worst insult a woman can hand a man, and you don't know "why I should be angry"!' he mocked acidly.

'It was a perfectly natural conclusion to draw,'

Kelly defended herself. 'Especially when you'd
. . .'

'I'd what?'

He was watching her with a look in his eyes that
made her wish she'd never started the conversation. She moistened her dry lips with the tip of her
tongue, her fingers curling into her palms, tension
drawn through her nerves like fine wire.

'When you'd . . . made love to me,' she finished
huskily. 'You . . .'

'Made love to you?' He laughed incredulously,
'Ye gods, where have you been? That wasn't
"making love", Kelly!'

No, it hadn't been, she knew on a savage burst of
pain. It had simply been the sort of thing a man like
him would do . . . almost as second nature.

'However,' he added grittily, 'since we were
interrupted when we were, it seems I owe you
something on account, and since I never like to be
indebted to anyone . . .'

He reached her with three lithe strides, one hand
shaping the back of her head, his fingers winding in
her hair, so that she couldn't move, the other
stroking the exposed column of her throat as he
gradually tugged her head back, his eyes watching
the play of emotions over her face.

A tremor of fear pulsed through her. Colin had
held her like this. She swallowed nervously, her
muscles tightening in dread as Jake bent his head.

'No!' She sobbed the word in panic-stricken
terror, watching the grey eyes darken and the firm
line of his mouth harden.

'No? Surely you aren't going to refuse me the
chance to repay my debts, Kelly?' he asked with

silky determination. 'You're not being very flattering, you know.' His lips captured the frantic pulse
throbbing beneath her skin, and instantly her fear
was gone, to be replaced by a languorous awareness of the pleasure being transmitted by the warm
male mouth as it moved sensually over her throat.

'Jake . . .'

She had meant his name to be a protest, but
somehow it sounded more like a plea. Jake
obviously interpreted it as such. His free hand
pushed aside the neckline of her loose dress,
caressing the curve of her breast. Instantly, Kelly
felt her nipples harden in excitement, her breathing
unsteady.

'Jake!' She tried to push him away, but her
fingers caught in the opening of his shirt, tangling
with the dark hairs on his chest. A molten fever
suddenly seemed to possess her, her senses blind to
everything but the warm silk of his flesh beneath
her fingers.

Jake's hand left her breast to find the hollow of
her back, holding her against him, the sensitive tips
of her breasts aroused by the intimate contact with
his body. His tongue stroked over her bottom lip,
her mouth parting achingly for his kiss.

She was being sucked down into a giddy whirl-
pool of pleasure, her whole world enclosed by the
heat of Jake's body and the pressure of his mouth
on hers. She arched helplessly against him, mind-
less in her desire to communicate to him her need.

When he suddenly released her the shock was so
great that Kelly clung instinctively to his shoulders.

'Oh no, Kelly,' Jake murmured slowly, his eyes
moving deliberately over her still aroused body.

'I've paid my debts. You hired me as a bodyguard, not a lover, remember.'

Nausea churned through her, humiliation a sour taste in her mouth. He knew that she had wanted him—he had deliberately aroused her just to prove to her that he could make her want him.

'I don't want you,' she lied bitterly. 'I could never want a man like you.'

'You're a liar, Kelly,' Jake told her softly. 'And you don't even begin to know the first thing about a man like me. One day you're going to stop living in the past with your ghosts, and you're going to admit that you're a real live woman, with real live emotions and feelings.'

He was gone before she could retort; before she could tell him that she would never feel anything for him. God, how she hated him, loathed him, loathed herself for responding to him! She walked blindly into the bathroom, shivering as she ran the water, but no matter how much she scrubbed her soft skin she couldn't wash away the memory of him touching her, caressing her, bringing her to life in a way she had never been before.

CHAPTER SIX

KELLY opened her eyes, tensing as she glanced at the motionless figure in the other bed, but Jake was still asleep, one brown shoulder visible above the thin cotton cover. She had been asleep when he came to bed. Her headache had grown worse during the evening and she had excused herself early, hating the mocking smile Jake gave her as she walked past him. Her body felt heavy and lethargic, aching with an emptiness she didn't want to acknowledge. Perhaps a dip in the pool would help refresh her?

Jake didn't stir as she slipped out of bed and gathered up her clothes. Their bedroom opened directly on to the patio by the pool, and Kelly slipped through the window as quietly as she could, expelling her breath slightly when Jake didn't move. She glanced at her watch; it was barely seven and she seemed to have the morning to herself. The air was pleasantly warm, small fluffy white clouds moving on the merest puff of wind.

The swimsuit she had put on was a new one—it had been years since she had last had a seaside holiday, and she had been pleased to discover an excellent selection of beachwear in the shops before her departure. She had been determined not to wear a bikini, but the swimsuit she had thought so sensible when she bought it was far more revealing then she had realised, dipping low at the front to

mould and accentuate her breasts and cut high at
the sides, lengthening her legs. If she had realised
how revealing it was, she would never have bought
it, Kelly decided, catching a glimpse of herself
mirrored in the azure water of the pool.

The water was pleasantly warm, and she swam
for several minutes before turning over to lie bliss-
fully on her back, paddling idly and letting the
tension flow out of her. It had been foolish to be so
concerned about her reactions to Jake. He was
after all a very handsome and experienced man, it
was only natural that she should feel some response
to him. It was unfortunate that he was here in Corfu
with them, but if she was sensible and level-headed
there was nothing to worry about. She bit her lip,
remembering his reaction to her accusation and the
swift reprisals which had followed. Her body quivered and she turned quickly, swimming strongly for
the side of the pool, dashing the water out of her
eyes as she pulled herself out.

'Good morning.'

A prickle of awareness shivered across her skin
as she looked up and saw Jake watching her. He
was dressed in cream jeans and a thin shirt opened
at the neck, and although he looked perfectly relaxed Kelly was aware of a difference in him. She
frowned as she tried to pinpoint exactly where it
lay; the nearest comparison she could come up with
was that he appeared to have changed from a
basking indolent jungle cat into a ferociously angry
predator deliberately stalking its prey.

He reached for her wrap before her, stretching
behind her to place it round her shoulders, his
hands lingering deliberately on her still damp skin,

tracing the shape of the bones beneath her skin. She shivered suddenly as her eyes met his and read the cynical message in their grey depths.

'Who chose the swimsuit?' he drawled, his eyes roaming with almost brutal sexuality over her body.

Kelly could feel her temper rising; resentment filling her.

'I chose it,' she gritted.

'Without trying it on?'

'What makes you ask that?'

'You look sexy in it.' He sounded quite bored, and looked it too, apart from the hard gleam in his eyes. 'Very sexy,' he added softly, 'sexy enough for me to . . .' His fingers tightened on her shoulders, pulling her hard against the length of his body, kissing her with a violence that robbed her of breath and even the will to resist. Her lips softened and parted and she was drowning in the sensual spell woven by Jake's touch, hungry for the feel of his skin beneath her palms. A fierce dry heat invaded her body and she didn't try to resist when Jake's lips left hers to explore the slim column of her throat. She couldn't understand what was happening to her, she thought, Jake only had to come near her and she melted; no, not melted, burned up, consumed by a heat that ached explosively through her body the way it was doing right now. So suddenly that it was a shock for her unprepared body Jake released her, lifting her hands from his chest to the lapels of her own robe where they trembled in rejection and humiliation.

'Hope I'm not interrupting?' Sue eyed her curiously and Kelly quickly tried to compose herself. 'I've just been having a swim,' she chattered over-brightly. 'The water was lovely, Jake . . .'

'I came down to see what she was doing,' Jake drawled laconically, propping his lean length up against one of the patio tables, 'but the pool's a little too public for the kind of swimming I prefer.'

Sue laughed. 'I came down to tell you that we've been invited out to a party tonight. Some neighbours who know Dad, and hadn't realised that he had lent the villa to us. They called round last night, and when I explained that we were borrowing they invited us all along instead. Should be fun. The villa belongs to Carne Wrayman, the television producer. He has a yacht which he keeps here as well. His villa has its own private mooring.'

'Sounds fun, doesn't it, darling?' Jake murmured before Kelly could speak.

'Oh, good. I'd better go and give Jeremy the news. He'll be quite pleased.' Sue pulled a face. 'He'll look upon it as a good opportunity to get new business. Don't worry about hurrying for breakfast. It's very much an alfresco meal—a help-yourself affair really,' she added as she hurried back to the house.

'She obviously thinks we want to continue what she interrupted,' Jake mocked, when Sue had gone. 'You'll notice that I don't charge extra for these convincing little touches.'

'No, but you were quick enough to accept the invitation to that party,' Kelly flashed back. 'You don't deceive me. You may have given up where I'm concerned, because you know I'm wise to your game, but no doubt you're hoping to find someone else to batten on to at the party—someone who doesn't know the truth and won't know it until it's too late.'

'You're right about one thing, Kelly,' he said contemptuously at last when the silence between them stretched as fine as wire, and Kelly's heart was pounding with nervous exhilaration. 'Where you're concerned I have given up. You know, I felt sorry for you at first, but not any longer. You deserve everything you get. I'll let you use the bedroom first,' he added with deliberate cruelty, 'and you needn't look at me like that—I have no intention of touching you. In fact, judging by your reactions to me just then the boot is most definitely on the other foot.

'What's wrong?' he goaded, when he saw her stricken expression. 'Do you find it hard to admit you actually want a man like me? I sympathise; but sexual desire has nothing to do with logic, Kelly. You can't feed it into a computer and come up with exactly the right reaction to the right man.'

'I don't want you,' Kelly flung at him. 'I don't want you or any other man. Not now . . . not ever!'

'Fancy coming shopping with me?'

Kelly looked at Sue. 'I thought you said we wouldn't need to buy anything for the first few days.'

'Oh, not for food,' Sue assured her. 'I mean proper shopping—clothes, silly—or at least a dress for this do tonight. I haven't brought anything suitable with me.' She sighed, her expression suddenly sombre. 'In fact it seems ages since I bought myself anything pretty at all. I was so wrapped up in having the baby . . .'

They were alone on the patio. Jeremy had announced after breakfast that he fancied a game of golf and had coerced Jake into going with him.

'I've been giving myself a firm talking-to lately,' Sue continued briskly, 'and I've come to the conclusion that if Jeremy is finding me boring, I've no one to blame but myself. Daddy gave me a birthday cheque before we came away, and there are some excellent dress shops on Corfu. A great many wealthy Greek women live here, so most of the fashions are Paris inspired. You just wait and see!'

'In that case I'd better buy something new myself. I've only brought a couple of casual things with me,' said Kelly.

'And who knows—make a good impression and you could pick up some more business. Is it serious between you and Jake—settling down and getting married serious, I mean, Kelly?'

'I . . . It's too early to tell,' Kelly told her, hating having to deceive her.

'Well, he's certainly keen on you. You should see the way he looks at you when you're not aware of it!' Sue sighed. 'I envy you, Kelly. You have so much—oh, not your money, I'd never envy anyone that. No, it's the way you've proved to yourself that you can live alone; that you're your own person. I sometimes feel that without Jeremy I'd only be half a person; a shadow.'

'Nonsense,' Kelly told her firmly, 'but if it makes you feel any better I'll let you into a secret. There are times when I feel very much alone, when I wonder if I've paid too high a price for success, especially recently.'

'It doesn't show! Do you want to come shopping?'

'I think I'd better,' Kelly laughed. 'Are we going to drive?'

'Yes. It isn't very far, but the bus service is pretty haphazard. We'll take Jeremy's hire car.'

Half an hour later Sue deftly parked the hire car outside a row of shops, and Kelly climbed out. The sun burned into her skin through the thin blouse she was wearing, and she was glad that she had had the foresight to bring a hat and her glasses.

'Hot, isn't it?' Sue commented as she joined her. 'Let's try in here, shall we?'

The shop she indicated was quite small, a simple silk suit the only garment in the window. Inside, it was decorated in couture shades of dove grey and silver, and the woman who came forward to serve them had the timeless chic of the French.

Sue explained that she was looking for a dress to wear to a party. 'Something simple but stunning,' she smiled. 'Can you help?'

Several outfits were produced for Sue's inspection and finally she settled on a simple silk dress in a soft shade of lilac blue which suited her colouring. While Sue was trying it on, Kelly's eye was caught by one of the other dresses the woman had produced. Also made of silk, it had tiny shoestring straps and a low-cut back, the skirt cut on the bias so that it floated gently in the draught from the air-conditioning. In shades of pink from palest blush to deep cyclamen, Kelly knew instantly that it would suit her. She touched the fabric almost wistfully. Once she might have bought a dress like this, but not now.

'Ah yes, this is one of our exclusive models,' the saleswoman told her, walking over to her. 'Would you like to try it on?'

She was just about to say 'no' when Sue pleaded eagerly, 'Oh do, Kelly! You'll look stunning in it, I know.'

The trouble was that she did, and she knew it too, Kelly reflected rather wryly ten minutes later surveying her reflection in the mirror. The dress might have been made for her, it clung so lovingly to her body, making her skin glow like the inside of a oyster.

'It is very nice,' she began reluctantly, 'but . . .'

'No "buts",' Sue interrupted firmly. 'You're having it, and then you and I are going to treat ourselves to a couple of hours in the nearest beauty salon. We don't want Jeremy or Jake looking anywhere but at us tonight!'

The saleswoman, no doubt pleased to have made two good sales, gave them the address of a beauty salon which she recommended, and the girls there certainly seemed to know their business, Kelly thought approvingly as Helena, the girl who was looking after her, deftly produced a nail polish which picked out exactly the soft pink of her dress.

'If you don't mind me making a suggestion,' Helena murmured half apologetically as she worked expertly on Kelly's nails, 'I think your hair would look very pretty left loose for your party, perhaps swept to one side with a comb?'

'Oh yes, Kelly, it would be lovely,' Sue enthused.

Somehow, Kelly found herself being persuaded into the new hairstyle, which wasn't what she would have chosen herself at all. For one thing, the long

dark sweep of hair, secured with a comb of mother-
of-pearl, gave her features a sultry sensuality she
had never expected. All at once her lips seemed
fuller and softer, her eyes slumbrous and softly
veiled. She looked . . . She looked as though she
had just been passionately kissed, Kelly thought,
startled by the knowledge.

'Kelly, you look fantastic!'

She gave Sue a vague smile. This wasn't how she
wanted to look at all. Looking like this made her
feel vulnerable.

Dusk was falling as they drove back to the villa.
They had spent most of the afternoon shopping and
then had a light meal, as Sue explained that she
thought the men would eat at the golf club.

There was no sign of the other hire car when they
returned. The party wasn't due to start until nine,
which gave them plenty of time to get ready, Sue
assured her, but Kelly decided that she would go to
her room and get changed now—with luck she
would be finished before Jake returned. What was
the matter with her, she wondered ironically. They
had shared a room; a bed; he had touched her and
she had responded to him—and yet suddenly she
felt afraid. But it was not the same sort of fear she
had felt with Colin. Frowning and uneasy, she
stripped off the clothes she had worn for shopping,
securing her hair on top of her head as she went to
turn on the shower.

Maisie had given her her favourite perfumed
showering gel as a goodbye present, and Kelly used
it lavishly. Even at her most austere she had not
been able to deny herself the pleasure of perfuming

her skin. Colin had never bought her perfume and
so there were no unpleasant associations, but
tonight as she smoothed the gel over her skin and
stepped under the shower's fine spray, the fine
needles of water against her body seemed almost
erotic, the perfume released by the warmth of the
water clinging to her flesh. If she closed her eyes she
could almost imagine that Jake was touching her,
arousing her already inflamed body with his skilled
hands, kissing the firm peaks of her breasts, letting
his mouth wander at will over her perfumed skin
until at last he possessed her lips. The dull thud of
the bedroom door as someone closed it jerked
Kelly back to reality, and a deep wave of colour
seared over her as she tried to deny the truth of
Jake's earlier claim that she wanted him.

'Kelly?'

She stiffened as he called her name, hurriedly
stepping out of the shower and reaching for a towel.

'I'm in here,' she called back, her mouth dry with
tension. He could so easily have simply walked in
and found her. And if he had done so would his
experienced eyes have noted the aroused state of
her body—and worse, known the reason for it? It
must be some sort of jet-lag she was suffering from,
she decided muzzily. She had never felt like this
before, not even with Colin. It was completely out
of character for her. Was it? She stiffened, trying to
blot out the tiny voice that mocked acidly that she
had never allowed her own sexual character to
develop. She had killed it at birth, refused to admit
it into her life, and now she was being paid back
with a vengeance.

Outside, she heard sounds of movement and

hurriedly pulled on a robe. 'Don't come in, I won't be a moment!'

She had barely finished speaking when Jake pushed open the door and leaned indolently against the frame.

'I asked you not to come in,' Kelly snapped angrily, trying to tie the sash of her robe. 'Or didn't you hear me?'

'Oh, I heard all right, but you've been around long enough to know that a remark like that is tantamount to asking for the opposite, and so as a mere employee what else could I do but oblige?'

It was the way he said 'mere employee', rather than the words themselves, that underlined the deep cynicism she could see etched alongside his mouth, but surely that couldn't account for the burningly intense anger that turned his eyes from flint to smoke and seemed to rob her of the ability to think or move with her normal efficiency?

'What's the matter?' Jake demanded smokily. 'You don't know what to do when you're confronted by a man who doesn't toe the line—your line—do you, Kelly? You just love calling the shots, don't you? Making men squirm, turning them on and then paying them off, but it won't work with me. So,' he drawled, folding his arms and studying her mockingly, 'if you want me to make love to you, lady, you're damn well going to have to ask this time.'

'Ask?' Kelly was too furious to be careful. 'You're the last man I'd ask for anything and . . . and besides,' she added on a flood of triumph, 'if I wanted a man to make love to me there's always Jeremy!'

'So there is.' His mouth went hard. 'You know, Kelly, I can't quite figure you out. One moment I think you genuinely care about Sue, and really want to protect her from finding out what a creep her husband is, the next I begin to think you're playing some deep game where the prize is Sue's husband with a ring through his nose and that you mean to win him.'

'Think what you like . . . You're here for one reason and one reason only, and that's because I'm paying you, and if you . . .'

'If I forget my place you'll dismiss me? No way. You try it and find out what happens.'

'Meaning you'll tell Sue about Jeremy? If I really did want to break up their marriage I'd let you, wouldn't I?'

'Not necessarily. You see, Kelly, you strike me as the type who likes her life all cut and dried. It wouldn't suit you one little bit to be known as the woman who broke up her friend's marriage and then stole her husband. No, you wouldn't want me telling Sue.'

'You're so sure of yourself . . . so damnably arrogant! Hasn't it occurred to you that you might be wrong?'

'Why should I?' he responded coolly. 'It never occurred to you, did it?'

With that enigmatic remark he started to step past her, his eyes flicking contemptuously over her still damp body as he did so.

'That's something else,' he murmured, smiling with hateful mockery. 'That "still wet from the shower" approach is old hat now—you're going to have to find a new routine—or start paying more.'

Kelly raised her hand automatically, shrinking herself as the sharp sound of it against his lean jaw fractured the silence, leaving a strained dangerous calm during which she watched the white imprint of her hand fade and slowly fill with angry blood until the marks throbbed hotly against the brown skin.

'Oh no, you don't,' Jake muttered thickly as she started to move away. His eyes were the colour of slate, hard and bitter, implacable determination underlining every movement as he placed his palms flat to the wall behind her, imprisoning her against it.

She could feel the heat coming off his body and knew she was trembling.

'Jake, please!' Was that hoarse, panicky voice really hers? She moaned huskily as he lifted one hand and slowly and quite deliberately pulled the pins from her hair until it cascaded on her shoulders. His thumb stroked along her jawline, his fingers forcing her downbent head up until she was forced to meet his eyes, and the murderous rage she saw in their depths told her without the need for any words that this parody of tenderness was a subtle form of punishment, and that he intended that she should never forget how he had repaid her for striking him.

'That's better.' His voice was slurred and Kelly trembled, longing for the strength to be able to push him away and run.

'All it needs is this,' he added, wrenching open her towelling wrap so that the curves of her breasts were exposed, 'and now you look the part completely. There was no need to slap me, though Kelly. Like I said before, all you had to do was ask.'

He bent his head and there was no way she could avoid the insistent stroke of his lips against her own, taunting and tormenting until her lips were parting on a groan, her arms going round his neck, her fingers curling into the thick silky hair at his nape as the torment continued until she couldn't endure it any longer, and she was arching against his body, her mouth clinging pleadingly to his, her small broken murmurs of pleasure filling the thick silence.

'Oh no . . . I'm not going to make it easy for you.'

Her hands were wrenched away, and suddenly she was free, her body aching with unfulfilled need, her mind totally disorientated by the power of the sexual feelings he had aroused.

Appalled, both by the intensity of her desire and the rage she could sense within Jake, she pulled away and darted into the bedroom, dimly registering the closing of the bathroom door behind her.

In the lamplit room her tousled, disordered hair and pale face stared back at her from the mirror. Her lips looked full and swollen, and as she hurriedly dressed in the clean underwear she had laid out Kelly was aware of the swollen fullness of her breasts, her nipples taut beneath the fine silk of her dress. She shivered, unable to believe that the woman staring back at her was her, the reflection was so unfamiliar; not merely because of the different hairstyle and silk dress. It was the more subtle difference that frightened her the most: the darkening of her eyes, almost all pupil, the sleekness of her skin, and the unmistakable softening of every feature. No man looking at her now would ever believe that she was the head of her own company, or

that she had kept her emotions in check for years. It
was like looking at a stranger, only the stranger was
elusively familiar, and Kelly shivered, her tongue
nervously touching dry lips. The woman staring
back at her—hadn't she seen her before, many
years before when she had still been a teenager and
Colin and her love for him and had filled her
life?

'No!'

Kelly wasn't even aware that she spoke the
denial aloud, the sound torn from her throat
against muscles tight with despair.

'Kelly, we're leaving in half an hour, are you two
nearly ready?'

Sue's voice outside the bedroom door steadied
her, turning her to something resembling normal-
ity, but her voice shook as she called out a response
and ten minutes later her hand still trembled as she
carefully tried to apply her eye make-up. Perhaps it
was because of that that her eyes seemed darker,
more exotic than usual, or perhaps it was simply a
trick of the lighting. The slither of silk against her
skin was a constant reminder of Jake's hands on her
body, and she fought against the memory, brushing
her hair with angry strokes and securing it with the
pearlised comb.

Sounds of movement from the bathroom had her
heading for the door, grabbing her bag as she did
so. There was no way she wanted to be in the
bedroom when Jake walked into it, neither was
there any way she could continue to share the room
with him. She didn't care what Sue thought, she
decided feverishly, she would have to tell her.
Perhaps she could make up some story about not

being able to sleep well—she could plead that she didn't want to disturb Jake.

'Oh, Kelly, you look gorgeous—doesn't she, Jeremy?' Sue asked, turning to him for corroboration.

Kelly hated the way Jeremy's eyes moved insultingly over her body in the thin silk.

'Gorgeous,' he agreed softly. 'The ice has melted with a vengeance! I'll have to get Jake to let me into the secret.'

As Sue's genuinely amused laughter filled the room, Kelly wondered how her friend could be so blind to the venom in her husband's eyes. Jeremy still hadn't forgiven her for rejecting him. Men were so vain; so arrogant in their assumption that they had the right to react like spoiled children simply because a woman did not find them desirable.

'Ah, here's Jake—now you'll be able to ask him,' Sue teased Jeremy as Jake strolled into the room.

He had changed into cream pants that clung to the powerfully lean thighs, his cream shirt open at the neck revealing the crisply curling hair that darkened his chest. In comparison to Jake's lithe maleness Jeremy looked flabby and out of condition.

'Ask me what?' Jake prompted, giving Sue a slow smile that appreciated her femininity in her new dress, and watching her friend glow with pleasure. Kelly felt a frisson of emotion she recognised bewilderingly as the beginnings of a knife-sharp pain.

'Oh, just how you managed to turn our ice queen

into a smouldering sex bomb,' Jeremy drawled unpleasantly.

Kelly wondered if anyone else noticed the way she shrank as Jake curled his arm round her waist, drawing her to his side, her nostrils teased by the warm male scent of his body.

'It isn't hard,' Jake told him equably, an excellent facsimile of tenderness softening his gaze as he turned to Kelly and added huskily, 'All you need is love, isn't that right, Kelly?'

She couldn't have moved even if someone had told her a bomb was about to go off next to her. Love! Her pupils dilated with shock, a sickening sensation of anguish filling her. Of course she didn't love Jake. The very idea was ridiculous. How could she? After Colin she knew better than to risk loving any man, least of all one like Jake who made his living from weak, foolish women.

They walked to the villa where the party was being held. Far larger than Sue's father's, its gardens backed on to his, and Sue explained that they owned the land right down to the sea itself, where the owner had a private mooring for his yacht.

The garden itself was illuminated with what seemed to be hundreds of pretty Japanese-style paper lanterns, and as always the absence of the sun seemed to enhance the scent of growing things, so that Kelly's nostrils were full of the scent of wild thyme and other aromatic bushes.

She was lost in a vision of how this island must have appeared to the first Greek adventurers, when Jeremy destroyed her dream by cursing vehemently as he caught his foot in an exposed root.

Kelly winced for her friend as he swore angrily, 'I

suppose it was your bloody stupid idea to walk here,' but to her surprise Jake said coolly, 'Actually it was mine.'

'Huh, I would have thought you'd have had enough of walking after this afternoon. We did the full eighteen holes.'

'Oh, Jeremy dragged you round the full course, did he?' Sue smiled sympathetically at Jake. 'I'm afraid he's something of a golf-aholic, although he tells me he only plays for business reasons. Are you a keen player?'

Kelly's heart turned over as Jake smiled back at Sue, a ridiculous surge of jealousy submerging her in its tormenting depths.

'Not really. I prefer squash.'

'No need to be that modest, old man,' Jeremy cut in acidly. 'He was good enough to beat me.'

Kelly hid a small smile of amusement. Jeremy prided himself on his golf—she had in the past been obliged to listen to him boasting endlessly about his prowess, and it was obvious that he was admitting Jake's superiority with grudging reluctance.

'Oh, we're nearly there—there's the pool,' Sue told them, with evident relief. 'It's full Olympic size—although I've heard that he rarely uses it.'

A short flight of steps brought them on to the same level as the pool and patio area, which was already thronged with other guests. The pool, as Sue had said, was huge, but Kelly doubted that many zealous swimmers would appreciate the design of it, which wasn't rectangular, but instead seemed to form an elongated figure of eight, the smaller circle disappearing inside the house in traditional Hollywood manner.

'That's so that they can use the pool in winter,' Sue informed her knowledgeably. 'Huge glass doors cut off that part of the pool and enclosed it inside. I believe it cost a fortune. And just have a look behind you,' she added, waiting with a knowing grin as Kelly obediently turned and gasped her amazement as she saw what appeared to be a floating white trelliswork gazebo in the centre of the second circle.

'Good heavens,' she managed weakly, while Sue laughed her appreciation. 'Mmm. Vintage Hollywood, isn't it? The third, or was it fourth Mrs Wrayman had the original villa almost torn down and all this done in its place, and just wait until you see the inside. Carne Wrayman is a fanatical collector of Byzantine religious relics and the like. He has some fantastic icons that were brought out of Russia during the Revolution—they're worth a fortune, but then of course he's a millionaire several times over.'

'Sounds just your type,' Jake murmured *sotto voce* against Kelly's hair. 'No worries about him wanting you for your money!'

'Perhaps you've got a point!' Kelly bit out the words, small white teeth snapping together as she fought against her anger.

'Jake darling! How wonderful! What on earth are you doing here?'

A lissom blonde girl extricated herself from the crowd by the pool and almost threw herself into Jake's arms. She was about eighteen, and Kelly knew beyond doubt that the feelings tearing at her with sharply venomous claws were pure feminine jealousy.

'Well, well,' Jeremy murmured tauntingly. 'A little bit of something from his past? You want to watch it, love,' he warned Kelly acidly, 'you might find she's making a takeover bid for the present and the future.'

'Jake, there's someone I want you to meet. Do come with me . . . You won't mind if I borrow him for a minute, will you?' the blonde asked Kelly with an arch smile that revealed surprisingly genuine dimples.

'Feel free.' Her face felt stiff and she knew her smile looked totally unnatural.

'I won't be long,' Jake told her casually before walking away, his arm round the blonde girl's shoulders, her face turned up to his full of laughter, and—Kelly was forced to admit it—love!

'Mmm, I wonder why he was so keen not to introduce her to us.' Jeremy was watching her with a triumph that was unmistakable, and it didn't take a genius to see what he was thinking. Even so, Kelly had to clench her teeth to stop herself retorting when he said with mock concern, 'Perhaps I'd better make a few enquiries. You can't be too careful, you know, Kelly, a woman of your wealth. Okay, I know he has all the trappings of success, but I would hate to see you taken in—again,' he added deliberately.

Kelly went white. The patio seemed to be whirling round, the noise of the party roaring in her ears. Struggling to re-assert her normal control, she managed a husky, 'What do you mean, "again"?'

'Oh, come on, darling!' Jeremy was really enjoying himself now, and Kelly wondered how long he had been storing up this bitterness, this need to cause her pain and inflict hurt. 'Old Ian told me—we were at a conference together, we'd had a few drinks, you know how it is. I happened to mention you, and he told me about what happened with Colin, how he deliberately set you up—married you for your money.'

'Jeremy!' Sue sounded shocked and angry, but Kelly was past caring. Amazingly, the old story lacked all the old pain. She couldn't care less what Jeremy had heard and it no longer caused her the slightest pang that Colin had not loved her. What she did feel was regret that she had been foolish enough to fall for what she could see now had been a clumsy charm at best, and sorrow that she had let it spoil so much of her life.

'It's quite all right, Sue,' she managed to say evenly. 'Jeremy's quite right, Colin did marry me for my money.'

'But Jake isn't the slightest bit like Colin,' Sue broke in hotly, 'and I can't think why Jeremy should suggest that he is. Perhaps it has something to do with the fact that he beat you at golf,' she suggested to her husband, who, Kelly was half amused to see, was regarding her with stupefied disbelief.

'You ought to apologise to Kelly, Jeremy,' Sue continued. 'Oh, saved by the bell,' she added. 'Here's our host.'

'Susan, my darling, you grow more lovelier every time I see you!'

'It's lovely of you to say so, Carne,' Sue responded to the well-built greying man who was embracing her, 'but we both know you're a liar.'

Carne Wrayman released her to shake Jeremy's

hand and then turned to Kelly, his eyes narrowing in appreciation as he smiled at her.

'You are here alone?' he questioned when Sue had introduced them.

'She is now,' Jeremy responded viciously. 'She's lost her partner to an eighteen-year-old blonde.'

'Is that so?' The hooded eyes studied Kelly again. 'Well then, his loss is my gain. Allow me to escort you to the bar. Sue, you know the way.'

CHAPTER SEVEN

'So, and what do you do with yourself when you're not holidaying on Corfu?' Carne Wrayman asked Kelly.

They were sitting by the patio drinking the driest Martinis Kelly had ever tasted in her life. She had lost sight of Sue and Jeremy, and Jake was just a painful blur on the edge of her vision; someone she tried not to see, just as she tried not to see the blonde girl clinging to his side.

'I . . . I'm in publicity. I have my own company,' Kelly told him briefly.

'A career woman.' Again that sharply hooded glance. 'You know, I find that an incredible turn-on,' Carne Wrayman told her, leaning closer to her, 'and as it happens I'm looking for someone to handle the British side of the publicity for a documentary we're doing. Fancy the idea?'

'I'd have to know more about it,' Kelly told him cautiously. 'You see, we only handle work we feel we can give our best to. I don't believe in making false promises to my clients, and the promises I do make to them I want to be able to fulfil.'

'Baby, I like what I'm hearing,' Carne breathed fervently. 'Something tells me that you and I are going to get along real fine together. Look, why don't we blow—we can go out to my yacht and talk this thing through. We'll get more privacy there. What do you say?'

121

Kelly's first instinct was to refuse. She glanced across the sea of faces and saw Jake dancing with the blonde girl, her body pressed provocatively close to his, and jealousy burned through her. Like an animal in pain she wanted only to escape, and her eyes were still on the slowly gyrating couple as she murmured distractedly, 'Yes . . . yes . . . fine . . .'

'Good. Good, let's go, then.' Carne Wrayman got up, and Kelly followed him along a path which led down through the gardens, giving the odd tantalising glimpse of the moon-silvered sea and the huge white yacht lit from stem to stern and drifting languidly at anchor.

'Hop in,' Carne instructed, indicating the small powerboat tied up at the jetty. 'The water in this cove is quite deep,' he told her as they headed for the yacht, 'but unfortunately not deep enough for the *Mary Belinda*—after wife number three I got sick of changing her name, and so, although the real Mary Belinda has long since left my life, her namesake remains.'

The small motorboat chugged noisily towards the yacht, Kelly entranced by the reflections of the stars in the midnight-blue water, the swell caused by the boat crested silver by the new moon.

'I've given the crew the night off,' Carne told her as they went on board. He saw Kelly's bemused expression and grinned boyishly. 'Would you like to see over her? She's one of my favourite toys, and I'm idiotically proud of her.'

With good reason, Kelly reflected half an hour later as Carne escorted her into what he described as the 'main saloon'. As large and lavishly equipped

as a small drawing-room, the room was decorated
in soft shades of green and toning cream.

'It's . . . it's like something out of a film,' she
managed at last. 'A floating stately home!'

Carne laughed. 'You should see some of the
yachts that put in to Corfu, they make mine look
very small beer indeed—but I still haven't shown
you my own private quarters.'

Still smiling, Kelly followed him through a door
and into a corridor carpeted in a thick pale cream
carpet.

As Carne opened a door she caught a glimpse of
the room beyond it; almost stark in contrast to the
pastel prettiness of the 'saloon', it was furnished in
a richly Oriental style with a low bed, and several
items of beautifully lacquer-worked furniture, including an antique 'medicine cabinet' and a screen.
The walls were painted a vivid scarlet, the bed
covered in black silk.

'Very sybaritic,' she murmured to Carne, 'and
quite different from the rest of the décor.'

'Yes, I had my own suite redecorated when I
divorced my third wife. Do you like it?'

A tiny frisson of warning prickled along her
spine. There was a look in Carne's eyes that she
recognised and distrusted.

'It's . . . it's very eye-catching,' she told him,
edging back towards the door. 'But hardly the place
to discuss business.'

'That depends,' Carne told her, watching her
intently. 'On the business, and the potential business partners. I could put a good deal of work your
way, Kelly . . .'

'Provided, in return?' she questioned evenly.

She was furiously angry, not so much with Carne as with herself by being stupid enough to get herself in this situation. Good heavens, how many times in the past had she been faced with the same potential hazard? More than she cared to remember, but this was the first time she had been idiotic enough to walk blindly into the trap as naïvely as a child.

'My dear,' Carne protested, 'need we be so crude? You aren't doing much for my ego, you know.'

'I shouldn't think it's in much danger from anything I can do,' Kelly said drily. 'I'm not stupid enough to believe you have any interest in me as a person, Carne. This is simply an exercise in power politics.'

'How astute you are!' He drawled the words pleasantly enough, but there was a look in his eyes that warned Kelly that he was annoyed. 'I thought you and I were two of a kind.'

'Perhaps it would be as well if I left . . .'

'From whose point of view?' There was no humour in his smile now. 'If you return to the villa now, having been seen leaving in my company, my guests, and even worse the inevitable press photographer who always manages to gatecrash these do's, will jump to the correct, and as far as I'm concerned, humiliating conclusions. I don't want you making a fool out of me by going back to the villa now, Kelly. You're a grown woman, you knew what you were doing when you agreed to come here with me. Okay, now you've changed your mind, but I haven't changed mine.'

He lunged for her, taking Kelly off guard as he grasped her arm. Pain jerked up her arm as he dragged her towards him. The urbane host who had amused and entertained her was gone. In his place was a man governed by vanity and obsessed with his public image, and she had been a fool not to read the truth in the weak mouth and greedy eyes before.

Common sense warned her against panicking; that was just exactly what he hoped she would do. Cool cynicism would be a far more effective weapon if she could just keep her head long enough to use it.

'Look,' she pleaded, playing for time, 'I can understand why you're annoyed—and some of the blame does lie with me. I wasn't thinking properly and I genuinely thought you did want to talk business. Let's go back to the villa together—that should stop any gossip, and I give you my word as far as I'm concerned that will be the end of the whole thing . . .'

'Your word!' He laughed harshly. 'My God, if there's one thing I've learned over the years it's that when a woman gives you her "word", it means exactly nothing. And besides,' he said softly, 'I want you. You're a very desirable woman—my kind of woman.'

'But you aren't my kind of man,' Kelly retorted pointedly. 'And now—I'm leaving, with or without you.'

'Brave words,' Carne sneered, 'but unfortunately for you no more than that. You can't start the boat without the ignition key, which I have here.' He patted his pocket. 'And besides, you couldn't outrun me, Kelly, but go ahead if you want to.'

His voice told her that he would love her to try

and make a run for it; that he would enjoy her panic and fear, and even though inwardly she was tense with anxiety and dread, Kelly forced herself to stand her ground and say calmly, 'I have no intention to staying here with you, Carne—or of allowing you to make love to me.'

His sneer almost made her panic.

'How are you going to stop me?' he mocked, tightening his grip on her arm. 'And don't start telling me you'll cry "rape", Kelly. The courts are getting tired of trumped-up charges from women who change their minds at the last minute.'

White-faced and thoroughly frightened, Kelly was forced to admit the truth of his comment. Even if she were to accuse him of rape she doubted that her case would stand much chance of success in court. By her own folly she had placed herself in a vulnerable position. She had come willingly with Carne to his boat, after all.

As though he read her mind and sensed victory, Carne pulled her towards him, triumph flaring in his eyes.

'Admit it, Kelly,' he breathed, nauseating her with his self-conceit, his wine-fumed breath reminding her that he had probably had a considerable amount to drink.

This was confirmed as he raised his free hand and started to fumble clumsily with the straps of her dress, and although what he had had to drink didn't appear to have affected his strength—he was still holding her arm in a bruising grip—it did seem to have affected his co-ordination.

A miasma of panic settled round her like a mind-paralysing cloud as she tried to fight free of him, her body tensing automatically against the intrusion of his hands against her skin, anger giving way to stark terror and the age-old human instinct to fight for survival.

'Hellcat!' Carne swore thickly at one point as Kelly scratched frantically at his face, his hand going automatically to the long red welts she had drawn along his skin. Momentarily free, Kelly reacted, instantly, racing for the open door, finding her way almost by blind instinct up the nearest companionway, lungs bursting, heart pounding with the fear that fuelled her flight. On the deck her flight was suddenly impeded by a solid mass that crushed the breath out of her body, the bite of strong fingers on her shoulders making her shudder with panic and despair.

'Kelly . . . Kelly . . . What the hell's going on?'

'Jake?' She stared at him in utter disbelief, suddenly galvanised into action as she heard Carne swearing and breathing heavily down below.

Jake registered her panic and smiled cynically.

'What's the matter? Did lover boy prove too much for you?'

'He told me he wanted to talk about business,' Kelly muttered, feeling foolish and very much on the defensive.

'And you're trying to tell me you fell for it?'

Kelly flinched as she heard angry footsteps on the companionway, clutching instinctively at Jake's arm, her eyes widening with fear.

'Oh, please, let's go!'

Carne had gained the deck and stood there, swaying slightly, his face livid with rage.

'Just who the hell are you?' he demanded thickly, advancing on Jake.

'I'm a friend of Kelly's,' Jake replied evenly. 'Thank the kind man for his hospitality, Kelly,' he drawled mockingly. 'It's time we left.'

For a moment, Kelly thought Carne was going to hurl himself at Jake and she held her breath, terrified by the thought of more violence. But half a dozen feet short of Jake Carne came to an uncertain standstill.

'Get her out of my sight,' he muttered angrily. 'Frigid little bitch, I didn't really want her anyway!'

All the way back in the boat the words reverberated endlessly through her mind, an acid refrain that seemed to burn through her frail protection, reminding her achingly of Colin and the taunts he had thrown at her, destroying the frail self-possession she had built up in the years between and leaving her as vulnerable to his rejection as she had been then.

She was shivering by the time Jake stopped the motorboat, barely aware of him standing up to throw anchor over the side.

'Come on, jump out, you'll have to wade the rest of the way.'

She shivered, backing away from him instinctively as he reached out his hand. The boat rocked wildly. Kelly heard Jake curse and then she was overbalancing, falling backwards into the cold dark water, her startled cry of protest choked off by the seawater filling her mouth and nostrils.

Her panic subsided almost instantly as her feet touched the sandy bottom, and by the time Jake reached her she had regained her balance. The cold water had the effect of shocking her back into an awareness of the present; of Jake's angrily icy face, and the bedraggled picture she must present in her seawater-doused hair and soaking dress. Why had Jake come to look for her and, more important, how had he known where to look?

'Sue was concerned about you,' he told her, obviously reading her mind. 'She couldn't find you, and she seemed to think you might be . . . upset, for some reason.'

Kelly was glad of the darkness as her face flamed. Sue meant that she had thought she would be jealous because Jake had disappeared with the blonde.

'That doesn't explain how you knew where to find me,' she retorted coolly, dragging the rags of her composure around her, retreating into the protection of the cold hauteur that had worked so well in the past.

'You were seen leaving with Wrayman,' Jake told her tersely, as he waded on to the beach and turned to help her. The moonlight fell sharply on his face and for a second his features seemed to tense, a muscle beating violently in his jaw. He looked angry, and more . . .

'Kelly, come on. We're both soaked through. We can't stand here all night. I take it you don't want to go back to the party?'

'Meaning you do? I'm perfectly capable of returning to the villa on my own,' she told him acidly, 'so if you want to return to your girl-friend . . .'

'My girl-friend?' He frowned, and then his expression changed, a mocking smile playing round his mouth. 'Ah yes, of course. But, Kelly, you are forgetting something. You are my girl-friend—at least, you are while I am still in your employ.'

For some reason she wanted to cry. She felt the tears sting the back of her eyes and knew with detached certainty that this was only the beginning of the pain she was going to experience. Where and why it had happened she didn't know, but she had fallen in love with Jake.

In a daze she followed him up the beach, barely aware of the fact that he had turned to wait for her, until she felt the warm clasp of his hand on hers.

'Cold?'

She nodded, wondering if she was hallucinating and imagining the tenderness in the word.

The night air was quite warm, but the sea and the shocks she had sustained had left her chilled to the marrow. By the time they reached the garden of Sue's father's villa she was shivering so much that her teeth were chattering. Jake, although equally wet, seemed impervious to the cold.

'Come into the sitting-room and I'll pour you a stiff drink,' he suggested curtly as they entered the house. 'It will help combat the shock.'

'No!' Kelly didn't want to tell him that she always associated the sort of drink he meant with the one the police constable had given her when he broke the news about Colin.

'I'll go and have a shower. I'm just cold, that's all.'

Jake shrugged, the powerful shoulders damply encased in the thin silk shirt, his jeans clinging to his body in a way that made her senses respond over-poweringly to the masculinity of him.

The shower helped, but she couldn't banish the

ice-cold knot of sickness lodged inside her heart.
Carne's final words had left a barb that festered
powerfully, no matter how she tried to blot them
out, and this, coupled with the knowledge of her
love for Jake, left her feeling totally disorientated
and achingly vulnerable.

She longed to go to bed and sleep so that she
could blot out what had happened—forget everything, but she knew that sleep would be impossible,
and then she remembered Sue saying that she had
some sleeping tablets her doctor had prescribed.
Ordinarily, Kelly wouldn't have dreamed of taking
medicine prescribed for someone else, but tonight
she couldn't endure to lie knowing that Jake was
either lying in the opposite bed or, more likely,
sharing the bed of the blonde girl who had made her
admiration of him all so plain.

She was heading for Sue's bathroom when the
living-room door opened and Jake emerged.

He frowned when he saw her, and Kelly was
absurdly aware of the brief towel she had wrapped
around her body—and the insulting remarks Jake
had made earlier. Her face burned as he looked at
her. Did he think she had done this purely to attract
his attention?

'I wanted to borrow a couple of Sue's sleeping
pills,' she muttered jerkily. 'I'm sure she won't
mind, and I . . .'

'Want to forget what happened on board the
yacht, is that it? What did happen, by the way?
Were you genuinely running from Wrayman or
were you simply egging him on?'

A sudden rush of tears to her eyes blinded her
momentarily, and she smothered a tiny, betraying

protest, turning swiftly on her heel. It was too dangerous to risk bandying words with Jake feeling the way she did at the moment—she could only lose.

'Kelly!'

It seemed he wasn't content with reducing her to tears. His fingers grasped her arm, spinning her round so hard that she gasped, fingers clutching nervously at her towel as it slipped precariously low over her breasts.

'Do these mean that it was genuine?' Jake demanded softly, his fingers oddly gentle as they brushed the dampness from her cheeks.

She tried to speak, to tell him coldly that if she was crying it was simply reaction, but instead, to her horror, the tears flowed even faster, like a dam bursting, falling harder as she struggled to suppress them and the emotions storming through her.

'Kelly!'

Jake spoke her name with unmistakable urgency.

'I know—you hate seeing women cry,' she tried to joke—but suddenly it wasn't a joke any longer as Jake smothered a curse, pulling her savagely into his arms as he muttered hoarsely, 'I hate seeing *you* cry. God, if Wrayman had hurt you . . .'

'It was my own fault. I should never have gone with him. God knows I've spent enough time avoiding similar situations, but tonight . . .'

Within the circle of Jake's arms, she shrugged, realising in amazement how easily she had confided in him.

'Would you like me to stay with you—until you fall asleep?'

Oh, she was tempted!

'Let's start again, Kelly,' Jake was murmuring softly. 'Somehow we got off on the wrong foot and we've stayed that way ever since, apart from one or two illuminating incidents. I could have killed Wrayman when he walked off with you tonight.'

'You saw us?' Kelly was astonished, and raised her head to look at him.

He grimaced slightly, his eyes darkening as they probed the shadowy swell of her breasts where her towel had slipped.

'I saw you,' he confirmed. 'I thought you were doing it to annoy me.'

When she looked puzzled, he said softly, 'Oh, come on, Kelly, you know how much I want you, you aren't blind—but then, of course, I'm not keeping to my place if I want you, am I? I'm only the hired help.'

'Jake?'

Her voice was wondering, hesitantly hopeful. Jake wanted her. She searched his face distractedly for signs that he was lying, but there were none. She could see the sharp hunger in his eyes, echoed in the tautness of his body against hers, as he held her.

'Don't play with *me*, Kelly,' he warned her, his voice rough with emotion. 'Let's have no misunderstandings this time. I want you, and . . .'

'And I want you, Jake,' Kelly told him huskily, her fingers trembling as she touched his face, trying to reassure herself that he was real, 'but first there's something I have to tell you.'

She wanted to tell him about Colin, about why she had been so bitterly suspicious of him. It didn't matter that he had no money, or how he earned his living, she decided passionately. What mattered was the way they felt about one another. He wanted her, and every feminine instinct she possessed told her that she would be a fool if she turned her back on this chance of happiness simply because of pride and money. What did it matter if she was rich and he was poor? What did it matter what anyone else thought? What did anything matter except for this wonderful, glorious happiness bubbling up inside her?

'Later, Kelly,' Jake was saying roughly, 'tell me about it later. Right now—right now . . .' he added huskily, 'I can think of better ways of communicating than simply by the spoken word.'

He lifted her in his arms and Kelly clung to the breadth of his shoulders, her heart pounding shakily as he pushed open the door to their room.

She was still in his arms when Jake bent his head to kiss her, her lips parting eagerly beneath his, her body trembling with heated urgency as he gradually slid her to her feet, every contour of her moulded against him so that she could almost feel his pulse beat.

'Kelly.'

She let him unfasten her towel, her own fingers making eager inroads into the buttons on his shirt, peeling it back, her eyes mesmerised by the sight of his body. His hands cupped her breasts and they swelled instantly to his touch. Her skin felt as though it were on fire with a burningly dry heat, the frenzied kisses she pressed against Jake's throat and shoulders eliciting a husky imprecation and the fierce assault of his mouth against her skin, his hands moving hungrily over her body, touching and exploring, bringing her to a fever pitch of sexual excitement.

Kelly was completely lost in the storm of sensual pleasure Jake evoked, stroking his torso feverishly as he savaged her mouth in explicit demand, releasing her lips to mutter hoarsely, 'For God's sake, Kelly, what are you doing to me?'

And then he was lifting her in his arms, and striding towards the bed, lowering his head to capture one taut nipple with his lips before he released her, savouring its burgeoning sweetness until Kelly sobbed out loud with pleasure, her stomach muscles cramping excitingly, her body throbbing tormentingly as Jake lowered her on to the bed.

She shivered for a moment as the coolness of the night air struck her skin, and then Jake was beside her, covering her trembling flesh with the warmth of his, and the feel of him against her was nothing like the humiliation she had known with Colin.

It was easy to give herself up to the seduction of his touch, to respond with caresses of her own, taking fierce delight from the harsh sounds of pleasure her fingers drew from his throat, and the kisses that followed them.

When his hand stroked along her inner thigh she tensed, nightmare memories flooding back, but her desire and love for Jake were more powerful than her fear, and intense waves of pleasure followed her initial fear, her body arching; wanting and inciting with age-old instinct the union of their flesh.

In the darkness she heard the ragged, charged quality of Jake's breathing, and felt the perspiration beading his skin as he muttered hoarsely beneath his breath, cupping her face and stroking her lips with his, until she clung mindlessly, exulting in the fierce thrust of his body and the savage passion of his kiss.

Somewhere, dimly in the recesses of her mind, she was registering pain, but she didn't care; she wanted this pain, wanted the fierce maleness of Jake with a need that overrode everything else, and when he tensed, withdrawing from her, she was plunged into a pit of bitter rejection, cringing away from him as he snapped on the bedside lamp.

'Kelly, look at me.'

She quivered under the harshness of his tone.

'Kelly . . .'

'No! Please, I . . .' To her horror she started to cry, not silent tears, but tearing sobs that shook her body and made her throat ache.

'Kelly, for God's sake!' She shrank beneath the whiplash of anger, shivering with self-loathing and humiliation. 'Why didn't you tell me?'

It was pointless and undignified trying to pretend she didn't understand.

'I tried to,' she managed wearily, 'but you wouldn't listen.'

'Are you going to tell me about it?'

'What do you want to hear?' Her voice sounded bitter and sour, but she couldn't help it, couldn't rid herself of the taste of rejection. 'Would you like to hear how my husband only married me for my money; how he tried to rape me on our wedding night, but how he couldn't bring himself to possess me in the end—he didn't really want me, you see, he only wanted my money, and making love to me was a price he found in the end he simply couldn't pay. So he left me and went to his girl-friend, only he was killed on the way. Funny, isn't it really . . .'

She started to laugh, a high bitter sound that went on and on, until Jake shook her roughly and then smothered the sound with his lips, kissing her until she was fighting for breath; fighting for the control to reject him as he had rejected her.

'You don't have to make love to me,' she told him when she finally managed to pull away. 'I'll still pay you.'

'I damn well ought to thrash you for that!' Jake ground out, and in the darkness she caught the burn of anger in his eyes, 'and besides, you're wrong. I do have to make love to you.' He said it so quietly that at first she thought she had misheard, but then he added slowly, as though he wanted every single word to sink in:

'I'm sorry for what happened with Colin and it explains a great deal I couldn't understand before—but, Kelly, I'm not Colin, and you can't spend the rest of your life punishing yourself because one man didn't want you. I want you,' he said quietly, 'and the only reason we aren't already lovers is simply that it threw me to realise that you were still a virgin.'

'Meaning that you'd prefer me to have more experience,' Kelly said bitterly. 'I'm sorry if I don't come up to your undoubtedly high standards, but . . .'

The crudity of the expression he used shocked her into silence. She stared across at him in the darkness, wondering if she was being a fool, but her body still ached for him, and she still loved him.

'Virginity is more a state of mind than an actual physical reality—at least that's my view, and my strongest feeling at the moment is one of pity—oh, not for you,' he said tersely, 'for Colin, for being fool enough to turn his back on you. No, I tell a lie,' he added drily. 'If I'm honest, my *strongest* feeling right now is my desire for you, but I don't intend to force any issues, Kelly. I want you—and badly, but I want you to want me too. I want you to experience pleasure in my arms, not simply give me pleasure. Do you understand what I'm trying to say?'

Her mouth had gone dry. Jake was being unfair, forcing her to make the decision, and yet inwardly she acknowledged that he was right; that it was her decision, and the fact that he had the strength to allow her to make it only increased her love for him.

'I . . . I want you, Jake.'

They were the hardest words she had ever had to utter, and for one terrifying moment when he made no response she thought it had all been a trick, a trap, and panic welled up inside her, fear crawling along her spine.

'Oh God, Kelly, I thought you were never going to be able to say it!'

She didn't know who moved first, but suddenly she was in his arms, his lips touching her hair, kissing the dampness from her cheeks, his thumb stroking the quivering fullness of her lips, and she knew joyously, overwhelmingly, that everything was going to be all right.

CHAPTER EIGHT

TOWARDS dawn, Kelly surfaced briefly. The comforting weight of Jake's arm lay across her ribs, securing her against him. Her body felt lethargic, totally relaxed, as bonelessly sensual as a small cat's, and she smiled secretly, remembering Jake's lovemaking and her own abandoned response to it. Jake moved, eyes still closed, nuzzling her throat, drawing her down against him, her body instantly pliant and responsive, as though it remembered the pleasure they had shared earlier.

The next time she woke up Kelly was alone. She padded across to the bathroom, recognising the faint tang of Jake's soap and cologne, and wondering why he had not woken her. Today they would have to talk. She loved him, and she wasn't going to let her chance of happiness slip away from her through pride. What good was her wealth if it separated her from the only thing that she really wanted—Jake's love? Did he love her? Kelly didn't know, but she wanted him to know that she was willing to share equally with him all her worldly goods. The sexes were equal nowadays, she reminded herself bracingly, she had always fought to be considered the equal of her male colleagues, and surely she wasn't hypocritical enough to want to revert to the typical male/female superior/inferior status now? What did it matter if they lived on her money? What did it matter if Jake had no career or profession to follow? Banishing all her niggling doubts, she showered quickly, marvelling at the difference a handful of hours could make. Even her flesh felt different—softer, more responsive, glowing with a soft radiance that was reflected in her face. But where was Jake?

She found Sue and Jeremy breakfasting on the patio, tension hanging almost visibly on the air.

'Morning, Kelly, did you enjoy the party?' Sue enquired in an over-bright, forced voice.

'How could she enjoy it? She didn't spend a good deal of time at the party, did she? Two millionaires in one night—that's pretty good going by anyone's standards, never mind a woman who's been fooling the world for years that she's as frigid as an iceberg!'

'Jeremy!'

'Two millionaires!'

Sue and Kelly spoke together, Jeremy ignoring his wife to turn and smirk at Kelly, 'You mean you didn't know?'

'Know what?' Kelly demanded. The phone started to ring and Sue got up hurriedly. 'It might be Dad,' she explained, 'he said he might ring. By the way, Kelly, Jake said to tell you he's just gone into town and that he won't be long.'

She got up and left, ignoring her husband, and Kelly wondered if the two of them had quarrelled during the party.

'So you didn't know, then?' Jeremy continued when Sue had gone. 'I thought not. Fooled you nicely, didn't he? That blonde girl he was with at the party knew all right . . .'

A cold tight feeling was gripping her.

'Know what, Jeremy?' she asked tautly.

'That Jake is a millionaire. She obviously recognised him straight away, and I made a few discreet enquiries at the party. It seems your Jake has extensive interests ranging almost worldwide, although he normally keeps a low profile. I bet he though it was hilarious when you walked into that agency and mistook him for one of the staff!'

She must not faint, Kelly told herself grimly. She must not give way in front of Jeremy, watching her, waiting to gloat over her.

'He told you about that?' she managed in a carefully controlled voice, while the icy cold invading her body almost burned in its intensity. She was shaking inwardly, but she daren't let Jeremy see it.

'How else would I know about it? He must have laughed his socks off afterwards! You hired him to keep me at bay, didn't you?

'Well, the joke's on you, Kelly,' Jeremy told her savagely, 'and how! You've fallen for him, haven't you? Let him inside your precious defences; let him make love to you, and all the time he was laughing at you—making a fool of you!'

It couldn't be true! Sickness boiled up inside her. It couldn't be true. Jake a millionaire. Jake deliberately deceiving her, encouraging her to fall in love with him. And yet Jeremy couldn't have made up something like that! But why had Jake confided in Jeremy?

'How does it feel to be a loser, clever lady?' Jeremy taunted. 'You should have stayed within your own league, Kelly. He'll be dining out on the story of how he fooled you for months. I wouldn't be surprised if he didn't deliberately encourage you to fall in love with him. Quite an amusing diversion for a man like him, especially with a woman like you, who wouldn't normally let a man of his type within a hundred miles of her.'

Kelly wanted to blot out the taunting words; words she knew were all too painfully true. Like a film played jerkily backwards she relived those moments when she had first walked into the agency; Jake's surprise at seeing her; the feeling she had had on several occasions that his manner was not in accord with his subservient role. Dear God, why had he done it?

She cringed to remember how she had revealed her innermost thoughts and feelings to him; how she had told him about Colin, and then trembled trustingly in his arms as he brought her to full womanhood, glorying in her joyous response to his lovemaking when it reached its peak of fierce intensity.

The vulnerable core of her ached for her foolishness. Hadn't she learned her lesson the first time with Colin? Why couldn't she be like other women she knew, content to take sexual pleasure where she found it, without experiencing the need to involve her heart and mind as well? She had loved Jake; had been prepared to share with him everything she owned, while he . . .

'You'd have been better off with me,' Jeremy repeated.

'Except that you happen to be married to Sue,' Kelly reminded him coldly, turning swiftly on her heel.

As she walked into the villa Sue was just emerging, looking tired and pale.

'Kelly?'

'I'm leaving, Sue,' Kelly told her shortly, 'I'm flying back to London on the first available flight.' Her mouth twisted bitterly.

'But what about Jake?'

Kelly laughed harshly, 'What about him?'

'Oh, Kelly, if you've quarrelled, I'm sure you'll make it up again. Why don't you wait until he comes back from town?'

'No.' Kelly was icily firm outwardly, but inwardly she was an aching mass of pain and confusion, still half unable to believe what was happening to her.

Less than an hour later she was on her way to the airport, her final goodbyes to Sue and Jeremy, brief and hurried.

She was lucky enough to get a cancellation on a flight leaving for London within the hour, and as she waited in the departure lounge Kelly tried not to think about what had happened. Was it really only last night she had lain in Jake's arms, feeling that at last she had come home?

Fool, fool, she chided herself bitterly. She ought to have known better. She of all people ought to have known. How Jeremy must have enjoyed learning the truth! When and why had Jake deliberately decided to deceive her, or had it simply been an impulse decision which had snowballed to the point where he had conceived the idea of making her fall in love with him?

Her flight was called, and she walked towards the terminal automatically, freezing as she recognised the blonde girl from the party. Today she was dressed casually in jeans and a tee-shirt, but there was no mistaking that blonde hair or those perfectly classical features.

And she wasn't alone. Kelly's heart jerked, ungainly as a puppet as she recognised the back of Jake's dark head, inclined now towards his companion. Even as Kelly watched, the blonde girl raised herself on tiptoe, flinging her arm round Jake's neck and kissing him enthusiastically.

Hot tears of jealousy scorched her eyes and, pain a living, tormenting thing inside her.

After a lifetime of agony in case Jake saw her, and witnessed her jealousy, she was safely on the plane and they were taking off. Fortunately, the blonde girl was nowhere to be seen. What had Jake told Sue to tell her? That he had gone to town? But he hadn't said anything about the reason for his visit, such as the fact that he was seeing his girl-friend off at the airport—but then there was so much he hadn't told her, and last night when those husky, passionate words of need had seared and melted her skin wherever his mouth touched, he had said nothing of love, nothing of the truth, while she, poor crazy fool that she was, had told him with every gesture and embrace that she was wholly and irrevocably besotted with him. She had thought the exquisite pleasure they had shared had been something unique to them. A dull flush of colour suffused her skin, and she writhed mentally, wondering if Jake would tell his girl-friend about what had happened; possibly laugh and joke about it; about *her* and the insecurities she had revealed all too plainly to him in the moments before the final throes of passion had swept aside restraint and selfconsciousness.

She cringed inwardly, huddling down into her seat, taking refuge behind a magazine, trying to convince herself that she was merely the victim of a bad dream; that when she returned to London she would wake up to find that Jake had never really existed.

'Kelly, have you seen this?'

Kelly frowned as her assistant thrust a letter under her nose, her manner one of contained excitement.

'What is it?' Kelly asked her, glancing at the letter, and stiffening a little as she did so.

'Isn't it fantastic?' Maisie demanded. 'I never dreamed we'd be invited to tender for a contract like this! Carew's is a huge multi-national organisation. I've always thought they were based in the States.'

'Mmm.' Kelly was nearly as impressed as her assistant, but since her return from Corfu she had found it difficult to throw herself as completely into her work. 'It seems that the chairman wants to meet me for preliminary discussions.' She frowned. 'I wonder why they chose us?'

'It could be something to do with that article they ran on us in that Sunday supplement,' Maisie suggested.

The article in question had appeared in one of the upmarket Sundays several weeks ago, and Kelly eyed her thoughtfully.

'Could be,' she conceded at last, 'although I shouldn't have thought the chairman of a multi-national like Carew's would be impressed by some-

thing he read in a colour supplement. I think I'll
have a word with Ian. I'm a bit wary of this one. We
could too easily find ourselves involved in heavy
preliminary expenses without anything to show for
it in the end. Including us in the tender might just
be a sop to some eccentric on the Board. Multi-
nationals normally run with their own kind, and
that being the case, why aren't they using one of the
large American companies?'

Two hours later she was putting the same question to Ian over lunch at the Ritz.

'Kelly, you're getting far too suspicious,' Ian
laughed when she had finished. 'Hasn't anyone
ever warned you about refusing gifts from the
gods? And that's what this contract could be. I
don't have to remind you about what the recession
is doing to your particular industry. Oh, I know
you've plenty of work in hand for the next few
months—but after that?'

Kelly knew he was speaking the truth, but why
would Carew's approach her? She was very small
fry indeed by their standards.

'It says in the letter they want me to fly to
Edinburgh. The company has offices up there.'

'They've got considerable interests in oil, Edinburgh is closer to the Scottish oilfields than London. Why are you such a doubting Thomas?' Ian
teased her. 'This could be a tremendous opportunity for the company. I don't know what's happened
to you recently. You've changed.'

'I'm getting older,' Kelly pointed out wryly. She
knew she had changed, and why she wasn't as
singleminded about the company as she had previously been, but despite the speculation in Ian's

eyes, she wasn't going to enlighten him. That was a
private pain; a deep and bitter ache that couldn't be
assuaged by discussion with someone else.

'Oh yeah?' Ian's voice was openly derisive.
'You're a very beautiful woman, Kelly. I've always
thought so, but recently there's been—oh, I don't
know, a softening; a more womanly look about
you.'

'We're here to talk about Carew's,' Kelly reminded him crisply, 'and there's no need to flirt
with me, Ian. You're in no danger of losing the
company's business.'

His hurt expression made her feel ashamed of
her outburst, but because she couldn't explain to
him that it had been to protect herself that she had
snapped at him, Kelly said nothing, simply directing several questions to him about the Carew
Organisation.

In response, she didn't learn much more than she
knew already; namely that Carew's were very big in
the petro-chemical world; that they had sub-
sidiaries all over the world and that the chairman
was an elusive, almost secretive man about whom
very little was known.

'He's English, oddly enough,' Ian told her.
'"R.J.", I believe his American colleagues call
him, although in actual fact he's . . .'

'Sir Richard Carew,' Kelly supplemented for
him. 'Yes, I've been reading up on him too, but I
couldn't find out very much, apart from the fact
that he built the company up practically from nothing.'

'Well, from very modest beginnings,' Ian agreed.
'When he came down from Cambridge he inherited

a small company on the Clyde involved in re-fitting ships.'

'Mmm . . . There's something of a myth about the company's success, isn't there?' Kelly mused.

'More a case of being in the right place at the right time and plenty of luck, coupled with a good deal of hard work, but I agree, it does make good reading. And you're to meet Carew himself, are you? You're very honoured, I hope you realise. He still insists on running them himself, although they say his son will soon be taking over. He's the one who engineered the company's success in the petro-chemical field.'

A week later, Kelly flew from Heathrow to Edinburgh, stomach clenching nervously as the shuttle flight came in to land.

A chauffeur-driven car collected her from the airport, the driver polite but withdrawn as he negotiated the Edinburgh traffic.

The Carew building was a large imposing one, and Kelly suppressed a flutter of nervousness as the car came to a halt. A receptionist smiled warmly at her as she entered the foyer, indicating that she take a seat, while she pressed some buttons on her telephone and spoke quietly into the receiver.

'If you'd just like to take the lift to the tenth floor Sir Richard's secretary will be waiting for you,' the girl told Kelly with another smile.

There was a mirror in the lift and Kelly couldn't resist checking her appearance swiftly in it. She *had* changed since her return from Corfu. For one thing, she had had her hair cut—not short, but in a softly curving bell that suited her classical features,

and the suit she was wearing was in soft muted
pinks, far more shapely and feminine than the
clothes she had previously worn. She had told
herself that she wouldn't allow what had happened
between Jake and herself to affect her at all, but
somehow she had found herself spurning the
clothes she had once favoured, her eyes drawn
almost hypnotically to softer shades, more feminine styles. Deep down inside her she knew that
Jake was responsible for this resurgence of femininity, but she hated having to admit it even to herself.

The lift stopped and the doors opened. Kelly
stepped into a starkly elegant foyer decorated in
shades of blue and grey.

A door opened and an immaculately dressed girl
came towards her.

'Sir Richard will be with you in a second,' she
told Kelly. 'Would you care for a cup of coffee
while you're waiting?'

Too nervous to really want a drink, Kelly nevertheless accepted. What on earth was the matter
with her? She had never felt like this before; but
then they had never been invited to tender for such
an important contract, and she was conscious of the
tension building up inside her as the girl disappeared and a heavy, almost oppressive silence
closed over the foyer.

A door opened, making Kelly jump, despite the
fact that she had been waiting for it. The man who
came towards her was dressed in a formal business
suit, dark grey with a thin chalk stripe, a silk shirt
and a toning striped tie, his dark hair curling against
his collar, the expensive styling of his jacket doing

nothing to minimise the power of the body it concealed.

Her heart in her mouth, Kelly watched almost mesmerised, her strangled 'Jake!!!' seeming to echo drily around the room as she struggled to her feet and stared at Jake in appalled disbelief.

'You seem surprised.'

He drawled the words casually, bending his dark head to remove a minute scrap of fluff from his sleeve, while Kelly's mind whirled, stupidly. What was Jake doing here?

'I don't know what you're doing here Jake, but I can't talk to you now,' she managed at last, fighting for composure. 'I have an appointment with Sir Richard to . . .'

'To discuss some PR work for the company?' Jake interposed smoothly. 'Yes, I know, and my father has asked me to handle it for him. He has been called away unavoidably—the Energy Minister.'

'Your father?' Kelly almost whispered the words. 'Your father is . . .'

'Sir Richard Carew? Yes, that's right. I'm Jake Fielding Carew. Ah, here's Helen with your coffee. Mrs Langdon will have her coffee in my room, Helen, and you can bring a cup for me as well if you will.'

Listening to the crisply authoritative tones, Kelly knew that she wasn't, as she had first thought, simply hallucinating.

Jake took her arm, steering her firmly towards the door he had just opened. His office was less austere than the foyer, but still very functional. Kelly, attuned to such nuances, could tell by the way Helen brought his coffee that the secretary not only admired him as a man, she also very evidently respected him. Kelly felt stunned, unable to take in what was happening.

'Look, what's going on?' she demanded angrily. 'I was told that Sir Richard wanted to see me.'

'And so he did,' Jake agreed smoothly, 'but, as I explained, something came up and he asked me to talk to you instead. How much do you know about Carew's?' he asked, watching her with eyes suddenly metallic and hard. 'Or were you simply hoping to charm my father into giving you a contract? You'll find me a much tougher proposition, Kelly.'

'Oh, I'm sure of it,' Kelly agreed bitterly, on the point of storming out of the room, but something kept her in her seat. Some deep-seated aching need to remain where she was simply drinking in Jake's familiar features, her heart pounding mercilessly as she remembered the heavy thud of it against her own; the lean, tanned hands now resting distantly on the blotter, caressing her, drawing from her a tumultuous response.

Her mouth tightened and she looked across the desk. 'How can you sit there and accuse me . . . When you deliberately deceived me, deliberately let me think that . . .'

'That I was available for hire?' Jake mocked, an acid smile twisting his mouth. 'Believe me, Kelly, you can't regret it anything like as much as I do.'

'I don't think there's any point in continuing this discussion,' Kelly said unsteadily, reaching for her bag. 'I can't pretend to understand why you've gone to these elaborate lengths to arrange this meeting, Jake—I am right in presuming you did arrange it, I suppose?' When he didn't answer, she rushed on, 'I'm surprised you had the audacity to arrange it after . . .'

'So am I,' Jake agreed curtly, cutting across her furious words, 'but nevertheless I did.'

'Haven't you already done enough?' Kelly choked, terrified by the feeling of her emotions rioting out of control, desperate to escape from the environs of his office, and the forceful presence of him.

She struggled to her feet, gasping in pain when Jake's fingers closed over her wrists, dragging her against him as he strode round to her side of the desk.

'Enough? No way,' he grated, transferring one hand to her chin and forcing her head backwards until Kelly thought her neck would snap under the strain.

'Although it's very gratifying to see that you're joining the human race again, Kelly, becoming a woman again.' He touched her hair and Kelly shuddered, her mind betraying her completely. Jake was only inches away. She could see the dark beard shadowing his jaw, smell the masculine scent of his skin. Her body ached to be held close against him, to bc carcsscd and kisscd.

She shuddered deeply, perspiration breaking out on her forehead. 'Let me go, Jake.' Her voice sounded odd and husky. 'I don't know why you brought me here . . .'

'You mean you think you know, but you're wrong, Kelly. I'm not so hard up for a woman that I need to procure them by force!'

'I know that!' She almost spat the words at him,

remembering the blonde girl and Jake's affectionate leavetaking of her at the airport, only hours
after she herself had lain in his arm, thinking they
were sharing something special and precious, but to
him all she had been was a challenge. She felt a
wave of familiar sickness, remembering the gloating look on Jeremy's face when he told her.

'All right, Kelly, I'll tell you what you're doing
here.' He released her and returned to his desk,
opening a drawer and removing several photo-
graphs which he placed purposefully on the desk.

Kelly stared at them. They seemed to be of an old
baronial building of some kind.

'I don't know how much you know about my
family—probably very little, because my father
shuns public life, but at one time our family owned
the Isle of Marne, off the west of Scotland. We lost
it before the First World War, but it then came up
for sale and my father bought it. This . . .' he
tapped the building in the photograph with one
long forefinger, 'was once a pele tower—later
embellished and embroidered into what it is today,
and my father has decided he wants to turn it into
an exclusive holiday retreat for exhausted business-
men. He's getting concerned about the fact that he
isn't yet a grandfather,' he added sardonically, 'and
I suspect this is his way of bringing that fact home
to me. He promised me the house and the island
for a wedding present,' he added, watching her
with what Kelly could only interpret as deliberate
cruelty.

'Perhaps you'd get to the point,' she interrupted
coldly. 'I didn't come here to listen to a potted
version of your family history, Jake.'

'God, to think I thought . . .' His jaw clamped on whatever he had been about to say, and he said instead, 'The point is, Kelly, that my father wants to consult a PR firm about the best way of bringing the hotel into prominence. He asked me if I could recommend a PR company who could handle the job.'

'And you recommended me?' Kelly couldn't keep the astonishment out of her voice.

'Why not?' Jake drawled, suddenly very much in control of himself. 'Call it payment for services rendered, if you like.'

Kelly went white.

'What's the matter?' he jeered unkindly. 'Or is it a different matter when you're the one who's on the receiving end of the insults?

'Where are you going?' he demanded when Kelly stood up shakily, reaching for her bag.

'Back to London,' she told him curtly.

'Running away? I expected better of you, Kelly. You know what I think?' he mused softly, 'I think you're frightened, Kelly; frightened of being a woman; frightened that you're not, after all, indifferent to me.'

'Of course I am.'

'Are you?' He asked the question smoothly, not giving her the opportunity to reply before he added, 'Then why run away? Your company is successful, Kelly, but not so successful that it can afford to turn down good business, and without even making the slightest effort to secure it. What would the rest of your Board say to that, I wonder? Something tells me they wouldn't like it.'

Kelly knew that he was quite right. She ran her tongue over her lips nervously.

'I'm not saying I'm not interested in the contract—merely that I suspect the motive for being offered a chance to tender for it.'

'Tell me, Kelly, have you ever trusted anyone?' She swallowed painfully, hating the cynical contemptuous look in his eyes. 'You can't spend the rest of your life punishing the whole world because one man let you down.'

'Haven't you done enough?' Kelly demanded, unable to keep up the façade of indifference any longer, aching with the need to reach out and touch him and hating him because of the way he had deceived her.

'Stop living in the past,' Jake told her ruthlessly. 'Prove to me that you've rejoined the human race. Prove to me that you're indifferent to me,' he added in a different tone. 'I'm flying out to the island tomorrow, I want you to come with me. My father is anxious to get things under way as quickly as possible. He can't handle it himself because he's tied up with talks with the Energy Minister. For God's sake,' he muttered, when he saw her face, 'do you think it's easy for me? Damn you, Kelly, don't you think I have any feelings?'

What could she say? If she said that he couldn't have any feelings and have treated her the way he had, he would guess how she felt about him.

'Your feelings are no concern of mine, Jake,' she managed at last, raising her head to add defiantly, 'and if tendering for this contract is what it takes to convince you of that, then that's what I'll do!'

CHAPTER NINE

SHE wasn't going to let Jake see how frightened she was, Kelly decided grimly, staring blankly ahead of her as the small aircraft gained height, and the mist that had greeted her when she woke up that morning pressed heavily against the cabin windows.

If she had had any sense she would have refused to come on this trip with Jake, but her pride wouldn't let her back down, not when he had come to collect her at her hotel this morning, smiling mockingly at her when she glanced hesitantly outside.

Now somewhere below them was Edinburgh and they were heading north to the Western Isles. Jake was sitting with the pilot and Kelly was free to study him unobserved, her heart aching as she remembered how he had deceived her. And he didn't even have the grace to apologise!

Why had he recommended her company to his father? As a means of making some kind of amends, or was his reasoning more subtle? Could he have guessed how she felt about him? Did he perhaps want to add to her torment? Why should he, she asked herself, but then why should he have deliberately allowed her to believe he was connected with the escort agency; why had he allowed her to think he was virtually penniless; why had he made love to her when Kelly had seen with her own eyes that there was someone else in his life? Pride prevented her from demanding answers to these questions, the same pride that had forced her into agreeing to accompany him this morning.

'Feeling all right?'

He turned quickly, catching her off guard and the dizzy weakness that filled her when he smiled told Kelly the real reason she had come with him. She still loved him!

'Kelly, are you all right?'

His voice sharpened and just for a moment Kelly allowed herself to think he might actually be concerned about her, quickly banishing the thought as she realised how improbable it was.

'I'm fine,' she told him huskily. 'How long does the flight take?'

'Twenty minutes or thereabouts, depending on the weather. Mists like the one we're seeing today can delay things a little.'

'Tell me a little more about the island,' Kelly suggested, forcing herself to sound businesslike. 'How did it originally come into the hands of your family?'

'It was originally owned by a Scottish arm of the family who were wiped out by Cumberland shortly after Culloden. The island was given to my ancestors by King George out of gratitude for supporting him instead of Bonnie Prince Charlie—it's remained in our family ever since. It's said that the original building was erected when Mary, Queen of Scots returned to Scotland from France, by an ancestor of ours who had been there with her at court. The original watch tower was extended and embellished in what is almost typically Scottish/French—lots of turrets and towers, the same sort of embellishments favoured by the French at the time. In fact, in those days the Scots, or those of them who made up Mary's court, were considered far more civilised than their English neighbours. During some restoration work ten years or so ago some documents were found relating to various purchases made for the castle; tapestries, carpets, all very expensive luxuries in their time. One wonders where a Highland laird found the money for them. It's rumoured that he was one of Mary's favourites. Whether that's true or not I don't know, but he certainly married well—a rich French heiress, and it was his son who founded the English side of the family. He quarrelled with his father and ran away from home. He joined Drake, became a staunch Protestant and found favour in Elizabeth's court.'

'It must be fascinating to be able to trace your family back so far,' Kelly responded eagerly, forgetting caution and doubt as she listened to Jake. A streak of romanticism, deeply hidden during the years since Colin, suddenly surfaced, and her face was unknowingly alight as she begged Jake to tell her more.

'My father's the one to talk to if you want to hear about the family history. It's his hobby, and he devotes most of his spare time to it. I think he's found considerable solace in it these last few years since my mother died. They were very close.'

Suddenly Kelly felt tears sting her eyes; not so much for the words as for the expression on Jake's face; shuttered, aloof, as though he were deliberately excluding her from something private.

'When my father complains because I haven't provided him with any grandchildren yet, I remind him that he didn't marry until he was well into his thirties. My parents' marriage was one of the fortunate ones. They say if your parents are happily married it adds to your own chances of marital happiness. Perhaps because it makes you far more selective, more demanding both of your partner and yourself.'

Kelly didn't know what to say. Was this some subtle way of pointing out to her that she did not fulfil his requirements? A way of reminding her that she fell far short of his standards?

She regarded him levelly and forced a cool smile. 'You'll have to be careful you don't turn into a crusty old bachelor, then, won't you?'

Jake's soft, 'Oh, I don't think there's much chance of that,' tormented her long after he had lapsed into silence. Was the blonde girl she had seen him with on Corfu a prospective bride?

'If you look down now you'll catch a glimpse of Marne.'

Jake's voice interrupted her miserable reverie and obediently Kelly glanced out of her window, her stomach lurching uncomfortably as a sensation of giddiness swept her, her eyes registering a small patch of greeny-grey dotting the steel blue sea, before she tore her glance away.

Jake watched her shudder unsympathetically.

'What's the matter?' he teased. 'Don't you trust the pilot? You know your trouble, Kelly?' he added sardonically. 'You've forgotten how to trust.'

'Perhaps it's just as well,' Kelly retorted bitterly. She had trusted him, hadn't she, and look where that had got her. She had even been ready to commit herself to him completely; to share with him everything she possessed; her money, the company. That was a laugh; compared with his wealth hers was a mere nothing, and yet he had deliberately let her believe that he was poor.

'If you suffer from vertigo, you'd better close your eyes now,' Jake warned as the small plane started to dip. 'The airfield is tiny, which is why we're using this particular type of plane. There's nothing to worry about,' he reassured her with a grin. 'It can land on a postage stamp—almost!'

Kelly felt the pilot was almost intent on proving the veracity of Jake's statement when she saw the tiny triangle below which Jake assured her was the airfield. As they dropped lower she had her first glimpse of the castle—not gaunt and severe as she had imagined, but delicate, sculptured out of stone, into a fairytale confection of turrets and towers, gilded by the sun suddenly breaking through the mist.

The tiny airfield was deserted. Jake stepped nimbly out of the plane and waited for Kelly to follow, helping her down, the touch of his hand on her arm electrifying, her body pulsing hotly from the point of contact.

'Okay, John, you can pick us up this afternoon,' Jake told the pilot laconically. 'Say four o'clock. That should give us enough time to see everything. There's a Land Rover in the shed over here,' he told Kelly, directing her gaze to the building at the edge of the airfield. 'Come on.'

As they walked towards it Kelly heard the plane taxiing for take-off and turned automatically to watch it.

'Where is everybody?' she queried as Jake pulled

open the door of the rough stone building he had referred to as a 'shed'.

'What do you mean, "everybody"?' He eyed her sardonically. 'The island is uninhabited now— "everybody" is you and me, and we're both here.'

'You mean we're alone here?' Kelly asked.

'My, my, how Victorian you sound!' Jake mocked. 'What's the matter, Kelly? Not as sure of your ground here as you were on Corfu, is that it?'

Before she could query what he meant, he had disappeared inside the hut, and was opening the door to a rather battered Land Rover.

'The island hasn't been inhabited for the last twenty years. It's too small to support enough livestock to bring anyone a decent living. There used to be a few crofters, but the children drifted away when they left school and eventually the others either left or died. That's one of the reasons why my father is so keen on this luxury recreational hotel idea. He reckons the island could provide a decent golf course. There's sea-fishing and a small inland loch; there's a grouse moor, although it's sadly denuded of birds at the moment. Someone comes over from the mainland once a week to check the place over; turn on the heating and give it an airing, that sort of thing, but my father wants to see it lived in.

'Come on, get in,' he ordered, opening the passenger door, and numbly Kelly went to join him.

There was no reason why the fact that they were the only two inhabitants of the island should unnerve her so much; it wasn't even as though they were intending to spend the night there, and even if they were she was perfectly safe from Jake. Her face burned as she remembered her response to his lovemaking, the unexpected sensuality he had revealed to her when he touched her.

It took just over ten minutes to drive to the castle. They entered it via a raised portcullis, driving into what had once been the keep but was now a garden with open cobbled spaces and a quantity of heathers and clumps of saxifrage.

'This garden was my mother's,' Jake explained curtly as he parked the Land Rover on the cobbles. 'She and my father lived here for a few years and then her brother, my uncle, was killed in a sailing accident one summer. After that, she couldn't bear to live here any longer.'

'You must have missed all this.' Kelly's glance encompassed the beauty of the cream stone, timelessly elegant, a child's dream; but Jake shrugged.

'I was away at boarding school most of the time. My parents moved to London. It was more convenient for my father's business interests. It's only been in these last few years that our petro-chemical interests have made moving our head office to Edinburgh a viable proposition.

'I'll show you over the place, and then we'll drive round the island, let you get the feel of it.'

'Jake, why did you suggest us—me—to your father for this, and I know you must have done?' Kelly continued, not letting him interrupt, 'because in his terms we're a very small concern indeed. I doubt he would even have heard of us.'

Jake didn't bother to deny her comment and Kelly shivered in the cold breeze which had sprung up suddenly, wishing she hadn't asked the question.

'Why?' he said harshly at last. 'For God's sake, Kelly, use your imagination! It shouldn't be hard to guess.'

He was gone before she could retort, striding across the cobbles and flinging open the arched oak door, heavily studded, and creaking in the authentic matter.

What did he mean, 'use your imagination'? Did he mean she ought to be able to guess that he was making some form of atonement, an apology without words, but that wasn't borne out by his behaviour which had swung from coldly cynical to barely restrained anger ever since they had met in the foyer to his office. He had known she was coming to Edinburgh; he had been prepared for their confrontation, whereas she . . .

She shivered again, telling herself that she mustn't allow herself to get caught in the same trap twice. This time she had no excuse; this time she knew that Jake wasn't interested in her as a person and never had been. At best she had merely been a 'specimen', an outdated freakish object in these permissive times, but he had been surprised when she told him that she was still a virgin and his lovemaking had been tender, or so she had thought at the time.

A gust of wind caught the open door, swinging it back with a bang. Kelly jumped, realising that she was alone in the courtyard. Telling herself firmly that she was here to do a job, and nothing else, she followed Jake into the house.

*

'And this is the Georgian wing,' Jake said drily, 'added by the same ancestor who was given the island by King George. He couldn't get a London architect up here, so he made do with a man from Edinburgh who had studied under Vanbrugh, and was by all accounts mightily pleased with the result.'

They were standing in a panelled library with uniform windows overlooking formal gardens.

'He wanted to knock down the original castle walls and give himself a better prospect, but his architect warned him that if he did, he'd be looking at barren earth. This side of the island catches the weather. Without the protection of the stone wall very little would grow.'

Privately, Kelly thought the formal garden was delightful. There was something very attractive about a walled garden, she decided, moving closer to the window. Perhaps because in her mind a walled garden was still connected with *The Secret Garden* which she had loved as a child. Modern-day educationalists probably didn't approve of such reading for children, she thought wryly, but she had certainly enjoyed it.

'We'd better take that drive now, I think,' Jake said behind her. 'The mist seems to be coming down again.'

Kelly hadn't noticed it, but he was right. The horizon was gradually blurring and she shivered, although in actual fact the library was quiet and warm.

'My father wanted you to see as much of the island as possible. No, we'll go out this way,' said

Jake, suddenly checking her as she turned towards the door.

His hand on her arm restrained her, her pulses thudding hectically, but Jake seemed unaware of her reaction as he indicated another door she hadn't seen. It led into a passage which brought them out at the back of the castle in the old and now deserted stable block.

'These buildings are soundly built and my father believes they can be converted into guest rooms.'

'But you don't agree with him?' Kelly said shrewdly.

'Well, let's say I had grown accustomed to thinking this place would be my home.'

'It still can be surely, if you marry,' said Kelly, remembering what he had told her.

'Mmm. You seem to like the house. How about taking me on with it?'

'The house I would enjoy, but you most definitely not,' Kelly lied quickly, bending her head so that he wouldn't see the betraying colour storming her cheeks. Her hand shook weakly as she reached for the door handle, but she was determined not to let him see how much his mocking comment had hurt.

'Why?' Jake almost snarled the word, his violence startling her, somehow intensified by the heavy mist pressing in on them. 'Because I remind you too much of Colin?' His mouth twisted. 'There's one regard in which I'm not like him, Kelly,' he told her brutally, the breath leaving her lungs on a painful gasp as he reached for her, fingers biting deeply into her arms as he held her against the length of his body, his mouth burning hotly against hers as he muttered, 'and that's this. He might not have wanted to touch you, but I damned well do!'

His mouth seemed to burn where it touched, her body on fire with an answering need, her fingers locking behind his neck, her heart thudding against the hard wall of his chest as he kissed her throat, the delicate shell of her ears, her eyelids, closed in mute ecstasy, and then the trembling softness of her lips, tracing their outline with his tongue, tasting them slowly like a connoisseur, before the harsh groan of his indrawn breath sent a shivering response through her, and they parted instinctively beneath the hungry pressure of Jake's.

An aeon, or was it only seconds, passed. Kelly was oblivious to everything but the possession of Jake's mouth, the controlled tension in his body which told her how much he wanted her. He broke the kiss, cupping her chin, his breathing harsh and ragged in the misty silence as he stared down at her.

'You want me, Kelly,' he said unsteadily, staring down at her. 'No matter what you told Benson, you want me.'

Kelly felt sick, instinctively pulling away. She might have told Jeremy in an effort to protect herself that she didn't want Jake, indeed she couldn't remember now what she had told Jeremy, but Jake had obviously seen her words as some sort of challenge. Waves of nauseous shivering racked her. This was how Colin had looked at her in those moments before he pushed her aside in disgust; angry and aroused, determined to force her to submit to him. Men hated being challenged where their sexuality was concerned, she should have remembered that.

'No!'

The sound was torn from her throat and she rushed headlong from the stableyard, not caring nor aware of where she was going. The gardens gave way to rugged hillside and scrub, the mist a thick wet blanket penetrating the cord jeans and warm jumper she was wearing. Behind her, she could hear Jake calling, but he sounded so angry that the sound of his voice only incited her to run faster. The ground rose sharply, and Kelly stumbled, catching her foot on a tussock of grass and falling heavily, the breath knocked out of her lungs, so that she was still lying on the damp hillside, fighting for breath, when Jake found her.

'Are you crazy?' he demanded roughly. 'You don't know a damned thing about the terrain here, you can't see more than a yard in front of you. You could have killed yourself! What the hell was all that about anyway?'

'I should have thought it was obvious,' Kelly managed icily between gulps of air. 'I didn't want you to touch me.'

'So you keep saying,' Jake agreed brutally, 'but your body says different. Can you manage to walk back to the castle? I'd carry you, but you don't want me touching you, do you?' he said sarcastically, glancing around as he straightened up. 'I think we're going to have to abandon our tour of the island. This mist is coming in fast and we wouldn't be able to see a thing.'

'Will the pilot be able to land?' Kelly asked. Her

teeth were chattering, her body shocked and cold.

'What's the matter? Afraid of being alone with me?'

'Certainly not,' Kelly retorted coldly. 'It's just that I told my office I'd be returning to London tonight.'

'No problem,' Jake assured her. 'If John can't land, he'll radio a message to us, and I'll have him radio one on to your office. Simple.'

With every step back to the castle the mist seemed to thicken. Kelly felt as though every bone in her body had been jarred by her fall. She ached in a thousand places and seriously doubted that she would have been able to find her way back without Jake. The mist cast an eerie atmosphere round the castle and she found herself shivering as Jake held open the main door.

'If you can wait half an hour I'll get the generator going and you can have a hot bath,' Jake told her laconically. 'You're soaked through.'

The mist hadn't penetrated his soft leather jacket, and Kelly wondered balefully if he had known what the weather was going to be like before they left Edinburgh. If so, he might have warned her. Her jumper seemed to have absorbed the damp rather than resisted it, clinging to her like a cold wet blanket.

'I'll pour you a drink and then I'll go and see about the generator,' Jake told her, walking her towards the library. A fire had been laid in the hearth and he knelt down, setting a match to it. 'Angus comes over every week to check the place over, and fortunately always leaves the fires ready.' He wanted for a few seconds until he was sure that the wood had caught, then got up lithely, walking towards one of the cupboards.

'Drink this,' he commanded, pouring some amber liquid into a heavy crystal tumbler. 'It's whisky,' he told Kelly when she stared at him rebelliously. 'Not enough to do you any harm, if that's what's worrying you, but it should take the chill off. Here.'

She took the glass, unnerved to discover how much her hands were shaking.

'Stay here by the fire, I won't be long,' Jake told her, watching her dispassionately for a few seconds before heading for the door. After it had closed behind him Kelly was startled to discover that she had been holding her breath. With Jake gone some of the tension drained out of her body, leaving it aching even more than before. Despite the whisky she was still cold, her jumper a wet soggy mass that seemed to clasp her with icy fingers, preventing her from gaining any benefit either from the fire or the whisky.

The lure of the flames proved too much and she inched nearer to their warmth, glancing anxiously at the door before tugging the wet jumper over her head and placing it on the hearth. She would hear Jake coming long before he reached the library— plenty of time for her to pull her jumper on again, and at least in the meantime she could have the benefit of the fire's warmth.

Gradually the blood seemed to seep back into her frozen body. Lulled by the warmth of the fire and the potency of the whisky, Kelly leaned back against a footstool. Jake had been gone longer than she had expected. Perhaps the generator was proving troublesome, she decided drowsily, barely aware that her eyes were closing.

When Jake opened the door she was soundly asleep, her skin gleaming silkily in the firelight. She didn't stir as he approached, the harsh planes of his face softening slightly as he watched her. He crouched down beside her, saying her name softly, his fingers tracing a line down her back.

Kelly opened her eyes, too comfortable and warm to move. She had been having the most wonderful dream. She had dreamed she was with Jake, in his arms. She sighed, stiffening as she realised where she was and that she wasn't alone, shock rippling through her as she realised part of it at least hadn't been a dream. She was in Jake's arms, her head pillowed against his chest, his fingers stroking softly along her spine. Her jumper! She stared helplessly at the hearth, cursing herself for falling asleep.

'Jake?'

'Don't talk,' he commanded thickly. 'Don't spoil it, Kelly.'

She was aware of him bending his head, of his lips against the back of her neck, awakening sensations she had tried to forget ever since she had returned from Corfu. His mouth moved downwards, lingering on each vertebra. Kelly felt him unfasten her bra, his hands cupping her breasts. Her body shook as she tried to withdraw, to cut herself off from the emotions his touch aroused, but it was too late; her body, weak and treacherous was already responding, overruling the dictates of her mind, and she was twisting in Jake's arms clinging wordlessly to him as his hands stroked over her body and it surrendered mindlessly to the pleasure of his touch.

'God knows how I've wanted this,' Jake muttered hoarsely against her throat, his hands on the waistband of her jeans, 'and you've wanted it to, Kelly, no matter how much you might try to deny it.'

She was past doing that; past doing anything but responding feverishly to his touch, her lips exploring the warm column of his throat, her body thrilling to the harsh sound of pleasure her touch elicited. And it was Jake who threw aside his jacket, ruthlessly tugging at buttons as he wrenched open his shirt, drawing Kelly down against him as he rolled on to the floor, placing her hands inside his shirt against the tangle of crisp hair darkening his chest.

His flesh tasted faintly salty against her tongue and Kelly shivered in pleasure as she felt his shuddered response, barely aware of him removing her jeans, totally engrossed in her delicate exploration of his body.

When Jake cupped her breasts, kissing the aroused peaks gently, desire cramped through her, her fingers curling into the waistband of his jeans as she fought to control her breathing, terrified of what her response might reveal to him, but it didn't seem to be enough to stop her from shaking like someone with a fever. And then she realised it was Jake who was shaking, his eyes dark with a passion which stirred her own senses, the brush of his tongue against her nipples making her abandon restraint.

He moved, rolling her underneath him, tugging

impatiently at his jeans, muttering something hoarsely under his breath, before he abandoned the attempt, guiding her hands to complete the task, his heart thudding against her like a sledge-hammer, making her own blood beat equally frantically.

His belly felt flat and hard, her tentative caresses eliciting a response that made Kelly ache with a need she had suppressed ever since her return from Corfu, only now she wasn't unknowing and inex-perienced and her responses were those of a woman, deeply desirous of a man intensely loved. The touch of Jake's fingers against her thigh in-voked a husky moan of protest, but he seemed not to hear, bending his head to savour the aching tips of her breasts, her whole body acutely attuned to his touch.

'Kelly, I'm not Colin.' His voice was slurred, his breathing raw and jagged, his mouth lifting from her breasts to her throat, her thighs parting instinc-tively as he moved against her, their hearts thud-ding in unison until the sound seemed to reverber-ate through the silence of the room.

Jake tensed, lifting his head, and then glanced at his watch. 'Damn,' he swore huskily. 'That's John back with the plane!'

Kelly pulled away, the spell woven by their love-making broken by the intrusion, reality crashing down on her as she reached hurriedly for her jumper.

'You wanted me, Kelly,' Jake told her harshly, as though he read her mind and wanted to impose upon it for all time his knowledge of her weakness.

She could have retorted that he had wanted her,

but men could want without love, women could not. As she pulled on her jumper she wondered what would have happened if she hadn't run away, hadn't got wet, hadn't taken her jumper off and then fallen asleep—and yet deep down inside, part of her refused to regret it; only that they had been interrupted when they had! In his arms, the fact that he had lied to her, made a fool of her, had meant nothing, and the knowledge of how easily her pride gave way to her love shocked and frightened her.

CHAPTER TEN

'OKAY, so it was too misty to see the island, but couldn't you have gone back? One or two of us are getting concerned, Kelly—both about you and the future of the company. Things aren't looking so good. We're in the middle of a recession and naturally enough the first thing people cut down on are the luxuries: the PR work and advertising. That contract was something we needed!'

Kelly stared disbelievingly at her oldest and most senior fellow director. Alan had said nothing to her of this when she left for Edinburgh. It was true that things were a little difficult at the moment, but surely nowhere near as serious as he was intimating?

'Look, Kelly, perhaps some of the blame lies with us. A few of us have seen what's coming, but we haven't wanted to worry you. In the last month we've had four cancellations—three while you were away in Corfu.'

Picking up the implied criticism Kelly replied drily, 'That was my first holiday in two years, Alan, but I take your point, even though I don't agree that you were right to conceal things from me. But now I do know we'd better call a board meeting to see how best we can put things right.'

'If they can be put right,' Alan Cormont said gravely. 'I don't want to be a wet blanket, Kelly, but I think we've a tough time ahead of us, the only consolation—if it is a consolation—is that we won't be alone.

'You look tired,' he added with belated consideration, his voice suddenly gruff as he added, 'You haven't seemed yourself for a while now, Kelly—ever since you came back from Corfu, in fact. Nothing wrong, is there?'

If only he knew! Kelly thought bitterly. She had left Edinburgh almost immediately the pilot had put down after the short flight back from the island, endured in a cold, gripping silence which left her too much time to think; to wonder what had possessed her, and worse, what Jake must have thought of her wildly abandoned response to him.

They had parted with brief, conventional words, and her heart had felt like a lump of lead in her chest ever since her return. And now Alan was berating her for not working harder to get the contract—a contract it seemed her company badly needed. The company, once the totally absorbing *raison d'être*, had taken second place in her life. She was worried about it, naturally, but nothing like to the extent she would once have been.

The headache which had been hovering all morning struck ferociously after lunch—a sandwich, eaten hurriedly at her desk and washed down with cold coffee—and on impulse Kelly decided to go home. She would worry just as efficiently there, she decided drily, gathering her bag and papers.

She was crossing Bond Street when she felt the hand on her shoulder. As she spun round quickly, her first thought was that someone was about to snatch her bag, but instead she found herself looking into the smiling face of the girl she had last seen at Corfu Airport with Jake.

'I thought it was you,' the girl exclaimed eagerly. 'I hope you don't mind me stopping you like that. You may not remember me—Corfu, a party . . .'

'Yes, yes, I do remember you,' Kelly told her. Her lips felt like cottonwool, her mouth unpleasantly dry as she tried to form the words without letting her lips tremble. 'You were . . . talking to Jake.'

'Yes, he was pouring out his troubles to me,' she agreed with a grin. 'Quite a role reversal! Look, have you got time for a cup of tea? I'm Lyn, by the way. I've heard all about your visit to Edinburgh from Uncle Richard and I'm dying to know what happened. Oh, I know you must think it frightfully inquisitive of me—but you see, it was me who told Jake not to give up. I was pretty sure you cared for him. A woman can always tell better than a man, can't she, and I was over the moon when my godfather, Uncle Richard, wrote to say that Jake had persuaded him to get you up there on some pretext or other. Oh . . .' She stared uncertainly at Kelly, who was motionless on the pavement, her face totally devoid of colour. 'Oh dear, have I said something wrong? You see,' she rushed on, 'I was so sure you loved Jake, despite what he told me. Oh . . .'

'I think that cup of tea was a good idea,' Kelly interrupted firmly, trying to gather her wildly disordered thoughts.

They found a small café off Bond Street, blessedly quiet after the lunch-time rush, and Kelly ordered for them, wondering as she did so if she was going mad, or had simply stepped into some sort of Looking Glass world.

'Now,' she said quietly when they had been served, 'let's start at the beginning. I saw you in Corfu, with Jake.'

'*With* Jake? You mean you thought Jake and I . . . Oh, no wonder you wouldn't have anything to do with him! Jake is almost an older brother to me. His father is my godfather and Jake has been marvellous, always helping me out of jams, you know . . . I got heavily involved with someone last year, I won't go into details, but when it all fell apart Jake was there to help me pick up the pieces. Every time we meet I always tease him, you know, ask him if he's met "the One" yet. This time he said "yes".' Lyn looked at Kelly. 'He told me how you'd met—all about you thinking he worked for the escort agency—oh, you mustn't mind, he let something slip by accident and I dragged the rest out of him. What a joke! I told him it was high time he realised how ordinary mortals live. Because his father is so rich a lot of women see him as a good catch, you know. I wanted him to introduce us, but he said he didn't want to panic you. He told me you didn't share his feelings.' She pulled a face and glanced hesitantly at Kelly. 'I thought differently, and I told him so. I was leaving Corfu in the morning and Jake promised to see me off. I told him then not to give up. He rang me a couple of weeks ago, and I asked him about you then. He told me things hadn't worked out. He was using that voice that says don't dare ask anything more, but I told him he was a fool if he let you go so easily. Was I right?'

Kelly managed a wan smile. 'Right and wrong,' she said shakily. 'Are you sure that . . .'

'That he loves you?' Lyn rolled her eyes heavenwards and laughed. 'Straight from the horse's mouth,' she confirmed. 'You know what Jake's like, close as the grave when he wants to be, but he did admit that he was worried about your reaction to the discovery that he wasn't some out-of-work actor and that he'd deliberately deceived you.' She grinned reminiscently. 'He actually unbent enough to admit to me that he fell in love with you on sight. He was just about to tell you that the agency had closed down and that he'd taken over the offices when he realised that if he did you would probably walk out of his life. He told me it was the most impulsive thing he's ever done.' She gave a gurgle of laughter. 'Poor Jake, you've certainly given him a run for his money! Not that it will do him any harm. Much as I love him there's no doubt about it—so far Jake hasn't had to try very hard when the feminine sex is concerned. But here I am prattling on without giving you a chance to say a word!

'Everything went well in Edinburgh and Jake got a chance to put his case. When he saw me off at the airport, he was so withdrawn and worried that I didn't want to ask him if he told you the truth.'

'When he was telling you about the agency,' Kelly asked her slowly, 'was anyone else with you?'

The other girl frowned. 'No. We were by the pool at the time, people all around us but no one actually with us—why?'

Perhaps something of her confiding manner had rubbed off on her, Kelly thought wryly, half amused and half alarmed by her own need to admit her doubts.

'It's just that a friend of mine told me that Jake had told him the truth; had in fact boasted of how he'd deceived me quite deliberately, and how . . .' Kelly fought to steady her voice, 'how amusing it would be to . . .'

'No! None of that's true,' Lyn cut in ruthlessly. 'I know Jake. He would never do anything like that. I'm not saying he can't be pretty miffy when the mood takes him, but he's never cruel or vicious. He's too male a man for that. But surely Jake himself explained . . .'

'I left Corfu on the same plane as you,' Kelly told her levelly.

'Oh, you mean you don't love Jake? I've really gone and put my foot in it, haven't I?' Lyn groaned.

'I do love him,' Kelly admitted huskily, 'and that was one of the reasons why I left. You see, I thought you and he—and then . . .'

'But you went to Edinburgh,' she interrupted.

'Yes,' Kelly agreed on a sigh. Was this girl right? Did Jake love her? According to the younger girl he had admitted as much to her, and Kelly knew enough of Jeremy to guess that he could have overheard their conversation and twisted it to his own ends. He was bitter and envious enough to have found pleasure in lying to her, but Jake? Why hadn't he come after her when she left Corfu? Why had he waited so long and gone to such lengths to get her to Edinburgh? And he had been so bitter. There were too many ends that just didn't tie up, Kelly thought, chewing at her bottom lip, but she already had an idea where she could unravel some of them.

'Look, do you mind if I rush off?' she asked quickly. 'There's someone I have to see.'

'And Jake?'

'Er . . .'

'He's due to arrive in London tomorrow. He has an apartment in the new Hartland block—more of a penthouse really. I was going to have dinner with him, but I can't make it.'

'I'll have to go,' Kelly told her, 'but thanks for telling me . . . everything.'

'Jake would probably kill me if he knew. I can't understand why he hasn't told you himself.'

'Perhaps he's decided he doesn't love me after all,' Kelly suggested in a shaky voice.

Lyn shook her head vigorously. 'No way,' she laughed. 'He loves you all right and, knowing Jake, it's a forever kind of love. That's the way he is.'

Jeremy's secretary answered the phone, putting Kelly through within seconds, and Jeremy's voice oozed satisfaction and self-esteem as he murmured her name.

'Has Sue been in touch?' he asked her. 'She's pregnant again, but this time the doc has told her to take things easy. I'm staying in town during the week to take some of the pressure off her.'

'Bully for you,' Kelly muttered sardonically under her breath. 'Look, Jeremy,' she told him curtly, 'I have to see you. There's something I want to ask you.'

'Well, well, and to think I thought you were never going to get round to it!'

Kelly had to grit her teeth to stop herself from bursting the bubble of self-assurance that surrounded him.

'Your place or mine?' Jeremy asked her.

'Neither,' Kelly told him, thinking quickly. 'What about the Savoy Bar?'

As she had suspected, Jeremy leapt at the suggestion of meeting her somewhere so prestigious and she managed not to retort when he said smoothly, 'Oh, of course, I was forgetting, it all goes down to expenses, doesn't it?'

'Look, Jeremy, do you want to meet me or not?' Kelly demanded, forcing herself to hold on to her temper.

'I'll meet you.'

Ten past seven. Kelly glanced impatiently at her watch. Where was Jeremy? Five minutes later she saw him walk into the bar, stopping to preen in the mirror. As different from Jake as chalk from cheese. Kelly felt a familiar stab of pity for her friend combined with contempt for Jeremy.

'Ah, there you are.' He bent his head and, guessing that he intended to kiss her, she sidestepped swiftly.

'This isn't a social occasion, Jeremy,' she said crisply. 'At least, not entirely. Cast your mind back to our holiday in Corfu if you will.'

She watched him frown as the waiter took their order and waited for him to leave before continuing. 'At that time you told me that you'd discovered that Jake had lied to me, pretending to work for an escort agency, while all the time he was an extremely wealthy man. You intimated that I represented some sort of challenge to him.'

'So?' Jeremy was watching her sulkily.

Kelly studied her drink for a few seconds. Her heart was thudding heavily—so much depended now on the gamble she was taking.

'So what, I wonder, did you tell Jake about me?'

She knew immediately that she had been right to gamble and that Jeremy had indeed said something to Jake.

'Oh, come on, Jeremy,' she pressed home her advantage. 'When Jake returned from the airport and found I'd gone he must have asked you where and why.'

'He may have said something,' Jeremy agreed. 'I told him we weren't your keepers. Sue was pretty upset—too upset to talk to him really, what with you rushing off.'

'So what did you say to Jake? Did you tell him I wasn't interested in him?' Kelly demanded, making a wild stab in the dark. 'Did you, Jeremy?' she demanded fiercely, watching the muscle twitch in his jaw and the nervous tic beneath his eye.

'He was like a madman,' Jeremy admitted sullenly, 'demanding to know where you were, what we'd said to you. I told him it was nothing to do with us.'

'Did you tell him what you said to me before I left?' Kelly asked sweetly.

Jeremy's face told her the answer.

'I ought to hate you, Jeremy, but you're simply not worth the effort. Poor Sue! What on earth has she done to be landed with a contemptible creep like you?'

'Bitch,' Jeremy muttered thickly. 'He's welcome to you!' He slammed his glass down and got up, shouldering his way through the press at the bar, leaving Kelly alone.

Jake was welcome to her, he had said, but did Jake still want her? Could she believe what Lyn had told her? Did she have the courage to believe it?

There was only one way to find out, she decided, getting up. She only hoped that her courage wouldn't fail her!

'Well, another day over.'

Kelly smiled at her assistant. 'Mmm.'

Darting Kelly a curious glance, the other girl started to tidy her desk. Kelly had been preoccupied all day, and yet there was an air of suppressed excitement about her, a glow that she hadn't seen before.

'Going anywhere tonight?' she asked idly as she headed for the door.

'Er . . . I may be.'

Would this outfit do? Kelly wondered, staring at herself in her full-length mirror. She had changed twice since getting home, delaying tactics even if they were heavily disguised, and now suddenly the outfit she was wearing, a silk dress in a pretty pastel pink which suited her colouring, over which she was wearing a soft silver silk jacket, seemed too dressy for a casual visit, but it was too late to change again. It was already after eight and if she left it much longer Jake might have gone out.

It took every ounce of courage she possessed to get in the taxi and give the driver Jake's address.

The huge office block looked cold and unwelcoming, the last batch of cleaners leaving as Kelly walked in.

A lift took her to the top floor, the doors opening on to a pale grey expanse of carpet and a curt sign reading 'Penthouse—private.'

Licking her dry lips, Kelly stepped out, crossing the carpet to ring the bell set into the marble wall.

An aeon seemed to pass before she heard any sound of movement, and as she heard the door chain rattle she had to fight down an urge to turn and flee. Panic filled her. What if she was wrong? What if Jake didn't want her? But it was too late now, the door was opening and she had a glimpse of Jake's towelling-clad back disappearing down a corridor as he called over his shoulder, 'Late as usual, Lyn! Come on in, then.'

With a tremendous sense of anticlimax Kelly followed him inside, closing the door behind her. Jake didn't stop walking until she had followed him into a huge living room, furnished in starkly masculine colours and shapes, greys and blues predominating.

'Sit down, then,' he commanded. 'I thought you weren't coming.'

'Did you, Jake?'

Her voice arrested his hand on its way to the decanter. He stiffened and straightened slowly, his face dark and inscrutable as he turned to look at her.

'Kelly?'

'I . . . I ran into Lyn the other day and . . .'

Oh heavens, she was making a complete mess of this! Why on earth had she mentioned Lyn? She could see Jake's face closing on her, his eyes hard and unreadable as he said hardly, 'I don't know that misplaced sense of pity brought you here, Kelly, but I don't need it. You know where the front door is,' he added curtly. 'Do us both a favour and use it.'

She wanted to cry out at the pain his words brought, stabbing a thousand needle-sharp wounds in her heart.

'Jake, please,' she whispered huskily.

'Jake, please what?' he mimicked harshly.

She couldn't ask him if it was true that he loved her; not in cold blood with him standing opposite her as an enemy. She was turning to leave when a tiny inner voice urged her not to give in, not to be so fainthearted. This was her whole life at risk and the quality of the happiness she would find in it.

'Jake, please answer me one question,' she managed calmly. 'Did you intimate at any time to anyone that you saw making love to me as a . . . a challenge?'

She could tell that her question wasn't what he had expected. His eyes narrowed and he watched her thoughtfully.

'Who told you that?' he asked at length.

Her mouth was dry with fear and tension. She longed to back down, but too much was at stake. She hadn't come all this way to take the coward's way out now.

'The same person who didn't explain to you why I'd left Corfu,' she told him evenly. 'Jeremy told me that he'd overheard you and Lyn talking. He deliberately misled me, allowing me to believe that you and Lyn were lovers.'

'Lovers?' Jake shook his head disbelievingly. 'But . . .'

'Jeremy played on my insecurities. He knew where to hurt me,' she admitted simply, taking a deep breath and holding it as she watched him levelly and said calmly, 'He knew I loved you.'

The silence lasted so long she began to despair, to think she had gambled everything and lost, and then Jake spoke, softly at first, and then more harshly as he demanded huskily, 'You loved me?'

Kelly nodded her head. 'And still do,' she admitted. 'Surely you could tell by . . . by the way I responded to you when you . . . when you made love to me?'

There was a huge lump in her throat, but she forced the words out, determined that she was not going to lose him this time by default. He might not love her, Lyn might be wrong, but she was still going to tell him the truth.

'That first day,' Jake said slowly, 'God—I was so furious with you! You walked into that office and it was like seeing a dream come to life. You were there, everything I'd always wanted, and then you started to talk. You hated men—that came across loud and clear, but you needed a man—an escort, so I jumped in with both feet. I wanted you so badly even then. Time enough later to tell you the truth, when I'd gained your confidence, but everything was so complicated. You'd been married—I thought you must still be deeply in love with your husband; and then there was Jeremy; and you kept throwing my poverty in my face. Ridiculously, I began to want you not just to love me, but to love me as you thought I was.'

'I did,' Kelly interrupted softly. 'Oh, I fought against it, but when we were in Corfu I forced myself to face the truth; that I loved and wanted *you*. That night I tried to tell you; I woke up wanting to tell you, wanting to admit to you that you mattered more than anything else. I was so happy . . .'

'That you ran away?'

'Jeremy told me who you really were; he laughed about it and said you had done too. Try to understand, it was more than my shaky self-confidence could take. I ran away. I saw you at the airport with Lyn and that just seemed to confirm everything Jeremy had told me.'

'Oh, Kelly! I ought to beat you for misjudging me so badly. You really love me?' He cupped her face in his hands, studying each feature.

'So very much,' Kelly told him softly. 'I hoped and prayed that you would come after me, explain . . . make everything all right . . .'

'Jeremy told me you never wanted to see me again. He said you told him I reminded you of Colin—you can imagine what that did to me. All of a sudden you weren't making love with me, you were consummating a marriage to someone else. I told myself I hated you, but I was lying. I managed to last out about a month before I gave in and persuaded my father to get you up to Edinburgh. I thought once I got you to myself on the island, we could work things out, I could prove to you that it was me you were responding to, not some shadow.'

'That was why you were so angry! I thought it was me—something I had said or done; I thought you must be laughing at me, knowing how I felt about you, and then I bumped into Lyn in London and she told me you loved me, and I couldn't believe it. I went to see Jeremy, guessing that if he'd lied to me he could well have lied to you as well. You were never a substitute for Colin,' she told him huskily. 'Everything I told you that night was true. I never really loved him, I've grown to see that over the years, but the scars he inflicted stopped me from making other relationships, from being able to trust, until I met you and I fell so hard that I couldn't help myself.'

'That's a very tempting admission,' Jake drawled, and Kelly was suddenly aware that all he had on was his robe, and that he was regarding her with a very disturbing glint in his eyes.

Her breathing suddenly changed, she murmured huskily, 'Meaning?'

'Meaning that for the first time since we've met I can hold you in my arms like this, without any deceit between us, and I can kiss you like this—' he bent his head, brushing her lips with his until she was clinging dizzily to his shoulders, her breath coming jerkily from half parted lips—'without feeling that you're thinking of Colin, or worse still, Jeremy. And I can touch you like this,' he muttered throatily, sliding his hands beneath the thin silk of her jacket, finding the full curves of her breasts and caressing them urgently as he drew her against his body, kissing her with feverish intensity, showing her without the need for words that everything Lyn had said was true.

'I love you, Kelly,' he told her thickly at last, releasing her throbbing mouth to trace a line of kisses downwards, slowly unfastening the tiny buttons closing her dress. 'So much that it's an ache in my guts. I fell in love with you on sight, and then you nearly destroyed me with your ice-cold reserve, but I knew there was a living, warm woman inside somewhere, and I was determined to find her.'

'And now that you have?' Kelly whispered, shivering delicately with the pleasure of his marauding mouth, tracing pathways over her breasts.

'Now that I have she isn't going to escape until she's promised to make an old man very happy—my father's heard all about you from Lyn and he says if I don't return to Edinburgh with you beside me, I can definitely forget about Marne *and* the chairmanship of the company. He admits that it's far harder to persuade a woman to change her mind than it is to run a company, but he says I'm not the right man to fill his shoes if I can't. Not that he's really thinking of vacating them—at least not until we provide him with a brace of grandchildren.

'Will you marry me, Kelly?' he asked roughly in a different tone. 'Will you?'

She raised herself on tiptoe, twining her arms round his neck, drawing his head down until she could reach his lips, murmuring her assent against them, feeling her body take fire from his as he tensed in response, letting her take the initiative until, with a groan, he pulled her tightly against him and her body melted into his, alive with the pleasure of the contact, revelling in the hardness of him against her without the barrier of his robe, her response urging him to swing her up in his arms and carry her—not to the bedroom, but to the fire, where the lamplight played revealingly over his features as he placed her carefully on the floor, bending tenderly over her as he drawled unsteadily, 'This time there aren't going to be any interruptions—I hope!'

'Well, they certainly won't come in the form of planes landing,' Kelly agreed with a chuckle. 'Oh, Jake,' she whispered urgently, 'love me, please love me!' She reached up to pull him down against her, revelling in the tenseness of his body, the fine film of perspiration dewing his skin, the hungry pressure of his mouth as it possessed hers, obliterating all that was past and welcoming the future.

PASSIONATE PROTECTION

BY
PENNY JORDAN

WORLDWIDE BOOKS
LONDON • SYDNEY • TORONTO

First published in Great Britain in 1983
Reprinted in Great Britain in 1992
by Worldwide Books, Eton House,
18-24 Paradise Road, Richmond, Surrey TW9 1SR

© Penny Jordan 1983

ISBN 0 373 58587 X

99-9205

Made and printed in Great Britain

CHAPTER ONE

'HONESTLY, Jess, I don't know what that family of yours would do without you,' Colin Weaver told his assistant with a wry smile. 'Well, what is it this time? Has your aunt locked herself out again, or your uncle forgotten to collect his new cheque book?'

'Neither,' Jessica Forbes told him, hiding her own smile. It was true that her aunt and uncle did tend to ring her at work for assistance every time there was a family crisis, but they weren't really used to the hectic pace of the modern-day commercial world—Uncle Frank, for instance, still lived in a pre-war daydream fostered by the leisurely pace of life in the small market town legal practice he had inherited from his father, and Aunt Alice wasn't much better; nervous, dithery, she was given to complaining in bewilderment that life had changed so much, she barely recognised it any more, and as for Isabel! Jessica sighed; the problems dumped on her by her eighteen-year-old cousin made those of her aunt and uncle seem mere nothings.

'Okay, okay, I'm sorry for criticising your beloved family,' Colin apologised with a wry smile. 'I suppose I'm just jealous really,' he admitted plaintively. 'Would you drop everything and come running for me if I locked myself out?'

'It wouldn't do any good if I did,' Jessica pointed out with a grin. 'You live in a penthouse apartment, my aunt and uncle live in a rambling old vicarage with a pantry window that simply won't close, but which neither of them can fit through, whereas yours truly . . .'

'Umm, I'm beginning to get the point,' Colin agreed, glancing appreciatively over her slender five foot eight frame, 'but that doesn't stop me from wishing they would stop depriving me of your valuable assistance.'

'I have to go this time—it's Isabel.' Jessica frowned, chewing the soft fullness of her bottom lip, dark eyebrows drawn together in a worried frown. The problem was that her aunt and uncle had been slipping gently into middle age when Isabel had arrived unexpectedly on the scene and neither of them had ever totally recovered from the shock.

'Oh, Isabel,' Colin said grimly. 'That girl's lethal,' he added with a grimace. 'I remember when you brought her here . . .'

'Here' was his exclusive London salon where he showed the alluring ranges of separates that bore his name. Jessica had worked for him ever since she left art school. She loved her job as his assistant, and if he needed mollycoddling occasionally, he more than made up for his lapses when they were over. In Jessica's view there was no one to match him in the design of separates. His secret, he had told her on more than one occasion, lay as much in the careful choice of fabric as the style the materials were eventually made up in. 'Couture Classics' were how *Vogue* described them, and Jessica reckoned there could be few wealthy women in Britain aspiring to the well-dressed lists who didn't have something of his in their wardrobe. For some clients he designed individual ranges, but it was, as Jessica knew, his great dream to take his designs and elegance into the high streets at prices every woman could afford.

'She is a little immature,' Jessica agreed, repressing a sigh at the thought of her cousin— pretty, headstrong Isabel, who reminded her of a frisky lamb, throwing herself headlong into whatever came her way on a momentary whim.

'She's exactly two years younger than you were when you first came to work for me,' Colin reminded her a little grimly. 'You all keep that girl wrapped up in too much cotton wool, Jess, you spoil her, and she laps it up. What were you doing at eighteen? I bet you weren't still living at home, financed by Mummy and Daddy?'

'No,' Jessica agreed sombrely. Her parents had died three months before her eighteenth birthday. They had been killed in a car crash on their way home from visiting friends. She could still remember Uncle Frank trying to break the news; Aunt Alice's white face. They had offered her a home, of course, but by then she had her career planned, first art school and then, she hoped, a job in fashion design, and so instead she had used some of the money left to her by her parents and had bought herself a small flat in London, but she had stayed in close contact with her aunt and uncle; after all, they were the only family she had left, and as she grew older the ties between them had strengthened. Family came to mean a lot when there was so little of it left.

Isabel had been a little girl of ten at the time of the accident, too young to remember very much about Jessica's parents, and somehow Jessica had found that as the years went by she was called upon to mediate between impatient youth and dismayed late middle age in the storms that swept the household as Isabel grew into her teens, Isabel urging her to support her on the one hand, while her parents were pleading with Jessica to 'make Isabel realise' on the other.

The plan was that Isabel would go on to university after leaving school, but in the sixth form she had suddenly decided that she was tired of studying, that she didn't want a career at all, and so at eighteen she was working in her father's office, and complaining bitterly to Jessica about it whenever they met.

'I wanted to talk to you about our visit to Spain as well,' Colin said sulkily, interrupting her train of thought. Jessica gave him a teasing smile. At forty-eight he could sometimes display all the very worst characteristics of a little boy in the middle of a tantrum, and he was not above doing so to make her feel guilty or get her attention when he felt the need arise. Jessica excused him on the grounds that he was a first-rate designer and an excellent employer, flexible and with sufficient faith in her ability to make her job interesting. The Fabric Fair was something he had been dangling in front of her for several months. Initially he had planned to go alone, and then he had suggested that she should go with him. He heard by word of mouth about a Spanish firm who had discovered a series of new dyes for natural fibres, and that the results were stunningly spectacular. Their fabrics were sold only to the most exclusive firms, and Jessica knew that Colin

was angling for an introduction to their Managing
Director.

'I don't know whether I'll be able to go,'
Jessica frowned, hiding a sudden shaft of
amusement as his manner changed from smug
satisfaction to anxious concern.

'Not that damn family of yours again!' he
protested. 'This time you'll have to tell them to
do without you. I need you, Jess,' he told her
plaintively.

'Very well, but no more unkind comments
about Isabel,' she reprimanded him severely. 'I
know she's a little headstrong . . .'

'Headstrong! Stubborn as a mule would be a
better description, but I can see nothing I have to
say is going to have any effect on you, so you may
as well finish early tonight.'

Colin really was a love, Jessica reflected fondly an
hour later, opening the door to her flat. They had
an excellent working relationship, and if she
sometimes chafed against his avuncular manner
it was a small price to pay for working with such
a talented and experienced man. There was no
one to follow him in the business, and he had
already mentioned that he might be prepared to
offer her a partnership if things went well. They
would make a good team, he had told her, and
Jessica agreed. In spite of his experience he
would always listen to her suggestions, and often
adopted them.

She grimaced at her reflection as she caught
sight of it in the mirror. She had hurried away
from the office without combing her hair or
renewing her lipstick, and both looked untidy;

her lipstick because she constantly nibbled on her lower lip, and her hair from running impatient fingers through its sable length.

Without doubt her hair was her greatest asset, in her eyes; long, thick and glossy, it fell smoothly past her shoulders in a gentle bell. Sometimes she twisted it into an elegant chignon, on those days when Colin wanted her to meet clients and she wanted to create the right impression. One of the bonuses of working for a well known designer was the fact that she got most of her clothes at cost; another was that her lissom shape and long legs were ideally suited to the subtle tweeds, silks and linens Colin preferred to use.

'I do love seeing my clothes on a real woman,' he had told her once, appreciatively. 'Models are caricatures of the female species, clothes-horses, the complete antitheses of the heavy county types who buy from me, but you ... You might have been made for them,' he had told her.

Isabel laughed about her cousin's employer. 'An old woman' was how she referred to him, and while it had traces of truth, Jessica chided her. Colin was shrewd and extremely talented, and while he might not be as charismatic as many of the men Jessica came into contact with, he was genuine, with a genuine love for his chosen career.

Another thing Isabel derided was Jessica's own fastidious reluctance to indulge in what she was pleased to term 'fun'.

'Fun' to Isabel encompassed a wholly idealistic impression of what it was like living alone in London. In Jessica's place there was no end to the 'fun' she might have, but unlike Jessica, who was footloose and fancy-free, she was tied to the boring old parents, and dull Merton with its farmers and relaxed pace of life.

After one or two attempts to correct her misapprehensions Jessica had acknowledged that her cousin had no intention of letting herself be disillusioned, and besides, Jessica's 'freedom' was a useful tool to wield against her parents when rebellion stirred. It had struck Jessica more than once lately that her aunt and uncle were beginning to look tired. Uncle Frank was talking about retiring, and Jessica sensed that in some ways it would be a relief to them when Isabel eventually married and someone else took on the responsibility of their rebellious daughter. But so far Isabel had shown no signs of wanting to marry, and why should she? Jessica reflected. In her opinion eighteen was far too young—or perhaps that was just one of the penalties of still being single at twenty-six; one became super-cautious of marriage, of the risks and dangers involved in making such an enormous commitment to another human being, and demanding so much from them in return.

Jessica was aware that Isabel had a far lighter approach to life than she did herself and would consequently probably have a much easier ride through life. She sighed, and chided herself for getting old and cynical as she showered quickly, barely sparing the briefest glance at the slender length of her body before draping it in a towel and padding into her bedroom.

Jeans and a tee-shirt would suffice for the drive down to her aunt and uncle's, and she pulled them on quickly, zipping up the jeans before brushing her hair with a swift economy of movement. Her skin was good, thank goodness, and she rarely used much make-up; less when she was 'off duty'. Her eyes were a tawny gold—an unusual combination with the satin sable hair, oval and faintly Oriental, adding a dash of piquancy to her features, even if she did lack Isabel's pretty pouting beauty.

It was just after eight-thirty when she turned her small car into the familiar road leading to the Vicarage. She frowned as she remembered her aunt's tearful telephone call. What on earth had Isabel done this time?

Silence greeted her as she stopped the car and climbed out. Nine o'clock was normally supper time, so she walked round to the back of the house, knowing she would find her aunt in the kitchen.

Alice James gave a small start, followed by a relieved smile as she saw her niece, enveloping her in a warm hug.

'Jess! You made it—oh, I hoped you would! We've been so worried!'

'Is Belle here?' Jessica asked her, pulling a stool out from under the kitchen table and perching comfortably on it. She knew from old how long it took to drag a story out of her aunt.

'No. She's out, with . . . with John Wellington, he's the young partner your uncle's taken on. Belle seems pretty keen on him.'

'And that's a problem?' Jessica enquired humorously, correctly reading the note of doubt in her aunt's voice. 'I thought this was what you'd been praying for for the last couple of years—that she'd find someone safe and steady and settle down.' She was still at a loss to understand the reason for her aunt's concern. 'Isn't that what you've always wanted for her? A nice safe marriage?' she prompted again.

'Everything we wanted for her,' her aunt confirmed. 'And now it's all going to be spoiled, because of that wretched holiday!'

'Holiday? What holiday?' Jessica asked, a frown creasing her forehead.

'Oh, it was several weeks ago. She wanted to go to Spain with a girl friend. John didn't want her to go—he's quite jealous—but you know what she's like. The very fact that he didn't only seemed to make her keener. Anyway, she went, and it was while she was there that it happened.'

'What happened?' Jessica asked patiently, quelling her rising dismay, her mind alive to all the fates that could befall a girl like her cousin, bent only on 'having a good time'.

'She got herself engaged—well, almost,' her aunt amended. 'To some Spanish boy she met over there. They've been writing to one another— none of us knew a thing about it, until she showed me his last letter. Jessica, what on earth are we going to do? She's as good as promised to marry John, and if he finds out about this . . .'

'Why should he?' Jessica asked practically, mentally cursing Isabel. Trust her to have two men dangling; she was all for the competitive spirit, Jessica acknowledged wryly. 'All she has to do is to write to this Spanish boy and simply tell him that it's over.' Privately she was surprised that Isabel's Spaniard had bothered to write; most of them made a hobby out of 'falling in love' with pretty tourists.

'She daren't. She's terrified that he'll come over here to find out what's happening, and then what on earth will she tell John?'

If Isabel didn't feel able to tell John the plain truth now, it didn't bode well for their marriage, was Jessica's private opinion, but she refrained from voicing it, practically deciding that her aunt's obvious distress was what needed her attention right now.

'Don't worry about it,' she soothed her. 'It will all be all right.'

'Oh, Jess, I knew you'd be able to sort it all out,' her aunt confided, promptly bursting into tears. 'I told Isabel you'd help.'

Jessica spread her hands ruefully. 'Of course, but I don't see what I can do . . .'

'Why, go to Spain, of course,' her aunt announced as though she were talking about a trip to the nearest town. 'You must go and see him, Jess, and explain that Isabel can't marry him.'

'Go to Spain?' Jessica stared at her. 'But, Aunt . . .'

'You were going anyway,' her aunt said hurriedly, avoiding her eyes, 'and you can speak Spanish, Jessica, you can explain to him in his own tongue, soften the blow a little. Think what it would do to Isabel if he were to come here. She genuinely cares for John, and I think he has the strength she needs.' She sighed. 'I sometimes think your uncle and I should have been stricter with her, but . . .' she broke off as the kitchen door suddenly burst open and a small, fair-haired girl hurried in. She stopped dead as she reached the table.

'Jess!' she exclaimed joyfully. 'Oh, you've come—thank goodness! Has Mum told you . . .'

'That you're being pursued by an ardent suitor? Yes,' Jessica told her cousin dryly. 'Honestly, Belle . . .'

'I really thought I loved him,' Isabel began defensively. 'He was so different from John, and it was all so romantic . . . Oh, there's no need to look like that!' She stamped her foot as Jessica raised her eyes heavenwards. 'It's different for you, Jess, you'd never get involved in anything like that, you're so sensible, so unromantic, but me . . '

Jessica winced a little as her cousin's unthinking comment found its mark. How often had she heard that comment 'You're so unromantic'? Every time she refused to go to bed with her escort? Every time she refused to get involved? And yet she had always thought secretly that she was too romantic; that her ideals were too high.

'You're really sure then about John?' Jessica questioned her cousin later in the evening when they were both preparing for bed.

'As sure as I'm ever likely to be,' Isabel told her with a rare flash of honesty. 'But it will spoil everything if Jorge decides to come over here to find out why I've stopped writing to him. You will go and see him, won't you, Jess?' she appealed. 'I don't think I could bear it if I lost John!'

There were tears in her eyes, and unwillingly Jessica felt herself giving way. She supposed it wouldn't hurt to try and see this boy while she was in Spain; even perhaps add a few days to the trip to make sure she did see him, although she was quite convinced that it was highly unlikely that he would turn up in England.

'But you don't understand,' Isabel wailed when she pointed this out to her. 'We were practically engaged. He will come over, Jess, I know he will!' She practically wrung her hands together in her fear, and Jessica, feeling immeasurably more than only eight years her senior, sighed.

'Well, I'll go and see him then, but honestly, Belle, I'm sure you're worrying unnecessarily.'

'You mean to tell me you actually agreed to go and see this impetuous Romeo on your cousin's behalf?' Colin expostulated three days later when she explained to him that she would like to add a couple of extra days' holiday to their trip to Spain. 'Can't she do her own dirty work?'

'Not in this case,' Jessica assured him, quickly outlining the facts. 'And of course, I do speak Spanish.'

In actual fact she spoke several foreign languages. They were her hobby and she seemed to have a flair for them.

'Well, I can see that nothing I can say is going to cure you of this protective attitude towards your family,' Colin admitted. 'All I can say is— thank God I don't have one!'

'And my extra days' holiday?'

'They're yours,' he agreed. 'Although I'd much rather see you spend them on yourself than squander them on young Isabel. She's a leech, Jess, and she'll suck you dry if you let her. You must see that, so why?'

'She's family,' Jessica said simply. 'She and my aunt and uncle are all I have left.'

Often she had wondered after her parents' shocking deaths if the accident had somehow not only robbed her of her mother and father, but her ability to love as well, because ever since then she had held the world at a distance, almost as though she was afraid of letting people get too close to her; afraid that she might come to depend on them and that she would ultimately lose them.

Seville was a city that appealed strongly to the senses. Jessica fell in love with it almost from the moment she stepped off the plane into the benevolent spring sunshine. Madrid was more properly the home of Spanish commerce, and Jessica had been there on several previous occasions, but Seville was new territory to her.

Initially she had been surprised when Isabel told her that Jorge lived in Seville; she had expected to find him somewhere on the Costa Brava, but Isabel had told her that Jorge had been holidaying like herself at the time they met.

Colin, running true to form, had insisted on her staying at the hotel the extra few days at his expense, and although Jessica had demurred, he had insisted, and in the end she had given way. Knowing Colin, the hotel he would have chosen would be far more luxurious than anything she could have afforded, and this supposition was proved correct when her taxi drew up outside an impressive Baroque building.

Her fluent Spanish brought a swift smile to the face of the girl behind the reception desk, and in no time at all she was stepping out of the lift behind the porter carrying her case and waiting while he unlocked the door to her room.

The hotel had obviously once been a huge private house, and had been converted tastefully and carefully. Jessica's room had views over the city; the furniture, although reproduction, was beautifully made and totally in keeping with the age and character of the room. There was a bathroom off it, rather more opulent than she would have expected in the hotel's British equivalent, a swift reminder that this part of the world had once been ruled by the Moors, who had left behind them a love of luxury and a sensuality that had been passed down through the generations.

Once she had unpacked Jessica went down to the foyer, where she had seen some guide books and maps on sale. The evening meal, as she was already aware, was the all-important meal in the Spanish home, and she wanted to make sure that her visit to Jorge did not clash with this.

As she had suspected, the receptionist was able to confirm that in Seville it was the general rule to eat later in the evening—normally about ten o'clock—which gave her the remainder of the afternoon and the early evening to make her visit, Jessica decided.

She had already formulated a plan of action. First she intended to discover if Jorge's family were listed in the telephone directory. If they were she would telephone and ask when she might call, if not she would simply have to call unannounced.

She lunched lightly in the hotel's restaurant—soup, followed by prawn salad, and then went up to her room to study the telephone directory. There were several Calvadores listed in the book, but none under Jorge's address, and Jessica was forced to the reluctant conclusion that she would simply have to call unannounced.

A call to the reception desk organised a taxi to take her to her destination. She showered and changed into soft jade green silk separates, from Colin's new range; a pleated skirt that swirled softly round her legs and a blouson top with full sleeves caught up in tight cuffs. The colour suited her, Jessica knew, and to complement it she brushed toning jade eye-shadow over her lids, thickening and darkening her lashes discreetly with mascara.

Soft kid sandals of jade, blue and cerise completed her outfit. It was warm enough for her to be able to dispense with a jacket, and she was just flicking a comb through the silken length of her hair when her phone buzzed and the receptionist announced that her taxi had arrived.

Because she spoke Spanish so well, Jessica had no qualms about giving the driver instructions herself, but she began to wonder if, after all, she had made some mistake, when they drove into what was obviously a very luxurious and exclusive part of the city. Imposing buildings lined the streets, here and there an iron grille giving a tantalising view of the gardens beyond. Fretworked balconies and shutters lured the eye, but Jessica was left with an overall impression of solitude and privacy strictly guarded, so that it was almost as though the buildings themselves seemed to resent her intrusion.

At last the taxi stopped, and rather hesitantly she asked him if he could return for her in half an hour. That surely would give her sufficient time

to explain the situation to Jorge? She only prayed
that he was in!

Quickly checking the address Isabel had
written down on the scrap of paper she had given
her, she climbed unsteadily out of the car and
glanced hesitantly at the imposing frontage of the
building. There was no need for her to feel
nervous, she reassured herself; the building,
impressive though its outward appearance was,
probably housed dozens of small apartments.
However, when she reached the top of the small
flight of stone steps there was simply one bell.
She pressed it and heard the faint ringing
somewhere deep in the recesses of the building.
An aeon seemed to pass before she heard sounds
of movement behind the large studded door.

Honestly, it was almost like something out of a
horror movie! she reflected as the door swung
back, creaking on its hinges.

The man who stood there had 'upper class
servant' stamped all over his impassive counte-
nance. He looked disapprovingly at Jessica for
several seconds and appeared to be on the point
of closing the door in her face when she babbled
quickly, 'My name is Jessica James and I've come
to see Señor Calvadores. Is he at home?'

The man seemed to consider her for an age
before grudgingly opening the door wide enough
for her to step into a hallway large enough to hold
her entire flat. The floor was tiled with the
famous *azulejo* tiles, so beautiful that she almost
caught her breath in pleasure. If only Colin could
see these! The colours were fantastic, shading
from softest blue to a rich deep azure.

'If the *señorita* will please wait,' the manservant

murmured, opening another door and indicating that Jessica was to precede him into the room. Like the hall, it was enormous, furnished in what she felt sure must be priceless antiques. Whoever Jorge was, he quite obviously was not a poor man, she reflected, gazing in awe at her surroundings.

'Señorita James?' he repeated slowly. 'I will see if *el Señor Conde* can see you.'

'*El Señor Conde!*' Jessica stared after his departing back. Isabel had said nothing to her about a title. What was the matter with her? she asked herself sardonically several seconds later; surely she wasn't impressed by something as outmoded as an inherited title? She, who had always despised those who fawned on the county and titled set, because of who they were rather than what they were!

She was lost in a deep study of a portrait above the fireplace—a Spanish don of the seventeenth century if she was any judge, formidable and with a magnetism that refused to be confined to the canvas—when she heard footsteps outside the door, firmer and far more decisive than the manservant's. She felt herself tense. Now that the moment was almost upon her she felt ridiculously nervous. What on earth was she going to say? How could she simply say baldly that Isabel no longer wanted him; and that in fact he was an embarrassment to her, now that she was on the verge of becoming engaged to another man.

The door opened and the man who stood there took her breath away. Her first impression was that he was impossibly arrogant, standing there staring down the length of his aristocratic nose at her, his lean jaw tensing, as though he was controlling a fierce anger. Ice-cold grey eyes flicked disparagingly over her, the aquiline profile inclining slightly in an acknowledgement of her presence, which was more of an insult than a courtesy.

He was tall, far taller than she had expected, his hair dark, sleek as raven's feathers, and worn slightly long, curling over the pure silk collar of a shirt she was sure had been handmade especially for him.

Everything about this man whispered discreetly of wealth and prestige, and never in a million years could Jessica imagine him holidaying on the Costa Brava and indulging in a holiday romance with her cousin.

For one thing, he must be almost twice Isabel's age—certainly in his early thirties—and nothing about him suggested the type of man who needed the admiration of a very young girl to boost his ego. This man did not need any woman; his very stance suggested an arrogant pride which would never admit to any need of any kind. He was the result of centuries of wealth and breeding of a type found almost exclusively in the great Spanish families, and Jessica felt her blood run cold at the thought of telling him that her cousin had decided she preferred someone else.

'Señorita James?'

He spoke perfect accentless English, his voice clipped and cool, and yet despite his outward control, Jessica sensed that beneath the ice-cold surface raged a molten torrent of barely held in rage. But why? Or had he guessed her purpose in coming? This man was no fool, surely he must have realised from the recent tone of Isabel's letters how the land lay?

'Señor Calvadores?'

Her voice was no way as controlled as his, and she had the dismal conviction that he knew he had unnerved her and that he deliberately intended to.

It was obvious that he didn't intend to make things easy for her. So much for Spanish hospitality! Jessica thought indignantly. He hadn't even offered her so much as a cup of coffee. Well, there was nothing for it but to plunge in; there was no easy way to say what had to be said, and all she wanted to do now was to say her piece and make her escape. His attitude and hauteur had killed all the sympathy she had initially felt towards him. Never in a thousand years could she imagine her flighty young cousin holding her own against this man whose very stance exuded an arrogant contempt that filled the air around them.

'I've come to see you about . . .'

'I know what you've come to see me about, Miss James,' he cut in brutally, not allowing her to finish, 'and no doubt you want me to make things easy for you. No doubt you hoped to sway me with your large, worried eyes, no doubt you've been led to believe that I can be persuaded to give way. Unfortunately—for you—that is not to be. To put it in its simplest form, Miss James, and having seen you for myself, having had confirmed every one of my very worst fears—that is to say, having seen for myself that you are a young woman who likes expensive clothes, and doubtless everything that goes with them; that you are at a guess somewhere in your mid-twenties; that you are bold enough to come here demanding to see me; there is simply no way I shall allow you to ruin my brother's life by trapping him into marriage simply because of an affair you had with him several months ago!'

Jessica was totally lost for words. His brother, he had said. That meant he wasn't—couldn't be Jorge de Calvadores, but he obviously thought she was Isabel. She was on the verge of correcting him when she realised what else he had said. 'An affair'. Isabel had said nothing about an affair to her; indeed, Isabel had given her the distinct impression that Jorge was the one pressing her into an unwanted engagement, whereas his brother seemed to think the boot was very much on the other foot. Clearly there were some misunderstandings to be sorted out!

CHAPTER TWO

SHE took a deep breath, wondering where to begin. Perhaps if she were to explain to him first that she wasn't Isabel. How contemptuous he had been about her cousin! He really was insufferably proud and arrogant; she didn't like him at all, she decided, eyeing him militantly.

She opened her mouth to explain, but was stunned into silence by the cynical way he was looking at her; a way no man had ever looked at her before, she realised, feeling the heat rising through her body. His study was an openly sexual one, and not merely sexual but contemptuous. Dear God, it could have been Isabel exposed to that merciless scrutiny that made no allowance for feminine modesty or embarrassment! And she had thought Spaniards were supposed to be reticent, cultured and, above all, respectful to women!

'You don't understand,' she began shakily when she had recovered her composure, anger fanned into tiny, darting flames by the look she had seen in his eyes.

'On the contrary, I understand all too well,' came the crisp response. '*Dios,* do you not think I know what goes on at these holiday resorts?' His finely cut mouth curled sneeringly downwards. 'You must have thought yourself extremely fortunate to meet a young man as wealthy and unworldly as my young brother, but unfortunately for you, Jorge does not come into his inheritance for half a dozen more years, when he reaches his twenty-fifth birthday. Until then I stand guardian to him, and you may take it that I shall do everything in my power to free him from your clutches. I must say I am surprised at your coming here,' he added. 'I thought Jorge had already made it clear to you that the affair was over. You should have persuaded him to pay for his pleasure at the time, Miss James,' he told her contemptuously. 'Now it is too late; now he sees you for what you really are.' His lip curled, and Jessica went hot and cold to think of Isabel being forced to stand here and listen to these insults.

'Your brother loved m-my ... me,' she corrected herself hurriedly. 'He . . .'

'—Desired your body,' she was told flatly, 'and in his innocence mistook such desire for a far different emotion—a fact which you used to your advantage, using his lust for you to force him . . .'

'Just a moment!' she inserted, with a sudden resurgence of her normal coolness. 'If you are implying that Jorge was forced into ...'

'Oh, I am aware that there was no question of "force" as such,' the icy voice agreed. 'Bemused, dazzled, dragged out of his depth—these would perhaps be better descriptions. You are an attractive woman,' he told her, openly assessing the shape of her body beneath the thin silk, 'not perhaps in Jorge's usual style, but no matter ... Of course I realise why you are here. I suppose you thought that a personal appearance might be just the goad he needed. Absence makes the heart grow fonder—of someone else, is that it?'

Matters had gone far enough. There was a

limit to the amount of time she intended to simply stand there and allow him to insult her.

'Before we go any further, I ought to tell you that I have no desire at all to become engaged to your brother,' Jessica told him truthfully, 'In fact . . .'

'Oh, come, you cannot expect me to believe that?' he said softly. 'Perhaps I should refresh your memory. I have here your last letter to Jorge. He brought it to me in a very troubled frame of mind. It seems that while he enjoyed your . . . company, the constant pressure you put on him to announce your engagement has panicked him into confiding in me.'

'You having considerable experience of ridding yourself of unwanted women, I suppose?' Jessica supplied sweetly. 'One of the penalties of being wealthy!'

The dark flush of colour beneath his skin brought her a fierce sense of satisfaction. He hadn't liked her implication that women would only find him attractive for his wealth, and she knew it wasn't true. He was too intensely male for that. She found herself wondering if he was married, and then squashed the thought as being of no concern to her.

'You must accept that Jorge no longer wishes to have anything to do with you,' she was told implacably, 'and even if he did, I would do everything in my power to dissuade him from marrying a woman like you. What attracted you to him the most? Or can I guess?'

'If you did you'd be wrong,' Jessica told him in a clipped voice. 'As I've already said, I have no desire to marry your brother.'

'No?' With a swift movement he reached inside his jacket and removed a folded piece of paper. 'Read this—perhaps it will help you remember,' he said contemptuously.

Unwillingly Jessica took the letter, her fingertips brushing his as she did, strange quivers of sensation running up her arm as she recoiled from the brief contact.

Matters had gone far enough. She would have to tell him the truth. She opened the letter, and her heart dropped. She had barely done more than read the first couple of lines, skimming quickly over them, but it was enough to bring a burning colour to her face. Isabel and Jorge had been lovers—that much was obvious; as was Isabel's impassioned plea for Jorge to marry her. What on earth had possessed her cousin to write a letter like this? Jessica felt sick at the thought of her aunt and uncle reading it; and what about John? Why on earth hadn't Isabel warned her? And why had she been so convinced that Jorge intended to come to England? To judge from his brother, the young Spaniard wanted to escape from the relationship just as much as Isabel herself.

'Edifying, is it not?' her persecutor drawled insultingly. 'And I understand from Jorge—although he was reluctant to admit it—that he was far from being your first lover.'

Jessica's eyes widened, mirroring her shock. Was it true?

'So, obviously realising that your letter had failed, you decided to come in person. Why, I wonder? It must surely be obvious to you by now that Jorge does not wish to marry you.'

What on earth had Isabel got her into?

For a moment she contemplated telling the truth, but to do so meant betraying her cousin. She had protected Isabel for too long to stop now.

'Perhaps, failing marriage, you had something else in mind?' The soft suggestion held a trace of bitter contempt. 'I know Jorge has told you of the marriage his family had hoped might take place between him and the daughter of a close friend of ours—a marriage, I might add, which would stand a far greater chance of success than the one you proposed. Perhaps you hoped to turn this fact to your advantage. Barbara's family are very old-fashioned. They would be intolerant of any folly on Jorge's part.'

Jessica went white, reaching out blindly to grasp the back of a chair for support as the meaning of his words sank in.

'You thought I'd use blackmail!' she whispered disbelievingly. 'You thought I came here to . . . to . . .'

'Very affecting,' the cool voice mocked. 'But I am not Jorge, to be easily impressed by a pair of huge amber eyes that plead with me to believe in an innocence I know they cannot possess. You are several years older than my brother; you used his inexperience and calf-love for you to further your own ends. You must have known that his family would never tolerate such an alliance—so, Miss James, let us get down to business, shall we?'

'If by business you mean you'll pay me to forget any claims I might have on your brother, you're wasting your time!' Jessica told him furiously, too angry to care about the danger

emanating from him as she pushed bitterly past
him, blinking away tears of rage as she wrestled
with the huge front door. She could hear him
behind her, and the terrible fear that he would
never allow her to leave made the blood pound in
her head, her fingers trembling as she tugged at
the door.

He swore harshly and she felt his hand on her
shoulder, sobbing with relief as the door yielded
and she half stumbled into the street. Her taxi
was waiting and she flung herself into it without a
backward glance, not caring what conclusions her
driver might be drawing. The first thing she
intended to do when she got back to the hotel was
to put a call through to her cousin and find out
exactly what was going on.

Fortunately, it was her aunt and uncle's bridge
night, and Isabel answered the phone, her
pleasure turning to petulance as she recognised
the anger in Jessica's voice.

'You saw Sebastian?' she exclaimed nervously.
'Oh, no, Jess, what did he say?'

She had a good mind to tell her, Jessica thought
wrathfully. So Sebastian was his name; it suited
him somehow.

'Nothing flattering,' she assured Isabel grimly.
'In fact he seemed to think I was you. Oh, Belle,'
she exclaimed as the scene in the vast and opulent
drawing room flashed quickly through her mind,
'you should have warned me, told me the truth.
Why on earth did you want me to come here?
Sebastian told me that Jorge had no desire to
become engaged to you, he even showed me your
letter.'

She knew from the sudden catch in her breath

that Isabel hadn't expected that, and yet true to form her cousin, even now, seemed to be trying to turn the situation to her own advantage.

'You didn't tell him he was wrong, did you?' she asked quickly, 'about us, I mean, Jess?'

'I wasn't given the opportunity,' Jessica told her dryly. It hadn't been pleasant listening to what the arrogant Conde had to say, and some of his more stinging barbs still hurt.

'He mustn't know,' Isabel was saying positively. 'Oh, Jess, try to understand—when I wrote that letter to Jorge, I was desperate—I thought I might be pregnant . . . Jess . . . Jess, are you still there?'

Trying not to betray her shock, Jessica murmured an assent. 'Oh, you don't understand at all,' she heard Isabel saying crossly, obviously correctly interpreting her silence. 'Honestly, Jess, you're so old-fashioned it just isn't true! Living like a frigid spinster might suit you, but it doesn't suit me,' she told her frankly, 'and why shouldn't I have fun if I want to?'

'Was it fun, thinking you might be pregnant and unmarried?' Jessica asked her bluntly. Isabel was still very much a spoiled child, and it did neither of them any good thinking now that she should have been treated far more firmly as a child—the damage was done, and Isabel seemed to think she had a God-given right to indulge herself in whatever she chose.

'No,' she heard Isabel admit sulkily. 'But what else could I do? I had to write to him—he was as responsible as me.'

'Go on,' Jessica told her briefly. The more she heard, the less able she felt to defend her cousin—but then there were her aunt and uncle to think of. Both of them would be unbearably shocked if they heard the truth.

'Oh, nothing.' She could almost see Isabel's petulant shrug. 'I discovered it was a false alarm, by that time I had met John, and so . . .'

'So you asked me to come here to see someone I thought you were on the verge of becoming engaged to. I don't understand, Belle. There must be something more to it.'

There was a long silence during which mingled exasperation and fear gripped her, and then at last Isabel admitted sulkily,

'Oh, all right then, when I wrote to Jorge he didn't write back, but his brother did. Jorge had shown him my letter, he said, and he wanted to know what proof there was that any child I might have was Jorge's—beast!' she added vitriolically. 'It was a hateful letter, Jess, and I was scared— Jorge had told me about him, that he was his guardian and that he was very strict. I was terrified he might come over here—come and see me because of what I'd written—so I panicked. I thought if you could see Jorge and tell him that I didn't want him any more then he would tell Sebastian and . . .'

And she would have been safe, without having to endure the unpleasantness of an interview with either Jorge or Sebastian, Jessica reflected bitterly. Trust Isabel to want to wriggle out of the situation with the minimum amount of discomfort to herself!

'You do understand, don't you, Jess?' Isabel pleaded. 'I couldn't run the risk of Sebastian coming over here. If the parents or John had seen him . . .'

'So you sent me into the lion's den instead,' Jessica supplied dryly. 'Thanks!'

'I didn't know that you'd see Sebastian or that he'd mistake you for me,' Isabel defended herself, 'but perhaps it's all worked out for the best,' she added with what to Jessica was colossal selfishness. 'Now he's seen you and you've told him that you don't want Jorge, he won't bother us again. What was he like?' she asked curiously. 'To hear Jorge talk about him anyone would think he was God!' She giggled. 'I quite fancied meeting him; Jorge said all the women were after him. He's immensely wealthy, and the title goes back to the days of Ferdinand and Isabella. He sounded fearfully haughty and proud.'

It was becoming obvious that Isabel knew far more about the Calvadores family than she had told her, Jessica realised. She was furious with her cousin, but as she knew from past experience, it was pointless getting angry with Isabel. Even if she were to drag her out here and make her face Sebastian and Calvadores herself, what possible good could it do? Isabel was probably right, it had all turned out for the best, although Jessica doubted that he would ever have felt sufficient concern about her hold over his brother to go the lengths of seeking her out in England.

'He sent me the most hateful letter,' Isabel was saying, her voice quivering slightly. 'He said that he didn't believe I might be pregnant and that it was just a trick to get Jorge to marry me. At least it's all over with now, Jess,' she added on a happier note, 'I'm so relieved. By the way,' she added coquettishly, 'John proposed last night and I've accepted him—the parents are over the moon!'

Privately Isabel thought her cousin far too young to be thinking of marriage. It was plain that Isabel was far from mature, and she doubted that John was the right husband for her, but she knew better than to interfere.

'When will you be back?' Isabel demanded. 'We're having a proper engagement party, and I want you to be there, of course.'

A sop to ease her conscience, Jessica thought wryly. She had done the dirty deed for her and now she was to be rewarded; Isabel couldn't get engaged without her. Had her cousin the slightest idea of what it had felt like to have to stand there and listen to Sebastian de Calvadores' insults? To be told that her morals were questionable, that she was motivated by financial greed—no, she thought grimly, Isabel didn't have the slightest conception.

Since she had allowed herself two days to sort out Isabel's romantic problems, Jessica found herself with a day on her hands. She wasn't going to waste it, she decided as she breakfasted in her room on warm rolls and fresh honey. She would explore Seville.

She already knew a little about it; that it had once been ruled by the Moors who had ruled all this part of Spain; that during the Middle Ages it had had a fine reputation as a centre of medical learning. Once Colin arrived there would be scant time for sightseeing, which in any case did not interest him, so after checking the time of his flight, which was due in early in the evening, Jessica collected her guide books and set out to explore the city.

But as she wandered the Moorish Alcazar,

instead of simply being able to drink in its beauty, at almost every turn she was forcibly reminded of Sebastian de Calvadores; it was from the men who had built the civilisation from which this beauty had sprung that he drew his arrogance, she thought as she looked around her. There was Moorish blood running in his veins, underlining and emphasising his total masculinity. She shivered, suddenly feeling cold, clad to step out into the warmth of the sunshine. Forget him, she told herself, why worry about what had happened? She knew that he had been totally mistaken about it, and that should have been enough. But somehow it wasn't. She could forget the contempt in his eyes, the explicitly sexual way they had moved over her body and yet at the same time had remained so cold, as though he had been saying, see, I know everything there is to know about you as a woman and it does nothing for me, nothing at all.

If it wasn't for the fact that by doing so she would betray Isabel she would have gone back and told him how wrong he was about her; then it would be his turn to feel her contempt, her condemnation.

Seville was a beautiful city, but she wasn't in the mood to enjoy it. Almost everywhere she looked she was reminded of Sebastian de Calvadores; Moorish faces, sternly oppressive, stared back at her from paintings; Moorish men who had guarded their women like precious jewels in rare caskets and who would never in a million years permit them the kind of freedom Isabel enjoyed.

Chastity and desire burned strongly in twin

flames in these people; either saints or sinners, but knowing no middle road; their history was a proud one and there could be few natives of Seville who did not boast some Moorish blood, some fierce elemental strain they had inherited from their forebears. They had been a race who, even while they tasted the cup of pleasure to the full, always remained a little aloof, knowing that where there was pleasure there was pain. A cynical, sophisticated race who had kept their women closeted away from the world to be enjoyed by them alone.

Jessica was glad when the time came to go and meet Colin's plane. He seemed so solid and safe somehow as he came towards her, carrying his briefcase, frowning uncertainly until he saw her.

'Jessica!' His hug was affectionately warm. 'Everything sorted out?' he asked her as they got into their taxi, his tone implying that he wouldn't be surprised to find that Isabel in her tiresomeness had allowed her problems to overflow into Jessica's working life.

'I think so.'

His relief made her laugh. 'Thank goodness for that! I was terrified that we'd have a tearful besotted Latin lover on our hands!'

Just for a moment Jessica compared this image to the reality of Sebastian, and wondered if Jorge was anything like his formidable brother. Probably not. She couldn't see Sebastian allowing himself to be manipulated in the way she was coming to suspect that Isabel had manipulated Jorge. No, when it came to the woman in his life, Sebastian would be totally in control. Was he married?

'Jess?'

Stop thinking about him, she chided herself, giving her attention to Colin. She was in Seville to work, not concern herself with the private life of a man who was virtually a stranger. Stranger or not, for those first few pulsating seconds when she had seen Sebastian she had been aware of him in a way that still had the power to shock her. For all his repressive arrogance there was a sensuality about him, a total maleness and a dangerous allure, reminiscent of that of a jungle cat for its prey.

Colin was tired after his flight and it was decided that he would dine in his room and have an early night.

'Have you been to the exhibition centre yet?' he asked Jessica. She shook her head. 'Well, the exhibition doesn't open until tomorrow. We've got an appointment with Calvortex after lunch. Keep your fingers crossed, won't you?' he asked her. 'I've done all next season's designs with their fabrics in mind. If they're anything like last season's we'll be on to a real winner—especially if he gives us the exclusive use of his stuff for the U.K.'

'How much do you know about them?' Jessica asked him as they stepped into the hotel foyer.

'Very little, and most of that word of mouth. The Chairman of the company handpicks his clients, from what I've been told. The company is a small family-run business; apart from that I know nothing, except that they produce the sort of fabrics that fill the dreams of every designer worth his or her salt. I'm relieved to hear you've sorted out all that business with Isabel,' he added as they headed for the lift. 'Tiresome girl! Why should you run round after her?'

'Well, I won't have to much longer,' Jessica told him. 'She's got herself engaged.'

'God help the man!' was Colin's pious comment as the lift stopped at their floor.

Their rooms were not adjacent and outside the lift they went their separate ways.

In her own room, Jessica tried to concentrate on the morning and the textile show, but somehow Sebastian de Calvadores' aquiline features kept coming between her and her work. A hard man and a proud one, and her face burned with colour as she remembered the way he had looked at her, the insulting remarks he had made to her.

She went to bed early, and was just on the point of falling asleep when she heard someone knocking on the door.

'Jess, are you awake?' she heard Colin mutter outside. 'I've got the most dreadful indigestion, do you have anything I can take?'

Sighing, she went to her suitcase and found some tablets. If Colin had one fault it was that he was a hopeless hypochondriac and that he refused absolutely to carry even aspirins about with him, preferring instead to play the martyr for the uninitiated. Jessica had got wise to this within her first few months of working from him, and had grown used to carrying what amounted almost to a small pharmacy around with her whenever she travelled with him.

She opened her door and handed him the small packet.

'You're an angel!'

Colin bent forward, kissing her cheek lightly, and as he did so out of the corner of her eye Jessica glimpsed the couple walking down the corridor towards them; the woman small and petite with smoothly coiled dark hair and an expensive couture evening gown, her escort tall, with raven's-wing dark hair and a profile that made Jessica's heart turn over thuddingly as she stared at him.

Sebastian de Calvadores! What was he doing here, and who was he with?

Her face paled as he stared contemptuously at her, suddenly acutely aware of her thin silk nightgown and tousled hair, Colin's hand on her arm, his lips brushing her cheek. Her face flamed as she realised what interpretation Sebastian de Calvadores would be placing on their intimacy, and then berated herself for her embarrassment. Why should she care if he thought she and Colin were lovers? What possible business was it of his? And yet his steely glance seemed to say that he knew everything there was to know about her, and that he doubted that her motives for being with Colin were any less altruistic than those he had accredited her with in his brother's case.

'Jess, is something wrong?' Colin asked her with a frown, sensing her lack of attention. 'You've seemed strangely on edge ever since I arrived. It's that damned cousin of yours, I suppose.'

'Nothing's wrong, I'm just a little tired,' she lied huskily, glad when Sebastian and his companion turned the corner of the corridor. 'I'll be fine in the morning.'

CHAPTER THREE

As a prediction it wasn't entirely true; Jessica felt strangely on edge and tense, her muscles clenching every time someone walked into the dining-room where they were having breakfast.

She would be glad to get back home, she thought wryly as her nerves jumped for the third time in succession at the sight of a dark-haired man. Arrogant brute! He hadn't even given her an opportunity to explain, denouncing her as though she were some female predator and his brother her completely innocent victim. She thought about what she had learned from Isabel and grimaced slightly. How could her cousin have behaved in such an unprincipled way? She had always had a streak of wildness, a tendency to ignore any attempts to curb her headstrong nature, but to actually try and force Jorge into marriage . . . And that was what she had done, no matter how one tried to wrap up the truth, Jessica admitted unhappily. Even so, that was no reason for Sebastian de Calvadores to speak to *her* in the way he had.

'Time to leave for the exhibition,' Colin reminded her, dragging her mind back to the real purpose of her visit to Seville.

Half an hour later they were there, both of them lost in admiration of the fabrics on display.

'Just feel this suede,' Colin murmured to her.

'It's as supple as silk. It makes my fingers itch to use it!'

'And these tweeds!' Jessica exclaimed. 'The wool comes from South America, I believe?'

'Many Spaniards have family connections in South America,' Colin reminded her, 'and I suppose it's only natural that they should turn those connections to commercial advantage, in this case by importing the wool in its raw state, and dying and weaving it here in Spain.'

He drew Jessica's attention to the display belonging to the company they were to see. 'In a class of its own, isn't it?' he asked, watching the way she handled the supple fabric. 'And those colours!'

'They're incredibly subtle,' Jessica agreed with a touch of envy.

On leaving college her first intention had been to find a job in a design capacity with one of the large manufacturers, but such jobs were hard to come by—even harder with the downturn in the textile industry in Britain, and although her languages had stood her in good stead, she had found that without exception the Continental firms preferred to take on their own young graduates. Now working with cloth in its raw stages was only a pipe-dream.

There was quite a busy throng around the Calvortex display and it was several minutes before Colin could talk to one of the young men in charge. He explained his purpose in Seville, producing the letters of recommendation he had brought with him, while Jessica swiftly translated.

'Unfortunately I am merely a member of the staff,' the young man exclaimed regretfully to

Jessica, 'but I will certainly mention this matter to my superiors. If we have a telephone number where we can reach you?'

Handing him both his card and their telephone number at the hotel, Colin announced that they had done enough for one morning and that it was time for lunch. Typically he decided that they would lunch, not at the restaurant within the exhibition, but at another one, far more expensive and exclusive, as Jessica could tell at a glance when their taxi stopped outside it.

She was wearing another of his outfits, and attracted several admiring looks from the other diners as they were shown to their table, Colin beaming delightedly at the attention they were receiving.

Over lunch though he was more serious. 'I hope to God I do manage to get to some arrangement with Calvortex,' he confided.

Jessica, sensitive to his mood, picked up the tone of worry in his voice.

'It would be very pleasant,' she agreed, 'their fabrics are fantastic, but it won't be the end of the world if we don't, will it?'

'It could be,' Colin told her gravely. 'Things haven't been going too well this last couple of years. The people with money to spend on haute couture are getting fewer and fewer, and we don't exactly produce high fashion stuff. Calvortex fabrics have a world-wide reputation, if we could use them for our clothes I'm convinced it would help boost sales—I've already had one approach from the Americans, with the proviso that we use Calvortex. Somehow they got to hear that we hoped to do so, and they've suggested an

excellent contract. There'd be enough profit in it
for us to start a cheaper line—bread and butter
money coming in with the designer collections as
the icing.'

What he said made sense, and Jessica knew
enough about the fashion world to know he wasn't
exaggerating. Several of the larger fashion houses
were cutting back; designers came, were acclaimed for a couple of seasons, and then simply
disappeared, but it was like chilly fingers playing
down her spine to realise that Colin might be in
financial difficulties.

'Well,' Colin told her when they had finished
eating, 'let's get back to the exhibition and see if
we can find something to fall back on if we don't
get anywhere with Calvortex, although I'm afraid
if we don't we'll lose the American contract—and
one can see why. The texture and colour of those
tweeds they were showing . . .'

'Mmm,' Jessica agreed, 'they were marvellous.
I wonder how they manage to get such subtle
colours?'

'I don't know. I've heard it's a closely guarded
secret. Their Chairman is also their main
designer and colour expert. It's quite a small
concern really, but as I said before, extremely
exclusive.'

The rest of the exhibition, while interesting,
fell very far short of the standard of the Calvortex
display, although Jessica did think that some of
the supple leathers and suedes might prove useful
to them. For some time she had been trying to
persuade Colin to try a younger, more fashionable
line, and she could just see those suedes, in
pewters, steel-blues and soft greens, in flaring

culottes and swirling skirts, topped with chunky hand-knits.

It was shortly after dinner that Colin received a message from reception to say that there had been a call from from Calvortex.

'Stage one completed successfully at least!' he announced to Jessica when he returned to the bar, faintly flushed and obviously excited. 'I've spoken to the Chairman and he's agreed to see me tomorrow. I've explained to him that I've got my assistant with me, so he's arranged for us to tour the factory, and afterwards we can talk.'

She wouldn't be included in the talks, of course, Jessica reflected, but it wouldn't be too difficult a task to occupy herself for a couple of hours—in fact she would enjoy seeing how such beautiful fabrics were made.

Although Colin had not suggested that she did so, she dressed with particular care for the visit—an outfit chosen from their new season's designs, a cream silk blouse and a russet velvet suit with a tiny boxy jacket with narrow puffed sleeves and scrolls of self-coloured embroidery down the front. The skirt fell smoothly in soft loose pleats from the narrow waistband, and it was an outfit that Jessica knew suited her.

Colin obviously thought so too, because he beamed with approval when he saw her.

'Very apt,' he approved as he looked at her. 'The jacket has a certain matador air, very much suited to this part of the world, and I must say I'm very pleased with the way that embroidery has worked out. The colour suits you as well.'

'I thought about the tweed,' Jessica told him, referring to a tweed suit which was also part of the new collection, 'but as it doesn't compare favourably with their fabrics, I thought . . .'

'Quite right,' he approved. 'Now, I've ordered a taxi for us, we've just about got time for a cup of coffee before it arrives.'

He looked more like an Old Etonian than a famous designer, Jessica reflected, eyeing his sober Savile Row suit and immaculate silk shirt. Colin belonged to an older generation that believed in dressing correctly and that one could always tell a gentleman by his clothes; in Colin's case expensive and discreet clothes—Turnbull & Asser shirts and handmade shoes.

The factory was situated just outside Seville, surprisingly modern and with access to the river and the port. It was, as Colin pointed out, very well planned, close to main roads and other facilities, and when he gave in their names at the gates they swung open to allow their vehicle to enter.

They were met in the foyer by a smiling dark-haired young man, dressed formally in a dark suit, his glance for them both extremely respectful, although there was a gleam of male interest in the dark eyes as they discreetly examined Jessica.

Having introduced himself as Ramón Ferres, he told them that he was to escort them round the factory.

'Unfortunately the Conde cannot show you round himself,' he explained in the sibilant, liquid English of the Spaniard, 'but he will be free to have lunch with you as arranged,' he informed Colin. 'Forgive me if I stare,' he added to Jessica, 'but we did not realise when Señor Weaver mentioned an assistant that he was talking of a woman. I'm afraid you might find the chemical processes of the factory a little boring . . .'

'Never,' Colin interrupted with a chuckle, while Jessica suppressed a tiny flare of anger at their escort's chauvinistic remark. Of course in Spain things were different. On the whole women were content to take a back seat to live their own lives, especially in the more wealthy families. No doubt someone such as Sebastian de Calvadores' wife, if indeed he had one, would never dream of interfering in her husband's life, or of questioning him about it. That was how they were brought up; to be docile and biddable, content with their families and their homes.

'You'll find that Jessica is far more knowledge-able about the manufacturing process than I am,' Colin added to their guide. 'In fact I suspect she prefers designing fabrics to designing clothes, if the truth were known.'

'Both fascinate me,' Jessica said truthfully.

The next couple of hours flew past. There was so much to see, so much to learn. The factory was the most up-to-date she had ever seen, the equipment of such a sophisticated and superior type that she could only marvel at the tech-nological advances made since she had left college.

They were shown the dying vats, but prudently Ramón Ferres said nothing about how they managed to produce their delicate, subtle colours. All he would say in answer to Jessica's questions was that in the main they used natural and vegetable dyes.

'But surely there's always a problem in stabilising such colours?' she pressed him.

He smiled and shrugged slim shoulders. 'This is so,' he agreed, 'but we have been lucky enough to discover a way of stabilising them—I cannot tell you how, you understand, but be assured that we have done so.'

'And next season's range?' Jessica queried. 'Could we . . .'

Again Ramón Ferres shook his head. 'That is for the Conde to decide,' he explained. He glanced at his watch. 'I will escort you back to the foyer, it is almost time for lunch.' He glanced at Jessica. 'Originally it was intended that we should lunch together, but as I explained, we had expected Señor Weaver's assistant to be a man.'

It was plain that he had expected Colin's assistant to want to talk shop over lunch, and it exasperated Jessica that he should think that simply because she was a woman she was merely paying lip-service to appearing interested.

'I should love to have lunch with you,' she said firmly. 'There are several points I should like to clarify regarding the manufacturing processes; problems you might have in maintaining the quality of your wool, for instance . . .'

They were back in the foyer, and an elegant, dark-haired secretary came to conduct Colin into the Chairman's private sanctum, leaving Jessica with Ramón Ferres.

A little to her surprise he guided her out to car, explaining that although the factory had a restaurant, they operated a scheme similar to that adopted by the Japanese, in that all the staff dined together.

'While the food is excellent, the atmosphere is no conductive to a serious discussion. However, there is a restaurant not far from here.'

'And the Chairman?' Jessica asked curiously, visions of Colin in his Savile Row suit sitting down to eat with several hundred noisy Spaniards.

'He has a private dining room in his suite which he uses for business entertaining.'

As Ramón Ferres had said, the restaurant was not very far away. It had once been the shipping office of a wine exporter, he explained when Jessica expressed interest, but had now been converted into a restaurant.

As they walked inside the unusual barrel-vaulted ceiling caught Jessica's attention, and as they were shown to their table Ramón told her that there were deep cellars beneath the ground.

'Almost every house in Seville has its cellars—a legacy from the times of the Moors—places of sanctuary and safety.'

'And sometimes prisons,' said Jessica, shivering a little. Like most people she found something distinctly frightening about the thought of being imprisoned underground.

'That too,' he agreed. 'The thought distresses you? There are not many of our leading families in Seville who have not had recourse to their cellars, for one reason or another, at some time in their history.'

'This is a very fascinating part of Spain,' Jessica commented as they were served with chilled *gazpacho*. 'A true mingling of East and West.'

'Not always with happy results,' Ramón told her. 'The Moorish character is a proud one, sombre too, and those in Seville who can trace their line back to the Moors are inordinately proud of their bloodlines. It has not always been so, of course. There was a time, during the Inquisition in particular, when to own to Moorish blood was to sign one's own death warrant.'

'Do you have Moorish ancestors?' Jessica asked him, genuinely interested.

He shook his head ruefully. 'No, my family was originally from the north, but the Conde can trace his family back to a knight attached to the Court of Pedro the Cruel. It is said that he ravished away the daughter of his arch-enemy, although there is a legend in the Conde's family that this was not so; that the girl was seduced by her cousin and in fear of her father she laid the blame at the door of his most bitter enemy. The Conde's ancestor was a proud man, and rather than endure the slur on his good name he offered to marry the girl—that is the story passed down through the Conde's family.'

And it bore a sombre echo of truth, Jessica thought wryly. She could well imagine a man who could not be moved by any other emotion being moved by pride; pride in his name and his race. She could almost see the dark flash of bitter eyes as he was faced with his crime . . . She shook herself mentally; what was the matter with her? For a moment in her mind's eye she had mentally imagined Sebastian de Calvadores as that accused ravisher. She would really have to stop thinking about the man. What was the matter with her? She was behaving like a teenager! If she felt anything for him it could only be contempt—and yet when he had stood there saying those dreadful things to her she had longed to tell him the truth, to see him smile instead of frown.

It was Jessica's turn to frown now. Why should she care whether Sebastian de Calvadores frowned or smiled? It was immaterial to her; not that she was ever likely to see him again anyway!

Ramón Ferres was an entertaining companion, and although Jessica suspected that he did not entirely approve of a woman in what he plainly considered to be a man's world, he answered all her questions as pleasantly and fully as he could.

'Much of this you will have to ask the Conde,' he told her with another of his shrugs, when she had asked several highly technical questions. 'I'm afraid I am employed more as a public relations manager than a technical expert. The Conde, on the other hand, knows everything there is to know about the manufacturing process. The whole thing was his brain-child; he conceived the idea when he was in South America working on the *rancho* of his godfather—it is from there that he gets the wool; it is of the highest quality and the partnership is a good one. It is said that Señor Cusuivas would like it to be even closer— he has a daughter who would make the Conde an excellent wife. Forgive me,' he added hastily, 'I should not have said that. The Conde . . .'

'I've forgotten it already,' Jessica assured him, amused that he had so far forgotten himself to gossip a little with her. As he had said himself, he was not from Southern Spain, and perhaps a little homesick here among the more taciturn, secretive people of Seville, who had lived too long in the shadow of death and danger not to weigh their words carefully. Centuries of blood-shed had stained this soil, leaving the inhabitants

a legacy of caution—deep-seated and ineradic-
able.

'I shall have to leave you in the foyer for a few
minutes,' Ramón apologised to her when they got
back to the factory. 'Señor Weaver should not be
long, and I'm afraid I have some business to
attend to, but I shall leave you in Constancia's
capable hands.'

Constancia was the secretary. She gave Jessica
a brief smile, and offered a cup of coffee. Jessica
accepted; the wine with their lunch had left her
feeling thirsty.

The girl had been gone about five minutes
when the door behind her desk was suddenly
thrust open.

'Constancia . . .'

Jessica felt her heart lurch in recognition of the
voice, less grim than when she had heard it last, but
recognisable all the same. She was halfway out of
her seat, the blood draining from her face, when
Sebastian de Calvadores turned and saw her,
frowning in disbelief. '*Dios!*' he swore angrily.
'You would pursue me even here? Have you no
pride, no natural feminine reticence? I have told
you as plainly as I can, *señorita*, that my brother has
no interest in you. And nor will you find him here.
He is away from home at the moment, visiting the
family of his *novia*-to-be,' he added cruelly, 'a
young girl of excellent family who would rather die
than tell a man to whom she was not married that
she was to bear his child.'

This last gibe brought the hot colour back to
Jessica's face.

'Did you send your brother away so that he
couldn't see . . . me?' she asked heatedly.

'Hardly. I had no prior warning of your arrival. However, I am sure that had we done so, Jorge would have thanked me for saving him from an unpleasant confrontation. What did you hope for by coming here? To browbeat him into changing his mind and offering you the protection of his name—our name?' he added proudly.

Before Jessica could retaliate the door opened again and Colin came out, beaming as he caught sight of her.

'Ah, Jessica my dear, you're back. Conde,' he smiled, turning to Sebastian de Calvadores and astounding Jessica, 'allow me to introduce my assistant to you. Jessica—the Conde de Calvadores, Chairman of Calvortex!'

'This is your assistant of whom you have spoken so highly to me?' Just for a moment Jessica saw that Sebastian was practically dumb-founded, although he managed to conceal his shock faster than she could hers.

He was the Chairman of Calvortex! He was the person on whom the future success of Colin's business depended. Her heart sank. She couldn't see him agreeing to anything that involved her, no matter how remotely.

'Yes, this is Jessica,' Colin was agreeing happily, plainly unaware of any undercurrents. 'Like Señor Ferres, the Conde expected my assistant to be a man,' he added to Jessica.

'Perhaps because I'm a woman he would prefer to see me shut away behind a locked gate—or better still, in one of Seville's many dungeons,' Jessica said lightly, and although Colin laughed, she knew from the tiny muscle clenching in the

Conde's lean jaw that he had not missed her
point.

'The Conde has invited me to join him for
dinner this evening,' Colin told her. 'We have
still not discussed everything.'

Jessica's heart pounded. Was the discovery that
she was Colin's assistant going to affect his
decision adversely? Surely as a businessman
Sebastian de Calvadores would make his final
judgment on commercial grounds only, and yet
she couldn't help remembering what Ramón
Ferres had said about his family and how it tied
in with her own impression that he was an
inordinately proud man. Would he turn Colin's
suggestions down simply because Colin employed
her?

Constancia returned with her cup of coffee and
Jessica took it, grateful for an excuse to turn away
from Sebastian de Calvadores' bitter eyes.

What an appalling coincidence! She had never
imagined for one moment that Jorge's arrogant
brother and the head of Calvortex would be one
and the same man.

'. . . and of course, Jessica is of particular help
to me because she speaks several languages
fluently,' she suddenly heard Colin saying, and
her fingers trembled as they curled round the
coffee cup and she realised that the two men were
discussing her.

'Most fortuitous,' she heard Sebastian de
Calvadores replying, cynicism underlining the
words, and bringing a faint flush to her pale skin.
'I believe you told me that she was also fully
qualified in textile design and processing?'

'Oh yes,' Colin beamed. 'In fact that's really

her first love, but as I'm sure you know, we have nothing in England to rival anything such as Calvortex.'

'I believe you mentioned that you would like to use the telephone,' Jessica heard Sebastian murmuring to Colin. 'If you would care to go with my secretary, she will help you with your calls.'

As Colin followed Constancia into her office, Jessica had a cowardly impulse to beg him not to leave her alone with Sebastian de Calvadores.

'Quite a coincidence,' he observed coldly when they were alone, 'and one that makes me even more suspicious of your motives. You knew, of course, when you first met Jorge of his connection with Calvortex and from that doubtless deduced that he was a comparatively wealthy young man. For all your much vaunted feminism and independence I find you are very little different from our own women in that you are looking for a man who will support you and ease your way through life, although unlike them you do not have the honesty to admit it, nor the accomplishments to make the bait tempting, especially not to a Spaniard, who expects to find his bride pure and innocent. No wonder you went for a boy like Jorge! He is still young enough to find a certain charm in experience—of course it is expected that young men will ... experiment, but you are singularly foolish if you honestly believe that Jorge would marry a woman such as yourself.'

Jessica's hand snaked out—she couldn't help it—anything to destroy that cynical, infuriating smile. But the instant her palm made contact with the lean tanned cheek, a sick wave of self-disgust swept over her. What on earth was happening to her? She had never struck anyone in anger before, no matter how much she had been provoked.

And it seemed that Sebastian de Calvadores shared her shock. His fingers touched the faintly reddening flesh, his eyes darkening rapidly to a fury that scorched and terrified her, but Jessica refused to be cowed. No matter how much she was trembling inwardly, he would never be allowed to know of it!

'*Dios*, vixen!' The words were breathed harshly, fastidious disgust etched in every line of the aristocratic features. 'Nobody strikes a Calvadores and is allowed to escape without retribution!'

He moved, silent and agile as a cougar, grasping her wrists and pinioning them with hard fingers that bit into her tender flesh. She tried to pull away, infuriated by her sudden imprisonment, and with a speed that left her startled and breathless she was jerked forward, the fingers that had held her wrists, biting into her shoulders, the dark grey eyes smouldering with an anger that touched off something elemental deep within her own body, mutual antagonism crackling between them.

'*Cristos!*'

She heard Sebastian swear and then his mouth was on hers, angry and hatefully contemptuous—the very worst kind of punishment, letting her know that she was less than the dust beneath his feet, her breasts were crushed against the fine wool of his suit and it appalled her that such a bitter and punishing embrace should still have the power to ignite a powerful sexual chemistry so that she was aware of Sebastian de Calvadores as a man in a way that she could never remember being aware of any man before. The expensive suit and silk shirt were simply the trappings of civilisation masking the true nature of a man who was still every bit as much a conqueror as his ancestors had been. He was enjoying using his body to punish her—she could sense it, feel it in the hard arrogance of his flesh against hers, forcing her to submit.

Against her will her lips softened, trembling slightly beneath the determined assault. Almost instantly Sebastian drew away.

'I am not my brother, Señorita James,' he told her sardonically. 'The warmth of your mouth trembling beneath mine leaves me cold—especially when I know that I am far from being the first man to have tasted its sweetness.'

'How hypocritical of you!' Jessica flashed back, walking unsteadily away from him. 'You obviously expect your wife, when you eventually marry, to be as pure as the driven snow, but you, I feel sure, can make no such claims!'

'Would you give a Stradivarius violin or a Bechstein piano to a mere beginner?' he mocked back, astounding her with his cynicism. 'And I think you need not concern yourself with the views of the woman who will be my wife, Señorita James. You and she will be worlds apart in your views on life.'

'Just like me and the girl Jorge is to marry,' Jessica stormed at him, irrationally hurt by his comment. 'How do I know Jorge really wants to marry this girl? How do I know it's not simply your idea?'

'Jesu Maria!' Sebastian breathed, as though imploring the heavens for patience. 'Jorge has told you himself!'

'Perhaps because you insisted,' Jessica told him doggedly, not sure why she was needling him like this, except that it had something to do with the contempt in his eyes when he had released her after kissing her. 'Perhaps I should get in touch with Jorge myself, talk to him . . .'

'Never! I will not allow it!'

He looked so grimly implacable that Jessica felt a tiny frisson of fear. Why on earth had she goaded him like that? She knew she had no intention of saying anything to Jorge! And yet something seemed to drive her on, so that she shrugged and said nonchalantly:

'You couldn't stop me.'

She almost flinched when she saw the look of utter fury in his eyes; eyes that had darkened almost to black, only the pale grey rim shimmering with barely suppressed rage as he stared at her.

'You dare to challenge me?' he demanded with awesome control. 'You are not only venal, you are a fool as well!' he told her softly.

CHAPTER FOUR

'YOU'RE quite sure you'll be all right?' Colin asked her fussily for the fourth time.

Jessica sighed. 'You're going out for the evening, not leaving me on the steps of the workhouse,' she reminded him dryly. 'Of course I'll be all right, what on earth could possibly happen to me?'

It was eight-thirty before Colin left for his dinner engagement with Sebastian de Calvadores, and after he had gone Jessica leaned back in her chair in the bar and tried to relax.

Her nerves had been like coiled springs ever since they left the factory. She had alternated between longing to confide in Colin and a firm determination not to involve him in her private affairs.

Sebastian de Calvadores couldn't possibly deprive Colin of the contract simply because he employed her, surely? And yet there had been a look in his eyes just before Colin had rejoined them which suggested that he would be perfectly willing to journey to hell and back again if he thought that by doing so he could punish her.

And what better way of punishing her could there be than putting Colin's business at risk? It wasn't inconceivable if things didn't improve that Colin would be forced to let her go, and she had no delusions about herself. In spite of her qualifications and experience she would find it extremely difficult to get a job of equivalent standing.

Against her will she found herself remembering Sebastian's kiss—in no way meant to be an affectionate embrace, but rather a gesture of disdain and condemnation—her memory lingering on the hard length of his body against hers, disturbingly male.

She went up to her room before Colin returned, mentally crossing her fingers that all would go well. He had been full of optimism when he set out, and she only hoped that it was well founded.

'So how did things go last night?'

Colin looked up from his breakfast, and it seemed to Jessica that he avoided her eyes as he answered, 'Quite well. The Conde seemed very interested in my proposals.'

'Did he agree to them, then?' Jessica pressed, for some reason alarmed by Colin's hesitancy.

'In a manner of speaking, although there were certain conditions . . .'

'Only to be expected in view of his company's reputation,' Jessica agreed, her spirits lightening. 'What were they?'

For a moment Colin didn't speak, and several seconds later when Jessica replaced her coffee cup she found him regarding her with an expression compounded of uncertainty and appeal. Suspicion sharpened her gaze, fear sending the blood pounding through her veins. Sebastian had told him he would only give him the contract if Colin got rid of her!

'He wants you to fire me, doesn't he?' she said calmly. 'Oh, I . . .'

'No, no, Jessica, it's not that,' Colin quickly reassured her. 'Quite the contrary. It seems that they're having problems with the designs for their next collection of fabrics. The Conde works on them himself with the help of another designer, whom he has recently lost to a rival organisation. As you can imagine, the Conde is most anxious to complete the work on the season's designs, and he's asked me if I would be agreeable to you working for him until this is done.'

Whatever Jessica expected to hear it was not this! For a few minutes she was too astounded to say anything.

'You see, you were quite wrong in thinking he disapproved of you,' Colin told her. 'He seemed most impressed when I told him about your qualifications. Over dinner tonight he questioned me in detail about you—where you'd trained, how long you'd worked for me. I must admit that I had no idea what he was leading up to, but it seems that Ramón Ferres had told him how interested you were in the manufacturing processes and how knowledgeable, and he confided to me the difficult situation he finds himself in.'

'But surely a firm such as Calvortex would have no trouble at all in finding a junior designer,' Jessica suggested, feeling a tinge of suspicion. Why did Sebastian want her to work for him? She couldn't understand it, especially when he had let her know how much he despised her and how determined he was to keep her away from his brother.

'Certainly,' Colin agreed, 'but it seems he's reluctant to take someone on on a permanent basis at this stage—employing someone on a temporary basis would suit him admirably, but as he admitted to me, it's very difficult to find an accomplished designer willing to be employed for a mere matter of weeks. It seems the Conde has a brother who may eventually take the place of the departed designer, but he needs a designer now to help him complete the new season's range of fabrics. It's quite an honour that he should ask for you,' he pointed out logically, 'and you've always said how much you'd like to work in textiles. It would only be for a few weeks—I should hold your job for you, of course—we can do nothing on next season's designs in any case until we know what fabrics Calvortex will produce.'

'Is your contract dependent on my agreeing to work for the Conde?' Jessica asked, frowning. She could not understand why the Conde would make such a stipulation, but if he had it could not be for any reason that would benefit her.

'Not in so many words,' Colin told her wryly, 'but I suspect if you did refuse . . .'

He left the sentence unfinished, but Jessica felt she knew enough about the Conde to guess at the pressure he would bring to bear on her employer. Despite her love of textiles she had not the slightest desire to work for Sebastian de Calvadores. But if she refused Colin's company might well fold. What should she do? Not for the first time she found herself wishing there was someone she could turn to for advice, instead of always being the giver of advice to others.

'What's wrong?' Colin asked her hesitantly. 'I thought you'd jump at the chance.'

'It's such a surprise,' Jessica told him, not untruthfully. 'How long would it mean staying in Spain?'

'I'm not sure. The details would have to be arranged with the Conde. Initially he is merely enquiring if I would be prepared to let you go on a temporary basis, and if you would be prepared to work for Calvortex. One other thing . . .' he paused and glanced at her uncertainly. 'He did suggest that he would be prepared to pay you extremely well.'

He would, Jessica thought cynically, her fingers curling into her palms, an irate expression in her eyes, and for one heady moment she toyed with the idea of telling the Conde exactly what he could do with both his job and his money. And then common sense intruded, bringing her back down to earth. Colin was watching her with a heartrendingly pathetic expression, and she knew she simply hadn't the heart to tell him she was going to refuse. It was a golden opportunity, she told herself, trying to cheer herself up; she would undoubtedly learn a considerable amount, and in years to come it would stand her in good stead to say she had worked for Calvortex, no matter how briefly, if she wanted to obtain another job.

'You'll do it?' Colin said eagerly, correctly interpreting her expression.

'I don't see that I've got much option,' she agreed dryly.

'Good! I'll telephone the Conde and give him the good news. Doubtless he'll want to talk to you to finalise all the arrangements.'

'Doubtless,' Jessica echoed ironically. She

could well imagine the sneering expression and suffocating arrogance Sebastian would adopt when he knew that she had agreed to his suggestion.

A tiny seed of doubt had taken root in her subconscious, warning her that she would regret this weakness, but she couldn't see what Sebastian could possibly do to her other than attempt to make her life a misery with his cynical remarks and contemptuous eyes, and she would soon show him that she was completely impervious to both.

Jessica had just stepped into the shower when she heard someone knocking on her door. Thinking it must be the maid with the light meal she had ordered, she shrugged on her towelling robe and quickly opened the door.

To her consternation it was not a maid who stood there, but Sebastian de Calvadores, looking cynically urbane as he lounged carelessly against the open door, his eyes slowly appraising her.

'I thought you were room service,' she stammered, feeling as gauche as a raw teenager. 'I . . . what did you want?'

'To speak to you. Surely Colin has already apprised you of my suggestion?'

'You want to speak about that? But Colin said you were going to telephone . . . at least . . .' She couldn't remember now exactly what Colin *had* said; Sebastian's unexpected appearance had thrown her completely, her thoughts were a chaotic muddle.

'Are you going to invite me in, or shall we hold our discussion here in full view of the other guests? On balance I think we would be better inside,' he drawled, walking past her and calmly closing the door.

'But I'm not dressed . . .' Jessica protested, hot colour storming her face as he looked her over thoughtfully.

'An age-old ploy, but one that unfortunately does not work on me. I'm immune to women who use their bodies as you use yours.'

'And yet you still want me to work for you? I should have thought I would be the last person you would want in your employ.'

'Sometimes it is necessary to give way to expediency,' he told her crisply, 'Now, could I trouble you for your decision?'

He really was the most unbearably arrogant man she had ever met in her life! Jessica thought wrathfully. Anyone with the slightest pretensions to consideration would have suggested that they meet downstairs, or at least have given her an opportunity to dress, but not Sebastian de Calvadores. No doubt he enjoyed having her at a disadvantage!

'I can't believe you want me to work for you,' she protested, wishing he would not watch her so closely. She felt like a particularly obnoxious life form being viewed beneath a microscope.

'Come, I'm sure I do not need to boost your ego by paying you flattering compliments. I am assured by your employer that you are a first-class designer. He is a man whose judgment I trust—I need a designer badly enough to be prepared to overlook certain aspects of your personality. It is as simple as that.'

'You must want me very badly if you were

prepared to threaten Colin that you would withdraw the contract!'

'As I said before, it is a matter of expediency. I am already behind with work on next season's fabrics. There have been problems with some of the dyes. Primarily I am a chemist, not a designer, and the work I have had to do on this side of things has meant that there have been delays in the design end of things. Like any other manufacturer, I have deadlines to meet. My suggestion to Colin was based purely on commercial necessity. He understands this even if you don't. I am prepared to help him if he will help me, there is nothing out of the ordinary in that.'

Nothing at all, and yet still Jessica felt uneasy, as though there was something she wasn't being told; something hidden from her.

'And you will merely want me to work for you for a matter of a few weeks?' she pressed.

'Two months at the most. Señor Weaver has said he can spare you for this length of time—the rest is up to you.' He gave a comprehensive shrug. 'I doubt that I would ever be your choice of employer—Señor Weaver obviously has no idea of your true personality—but if you wish to save his business I am sure you will see the wisdom of agreeing.'

He must want a designer very badly, was Jessica's first thought, but then he had already admitted that he did. So why did she have this nagging feeling that there was something else?

'You . . .' she began.

'I have no time to waste in answering further arguments,' he interrupted her with an arrogance that had her spine prickling as defensively as a ruffled kitten's. 'Either you agree or you refuse, but if you refuse, be very sure at what cost.'

It really wasn't fair, Jessica thought, shivering a little, as she hugged her robe even more firmly around her slender body. What choice did she have?

'I . . . I agree,' she said huskily at last, the tiny thread of disquiet she had felt earlier exploding into full-blown fear as she saw the triumph glittering briefly in his eyes.

'Most wise. So . . . if you will be ready to leave in the morning, I shall collect you at nine, that will leave us enough time to . . .'

'Leave?'

'Ah yes, didn't I tell you?' he drawled mockingly. 'I intend to spend the next two months working from my *hacienda*. I have . . . responsibilities there, and the peace and quiet of the *hacienda* is more conducive to design work than the factory. Besides, it is there that I have my laboratories where we experiment with the dyes.'

'I'm not going with you.'

'Oh, but I think you are,' came the silky response. 'Only five minutes ago you told me that you were prepared to work for me. Surely the mere fact that you have learned that you are to be a guest in my family home instead of living alone in a hotel cannot be the reason for this sudden turn-around. Think of Colin,' he told her hardily, 'think of your own future, just as I am thinking of my brother's.'

'Jorge?' Jessica looked bewildered. 'What does he have to do with this?'

'Everything,' he told her succinctly. 'Did you honestly think I would allow you to remain in Seville to further harass my poor brother upon his return, spreading the lord only knows what rumours about his relationship with you— rumours which could well reach the ears of his *novia*? Seville is a very enclosed society and a very rigid one. Barbara's father would never consider Jorge as a husband for his daughter if he were to learn of his relationship with you.'

'I should have thought it was Barbara's opinion that mattered, not her father's,' Jessica remarked sardonically, watching him look down the aquiline length of his nose at her, 'and besides, I had no intention of staying in Spain.'

'You tell me that now, but you cannot deny you came here initially with the express purpose of seeing my brother, when he had already written to you telling you that your association was at an end? No, even if you swore to me that you would never try to contact Jorge again I would not believe you. There is only one way to end your interference in our lives.'

'And what may that be?' Jessica asked tartly. 'Or does the mere fact that I'm in your employ mean that no one would ever believe a Calvadores guilty of demeaning himself by becoming involved with a mere wage-slave?'

Her sarcasm brought a dark tinge of angry colour seeping beneath his tan, his eyes as cold as granite as he stared at her aloofly.

'By no means,' he said at last, 'but what they will think is that Jorge would never stoop to become involved with my mistress.'

'Your . . . You mean you'd let people think I

was your mistress?' Jessica gasped. 'Oh, this is infamous! You wouldn't dare!'

A muscle clenched in his jaw, beating angrily against the taut skin, and her eyes were drawn betrayingly to it, as it echoed the uneven pounding of her own heart.

'I thought you might have learned by now not to challenge me,' he told her softly, and she knew that he did dare—anything—if he deemed it necessary.

Heavens, it was like a Restoration comedy! First of all he accused her of being his brother's mistress and now he was saying everyone would think she was his!

'You're exaggerating,' she said positively. 'No one would believe, because I was working for you, that I was your mistress.'

'Of course not,' he agreed smoothly, 'if we were working at the factory. But we shall be working at my home, and I shall take good care to make sure that our relationship is not merely that of employer and employee.'

'But this is all so unnecessary!' Jessica cried heatedly.

'To you perhaps, but not to me. The Calvadores name means a great deal to me, and I will not have it dragged in the mud because some greedy woman tries to blackmail my brother into marrying her.'

His last unforgivable words infuriated her. By what right did he presume to stand in judgment on her?

'Well, if you expect to stop me by dragging me off to your *hacienda*, you're in for a big disappointment,' she told him coldly, 'because

I'm not coming with you, and there's no way short of using physical force that you can make me.'

'You've already agreed to work for me,' he pointed out icily, '—of your own free will. If you don't . . .'

'I know,' Jessica agreed wearily. 'Colin will lose the contract.'

'No doubt he will understand—when you explain to him your reasons for refusing,' he told her smoothly, and a sick dismay filled her. Of course she could not explain to Colin why she had refused, it was all far too complicated now, and he would probably simply tell her to tell the truth. How could she do that now? How could she expose Isabel to his wrath? For one thing, she would not put it past him to go to England and terrorise Isabel into doing something foolish. And what about John? How would he react to the news that his fiancée had been having a brief fling in Spain when she was supposed to be thinking over his proposal, and moreover that she had actually thought that she might be pregnant by her lover? No, she could not tell the truth, and the only alternatives were to either accept the proposition and everything that went with it, or refuse it and risk jeopardising Colin's business. Some alternative!

She knew she really had no choice, but it infuriated her to have to give in to such outrageously buccaneering tactics.

'I will come with you,' she said coolly at last, 'but if you attempt to give anyone the impression that we're anything other than business colleagues, I shall be forced to contradict you.'

'Who said anything about "telling" anyone?' he mocked her softly. 'There are other, more subtle ways—like this, for instance.'

Before she could stop him, he had jerked her against his body, his hands locking behind her, holding her against him. She could feel the steady thud of his heart, so much at variance with her own which was racing unsteadily, the breath constricted in her throat, her eyes on a level with the plain severity of his tie. Her heightened senses relayed to her the sharp, clean fragrance of his cologne, the pristine freshness of his shirt, and the smooth brown column of his throat. She lifted her eyes. There was a dark shadow along his jaw suggesting that he might find it necessary to shave night and morning, and she shivered at the thoughts the knowledge conjured up in her mind.

'Let me go!' Her voice was husky, edged with anger and pain. She saw the curling mockery of his smile, the darkness of the cold grey eyes, and knew there was about as much chance of her plea being answered as there was of a hawk dropping its prey.

'You are trembling.'

It was a statement that held an edge of surprise, accompanied by a quick frown. The hand that wasn't securing her body against the hard length of his moved to her shoulder, flicking aside the collar of her robe to reveal the silky paleness of her skin.

'You didn't do much sunbathing when you were on holiday, or is it simply that Jorge told you how much we Latin races admire a palely beautiful skin? Yours has the translucency of a pearl.'

His fingers stroked lightly across her exposed collarbone, tiny tendrils of fear curling insidiously through her lower stomach. Dear God, she thought achingly, what was he trying to do to her? What *was* he doing to her? She had been touched before, for heaven's sake—but never with such explicit sensuality; never as though the male fingers drifting against her skin were touching the softest silk.

'*Dios*,' she heard him murmur smokily, 'one would think you had never been touched by a man before. But we both know that is not true, don't we, *señorita*?'

And then, shockingly, his mouth was where his fingers had been, the eroticism of his touch sending tiny shivers of pleasure coursing through her body. Mindlessly Jessica allowed him to mould her body to his, her head falling back helplessly against his arm, his eyes darkening to obsidian as the neckline of her robe dipped, revealing the pale curves of her breasts.

'Like marble,' he murmured huskily, trailing his fingers seductively along the hollow between her breasts, ignoring her stifled gasp of shock, 'but unlike marble, your skin feels warm to my touch.' His fingers tightened ruthlessly on her hair, his voice hardening as he demanded savagely, 'Tell me now that someone walking in here would not immediately think that we were lovers!'

She shivered bitterly with reaction, hating herself for the way she had yielded so completely to his superior strength, hating her body's purely female response to his masculinity.

His sardonic, 'Perhaps you need further

convincing,' made her stomach muscles coil
tensely, her body stiffening as he grasped her
chin, tilting it so that there was no way she could
avoid the hard punishment of his lips, and yet
even knowing that he was punishing her,
something elemental and fierce sprang to life
inside her the moment his mouth touched hers.
Her robe was pushed aside, tanned fingers
cupping the soft swell of one breast. Jessica
shuddered uncontrollably and pushed frantically
away, and by some miracle Sebastian released
her, surveying her flushed cheeks and furious
eyes with cynical amusement.

'What is wrong?' he drawled. 'Surely I took no
liberties that have not been permitted to
countless others?'

The truth of the matter was that he had; but
Jessica wasn't going to admit as much.

'As you've pointed out,' she responded icily,
'*they* were permitted them, you weren't.' Not
even for Colin's sake could she agree to work
with him now; she would never know a moment's
peace, never be able to relax . . .

'I'm not going to work for you,' she told him
quickly, huddling into the protection of her robe,
and avoiding his eyes. 'I . . .'

'You are trying to tell me you won't work for
me because of that?' He was openly incredulous
and disbelieving. 'You are behaving like an
affronted virgin; quite unnecessary, you cannot
imagine you stand in any danger of receiving
unwanted advances from me? If I haven't
already made it clear, perhaps it's time I did,'
he told her with deadly silky venom. 'I am not
interested in other men's leavings—whether it is

one man or a hundred. You are as safe with me as you would be locked up in a convent. Don't mistake a timely warning for any desire for you, and that was all that was—a warning. You will come with me,' he added softly, 'I promise you that. Be ready—I shall pick you up tomorrow morning at nine.'

If she had any pride, she would be on a plane back home right now, not sitting staring at her suitcases and wondering if she was doing the right thing, Jessica decided as she glanced round the impersonal hotel bedroom. A glance at her watch showed that it was half past eight. Colin had already left for the airport, full of praise and gratitude—they had talked all evening, and she had tried on several occasions to tell him that there was simply no way she could work for Sebastian de Calvadores, but every time her nerve failed her.

A knock on her door startled her. The porter entered and picked up her cases. Nervous dread fluttering through her stomach, Jessica followed him to the lift.

To try and calm herself a little she ordered herself a cup of coffee, but when it came she felt totally unable to drink it. She hadn't had any breakfast either. Why, oh, why hadn't she left Spain with Colin? He would have understood if she had explained. But she hadn't been able to disappoint him, to know that she was destroying everything he had come to Spain to achieve. She was a coward, she berated herself. She should have told him, and if she had, she wouldn't be here now, waiting . . . her heart leapt into her throat as she saw the familiar tall figure striding towards her.

'Come!'

It was the first time she had seen him wearing anything other than a formal suit; the dark, narrow-fitting pants clinging to the taut muscles of his thighs, the thin silk shirt hinting at the shadow of hair across his chest. Her stomach muscles tensed protestingly, and she was vividly reminded of how she had felt when he touched her. A fine linen jacket emphasised the breadth of his shoulders, and Jessica suddenly felt acutely nervous. What did she know of this man, apart from the fact that he had an almost obsessive pride in the good name of his family? Nothing!

'You may cease looking at me as though I had suddenly grown two heads. I assure you, you are quite safe,' he told her urbanely. 'Just as long as you behave yourself.'

'And if I don't, you'll do what?' Jessica demanded huskily. 'Punish me as you did yesterday, by forcing yourself on me?'

'Be careful, Señorita James,' he warned her softly. 'You challenge me so recklessly that I wonder if you find the "punishment" as unpalatable as you claim. You have a saying, do you not, "Any port in a storm", but I will not be the port for your frustrated desires, no matter how much you goad me.'

Jessica stared at him fulminatingly. Did he dare to suggest that she actually wanted him to touch her? To . . .

'You're quite wrong,' she told him bitterly. 'I would rather endure the worst tempest that can rage than seek a haven in your arms!'

Just for a moment she thought she had disconcerted him. There was a brief flash of surprise in his eyes, but then it was gone, and he was ushering her through the foyer to the main entrance of the hotel. Outside, he guided her towards a gleaming Mercedes, while a porter brought out her luggage.

Jessica glanced at the car and shivered slightly. Once she was inside it there would be no going back, no chance to change her mind. She hesitated, torn between a longing to escape no matter what the cost, and a feeling that she owed it to Colin to stay.

'Do not do it,' a dulcet voice murmured in her ear. 'Where would you run to? Come,' Sebastian added, 'get in the car, and stop regarding me as though I were a convicted felon. I assure you I am quite harmless when I am treated with respect.'

Blindly Jessica groped for the rear door handle, but to her surprise, he opened the front passenger door.

'What's the matter?' she asked him bitterly as she climbed in. 'Surely you aren't afraid I'll try and escape?'

'We are supposed to be lovers,' he told her succinctly. 'That being the case, you would not sit alone in the rear of the car.'

'Certainly not,' Jessica agreed sarcastically. 'That, from what I recall of Spanish life, is a privilege accorded only to wives!'

They drove for several kilometres in silence, Jessica's nerves tensing every time Sebastian glanced at her. He was a fast but careful driver. sSe looked surreptitiously at him, flushing when she discovered that he was watching her.

'I have already told you,' he said harshly, 'you have nothing of a sexual nature to fear from me.'

'I don't,' Jessica told him, surprised by the anger in his eyes and the rigid line of his mouth.

'No? You are clutching the edge of your seat as though you expect an imminent assault on your virtue. Or are you simply trying for an effect? If so, it won't work,' he told her laconically. 'Even if I did not know all about you from Jorge, I could never believe that a Northern European woman in her twenties had retained the virginal innocence you are trying to portray.'

'Why not?' Jessica snapped at him. 'That comment has about as much basis for truth as saying that all Spanish girls are virgins when they marry—it simply doesn't hold water.'

'I shall not argue about it,' she was told evenly, 'but if I were you I would not tax my patience too greatly by trying to assimilate a personality we both know you do not possess!'

Jessica didn't know how long it would take them to reach the *hacienda*, but when eleven o'clock came and went and they were in the depths of the country she started to realise how difficult it might be for her to leave the *hacienda* if she wished.

'Not much farther now,' Sebastian told her. 'Another hour, perhaps.'

'How on earth can you work so far away from the factory?' Jessica asked him.

'There are such things as telephones,' he told her dryly. 'The *hacienda* has been in my family for many generations. We still grow the grapes that go to make one of our fine local sherries, although now this is not produced exclusively from Calvadores vines.'

Jessica had already noticed the vines growing in the fields, but pride had prevented her from asking too many questions—that and a growing nausea exacerbated by the fact that she had had no breakfast. In fact she was beginning to feel distinctly lightheaded, but she forced herself to appear alert and interested as Sebastian told her about the local wines, and the art of making sherry.

It was almost exactly twelve o'clock when they turned off the main road, throwing up clouds of dust as they bumped down an unmade-up track. Vines covered the ground as far as the eye could see, and it was only when they crested a small incline that Jessica got her first glimpse of the hacienda.

For some reason she had expected a simple farmhouse-type building, and she caught her breath in awe as she stared down at the collection of Moorish-style buildings, shimmering whitely in the strong sunlight, the cupolas gilded by the sun, for all the world as though the entire complex had been wafted from ancient Baghdad on a magic carpet.

'The original building was constructed many centuries ago by an ancestor of mine,' Sebastian told her. 'He was given this land as part of his wife's dowry and on it he built the first house. Since then many generations have added to it, but always retaining the Moorish flavour—of course there have been times, for instance during the Inquisition, when it was not always wise for people to admit to their Moorish blood, when it has even perhaps been expedient to deny it.'

Looking at him, Jessica couldn't imagine that he would ever deny his heritage; indeed, she could far more easily see him condemning himself to the flames of the *auto de Fe* than recanting his Moorish blood and his proud ancestors.

They drove under a white archway and into an outer courtyard, paved and cool. As Sebastian opened her door for her, Jessica was aware of movements, of a door opening and people hurrying towards them. A wave of dizziness struck her, and she clung hard to the nearest solid object, distracted to realise it was Sebastian's arm, and then, catching her completely off guard, Sebastian bent his head, coolly capturing her lips and plundering the unguarded sweetness of her mouth.

Just for a moment time seemed to stand still, crazily improbable emotions racing through her heart. What was happening to her that she should want to cling to those broad shoulders and go on clinging? And then her lips were released and Sebastian was saying lazily, in English, 'Ah, Tia Sofia, allow me to introduce Jessica.'

And Jessica was being scrutinised thoughtfully by a pair of snapping dark eyes, very much like Sebastian's, although in a feminine and less arrogant face.

'You are on time, Sebastian,' was all his aunt said. 'The little one is so excited I have had to tell her to go and lie down for a little while. It is always the same when she knows you are coming.'

'My aunt refers to my ... ward,' Sebastian explained to Jessica. 'She lives here at the *hacienda* with my aunt and will do so until she is old enough to go to school.' His fingers rested lightly on her arm, and although she was looking discreetly away, Jessica knew that his aunt was aware of their intimacy.

'I have had Rosalinda's rooms prepared for your guest,' she was saying to Sebastian, glancing uncertainly at him.

'Rosalinda was the first Calvadores bride to occupy the *hacienda*,' Sebastian told Jessica. 'Her rooms are in one of the towers, quite secluded from the rest of the house with their own courtyard and stairs leading from it.'

Jessica's face flamed as the implication of his words sank in, and out of the corner of her eye she saw his aunt frown a little and glance at her uncertainly. There was no doubt at all in Jessica's mind that his aunt thought that they were lovers. Lovers! A sharp pain seemed to stab through her heart, her muscles tensing in protest at the images the word invoked. But she and Sebastian were not lovers, she reminded herself, nor ever likely to be. For one thing, he felt nothing but contempt for her, while she, of course, equally detested him ... Just for a moment she remembered her mixed emotions when he had kissed her, quickly banishing the treacherous suggestion that there had been something infinitely pleasurable in the pressure of his mouth against hers. How could it have been remotely pleasurable? He had kissed her in punishment and she had loathed and resented it! Of course she had.

CHAPTER FIVE

IT was Sebastian's aunt who showed Jessica to Rosalinda's tower, much to her relief.

They approached the tower via a narrow, spiralling staircase, the smoothly plastered walls decorated with decorative frescoes and friezes in the Arabic style.

At the top of the stairs, Tia Sofia opened a door and gestured to Jessica to precede her. Once inside Jessica caught her breath on a gasp of pleasure. The room was large and octagonal in shape, an arched doorway leading to another room, and the view from the mediaeval slit windows stunned her with the magnificent panorama spread out below.

'This room is the highest in the house,' Sofia de Calvadores explained. 'Although latterly it has not been used—it is too impractical for a married couple, and there have been no daughters of the house to make it their own as was the custom in the past.'

'It's beautiful,' Jessica said reverently, gazing at her surroundings. The walls were hung with a soft apricot silk, matching rugs on the polished wood floor. This room was furnished as a small sitting room, and she guessed that beyond it lay the bedroom. Bookcases had been built to fit the octagonal walls; one of the larger window embrasures was fitted with a cushioned seat, and it wasn't hard to imagine a lovely Spanish girl sitting there perhaps playing her mandolin while she gazed through the window waiting for her husband to return home.

Her guide opened the communicating door to show Jessica the bedroom, once again decorated in the same soft apricot, the huge bed covered with a soft silk coverlet.

'There is a bathroom through there,' she told Jessica, indicating another door set into one of the walls. 'It is fortunate that when the idea of this octagonal room was conceived it was built within the existing square tower, so we have been able to make use of the space between the walls to install modern plumbing. I shall leave you now—Maria will come and unpack for you, and we normally have lunch at one.'

Taking the gentle hint, as soon as she was alone Jessica opened the bathroom door, gasping with fresh delight when she saw the sunken marble bath and mirrored walls of the room, reflecting images of her whichever way she turned, the mirrors possessing a greenish tinge, given off by the malachite.

She washed quickly, then changed into a linen skirt in a buttercup yellow shade that complemented her colouring, adding a delicate short-sleeved embroidered blouse. She was going to need more clothes if she was to stay here for the time stipulated. She would have to write to her aunt and ask her to arrange to send some of her things on.

She checked her make-up, renewing her lipstick, chagrined to see how little of it was left after Sebastian's kiss, and having brushed her hair she walked through the sitting room to the top of the stairs, conscious of a nervous butterfly sensation in her stomach, and something faintly akin to anticipation tingling along her spine, as she steeled herself to face her host and new employer.

Whatever his aunt might privately think of Jessica's presence, it was plain to Jessica that she was a Spanish woman of the old school, and that the will of the male members of her family was law. She greeted Jessica pleasantly when she reached the bottom of the stairs and explained that she was waiting to show her the rest of the house, 'Which is rather rambling,' she told her, 'so I will show you round so that you will not get lost.'

Jessica followed her into the main *sala*, furnished with rare antiques, and with a silkily beautiful and probably priceless Aubusson rug on the floor. Beyond the windows lay a courtyard similar in design to the one beneath Jessica's tower, only this one was larger, encompassing several formal beds of flowers, and whereas Jessica's boasted a fountain and a small pool, this one possessed a shimmeringly blue swimming pool and a terrace.

'This is the main courtyard,' Sofia de Calvadores told her. 'There are others, because the Calvadores are first and foremost a Moorish family and for many centuries strictly segregated the differing sections of the family; privacy becomes of prime importance when a house is shared by several generations, and while this *sala* and its courtyard has always been considered a gathering place, there are several small, secluded courtyards which in the past were the private domain of various family members.'

'Just as the tower belonged to Rosalinda,' Jessica suggested. 'It must be fascinating to be able to trace one's family history back so far,' she added genuinely, suddenly remembering what Ramón Ferres had told them about the first Calvadores bride.

'Sometimes—sometimes it is not so pleasant to have the world privy to all one's secrets.'

'But the first Calvadores was one of Pedro the Cruel's knights, wasn't he?'

'Ah, you have heard that story,' Sofia smiled. 'Yes, indeed, that was so. He married the daughter of a Christian knight and it was for her, Rosalinda, that the tower was built.'

Jessica longed to question her further, but refrained, not wanting to appear too curious. What was it Ramón Ferres had said about the girl? That she had claimed her father's enemy had ravished her, and that rather than endure the taint of such an accusation he had married her?

'There you are!' a tiny voice suddenly piped up childishly, from the back of the room. 'Tio Sebastian sent me to look for you.'

'Lisa!' Señora Calvadores' voice reproached. 'Please remember we have a guest.' Her face relaxed into a faint smile as she turned to Jessica and explained in English, 'She is a little unthinking at times, and as always is excited by Sebastian's arrival. Lisa, come and meet Miss James, who is to work with Sebastian.'

A small, dark-haired child, with unexpectedly shadowed brown eyes, stepped forward and gravely offered her hand. She was immaculately if somewhat impractically dressed in a flounced white dress, matching ribbons securing her long hair, gleaming white socks and little black patent shoes such as Jessica couldn't remember seeing a little girl wearing since she herself had been a child.

She regarded Jessica with anxious gravity for several seconds and then burst out impetuously, 'Tio Sebastian won't be working all the time, will he?'

'Not quite,' Sebastian announced, startling Jessica with his silent entrance. 'You were so long, *pequeña*, I thought I should come and look for you.'

'Then, if you are not to work all the time, this afternoon we may go for a ride?' Lisa suggested with innocent coquetry. 'Please, Tio Sebastian! No one else lets me ride as fast as you.'

'We shall see, after lunch,' he told her. 'First your aunt must tell me if you have been a good girl while I have been gone.'

The child ran across to him, clinging to his arm while she assured him that indeed she had, and Jessica was shocked by the sudden wave of longing she experienced to be part of that charmed circle, with Sebastian's free arm securely round her.

The feeling was gone almost immediately, superseded by the knowledge that she was indulging in a ridiculous daydream, probably brought on by the fact that she was virtually alone in an alien land, excluded from the intimate family scene being played in front of her.

'Sebastian spoils her,' Sofia Calvadores complained as she and Jessica followed them out of the room, 'but in the circumstances it is easy to understand why. She is the image of her mother and . . .' She broke off as though feeling that she had said too much, drawing Jessica's attention to the doors leading to some of the other rooms as they walked into the hall.

'This is Sebastian's study,' she told her, opening one door and giving Jessica a brief glimpse of highly polished heavy furniture and a stained wooden floor covered in rich animal skins. 'But of course he will show you that himself later.'

The dining room seemed huge, the glittering chandeliers and frank opulence of the heavy mahogany table, polished until one could see one's reflection in it, making Jessica blink a little in dismay. She had forgotten how formal life could still be in the great Spanish houses.

'First an aperitif,' Sebastian announced, pouring small measures of golden sherry into small glasses and handing first his aunt and then Jessica one. 'This is made with the produce from our vines,' he told Jessica as she sipped hesitantly at the amber liquid. She had had nothing to eat all day and was beginning to feel the effects. A glass of sherry on an empty stomach was the last thing she wanted, but rather than cause offence by refusing she sipped hesitantly at the rich liquid. It slid warmly down her throat, but any hopes she had had of simply sipping a little and leaving the rest were dashed when Sebastian said ominously, 'Perhaps it is not to your liking?'

As though she would dare not like it! she thought half hysterically, and quickly drank the rest, and wishing she hadn't when her head started to spin muzzily.

It was still spinning when Sebastian indicated

that she should sit down at the table. A servant was holding her chair for her, and she walked hesitantly towards it, appalled to realise how disorientated the sherry had made her feel. Surely it was far more potent than anything she had drunk at home?

'Jessica!' Sebastian's voice cut sharply through her muddled thoughts.

'I ... it's ... I'm so sorry,' she managed to gasp as the world started whirling round dizzily and she reached for the first solid thing she could find, her fingers tightening convulsively on Sebastian's jacketed arm.

She heard him swear mildly, and then to her relief the mists started to clear.

'It was the sherry,' she managed to explain apologetically. 'I didn't have any breakfast, and . . .'

'It is very potent if you are not used to it,' Sebastian's aunt agreed. 'Sebastian,' she directed her nephew, 'it is your fault for insisting she drink it, but you will feel better directly, my dear,' she comforted Jessica.

What a terrible impression she must be creating, Jessica thought with burning cheeks, and she released Sebastian's arm as though it were live coals. She didn't miss the flash of sardonic comprehension in his eyes and shrank back when he bent his head and murmured softly, 'You cling to me as fiercely as a dove to the branch that gives it shelter, but I am not deceived by your air of helpless dismay. Jorge told me of the wild beach barbecues you both attended, when drinking raw Sangria was the order of the day, so please do not expect me to believe that one single glass of sherry could have such a calamitous effect.'

What was he trying to imply? That she might have some other motive for clinging to him? But what?

'If you are having second thoughts,' he added, supplying her with the answer, 'and thinking that any man in your bed is better than none, do not, I beg you, even think of nominating me for the role. As I have already said, I am particular about with whom I share the pleasures of the act of love.'

'Tio Sebastian, what are you saying to Miss James?' Lisa piped up curiously. 'She is looking all pink and funny!'

His aunt quickly shushed the child, but not before Jessica had pulled away and slid into her chair. What must his aunt think of her? she wondered bitterly; or was she inured to her nephew's habits? Did she perhaps simply ignore the real role in his life of the women whom he brought home? They would think they were lovers, he had told her, and she was forced to admit that he had been right, but how did one correct such insidious suggestions? By simply and frankly correcting them? How could she tell his aunt they were not lovers? It was impossible!

After lunch Sebastian suggested that he should show her round the laboratory.

'Can I come too, Tio?' Lisa pleaded. 'I promise I will be good.'

'If you have no objection?' he murmured enquiringly to Jessica.

She shook her head. In truth she would be glad of the little girl's company, because her excited chatter broke the constrained atmosphere that stretched between them.

The laboratory was situated at the back of the *hacienda*, in what had originally been an immense stable block but which Sebastian explained to Jessica had been converted into garages and his laboratory.

The door was padlocked and bolted, and he told her as he unlocked it that because of the dyes and processes used he allowed no one apart from himself to enter the building.

'At the moment we are working on a new generation of dyes, almost entirely based on natural substances, but there is still some problem with the stabilising agent, although that should not take too long to sort out.'

'You are the only company I know that uses only natural dyes,' Jessica mentioned. 'It's quite rare, but of course that's why no other concern can match you for delicacy of colour.'

'This is so,' Sebastian agreed, 'and that is why the exact blending and stabilising of the various agents is a closely guarded secret. Indeed, I am the only person in the company who possesses the complete formula—it is as valuable as that to us.'

Jessica could well understand why. The subtlety and delicacy of their colours was one of the things that helped to make their range of fabrics so successful.

The laboratory was well equipped, and she followed with interest Sebastian's description of the work he was carrying out, although her prime interest lay not so much in the dying of the fabric but in the design of it.

PASSIONATE PROTECTION 89

There was an office off the laboratory with a
row of metal filing cabinets, and Sebastian
unlocked one, producing some detailed sketches
and swatches of fabric which he handed to her.

'These are the colours we are hoping to
produce for next season's fabrics—as you know,
the Colour Council normally decide a season's
colours two or three years in advance. These are
the colours suggested by the last Council
meeting. What we have to do now is to
incorporate them into the design of the fabric.
What I should like you to do initially is to work
on them and produce some suggestions for me.'

Jessica nodded, excitement stirring as, against
her will, she became fascinated by the project
ahead. She did know that the Colour Council
worked two years ahead of the fashion designers,
selecting the spectrum of colours for a particular
season, and the swatches Sebastian had handed
her made her mouth water in anticipation. They
were autumn and winter colours; black, charcoal
grey, softly muted heathers and a bright peacock
blue shading to mauve.

'You can use the office here, or the sitting
room in the tower, whichever you wish,'
Sebastian told her carelessly, glancing down at
Lisa as she tugged impatiently at his hand.

'You said we could go riding,' she reminded
him, pouting a little. 'You promised!'

'You are forgetting that we have a guest,'
Sebastian reminded her firmly. 'Would it not be
polite also to ask Miss James if she would care to
come with us?'

The question was for Lisa's benefit and not
hers, Jessica acknowledged. Like other Latin

races Spanish children were petted and indulged, but good manners were considered paramount. Hesitantly Lisa asked if she would like to join them, her relief patent and winning Jessica a wide relieved smile, when she gently refused.

'I'll take these up to the tower with me,' she told Sebastian, adding to Lisa, 'Enjoy your ride.'

She didn't go straight back to the tower, but found her way instead to the small enclosed courtyard she could see from her bedroom window. Jacaranda bloomed profusely against the walls, mingling with the bougainvillea, while two doves cooed melodiously on the rim of the pool. The courtyard had a secluded, mysterious air, as though it preferred moonlight and the seductive whispers of lovers to sunshine and birdsong. Had Rosalinda ever walked here with a lover—the husband who had married her so unwillingly, perhaps? Had they ever found love together?

When she returned to the house she met Sebastian's aunt in the hall. 'Lisa and Sebastian are going riding,' she told her, adding impulsively, 'Lisa is a delightful child.'

'Charming—when she wants to be,' Sofia Calvadores agreed dryly, 'but Sebastian spoils her. It is natural, I suppose. He is all she has.'

'Her parents are dead, then?' Jessica asked sympathetically.

Was it her imagination or did the Señora hesitate briefly before saying, 'Yes, I'm afraid so, she is Sebastian's ward. It could be difficult for her should Sebastian marry and have children of his own.'

'But surely, when he does, his wife will

understand and accept that Lisa is bound to find it hard at first,' Jessica suggested.

Señora Calvadores smiled. 'One would hope so, but it would depend very much on the wife. Sebastian must marry, of course, to carry on the name. He was betrothed once, but his betrothed died—a tragic accident in a car.' She sighed and shook her head. 'It was all a long time ago, and best forgotten now.'

It was late afternoon before Lisa and Sebastian returned to the *hacienda*. Jessica had been working in her sitting room when a maid had knocked and told her that it was the custom for the ladies of the household to drink sherry and eat almond pastries at this particular time of the day, adding that Señora Calvadores was waiting for her in the main courtyard.

She hadn't realised how cramped her limbs had become, and she was still a little stiff when she emerged into the sunshine to find that Lisa and Sebastian had returned and were sitting with the Señora.

Sebastian moved and Jessica realised there was someone else with them; a tall stately woman in her early thirties, her thick dark hair drawn back in a chignon, her cold dark eyes appraising Jessica as they moved over her.

Jessica recognised her from the hotel in Seville, and wondered who she was.

'Ah, Jessica, there you are. Allow me to introduce Miss James to you, *cara*,' he said to his companion. 'She has come here to work for me for several weeks.'

'I hope she realises her good fortune,' was the brunette's acid response.

'Jessica—Pilar Sanchez, a close friend and neighbour of ours.'

'Merely a close friend,' Pilar pouted, slanting Jessica another acid glance. 'Come, our relationship is stronger than that. If poor Manuela had lived we would have been brother and sister.' Scarlet-tipped fingers lay provocatively along Sebastian's forearm, the look in her eyes as she gazed up at him anything but sisterly. There was a strange aching sensation in Jessica's stomach. They could be lovers. *Were* they lovers? Surely not; Pilar obviously came from a family as exalted as Sebastian's own; her sister had obviously been engaged to him. If he needed a wife surely he need look no further than Pilar. Or was there perhaps some bar on such a marriage because of his relationship with her sister? Jessica wasn't sure about the Catholic church's ruling on such things.

She was brought back to her surroundings with a jolt as Pilar scolded sharply, temper flags flying scarlet in her cheeks, 'Lisa, your fingers—don't touch my dress, child, you will ruin it!'

The little girl's face crumpled. She looked uncertainly at Sebastian, who was frowning, and then towards his aunt, who said gently, 'Lisa, go and find Maria. It is time for you to rest.'

'Really, Sebastian, that child is growing impossible!' Pilar commented sharply when Lisa had gone. 'You should send her to a convent where she could learn obedience.'

'As Manuela did?' Sebastian drawled sardonically, but Jessica couldn't understand the expression in Sofia's eyes or the reason for his aunt's suddenly tense body.

Jessica had to wait until after dinner to show Sebastian the work she had done during the day. To her surprise he didn't criticise it as thoroughly as she had anticipated, instead showing her some work he had done himself.

'Initially I didn't want to give you any guidelines,' he told her, 'because it is important that we work on the same wavelength. What you have done shows me that you have a natural sympathy for our fabrics and what we hope to achieve with them. Tomorrow we shall spend an hour together in my study talking about what line the new range will take. You like the tower?' he asked her unexpectedly.

Caught off guard by the absence of his normal cynicism and contempt, Jessica replied enthusiastically, 'I love it, but I can't help wondering if Rosalinda was happy there. She occupied those rooms alone . . .'

'Instead of sharing those of her husband?' Sebastian interrupted. 'This is true, but it was only in the initial days that she occupied the tower. You have obviously heard the story and you must remember that she had accused her husband of seducing her, when in fact he knew he had not. He had married her to protect his good name, but he swore he would remain celibate rather than touch an unwilling woman who had already given herself to another. So matters might have continued if Rosalinda hadn't found the courage to go to him and confess that she had lied to her father, but not to conceal any affair with another man, simply because she had fallen desperately in love with Rodriguez, and wanted him for her husband, but she knew that because

of the enmity that existed between him and her
father she had no chance of marrying him. So she
conceived her plan. She knew of the pride of both
Rodriguez and her father and knew that if she
were to accuse Rodriguez of dishonouring her he
would be forced to make reparation. It was a bold
step to take; she had to face dishonour herself—
admit to her lack of chastity, perhaps endure the
hatred of her husband for ever, when he knew
how he had been tricked.

'But Rosalinda was beautiful as well as bold.
Rodriguez could not resist her tears of contrition
for the trick she had played, and she told him that
she was still a virgin. She did not spend many
nights alone in her tower,' Sebastian added dryly.

'So she tricked him into marriage, just as
you've accused me of trying to trick Jorge,'
Jessica pointed out.

He looked at her angrily. 'The two cases are
entirely different. She was motivated by love,
which excuses much; you are motivated by
material greed, which is unforgivable.'

Why was it that no matter what subject they
discussed they always ended up quarrelling?
Jessica wondered tiredly as she gathered together
her designs and the swatches of fabric.

'You are looking pale,' Sebastian confounded
her by saying abruptly. 'My aunt tells me you
worked all afternoon and then into the evening.'

'You had a guest,' Jessica pointed out, without
reminding him that Pilar had looked anything but
pleased at his suggestion that she stay with them.
'And besides, I enjoyed it.'

'In future you will take proper exercise.' He
frowned. 'Can you ride?' Jessica shook her head.

'A pity, you could have joined Lisa when she rides with me in the morning.'

He made her sound like another child to be humoured and scolded, Jessica thought wryly.

'I can walk, or swim,' she told him. 'And besides, the sooner the work is completed the sooner I can leave.'

For some reason his mouth compressed angrily at that statement, and with one of those quickly shifting moods she was coming to dread Jessica felt a frisson of awareness steal through her. He had discarded his jacket, and the breeze from the open windows flattened his shirt tautly to his body, moulding the muscled power of his torso. His shirt was open at the neck, the pale glimmer of the white fabric emphasising the darkness of his skin. A pulse beat steadily at the base of his throat, drawing her eyes, a curious sensual tension enveloping her. She moistened her lips and watched as he moved slowly towards her.

'Jessica . . .' He broke off as the *sala* door was suddenly thrust open and a tall young man with a shock of dark hair and a mobile mouth hurried in, coming to a standstill as he saw Jessica.

'Jorge!' Sebastian exclaimed in surprise. '*Dios!* What are you doing here?'

Jorge! Jessica stared in disbelief at the newcomer. This was Sebastian's brother?

It was plain that he was slightly taken aback by Sebastian's attitude. He glanced uncertainly first at his brother and then at Jessica.

'I wanted to see you,' he said in a puzzled voice. 'I had no idea you were planning to come here. You never mentioned it when we spoke on the telephone.'

'Perhaps because I had no idea you were intending your stay with the Reajons to be of such a short duration. It was, I believe, to be for one month.'

Jessica felt sorry for the younger man as he flushed and looked uncomfortable. 'That is one of the things I wanted to talk to you about, Sebastian. I . . .' He broke off and glanced hesitantly at Jessica, then turned to his brother, saying gallantly, 'But you have a guest—and a very beautiful one. Aren't you going to introduce me?'

To say that Sebastian looked stupefied was an overstatement, but there was a certain amount of shock as he registered the words. He too turned to look at Jessica, and she quailed beneath the message she read in his eyes.

'I thought Miss James was already known to you,' he said in icy tones. 'In fact to such an extent it is not so long ago that you were pleading with me to help you remove her from your life.'

Jessica felt sorry for the young man when he flushed again, but it was obvious to her that Sebastian intended to spare her nothing.

'I am Isabel's cousin,' she explained to Jorge, ignoring Sebastian. 'There's been a slight misunderstanding and your brother mistook me for Isabel. When I learned what he had to say to her I decided not to enlighten him. For all her faults, Isabel is acutely sensitive . . .'

She didn't need to say any more. Jorge looked appalled, and turned horrified eyes on his brother. 'Sebastian, you said nothing about speaking personally to Isabel! We were agreed that a letter . . .'

'So we were, but then I had no idea that she intended to come and plead her case personally—or so I thought. Naturally my first priority was to protect you.'

'Another misconception on your part,' Jessica told him bitterly. 'Isabel ... didn't tell me the full facts. She was terrified that you intended to go to England to see her. She is now engaged to someone else ... and quite naturally ...' She was beginning to flounder, not wanting to betray Isabel's stupidity and lack of moral fibre, but Sebastian, it seemed, had no such qualms.

'What you are saying is that your cousin lied to you.'

'Not deliberately,' Jessica hastened to defend Isabel. 'She simply wanted to make sure there would be no repercussions from her letter to Jorge—written when she was feeling extremely worried and almost desperate. She wanted me to tell Jorge that she fully accepted that their liaison was at an end.'

It wasn't quite the truth, but it would suffice.

'You knew I had mistaken you for her, why did you not tell me the truth then?' Sebastian demanded, watching her with narrowed eyes.

'Because I didn't want to expose Isabel to the same sort of insults I had been forced to endure myself,' Jessica told him coolly. 'Just as you wanted to protect your brother, I wanted to protect my cousin!'

'We will speak of this later,' he told her silkily. 'For now ...'

'You naturally want to be alone with your brother,' Jessica supplied dryly, not adding that she was more than happy to leave them alone together.

Jorge's unexpected arrival had given her a bad shock. Whereas she ought to be experiencing relief and satisfaction that Sebastian now knew the truth, all she could think was that he might now send her back to England, and for some reason she didn't wait to analyse too carefully, she didn't want to go!

CHAPTER SIX

'Ah, there you are, I hope you will permit me to join you?'

Jessica glanced at Jorge's concerned face and smiled. She was sitting in her small courtyard, working on some of the designs, and enjoying the sunshine.

'Sebastian is working in his laboratory,' Jorge informed her, needlessly, since Sebastian himself had told her at breakfast that he could be found there should she want him. There had also been a look in his eyes that told her that there was still a reckoning to come, but that was something she was refusing to think about!

'I must apologise, for my . . . for my brother's behaviour,' Jorge managed at last, flushing a little. 'It is unforgivable that he should have involved you in this affair.' He bit his lip. 'He has given me the gist of what has happened between you, although why, feeling as he does, he has brought you here to the *hacienda* to work for him I do not know!'

He looked perplexed and unhappy, but Jessica didn't enlighten him. He might think Sebastian had told him the truth, but she knew differently.

'I was speaking to my aunt this morning and she seems to think . . . that is, Sebastian has given her the impression . . . that . . . that you are lovers,' he added uncomfortably, 'and yet plainly this is not so. I shall speak to him about it on your behalf. Isabel talked of you to me, I know you are not . . . that you do not . . .'

'That I'm not promiscuous?' Jessica supplied dryly, privately suspecting that Isabel had been far more unflattering in her description of her, but Jorge seized on the expression gratefully.

'*Si*,' he agreed, 'this is so . . . Sebastian cannot appreciate what my aunt thinks, for he would never expose a young woman of unblemished reputation to such an insult.'

Heavens, he sounded like something out of a Victorian novel! Jessica thought to herself. Surely he couldn't be serious? But apparently he was.

'I shall speak to him about it,' he added again. 'It is not right.'

Right or wrong, she couldn't see Sebastian being easily influenced by his younger brother, Jessica reflected when Jorge had gone.

She had been on her own for about half an hour when she glanced up, hearing footsteps coming in her direction. To her surprise she saw Pilar coming towards her, the older woman's mouth grimly compressed, two bright coins of colour burning in her otherwise completely pale face.

'You are wasting your time!' she hissed to Jessica without preamble. 'Sebastian does not really want you. He has only ever loved one woman—my sister, and . . .'

Jessica tried to interrupt, to assure her companion that she had no romantic interest in Sebastian. Something about the way the older woman was watching her triggered alarm bells in her mind. It struck her that there was something driven, something almost bordering on hysteria, in Pilar's manner.

'He was obsessed by her,' Pilar continued almost as though Jessica wasn't there, 'but one day he will have to marry, if only in order to have sons, and who better than the sister of the woman he loved?'

'But surely . . .' Surely there is Jorge, Jessica had been about to say, but once again Pilar didn't give her the opportunity to finish.

'You are thinking of Lisa,' she said bitterly, 'but she is only a daughter. Sebastian needs sons.'

Lisa was Sebastian's daughter? Shock coursed through Jessica, stingingly, followed by a hot, molten anger. How dared he question her morals when he . . .

'You didn't know?' Pilar started to laugh wildly. 'Of course he wouldn't tell you. No one is supposed to know about it. My sister Manuela had been his *novia* for many months and the preparations for the wedding were all in hand when she suddenly become ill. It was the strain of preparing for the wedding, our doctor told my parents, and Manuela was sent to Argentina to stay with relatives there. When she returned it was obvious that there was to be a child— Sebastian's child. My parents were bitterly hurt and shocked. Sebastian whom they trusted and treated like a son had taken Manuela's innocence before they were married. Preparations for the ceremony were speeded up. My mother begged Manuela to tell her why she had not confided in her before her visit to Argentina. I myself was married then. I too was shocked by Sebastian's behaviour, but I knew how much he loved her.

And then just two days before the ceremony Manuela asked me if she could borrow my car.' Pilar hesitated and for a moment there was a sly, almost gloating expression in her eyes.

'She was involved in an accident near Seville, and was taken immediately to the hospital. They were able to save the child, but by the time Sebastian reached the hospital Manuela was dead.'

Jessica couldn't conceal her shock and distaste. Poor Manuela! By all accounts she had been tragically innocent and young, and now she was dead and Sebastian was left only with memories of what might have been, and a child—his child! Why then had she been introduced as his 'ward'?

'Of course everything was hushed up,' Pilar continued. 'Only the closest members of the family know of the circumstances of Lisa's birth.' Her lips twisted, and Jessica was reminded of how much she seemed to dislike the little girl—a child who was after all her niece. 'Lisa is a constant reminder to Sebastian of my sister,' Pilar continued, and with a flash of insight Jessica realised that Pilar was jealous; jealous of her sister's child.

'It was a tragic year for our family,' she added. 'First Manuela and then my own husband and parents were killed when my husband was taking them to Minorca in his plane, but worst of all— Lisa.' She shuddered. 'It is just as well Manuela died. Had she lived she would have been shunned for her sin.'

Jessica could hardly believe her ears. What Pilar was saying was positively feudal—and what

of Sebastian, surely he was equally to blame, if
indeed 'blame' was the word. And poor Lisa! She
obviously didn't realise that Sebastian was her
father. Jessica felt an upsurge of anger against
him. How could he deny his daughter her right to
her relationship with him? Pilar said he had loved
Manuela, but in Jessica's opinion it was a poor
sort of love that denied the human evidence of
that love.

She was still trying to come to terms with what
Pilar had told her after lunch, when Sebastian
announced that he wanted to talk to Jorge in his
study.

Lisa was at a loose end, and asked Jessica if she
could sit with her. 'I will be very good,' she
promised, 'but it is Tia Sofia's day for having her
friends round, and it is very dull.'

Jessica was touched that the little girl should
want her company. Her work on the designs was
well advanced, and in fact she could do little until
she had spoken to Sebastian, so she suggested
instead that Lisa show her round the environs of
the *hacienda*.

The little girl was an entertaining companion.
Jessica had always liked children, and concealed
her pity carefully when Lisa commented on how
lonely she sometimes felt.

'Pilar wants to send me away,' she confided
fearfully, 'but Tio Sebastian will not let her.'

How could Sebastian deny his relationship
with his child?

It was late afternoon when they returned.
Sebastian's aunt was in the *sala* with her friends,
and Lisa politely listened to their questions,

responding demurely, quite different from the exuberant child she had been when she had been with Jessica.

Jessica could tell that she herself was the subject of a good deal of discreet curiosity.

'Jessica is a particular friend of Sebastian's,' his aunt explained.

'But I understand from my niece that you were here primarily to work for him,' one formidable matron said icily.

Jessica wasn't surprised to discover that she was Pilar's aunt. 'And your family don't mind?' she asked, apparently unable to believe it when Jessica assured her that they didn't. 'In Spain no young woman of good family would be permitted to stay in the home of an unmarried man without a female relative with her.'

'I am here to work,' Jessica reminded her coolly, uneasily reminded of what Jorge had said. Did these women think she was Sebastian's mistress? What did it matter if they did? And yet it was an uncomfortable sensation to have them studying her, perhaps talking about her when she wasn't there.

After they left the *sala*, Jessica went upstairs to her tower, while Lisa was whisked away by her maid for a rest.

The household ran like clockwork, and yet apparently without any effort on the part of Sebastian's aunt, although Jessica had noticed that the staff consulted her every day just after breakfast. It must be an enormous responsibility caring for the valuable antiques and art treasures that filled the *hacienda*, and she reflected that it was impossible not to admire the selflessness of

Spanish women when it came to devoting themselves to their homes.

She had wanted to see Sebastian about the designs she was working on and gathering up her work she went downstairs to his study. She could hear voices from inside, one of them recognisably Jorge's and bitterly defensive.

Now was obviously not the time to intrude, and she was just walking away when Rafael, the major-domo of the household, appeared.

'I was hoping to have a word with the Conde,' Jessica explained in response to his unspoken question, 'but . . .'

'I shall inform him when he is free,' Rafael assured her. 'Perhaps you would care for a tray of tea? In the past our English guests have often asked for tea at this time.'

It was six o'clock and as Jessica knew from experience, it would be several hours before they dined. Spaniards dined late, so she thanked Rafael and told him that tea would indeed be most welcome.

It arrived twenty minutes later—a bone china tea service and a plate of delicate almond cakes. Until she saw them Jessica hadn't realised how hungry she felt. She had just finished her second cup of tea when someone knocked briskly on the door. She knew without opening it, with some instinctive sixth sense, that it was Sebastian.

He looked preoccupied and bleakly angry, and her heart sank. Now was obviously not the time to discuss her ideas with him.

'Now,' he said, when he had closed the door with a precision that sent shivers of alarm feathering along her spine, 'perhaps you will be good enough to explain why you did not tell me the truth about your cousin?'

He was leaning against the door, arms folded across his chest, unconsciously straining the fabric, his eyes glinting metallic grey as they waited for her response.

'I've already told you,' Jessica said tightly. She had forgotten the implicit threat she had seen in his eyes when Jorge unwittingly revealed the truth, in the shock of listening to Pilar's disclosures.

'I wanted to protect Isabel . . .'

'Protect her, or her engagement?' he asked with devastating insight. 'Jorge has told me of this John—apparently she was contemplating becoming engaged to him when she met Jorge.'

'Jorge was simply a holiday romance,' Jessica told her firmly. 'Isabel is silly but not venal. I can assure you she had no mercenary interest in Jorge.'

'No? Then why did she threaten him with this child she says she conceived?'

'A mistake,' Jessica told him. 'Surely you can appreciate her position? She came back from holiday, and then discovered that she might be carrying Jorge's child, or so she thought, so she panicked . . .'

'And tried to force him into marrying her,' Sebastian concluded distastefully. 'And this is the innocent child you wished to protect? No, I cannot accept it.'

She wasn't going to tell him how Isabel had lied to her, Jessica decided angrily, her chin tilting defiantly as she stared up at him.

'It doesn't matter to me whether you do or not,' she told him unsteadily. 'All I want to do now is to put the entire incident behind me.'

It wasn't completely true—certain aspects of it would remain to haunt her always, and she was very much afraid that what she felt for Sebastian came dangerously close to love. Quite how or why it should have happened she didn't know, but these last few days had underlined, time and time again, that she was far from indifferent to him. She only had to register the way her pulses raced whenever he walked in a room to be aware of that! And yet he was the complete antithesis of all she admired in men. Arrogant, domineering and apparently incapable of facing up to his responsibilities.

'Easier said than done.' He frowned, unfolding his arms, and moved silently to the window. 'As Jorge has just been at considerable pains to point out to me, my aunt, and no doubt by this time, her cronies, all believe you to be my mistress.'

He seemed to be waiting for some response, and Jessica refused to acknowledge the hurting shaft of pain his indifference occasioned.

'We know differently,' she told him. 'And besides, the opinion of half a dozen or so people I've never set eyes on before and am not likely to see again doesn't trouble me.'

'I'm sure it doesn't,' Sebastian agreed grittily, 'but unfortunately, I do have to see them again and it does concern me, as everything touching upon the good name of our family must.'

It was on the tip of Jessica's tongue to tell him that this was something he should have thought of before, but instead she said unsteadily, 'Yes, I see that having a reputation such as yours must be a great burden to so proud a man.'

Instantly she realised she had gone too far. Fingers like talons gripped her wrist.

'Just what do you mean by that?' he demanded softly.

'I think you know,' Jessica managed bravely. 'There's Lisa, and people are not blind . . .'

'Ah, someone has told you about Manuela,' he said comprehensively, his mouth twisting in a cynically bitter smile. 'And of course you are quite right. There is endless gossip about Lisa, and her parenthood, and because of that I have to be extremely circumspect—for her sake as much as my own.'

'I can't see why you don't tell her the truth,' Jessica told him huskily. 'It's cruel not to do. She's bound to find out.'

'You are very concerned on her behalf.' Again the mockingly cynical smile.

'Because I happen to like her; and because also I know what it's like to lose both parents, and nothing, but nothing compensates for that loss. Any parent is better than none at all,' she told him fiercely, 'and you're depriving her of the right to that relationship.'

'Enough!' With a ferocity that jerked the breath from her lungs she was dragged towards him. 'I will not listen to any more. You will be silent!'

'How will you make me?' Jessica demanded breathlessly. 'By flinging me in your dungeons?'

'Oh no.' The soft way he spoke, and the insolently appraising look that accompanied the words, sent nervous tremors of warning chasing down her spine. 'Like this!'

He moved so suddenly that she couldn't evade

him, hard fingers tangling in her hair and tugging painfully until she thought her spine would crack under the pressure. His eyes searched her vulnerable, exposed features in silence, while hers spat the defiance she now dared not voice.

'It is too late for obedience now,' he told her silkily. 'You must take your punishment.'

His mouth on hers was brutally chastising, his fingers hurting as they bit into her waist, a savage anger that she had not seen before burning in the pressure of his mouth against hers.

She felt frozen and completely unable to feel, her eyes glazing as she tried not to mind that he was humiliating her like this, turning what should be a sensually exciting experience into a deeply humiliating one.

As though he sensed that somehow she had escaped his vengeance, the pressure of his mouth suddenly softened and then shockingly his lips left hers, his tongue slowly tracing their quivering outline, until she ached and yearned for the feel of his mouth. The anger had gone from his eyes, to be replaced by a slumbrous heat.

Her body seemed to melt against him entirely without her consent, her eyes closing as he feathered light kisses over the trembling lids.

'*Por Dios*,' he muttered hoarsely against her ear, 'there is a chemistry between us that refuses to be denied!'

Jessica knew she should make some protest, tell him to release her, but his fingers were stroking soothingly along her scalp, his mouth investigating the exposed vulnerability of her throat, releasing a fluttering fever of sensations that made her long only to cling to the breadth of his shoulders, and offer herself up to whatever he wanted from her.

Not even the heat of his fingers scorching the curves of her breasts had the power to alarm her. Instead she felt an elemental response to the caress, coupled with a primitive need to feel his touch against her skin without the constricting barrier of clothes. As though somehow her thoughts communicated themselves to him, Jessica heard him groan and saw with surprise the dark flush mantling his skin and the heated glitter of his gaze.

She made no attempt to stop him when he unbuttoned her blouse and slid it from her shoulders. Her lacy bra emphasised rather than concealed the curves of her breasts and her pulses seemed to quicken in elemental excitement as Sebastian's dark gaze lingered on the pale almost translucent skin.

'How much more attractive is this than the over-exposed bronzed bodies that litter our beaches! This,' he added emotively, stroking a finger over the pale flesh, 'is an enticement to man to touch and taste. The very paleness of your skin hints at a chastity that arouses the hunter in man, no matter how false that impression might be.'

Jessica gasped as he released the catch of her bra, exposing her breasts fully to his gaze. She knew she should feel shame; yet what she did feel was a tremulous, aching excitement; a need to have him touch her. As though he guessed her thoughts his hands cupped her breasts, her nipples hardening devastatingly at his touch. The stroke of his thumbs over the sensitised and aroused flesh incited a need to writhe and press herself close to his body, the husky moan torn from her throat shocking her with it sensuality.

'*Dios*, I despise myself for it, but right now I want nothing as much as I want to take you to bed, to feel your silkiness against my skin, like a soothing balm to overheated flesh. I want to lose myself in your softness . . . I . . . What is it about you that makes me forget what you are?' Sebastian muttered huskily, lifting her in his arms, his eyes moving from her face to the rosy peaks of her breasts and then back again.

She shouldn't be letting him do this, Jessica thought distractedly, but every nerve centre in her body was screaming for the satisfaction she knew only he could give. She felt the bed give under their combined weight, and all her muscles tightened in stunned protest as his mouth moved hungrily over the curve of one breast, the rough stroke of his tongue against the aching nipple causing her stomach muscles to lock in mute protest at the waves of pleasure crashing down on her, teaching her more about sensuality and her own body's response to it in two minutes than she had learned in twenty-odd years.

'*Dios*, I want you!'

He was only echoing her own thoughts, her own need. She had never felt this overpowering desire to know a man's possession before, and it shocked her that she should now. But then she had never loved a man as she loved Sebastian.

Loved! With sickening certainty she knew that it was too late to banish the treacherous and insidious truth. She *did* love him.

'Jessica?'

He was watching her, studying the flushed contours of her face, the arousal she felt sure must be there. She longed to touch him as intimately as he was touching her, and she reached out tentatively towards him, her fingers trembling as they encountered the rigidity of his collarbone.

'*Dios*, I have hungered for your touch against my skin,' he told her huskily, burying his mouth in the curve of her shoulder, 'almost from the very first. It is true, is it not, that there was a vital chemistry between us—a desire that neither of us can deny.'

Jessica wanted to say that it was not purely desire that motivated her, but Sebastian was wrenching open his shirt and her eyes were drawn to the naked virility of his body. Without the trappings of civilisation, the expensive suit and the silk shirt, his body was totally male, tautly muscled, his chest shadowed with dark body hair that tapered towards his waist.

'*Dios*, Sebastian, what is the meaning of this!'

They were so engrossed in one another that neither of them had heard the door open. Jessica's shocked eyes saw his aunt's disturbed face and behind her Pilar's glitteringly triumphant one.

'I told you you were wrong,' Pilar said triumphantly. 'I told you they were lovers!'

Sebastian was shielding Jessica with his body, but that didn't stop the shame coursing through her, burning into her soul as she realised how they must appear to their onlookers.

'Sebastian!' his aunt's voice was deeply reproachful. 'I am wounded beyond words that you would use your home as . . .'

'That is enough.' Quietly and calmly Sebastian silenced both women. 'If you will wait in the sitting room, there is something I must say to you both.'

He waited until they had gone and then quickly stood up, his back to Jessica.

'My apologies for that,' he told her curtly. 'I never imagined that . . .'

That what? Jessica wondered. That he would allow his desire to overrule his dislike of her as a person?

'I must speak with my aunt.'

He was gone, closing the door behind him, leaving Jessica to bitterly regret giving in to the wild clamouring tide of desire he had aroused in her. How on earth could she face his aunt or Pilar again? She felt humiliated beyond bearing that they should have witnessed such intimacies. She had wanted to give herself in love, but somehow their interruption had reduced her to the status of a kept plaything, whose only role was to satisfy the needs of her master who might enjoy her body while openly despising her mind.

'Jessica, could you give us a moment?' The quiet voice suggested that if she didn't he would come in and get her.

What was he going to say to her? she wondered nervously, checking in the mirror that she was properly dressed, before screwing up her courage and walking nervously into the other room.

From Sebastian's aunt she received a kind if somewhat sorrowful look. From Pilar she received one of blazing hatred.

'You cannot mean this, Sebastian,' she was saying as Jessica walked into the room. 'It is total folly!'

'That is something only I can decide,' Sebastian replied with iron inflexibility. 'I have just told my aunt and Pilar that we are to be married,' he told Jessica coolly, his eyes warning her against saying anything to contradict his statement. 'As Pilar and Jorge have pointed out to me, I have already been responsible for the destruction of one girl's good name. I will not have the Calvadores name dragged in the mud a second time.'

'But, Sebastian, to go to these lengths!' Pilar protested, glaring at Jessica. 'It is not necessary. You have only to send the girl away. Nothing will be said.'

'No, Sebastian is right,' his aunt interrupted firmly. 'You must not try to dissuade him, Pilar. Jessica, I am pleased to welcome you to our family.' She walked across to Jessica, grasping her hands, kissing her gently on either cheek. 'Come Pilar, it is time we left. Sebastian, if you will tell me what arrangements I am to make . . .'

'If he does intend to marry her he will want it done as quietly and quickly as possible,' Pilar said spitefully. 'He will not want another bride giving birth before he can get her to the altar!'

'Enough!'

Jessica quailed at the fury in Sebastian's voice, but Pilar seemed not to mind, merely shrugging insolently as she looked at Jessica. 'He may marry you,' she told her, 'but always you will know why. Can you live with that?'

She was right, Jessica thought as they left the room and Sebastian closed the door. Of course she could not marry him. And yet he had admitted that he desired her, surely from that something might grow? His family was one that for generations had endured arranged marriages, marriages with far less hope of success than theirs, and surely she had enough love for them both?

All these were wild and foolish thoughts, she admitted as Sebastian turned and she saw the bleak anger in his eyes.

'We don't really have to get married,' she faltered. 'I can leave . . .'

'And have everyone know that once again a Calvadores has betrayed his name?' he said bitterly. 'Never! I cannot believe that marriage to me will be so abhorrent to you. Sexually we are compatible,' he gave her a thin smile. 'At least we will not be bored in bed, and as for the rest,' he shrugged, 'I shall have my work, and please God eventually you will have our children.'

Why, when he said it like that, did it sound such a barren existence, so different from the one she had visualised?

'I should have listened to Jorge and not given into my need to feel the softness of your skin beneath my hands,' he added bitterly. 'We will be married just as quickly as it can be arranged, do you agree?'

Jessica wanted to say 'no'. She should say 'no', but it was a weak, hesitant 'yes' that finally left her lips, earning her a look of burning contempt.

'A wise decision. You will be the first Calvadores bride in nearly a thousand years of history who has not come to her marriage bed a virgin.'

'You once told me you would never marry a woman who had known other lovers,' Jessica reminded him with a dry throat, wondering if now he would change his mind.

'Circumstances sometimes dictate a lowering of one's standards. If I do not marry you now, doubtless I will be accused of despoiling two innocent young women.' His mouth twisted bitterly. 'I cannot allow that to happen, for the sake of my aunt and brother, if not for myself.'

'It's rather a high price to pay for family pride, isn't it?' Jessica queried numbly. Never in her wildest imaginings had she ever imagined herself in a situation such as this.

'For some things no price is too high,' he told her sombrely, 'and when we celebrate the birth of our first son perhaps I will be able to tell myself that there is after all some virtue in our marriage.'

She would never allow a child of hers to be brought up thinking that his whole life must be given over to upholding the pride of the Calvadores name, Jessica decided fiercely. Her child would not be sad and lonely like Lisa. Her child . . .

With a shock she realised that already she was thinking about bearing Sebastian's child, and she knew then that she would marry him, no matter how much common sense warned her against it.

CHAPTER SEVEN

THREE days later they were married in Seville. Sebastian had asked Jessica, with the same distant politeness he had adopted towards her ever since she had accepted his proposal, if there was anyone she wanted to invite to the ceremony.

She thought fleetingly of her aunt and uncle and Colin, and then regretfully shook her head. To invite them would lead to too many questions; too many doubts to add to those already crowding her mind. It would be far easier to simply tell them once it was over.

Over! She was viewing the thought of her marriage in much the same light as she would a trip to the dentist, and who was to blame? Ever since the afternoon she had agreed to marry Sebastian their marriage had been treated as though it were an unpleasant necessity. It was true that Lisa had greeted the news with unalloyed joy.

'I'm so glad you're going to marry Tio Sebastian,' she had confided Jessica only that morning. 'I would have hated it if he had married Pilar. She doesn't like me!'

But as far as the rest of the family were concerned, it had been all long faces and grave expressions.

Jorge had sought Jessica out and confided that he could not see what other course his brother could have taken.

'He should never have allowed you to become the object of Pilar's speculation in the first place,' he had told her. 'Sebastian knows how possessive Pilar is about him, how she would seek to discredit anyone who is close to him.'

Jessica scarcely felt that she came into that category, and if that had been the reason for Pilar bursting in on them in the manner she had, it had had completely the opposite effect from the one she had desired.

She glanced briefly at Sebastian, wondering what thoughts lay behind the shuttered face. They had been married this morning, she was now the Condesa de Calvadores. She touched the new band of gold on her finger, as though the touch of the shiny metal would make her new status more real.

A wedding breakfast had been arranged at Calvadores town house. Fifty-odd guests had been invited—all close family, Sebastian's aunt had assured her, and all of whom would be bitterly resentful if they were not invited.

'They look upon Sebastian as the head of our family,' she had explained to Jessica when she had protested. 'It will only cause problems later if they are not invited. There has already been so much turmoil in his life . . .'

She broke off, and Jessica sensed that she was thinking back to that other girl Sebastian should have married. In fact Sofia had done all she could to welcome Jessica into the family, her serene expression betraying no hint of the shocked reproach Jessica had glimpsed in her eyes in those few horrifying seconds when she had followed Pilar into the tower room.

Only this morning as Jessica was dressing for the service she had come into her room, proffering a pearl choker.

'You must wear them,' she had insisted. 'Every Caldvadores bride does.'

'But I'm scarcely the bride you can have wanted for your nephew,' Jessica had protested miserably. Today of all days she longed to have her aunt with her, longed for the misty white dress she had always secretly dreamed of wearing, instead of the expensive silk separates she had bought hurriedly in Seville—extremely beautiful in their way, but scarcely bride-like.

'You love him,' Sofia had stunned Jessica by saying quietly, 'and that is enough for me. Above all else Sebastian is a man who needs a wife's love. I know he can sometimes seem hard, arrogant even,' a small smile lifted her mouth. 'My own husband was much the same, it is a Calvadores trait, unfortunately, but Sebastian has had to endure much in his life. The loss of his parents was a terrible blow to him. He had to assume the role of guardian and mentor to Jorge; and then there was poor Manuela. So much misery and pain! I have hoped for a long time to see him married. You will make him a good wife, I know, because you love him.'

'But he doesn't love me!' Jessica hadn't been able to stem the anguished words.

'He desires you, who knows where that desire may lead?'

Who knew indeed? Jessica thought unhappily, glancing down the length of the table, listening half-heartedly to the hushed Spanish voices. She was a part of this family now, an important part, as one dowager had already reminded her, for she would be the mother of the next head of the family.

They were not having a honeymoon; Sebastian had deemed it unnecessary. They would return to the *hacienda*, at least for a few weeks, until he had completed his work on the designs, and then they would divide their time between the house in Seville and the *hacienda*.

Out of the corner of her eye she noticed Jorge. Sebastian was angry with him because Jorge had announced that he would not marry Barbara.

'Isn't it enough that one of us has married without love?' he had flung at Sebastian in the middle of their argument, and Jessica, who had been standing outside the study waiting to talk to Sebastian, had fled, just managing to reach the privacy of her room before she dissolved in tears.

What sort of marriage had she commited herself to? One where her husband took his pleasure of her body while ignoring her mind? Could she endure that?

The breakfast seemed unending, her head throbbing with the rich food and drink, her body aching with a bone-jarring tension that made her jerk away from Sebastian when he rose, to cup her elbow, when they eventually left.

'*Dios*,' he swore, his eyes darkening to graphite, 'why do you shrink from me like a petrified virgin?'

Because that's exactly what I am, Jessica longed to scream, but somehow the words wouldn't come. Why on earth had she allowed him to think otherwise for so long?

She had the long drive back to the *hacienda* to

dwell on her folly. She had no illusions about the nature of their marriage. It would be for life and there would be nothing platonic about it. Sebastian wanted children, he had told her so, and so did she, but up until now she hadn't allowed herself to think any further than the fact that she loved him. Now she was forced to concede that he believed her to be a sexually experienced woman; while in fact . . .

The hum of the powerful air-conditioning was the only sound to disturb the heavy silence of the car. Sebastian was driving the Mercedes himself, and his glance flicked from the road to her pale face, with dispassionate scrutiny.

'You are very pale. Do you not feel well?'

'A headache,' she managed to whisper, through a throat suddenly painfully constricted.

'That is the excuse of the married woman, not the bride,' Sebastian told her curtly. 'You are my wife, Jessica, and I will not have you reneging on our marriage now. There is something more than a headache troubling you—what is it?'

Was this the moment to tell him the truth? She cleared her throat hesitantly, wishing he would stop the car and take her in his arms. Somehow then it would be much easier to tell him that she was still a virgin.

'Stop playing games!' he warned her irately, swearing angrily as a cyclist suddenly wobbled into the centre of the road and he had to take evasive action. '*Por Dios*, my patience is almost at an end!' he muttered savagely. 'I can only thank God that I am spared the necessity of initiating a virgin. We were interrupted at a singularly inappropriate moment by my aunt and Pilar, and my need for the satisfaction their appearance denied me has been an aching hunger in my body ever since. But it is one which will be fully appeased tonight,' he added grimly, shocking her with his frankness.

'My payment for the privilege of bearing your name?' Jessica said tautly.

'Payment?' He frowned. 'What rubbish are you talking now? Your desire was as great as mine—you admitted it.'

And so she had, but that desire had been aroused by her love for him, and had been totally obliterated by her fear. How could she tell him the truth now?

'The others are a long way behind,' she murmured nervously at one point, glancing over her shoulder at the dust-covered road.

'They are indeed,' Sebastian agreed dryly, 'a full twenty-four hours behind. Tonight we shall be completely alone—my aunt's suggestion, and one I could not argue against. As it is, she points out to me that many of the family find it strange that we are returning to the *hacienda*.'

'I'm sure Pilar will acquaint them with the truth,' Jessica heard herself saying bitterly. 'That I trapped you into this marriage, just as you once thought I was trying to trap Jorge.'

'Pilar will say nothing,' Sebastian assured her coldly. 'And you are becoming hysterical—I cannot conceive why.'

No, Jessica raged inwardly, you wouldn't, would you? You're totally unfeeling and blind. If you weren't you'd know that I'm not . . .

They turned into the drive leading to the house. Dusk had crept up on them as they drove, and the evening air was full of the scent of the flowers, the chirp of the crickets filling the silence.

As Sebastian had said, the house was completely and almost eerily empty. She felt his eyes on her back as she headed for the tower, freezing as he drawled mockingly,

'You are going the wrong way. From now on you will share my suite.'

His suite. His bed! Almost suffocating with the fear crawling through her body, Jessica allowed him to propel her towards another flight of stairs.

This was a part of the house she had not previously seen. A large but austere sitting room looked out on to a secluded, darkened courtyard. Lamps threw soft shadows across the room. It was decorated in soft mochas and creams; modern furniture that was entirely masculine. Expensive Italian units lined one wall, two dark brown velvet-covered settees placed opposite one another across an off-white expanse of carpet.

'The bedroom is through here.'

Jessica stared disbelievingly. Surely when he had talked about his desire he had not meant that he intended to satisfy it now?

She stared blankly at the door. It was barely seven o'clock, far too early to ... A hundred confused thoughts jumbled through her mind. She had been hoping to find a way of telling him the truth; had hoped that during the course of the evening his manner might soften a little ...

'I'm hungry,' she lied wildly, 'I ...'

'So am I,' Sebastian agreed obliquely, 'and I thought I had already warned you about playing games with me ... What are you trying to do?' he demanded brutally, 'drive me to the point where I'll commit rape? Does the thought of that turn you on, is that it?'

'No!' Jessica was totally revolted. 'I . . .' 'I'm not ready' was what she wanted to say, but how could she? 'I'd like to shower and change, if you don't mind,' she managed with pathetic dignity. 'It's been a long day, and . . .'

'Of course I don't mind,' he said smoothly. 'The shower is through there.'

He indicated a door across the width of the bedroom. As she craned her neck to see it, Jessica was acutely aware of his proximity, of the maleness he exuded and her own tremulous reaction to it.

'If you'll just excuse me for a second,' he drawled mockingly, 'there's something I have to do.'

At least he was affording her some brief respite, Jessica thought thankfully as she saw the sitting room door close behind her. He probably realised she would prefer to prepare for what was to come in private. The bedroom was as masculine as the sitting room, echoing its colours, with sliding patio doors into the courtyard. She flicked the light switch and instantly the room was bathed in soft light.

What about her clothes? she wondered anxiously. She could scarcely put back on her silk suit. She had just reached the sitting room door and opened it when Sebastian seemed to materialise out of nowhere.

'Going somewhere?' he asked sardonically.

'Er . . . my clothes, I . . .'

'You will find them in one of the cupboards.

The maids will have attended to it during the day.' He watched her lazily. 'Why so nervous? It cannot be the first time you have been in such a situation.'

'It's the first time I've been married, though,' Jessica managed tartly, almost instantly wishing she had been less aggressive when she saw the way his eyes darkened.

'Rafael has left us some chilled champagne. I shall go and pour some out, although I doubt that it will be consumed in the spirit he anticipates. He probably left it thinking that to drink it would help allay your maidenly qualms,' Sabastian explained succinctly when she glanced hesitantly at him.

At last he was gone, and Jessica searched feverishly through her clothes, finding clean underwear and a fresh dress. Luckily some of her clothes had arrived, and although there was nothing remotely bridal among them they brought a nostalgic touch of home.

The bathroom was luxuriously masculine; a deep dark red and cream, the bath enormous. After one brief glance at it, she opted for the shower, wishing fervently that the bathroom door had a lock, and then chiding herself for her lurid fears. She was behaving like a swooning Victorian heroine faced with her would-be ravisher. She loved Sebastian, she reminded herself.

But he didn't love her; and he didn't know that he would be her first lover.

The sting of the shower spray cooled her heated skin. Someone had placed her toiletries with Sebastian's and she used her perfumed shower gell to soap her body, enjoying the fragrance, but reminding herself that she mustn't linger. She was just about to turn on the water to wash off the soap when a deep voice murmured provocatively, 'You've missed a bit!'

Sebastian! She hadn't heard him enter the bathroom, and she turned quickly, reaching instinctively for a towel.

'Such modesty!' he mocked, twitching it away from her, 'and so unnecessary . . . mm?'

'Sebastian, please!' Her voice was curiously husky, a strange deep heat pervading her body, her head oddly light.

'There is no need to beg me, *querida*,' he drawled huskily, deliberately misunderstanding the nature of her plea. 'You are a very desirable woman, a little slender perhaps,' he mocked, and Jessica wondered if he was thinking of Pilar's lusher charms, 'but very tantalising for all that. I like your perfume,' he added softly, his finger moving along the ridge of her spine.

Panic clamoured inside her, her body tensing under the explorative caress, but Sebastian appeared not to notice. His fingers moved rhythmically over her skin, and as though he sensed that she was about to protest, he said softly, 'Like I said, you've missed a bit. What's the matter?' he asked, frowning as he sensed her tension.

'I . . . I'd like to get dressed,' she muttered huskily. 'As I said before, I'm hungry, and . . .'

'Like I said, so am I . . . I hope you're not getting any foolish ideas about reneging on our marriage. I want you, Jessica,' he told her coolly, 'and I want you now . . . Perhaps you're right,' he added softly, 'and now is not the time to play games in the shower. Later—er—when we have more leisure for playing. Right now, all I want is the scented warmth of your body in my arms, your heart beating against mine . . .'

'No!'

Jessica managed a husky protest, but it was lost, smothered as he lifted her out of the shower, careless of the dampness of her naked body against his clothes, carrying her effortlessly into the bedroom and depositing her on the bed.

'Beautiful,' he murmured with pleasure as his fingers drifted exploratively across her skin. 'So soft and pale.'

Jessica looked imploringly at the lamps revealing her body in its most intimate detail.

'You want us to make love in the darkness?' Strangely the idea seemed to displease him. 'Why?' he demanded. 'So that you can pretend I am someone else? Oh no, *querida*,' he told her tightly, 'I want you to know who it is who possesses you, and besides, your body is so beautiful I want to enjoy it with my eyes as well as my hands and lips. Just as I want you to enjoy mine,' he added seductively. 'A pity you had decided to shower before I could join you. I would have enjoyed undressing you.'

'I'm a woman, not a doll!' Jessica protested fiercely, terrified by the images his words were conjuring, the pulsating sensations radiating to every part of his body.

'Tonight you are my wife, and no matter what has gone before, it shall be as it has been with no other man, so that by morning you will remember only the touch of my hands, my body . . .'

And Jessica remembered the Moorish blood in his veins, the blatant sensuality that would be part of his legacy from that blood, and every muscle in her body constricted in terrified dread. He expected her to be a sexually experienced woman, instead of which . . .

She shivered, and he frowned, moving away from the bed, and returning with a glass of frothing liquid.

'Drink this,' he commanded. 'You are cold.'

The champagne bubbled in her throat, tickling her nose. She coughed, spilling some and feeling it splash down on her skin.

'*Dios*, but I want you,' Sebastian murmured throatily, then he bent his head, his tongue touching the spot where the champagne had fallen in the valley between her breasts. Tension coiled through her, a cramping sensation stirring in her stomach, weakness invading her muscles as his fingers gripped her hips and his mouth continued its subtle exploration of her breasts, first one and then the other—light, delicate caresses, the mere brush of his lips against her skin, tormenting her with the ache of unappeasement they left.

Her fear was forgotten. All she wanted was right here within reach. She groaned a half protest as Sebastian's lips continued their teasing assault, her fingers locking into his hair as she tried to silently convey her need for something more.

'You are too impatient,' he murmured against her skin. 'We have all night before us, your skin is as sweet and tender as a fresh peach, tempting to the tongue and firm to the touch.'

His hand left her hip to stroke wantonly across the soft tension of her stomach, his lips following a downward path.

'Sebastian . . .'

'How sweetly you say my name,' he told her huskily, 'and how much sweeter it would be to feel your lips against my skin. Surely, *querida*, I don't have to tell you that?'

He moved, and Jessica was instantly aware of his arousal, but a languid yielding sensation was spreading through her, driving out fear. Her fingers trembled over the buttons of his shirt, exploring the moistness of the skin beneath. His skin was warm, silk shielding hard muscle and bone, and merely to let her fingers drift over the smooth muscles of his back provoked a racing excitement that seemed to invade every nerve. His skin burned against her palms, his husky moan inciting her to press quivering lips against the smooth column of his throat, tasting the salty male scent of him.

'*Dios*, Jessica,' he protested hoarsely as her tongue delicately probed the curve of his throat, her hands clinging to his shoulders, the soft movements of her body inviting his touch. His hand cupped her jaw, imprisoning her as his mouth possessed hers with hot urgency, forcing her lips to part, tasting the moist inner sweetness. His hands moved urgently over her body, desire burning hotly in his eyes as he urged her to help him with his pants. He had none of the self-consciousness she possessed, his body golden and taut in the light from the lamps as he stood up briefly, watching her eyes move wonderingly.

'You look at me as though you have never seen

a man before, *querida*,' he told her softly. 'Such a look is a temptation to any man, and I am more than willing to be tempted.' He leaned over her, tanned fingers gently cupping first one breast and then the other as he bent his head, stroking the pulsating nipples lightly with his tongue, his mouth finally closing over the aching core, and waves of sensation beat through her as she gasped and trembled at the sensations he was arousing. A need to press wild, scattered kisses against his body seized her, his husky growl of pleasure reverberating along her spine.

His mouth left her breasts to stroke delicate kisses across her stomach, quivering with shock at the unaccustomed sensuality of his touch, but it seemed it wasn't enough simply for him to kiss her, she had to kiss him, and the feel of the tautly male flesh against her lips seemed only to increase the deep ache she could feel inside her. Then, as though he sensed her need and shared it, Sebastian parted her thighs, the heated masculinity of him unbearably arousing, as his tongue brushed softly over her lips, making her moan and cling desperately to his shoulders, mutely imploring him to cease tantalising her.

His mouth suddenly hardened on hers, his body taut with a need that communicated itself to every part of her. He moved, and suddenly, starkly, all her fear returned. There was pain and anger in his eyes, an anger which she had to blot out by closing hers, and weak tears seeped through as the sharp pain ended, taking with it her earlier euphoric pleasure.

'A virgin! You were a virgin,' Sebastian accused her. He was standing beside the bed wearing a dark silk robe, his hair tousled, and his expression bitter. 'Why didn't you tell me?'

'How could I?' Jessica muttered. 'I was going to when you started telling me how glad you were that I was a woman of experience . . . Anyway, I don't see why you should complain,' she added acidly. 'It isn't many men who get to have two virgin brides . . . Although, of course, in Manuela's case . . .'

His jaw tightened in fury, all the muscles in his face tensing, and Jessica had the overwhelming suspicion that if she hadn't been a woman he would have hit her.

'You should be pleased,' she threw bitterly at him, refusing to give in to the tiny voice warning her not to go any further. 'I thought that was what all the Calvadores men expected in their brides—innocence, purity!'

'You should have told me,' he repeated icily.

'Why?' Tears weren't very far away, everything had gone disastrously wrong. In a corner of her heart Jessica had been hoping that somehow the discovery that she was a virgin might soften him towards her, but instead . . . 'So that you could have been less . . . excessive? Would it have made any difference? You would still have hurt me.'

It was a childish accusation, and her emotions were more bruised than her body, but his face closed up immediately, his expression grimly unreadable as he assured her curtly, 'In that case you may be sure that I will never . . . hurt you again. I want no unwilling sacrifice in my bed,' he added cruelly.

'And there is always Pilar, isn't there?' Jessica flung at him. 'She's no shrinking virgin, to be shocked and distressed by your ... your demands!'

He laughed mirthlessly. 'My demands, as you call them, are no more than any sensual aroused male experiences. My mistake was in hoping to share them with you. Plainly you prefer to remain frigidly prudish. Then you may do so!'

CHAPTER EIGHT

IT had all gone disastrously wrong, Jessica thought numbly, listening to Tia Sofia while Lisa perched on her knee. The three of them were in the *sala* that Sofia had claimed as her own, drinking coffee and eating the cook's delicious almond biscuits.

Tia Sofia had been explaining to Jessica that they were expecting a visit from Sebastian's godfather and his daugher.

'*Querida*, are you not feeling well?' she broke off to ask Jessica with concern. 'You look pale— you have been indoors too much working on Sebastian's wretched designs, you must go out more.'

'Yes, you promised you would go for a walk with me,' Lisa reminded her reproachfully.

Assuring them both that she was fine, Jessica forced a smile to lips that felt as though they would crack from the constant effort of having to smile when it was the last thing she wanted to do. How could two people live as intimately as she and Sebastian did and yet remain so far apart? Initially she had expected him to suggest that they have separate bedrooms—he could hardly want to share his with her now, but to her dismay he did no such thing. Perhaps the terrible pride of the Calvadores would not allow him to admit that he did not desire his wife. Whatever the reason, she was forced to endure the humiliation, night after night, of knowing that he was lying merely inches away from her, but his attitude towards her was so cold and dismissive that they could have been separated by the Sierras.

And the strain was beginning to tell. More than once she thought she had glimpsed sympathy in Sofia's eyes, and she wondered if the older woman suspected the truth. She roused herself when Lisa repeated insistently that she had promised to go out with her.

The little girl was wearing another of her dainty dresses, and while they looked enchanting, Jessica wished she could see her in shorts and tee-shirts, getting grubby; living a more natural life.

'I wish Tio Sebastian was with us,' Lisa confided as they walked through the courtyard and past the swimming pool towards the outbuildings. 'When will he be back from Seville?'

'Tonight,' Jessica told her, trying not to admit to the sinking sensation she experienced whenever she thought of Sebastian. She had thought she had seen him angry before, but it was nothing compared with the icy hauteur with which she was now treated. How foolish she had been to think that her love was the key to his heart! He wanted neither her love nor her body.

'I'm going to show you my secret place,' Lisa told her importantly. 'No one knows about it but us . . . And Tio Sebastian.'

Lisa took her hand and led her towards the stable block. Her pony whinnied as they walked past, and they stopped to stroke his nose and feed him carrots from the bucket by the door.

'A long time ago this was where they made the wine,' Lisa told her importantly, opening a door into what Jessica had thought must be part of the converted garages, but which in fact she realised was a store place of some description. There was an old-fashioned wine press which she recognised from pictures, several large vats and some decaying barrels. 'It's down here, come on!'

Urged on by Lisa, she followed her to a cobwebby corner of the building, startled when Lisa motioned to another door. Jessica opened it, almost overbalancing on the steep flight of steps leading down from the door. As she glanced down the narrow, dark steps she felt a shuddering reluctance to descend them. She had always loathed the thought of being underground, but Lisa displayed no such qualms.

'It's fun, isn't it?' she demanded, leading the way with an agility that suggested she knew every step by heart. Jessica had to duck quickly to avoid the low roof as the steps suddenly turned and then levelled out.

They were in a rectangular room, illuminated by one single bare bulb suspended from a wire which ran the length of the ceiling. The ceiling itself was arched and composed of crumbling bricks. Moisture streamed off the walls, and the air felt cold and damp. Lisa, completely oblivious to Jessica's dislike of her treasured hidey-hole, beamed up at her with evident pleasure.

'No one ever comes down here now,' she told her. 'They used to store the barrels here a long time ago.'

She was going to have a word with Sebastian about allowing Lisa to wander so freely somewhere so potentially dangerous, Jessica decided when the top of the stairs was gained and they had switched off the light. It made her blood run cold just thinking what might happen to her alone down there. For one thing, the ceiling hadn't looked too safe; there had been deep fissures in some of the bricks.

They were on the way back to the house when Jorge suddenly caught up with them. He had been out riding and his hair was tousled from the exercise. He was an attractive boy, Jessica reflected, smiling warmly at him, but he was not Sebastian.

'Tio Jorge, Tio Jorge, put me down!' Lisa squealed, laughing as he swung her up in his arms and whirled her round and round.

'Not until you gave me a kiss,' he threatened teasingly.

Obligingly she did so, while Jessica laughed. 'So that's the secret of your great charm, is it?' she mocked. 'Kisses by threats!'

'Be careful I don't do the same thing to you,' Jorge told her mock-threateningly, while Lisa announced earnestly, 'You can't kiss Jessica, Jorge, because she's married to Tio Sebastian!'

'Out of the mouths of babes,' Jorge drawled, sliding Jessica a sideways dancing glance. 'Not that I wouldn't like to try. My brother is a very lucky man.'

They were still laughing when they reached the courtyard, Lisa in the crook of one of Jorge's arms, while the other rested lightly on the back of Jessica's waist in a gesture more protective than provocative.

But the laughter drained out of Jessica's face

when she saw Sebastian's grimly angry face. He was sitting on the terrace with his aunt and Pilar, and all at once Jessica felt acutely aware of her untidy appearance, cobwebs no doubt clinging to her dress and hair, Jorge's arm on her waist.

'Jessica, had you forgotten Pilar was coming to see you this afternoon?'

Jessica shot a surprised glance at the Spanish woman's perfectly made up and bland face. As far as she knew they had made no such arrangements, nor was there any reason why they should do so. She didn't like Pilar and she knew the feeling was reciprocated. For one thing, she disliked the way Pilar treated Lisa, who was, after all, her sister's child.

To save any argument she apologised lightly, and was about to excuse herself to run upstairs and tidy up, when Pilar astounded her by saying, 'That is perfectly all right, Jessica. I quite understand. When one has an attractive man as an escort one tends to overlook engagements with one's woman friends.'

Sebastian looked thunderously angry, and Jessica bit her lip. Surely he didn't think she had deliberately ignored an engagement with Pilar? And Jorge—why was he looking at his brother in that evasive fashion, not explaining that they had simply met at the stables and walked back together?

Lisa, sensing the tension in the atmosphere, reached imploring for Sebastian's hand, her voice uncertain, her small face anxiously puckered. She was stretching on tiptoe and suddenly she over balanced, clutching the nearest thing to her for support, which happened to be Pilar's arm. The glass of *fino* Pilar was holding in her hand spilled down on to the cream silk dress she was wearing, and with a cry of rage she rounded on Lisa, taking her by the shoulders and shaking her furiously.

'This is too much, *querido!*' she complained to Sebastian. 'The child is uncontrollable and clumsy. I have told you before, she should be sent to a convent and taught how to conduct herself ... What may be suitable behaviour in an English household does not commend itself to our people. Perhaps you should explain that to your wife, for it is obvious that she has been encouraging Lisa to run wild. Clumsy girl!' she told Lisa, now pale and trembling, her dark brown eyes huge in her small face. 'When I was a child, I would have been whipped and sent to my room for the rest of the day for such unmannerly behaviour!'

Jessica longed to intervene. Her blood boiled in answering fury. How could Pilar terrorise Lisa so? It had been an accident; admittedly it was unfortunate that the sherry should have been spilled, but Jessica doubted that the cream silk was the only dress in Pilar's wardrobe, or that she couldn't replace it quite easily.

'Perhaps you are right, *querida*,' she heard Sebastian saying evenly. 'Lisa, you will apologise to your aunt, and then I think you will go to your room ...'

'It is probably more Jessica's fault than Lisa's,' Pilar added maliciously. 'Have you seen how grubby the child is? She is probably over-excited.'

'My wife does seem to have that effect on some

people,' Sebastian agreed coldly. 'Lisa,' he commanded, looking at the little girl, 'I have told you once to go to your room, I will not do so again!'

Jessica saw his aunt check a response, her expression unhappy, and all her own indignation boiled over.

'It was an accident,' she interrupted hotly. 'Poor Lisa is no more to blame than . . . anyone else. Sebastian, I . . .'

'Be careful, Jessica,' Pilar mocked. 'Sebastian does not like to have his decisions queried, do you, *querido*?'

Jessica ignored her. 'Come, Lisa, I'll take you upstairs,' she said softly, hating the hurt pain in the little girl's eyes. She had just seen her god topple from his plinth, Jessica suspected, still unable to understand why Sebastian had spoken so harshly.

Dinner was always a formal occasion in the Calvadores household, but it had never been as silently tense as it was tonight, Jessica thought to herself as she refused any caramel pudding in favour of a cup of coffee.

'Señor Alvarez and Luisa arrive tomorrow, will you collect them from the airport?'

'I have some work to complete on the designs,' Sebastian said curtly. He had hardly spoken to any of them during the meal, and Jessica thought she might be wrong, but there was a controlled tension about him she had never noticed before. Was it because of their marriage? Was he, like her, wishing it had never taken place?

'I could go,' Jorge offered. 'I could take Jessica and Lisa with me.'

'I think not,' Sebastian cut in coldly. 'The car will be cramped with five of you, and besides, it is time that Lisa learned that good manners are something that cannot be discarded simply at whim. She will remain indoors tomorrow as a reminder.'

'Does that apply to me too?' Jessica demanded, temper flags flying in her cheeks. 'Am I to be "sent to my room", for forgetting Pilar's invitation?'

Sebastian's mouth compressed into a thin hard line. 'Lisa is at an age where her nature can still be moulded and formed. Regrettably, you are not. Now, if you will excuse me, I have work to do.'

'Phew!' Jorge grimaced when he had gone. 'He has a black monkey riding on his back tonight, hasn't he? Have you two had a quarrel?'

Quarrel! Jessica suppressed hysterical laughter. To have a quarrel they would need to talk, to share an emotion. They weren't close enough to quarrel.

'Sebastian is tired,' Tia Sofia palliated. 'He has been working too hard. I have warned him before . . .'

'I didn't know Pilar intended to visit me,' Jessica explained to his aunt, not wanting her too to think she had been remiss.

'Pilar tends to be a little possessive towards Sebastian,' Sofia said gently, 'and sometimes that prompts her into actions of impulse. I'm sure she did not mean to cause any friction between you.'

Jessica said nothing. She was pretty sure that was exactly what Pilar had wanted to do, but she had no intention to saying so to the others.

'Has Sebastian said anything to you about Barbara?' Jorge asked her half an hour later as they wandered through the courtyard.

'Nothing,' Jessica told him, without adding that it was hardly likely that he would do so.

'He is annoyed with me, I am afraid, but I cannot marry a girl I do not love.'

It was a sentiment Jessica wholly appreciated. 'Of course not,' she agreed sympathetically.

The courtyard was illuminated by a full moon, bathing everything in soft silver light. The air was warm, almost too warm, and curiously still.

'We could be in for a storm,' Jorge commented as they headed back to the house. 'We need rain badly. It has been a very dry spring.' His sleeve brushed against Jessica's bare arm and he stopped her suddenly, his hand on her shoulder as he turned her towards him.

'You are so very different from your cousin,' he said softly. 'She is a taker from others, while you are a giver, but be careful you don't give my brother too much. He has a devil riding him that cannot be exorcised. He has been this way since Manuela died.'

What was he trying to tell her? That Sebastian still loved Manuela? Tears stung her eyes and she lowered her head, taking momentary comfort from Jorge's presence before turning to return to the house.

As always, she felt a reluctance to go upstairs. Sebastian was never there. He always worked late—avoiding the awful moment when he must join her, Jessica thought bitterly. If she had hoped that somehow the fact of her virginity might incline him towards her she had been bitterly disappointed. And the mutual desire he had spoken of so freely before they were married might never have existed. Jessica didn't know what was responsible for the change in him—but she hated the long, empty nights when she lay sleepless at his side, knowing she had only to stretch out her hand to touch him, and knowing it was the one thing she must never do. And humiliatingly she still wanted to touch him; it was there like an alien growth inside her, this need to touch and know. She couldn't forget his final cruel words to her on the night of their wedding, and there was still an unappeased ache within her that throbbed like an exposed nerve whenever she thought about how it had felt to be in his arms.

She opened the bedroom door, stiffening with shock as she saw the moonlit figure by the patio door.

'So you have returned.' Sebastian's voice was flat and unemotional. 'I thought after what I just witnessed that you might have decided to spend the night with my brother.'

For a moment Jessica stared uncomprehendingly at him, and then enlightenment dawned.

'Jorge and I were simply talking,' she protested, silenced by the harsh sound of his laughter.

'The way you had been simply talking this afternoon, I suppose,' he said savagely.

It was useless to tell him that she had simply met Jorge on the way back from her outing with Lisa, but at the thought of the little girl, she remembered the tear-stained face and trembling mouth when she had gone in to say goodnight to her, and read her the story they were both enjoying.

'You were very unfair to Lisa this afternoon,' she told him angrily, able to defend his daughter if she couldn't defend herself. 'It was an unfortunate accident, but she was in no way to blame. Pilar always contrives to upset her. She adores you, Sebastian, and you were viciously cruel to her. I can't understand why you turned on her like that.'

'You can't? Perhaps it's because a wounded animal does claw at other things in its agony; perhaps it's because I'm going out of my mind with frustration,' he told her bluntly. 'When I married you it was not with the intention that our marriage should be platonic.'

'I should have told you the truth,' Jessica admitted huskily. 'I wanted to, but . . .'

'But you preferred to let me find out the hard way—for us both—and then you turn to my brother for solace. Well, you may not find solace in my arms, Jessica,' he told her brutally, 'but I'm no saint to burn in the fires of hell when the means of quenching them is at hand. You were prepared to give yourself to my brother, now you can give yourself to me!'

Her panicky protest was lost against his mouth, storming her defences, sending waves of heat pulsating through her body. Instantly everything was forgotten but the wild clamouring in her blood, the need for his possession which had been aching inside her ever since their wedding night, although never fully acknowledged.

'I want you,' Sebastian muttered thickly against her mouth, 'and when I take you, you will think only of me, not my brother, not anyone but me. It will be my name you cry out in the fiery midst of passion; my body that gives yours the ultimate sweet pleasure.'

A shaft of moonlight illuminated his face, drawn and shadowed, so that Jessica could almost deceive herself that it was pain she saw in his eyes. Was he thinking of Manuela when he spoke to her? A sharp stabbing pain shot through her, her small moan of protest igniting a ferocity within him that shocked and excited as he stripped her swiftly, his face a mask of concentration, his hands only stilling when he had removed everything but her minute briefs.

The knowledge that he wanted her trembled though her on an exultant wave, and slowly she reached towards him, unfastening the buttons of his shirt, sliding her hands across the breadth of his chest and feeling it lift and tense with the sudden urgency of his breathing. Her marauding fingers were trapped and held against his heart as it pounded into her palm, and a curious sensation of timelessness gripped her.

This time she felt no shyness at the sight of his naked body, rather a desire to touch and know it, but his smothered groan as her fingertips stroked lightly against his thigh warned her of the intensity of his need. His hands cupped her breasts, his mouth following the line of her throat and shoulders, before returning to fasten hungrily on hers. His body burned and trembled against her, sweat beading his forehead and dampening his skin.

On a swiftly rising spiral of excitement Jessica explored the maleness of his body, feeling the increasing urgency within him; the blind hunger that made him shudder under her touch, and she knew beyond any doubt that this time nothing would appease the ache inside her but the hard, demanding pressure she could feel building up inside him.

She wanted his possession of her body with a need that went beyond anything she had ever experienced. Her hips writhed and arched, and Sebastian groaned against her throat, holding her, shaping her until she was formless and malleable, her only purpose in life to fulfil the explosive ache that possessed her every conscious thought and action.

'Sebastian . . .' She moaned his name under his caressing hands, trying to communicate her need, but instead of fulfilling her, he stilled. She opened desire-drugged eyes and stared at him uncomprehendingly, a tiny protest leaving her lips.

'Sebastian, please!' Her fingers curled into the smooth muscles of his back, her mind still shying away from actually telling him how much she needed him, while her body ached wantonly for her to do so, no matter what the cost.

'You want me.'

It was a statement rather than a question, but something forced her to respond to it, her nervous, husky, 'Very much,' making his eyes darken until they were almost black, his breathing suddenly altered and uneven. '*Dios*, Jessica,' he told her rawly, 'I want you, even though I know . . .'

She didn't want him to say more, to spoil what was between them with any words that might

make her face up to the truth. Now lying in his
arms, the full weight of his body pressed against
hers, she could almost convince herself that he
could love her, but if he spoke, if he said that
word 'want' again when she wanted to hear him
say 'love', it would burst her protective bubble,
and that was something she didn't want. So in
desperation she pressed her finger to his lips and
then clasped her hands behind his neck drawing
him down towards her, running her tongue softly
over his lips, tracing the firm outline of them,
until, suddenly, he muttered a husky protest,
capturing her face with his hands and holding it
still while his mouth moved hungrily over hers and
the heated pressure of his thighs ignited a heat
that spread swiftly through her body until it
welcomed his shuddering thrust, rejoicing in the
bittersweet mingling of pain and pleasure,
knowing with some prescient knowledge that this
time he was tempering his need so that she could
share fully the pleasure of their entwined bodies.

And then all thought was superseded as swiftly
urgent pleasure contracted through her body and
she was free-soaring into realms of delight she
had never dreamed existed.

When she woke up she was alone; there was a
dent in the pillow where Sebastian's head had
lain, but no other traces of his presence. Jessica
swung her legs out of the bed, surprised to
discover how lethargic and weak she felt. She
steadied herself as the room spun round, and
faintness overwhelmed her. Just for a moment
she wished Sebastian was there, to take her in his
arms, and kiss her with the tenderness a man

might reserve for the woman he had just made
wholly his, if he loved her, but then she banished
the thought. Perhaps last night would lead to
other improvements in their marriage. Perhaps his
desire for her might lead Sebastian to treat her
with tenderness and affection.

She had forgotten that he had said he was
going to Seville and was disappointed to get
downstairs and find him gone. Jorge was at the
breakfast table, trying to cheer up a tearful Lisa.

Jessica had started going with Tia Sofia when
she discussed the day's menus and work plans
with the staff. The *hacienda* was enormous, with
so many valuable antiques and works of art that
cleaning it had to be organised with almost
military precision. Many of the staff had inherited
their jobs from their mothers and fathers, and all
were devoted to the family. Jessica had found
that they treated her with respect and affection,
and when she murmured to Sofia that she was
sure she would never be able to cope as
admirably as she did, the older woman had
laughed.

'You will,' she had told her, 'and before very
long as well. You have a natural flair with
people.'

If she did, it didn't extend to include her
husband, Jessica thought ruefully.

Lisa was so unhappy that Jessica spent a large
part of the morning with her. Her part of the
designing work was now almost complete until
Sebastian came to a final decision. She had
received a delighted letter from her aunt and
uncle, full of exclamations and wishes that they
had been able to attend her wedding.

'Isabel gets married in three months' time,' her aunt had written, 'and of course you must be there. She was going to ask you to be bridesmaid, but now it will have to be matron of honour. John's parents are holding the reception at their house—there's to be a marquee in the garden, and John's mother is a splendid organiser, so I won't have anything to worry about other than finding an outfit.'

As she folded the letter Jessica sighed. Would Isabel be any happier than she was? She certainly hoped so.

In an effort to try and cheer Lisa up, she taught her to play Snap with an old pack of cards she had found, and although she played dutifully, her eyes kept straying to the door. How could Sebastian have been so cruel to her? Jessica fumed. His own child, even if he did refuse to acknowledge her. This cruel streak in a man who was so otherwise so strong was a weakness that caused her concern. His pride she could understand and even forgive, but his refusal to tell Lisa her true parentage was something that worried her.

'Will Tio Sebastian really send me away to a convent?' Lisa asked her at one point, her chin wobbling slightly.

'I'm sure he won't,' Jessica told her, trying to comfort her.

'But when you have babies, he won't want me,' Lisa appalled her by confiding. 'Pilar told me so.'

'Of course we'll still want you,' Jessica assured her, inwardly wondering how Pilar could be so deliberately malicious. 'What shall we do this afternoon?' she asked her, trying to redirect her thoughts. But Lisa refused to respond.

Jorge returned with the visitors from South America just after lunch. Señor Alvarez, Sebastian's godfather, turned out to be a genial, plump South American, who kissed both Jessica and Sofia enthusiastically, his eyes twinkling as he told Sofia that she didn't look a day older.

'Then you must need new glasses,' Sebastian's aunt told him practically, 'for it is over twenty years since we last met.'

'I remember it as though it were yesterday,' he assured her. 'You were then a bride of six months, and how I envied my cousin! Just as I'm sure many men must envy Sebastian,' he added gallantly, turning to Jessica. 'Jorge tells me that he has to work but that he will return in time for dinner. You must not let him work so hard—all work and no play, don't you English have a saying about that?'

'Sebastian has a black monkey on his back at the moment,' Jorge interrupted cheerfully. 'Poor Lisa felt the weight of his temper yesterday, and all because of that cat Pilar Sanchez.'

'Ah, Pilar!' Señor Alvarez grimaced. 'A very feline woman, is that one. I shall have to take care to guard my little Luisa from her claws!'

He drew his daughter forward to be introduced, and Jessica noticed the look in Jorge's eyes as they rested on her. Small and dainty, her glossy black hair was drawn back off her face, her huge pansy-brown eyes were nervous and hesitant as they were introduced. She couldn't be more than eighteen, Jessica reflected, but already she had the ripeness, the innocent sensuality of Latin women.

At Jorge's suggestion she allowed herself to be

detached from the others to explore the court-yards. The *hacienda* was so different from the style of architecture she was accustomed to that she was eager to explore.

'Your daughter is extremely lovely,' Jessica commented warmly when they had gone.

'She is a crimson velvet rose,' her father agreed poetically, 'but many men prefer the beauty of the golden rose that grows best in the cooler climes of the north.'

Señor Alvarez had come to Spain on business as well as pleasure, and when he discovered that Jessica had been helping Sebastian with his new designs he started to talk to her with great enthusiasm and interest about wool and South America. Jessica found it all fascinating; he was an entertaining companion; scholarly, and yet worldly enough to add a little salt to his speech, and like all Latins, he was an expert at turning a neat compliment. Sebastian had never compli-mented her, Jessica realised with a shock. He had never flirted with her either. The tiny cold lump of unhappiness she had felt on waking and discovering that he had gone grew and refused to be banished.

Sebastian eventually returned to the *hacienda* just before dinner. Pilar had been invited to join this celebratory meal, mainly because she knew the Alvarez family well, and as she was a widow, it was perfectly permissible for her to join a family party without a male escort.

She arrived just as they were sipping sherry in the *sala*, her black silk evening dress a perfect foil for her dark beauty and curvaceous figure. In comparison, Jessica felt pale and insignificant in her softly draped cream chiffon suit with its camisole top and loose jacket, even though she had loved it when she tried it on in the shop.

Luisa, as befitted a young girl, was wearing a plain dress in white, and pretty though it was, Jessica didn't think it did the younger girl's complexion justice.

Sebastian had been late joining them and had come into the room only minutes before Pilar, who, the moment she saw him, made a beeline for him, linking her arm with his in a very proprietorial manner, scarlet fingernails like drops of blood against the darkness of his jacket, as she laughed and joked with Señor Alvarez.

'Have you been in to see Lisa?' Jessica managed to ask Sebastian quietly before they went in to dinner. 'She's been moping all day because you were so cross with her.'

She didn't think anyone else had heard her until Pilar turned round suddenly, her eyes raking Jessica's face coldly, her voice falsely sweet as she said smoothly,

'I must go up and see her too before I go. Lisa is suddenly displaying a very naughty strain,' she added for Señor Alvarez' benefit. 'I'm afraid I had to be quite cross with her yesterday.'

Sebastian hadn't answered her question, and Jessica was afraid to ask it again. All her hopes that somehow last night might have had a softening effect on his attitude to her had been destroyed the moment he walked into the *sala*, his face grimly blank as he sought her out and with meticulous politeness enquired about her day. His very politeness seemed to hold her deliberately at a distance as though he wanted to warn her not to try to come too close. Had his love for Manuela been such that he could never love anyone else? Had her death frozen his emotions, making it impossible for him to feel anything other than desire for another woman?

Jessica sighed, reflecting that the evening ahead wasn't likely to be an easy one. Already she could see that Jorge was being more than simply politely attentive to Luisa and that she was responding with glowing eyes and happy smiles. Sebastian hadn't noticed yet, but when he did . . .

Jorge hadn't been forgiven for refusing to marry Barbara, although privately Jessica thought it was very wrong of Sebastian to attempt to dictate to his brother whom he should marry. But of course that was the Spanish way.

The night was hot and stuffy, thunder growling in the distance. Halfway through the meal Jessica was attacked by a wave of nausea and dizziness, which, fortunately, she managed to fight off. She didn't believe anyone had noticed, until she realised that Pilar was watching her with narrowed, assessing eyes. Trying to dislodge the cold feeling of disquiet she always felt when the other woman watched her, Jessica discreetly refrained from eating much more. Doubtless it was the overpowering heat and threatening storm that was making her feel so odd, and at least Sebastian seemed more relaxed, as he chatted to his godfather. She heard him mention her name and listened, wondering what was being said.

'Your husband has just been praising your ability as a designer,' Señor Alvarez told her, with a smile. 'He tells me that your ideas are nothing short of inspired.'

Again Jessica was conscious of Pilar's malevolent regard, but she tried to ignore it. Sebastian praising her! A tiny thrill of pleasure lightened the ice packed round her heart. Perhaps after all there might be some future for them; some basis on which they could build the foundations of a relationship.

CHAPTER NINE

'TIA SOFIA, have you seen Lisa?' Jessica had been looking for the little girl for half an hour, but no one had seen her since lunchtime. She glanced out of the window at the black sky and pounding rain. Surely Lisa wouldn't have ventured outside? The rain fell in sheets rather than drops, bouncing on the hard dry earth, and on the radio there had been flood warnings.

Sebastian had been concerned for the vines, although he explained that fortunately they were not at a stage in their development when too much damage would be done. The poorer growers might suffer some losses, Jorge had told Jessica later, but Sebastian, together with other wealthy landlords, had formed an association that could help the small growers through difficult patches.

'He takes his responsibilities as head of our family very seriously,' Jorge explained to her. 'Too seriously, I sometimes think, perhaps because he was so young when he had to take over from our father.'

And he had had to take over alone, Jessica reflected, without Manuela at his side.

'I'm getting worried about Lisa,' she confided in Sofia with a frown when no one could remember seeing the little girl. 'Where can she be?'

'She has been very upset recently,' Sofia

agreed, echoing Jessica's concern. 'I told Sebastian he had been too harsh with her, but he seems to have devils of his own to fight at the moment.'

'I think I'll go upstairs and check again that she isn't in her room—she might just have slipped out,' Jessica commented.

'If you don't find her, we'll organise a search. Children get odd ideas into their head when they're upset—even the most sensible of them.'

Lisa wasn't in her room, but Jessica bumped into the girl Maria, who looked after her, as she came out. She looked worried and upset.

'Have you seen Lisa?' Jessica asked her. The girl shook her head.

'Not since morning,' she told Jessica. 'She was very upset, the little one. Last night . . .' she bit her lip, flushing and hesitating.

'Yes, go on,' Jessica urged her. 'Last night . . .?'

'Well, it is just that Señora Sanchez came up to see her. I had gone downstairs to get her some hot milk to help her sleep, and when I came back I could hear their voices. Señora Sanchez was very, very angry. I could hear her shouting, but I didn't go in. When she came out she didn't see me, and I went into the room and found Lisa crying. The Señora had told her that she was to be punished for being naughty and that the Conde was to send her away—to a school where they would be very strict with her—and that she would never be allowed to come back.'

Jessica was appalled and looked it. How could Pilar be so heartless, and why had Sebastian not confided his plans to *her*? Of course Pilar was Lisa's aunt, but surely he might have consulted her before deciding to send Lisa away to school?

She had been intending to suggest that there might be a good school in Seville she could attend, and that during the week they could live in the house there to be with her. How could he treat his daughter so unkindly?

'I tried to comfort her,' Maria went on to say, 'but it was many hours before she went to sleep.'

'You should have come and told me,' Jessica said remorsefully, hating to think of Lisa lying awake and crying while they were dining downstairs unaware of her misery. 'Did she say anything this morning?' probed.

Maria shook her head. 'Not a word. She was very subdued and quiet, but she said nothing.'

Feeling more apprehensive than she wanted to admit, Jessica hurried back downstairs to give Tia Sofia the news.

She too looked grave when Jessica had finished. 'You say Pilar told her that Sebastian was to send her to school? I cannot believe he would come to such a decision without telling us first. Do you think she could have exaggerated?'

It was a thought, but Jessica felt that not even Pilar would have dared to tell such a barefaced and hurtful lie without some justification.

Jorge was summoned and told of their fears, and Señor Alvarez, who had accompanied him, was quick to suggest that they each take portions of the house to search.

'Sebastian must be told,' he added firmly.

'I'll telephone him,' Jorge agreed. 'Unless, of course . . .' he glanced at Jessica, but she shook her head. She didn't trust herself to speak logically to Sebastian at the moment; she was too concerned about Lisa. She thought of the little girl's misery and was overwhelmed by a sensation of nauseous sickness. She had felt slightly unwell when she first woke up and had put it down to the richness of the food at dinner last night and the fact that her system had still not grown accustomed to eating so late.

'You are not well?' Señor Alvarez had seen her pale face and hurried to her side.

'It's nothing,' she assured him. 'I'm fine now.' She saw the glance he and Sofia exchanged and was puzzled by it, until she murmured discreetly to her,

'I have noticed on a few occasions recently that you have not seemed well. Could it be . . .?'

It was a few minutes before Jessica realised what she meant. Could she be carrying Sebastian's child? Surely it was too soon to know, and besides, there had only been those two occasions . . .

One of which would have been more than enough, she reminded herself grimly, panic clawing through her at the implications. She wasn't ready yet for the responsibility of a child. Her relationship with Sebastian was too fraught with difficulties; they had no right to bring a child into such an insecure marriage. Children should be wanted, surrounded with love and care.

She was letting her imagination run away with her, she decided later, as she listened to Señor Alvarez speaking quickly to Sebastian. She probably wasn't pregnant at all.

'Sebastian is returning immediately,' he told them. 'Meanwhile we must do all we can to find her.'

Señor Alvarez quickly took command, much to Jessica's relief. They were each given different sections of the house to seach, apart from Luisa, who elected to help Jorge with his.

Jessica walked with them to the top of the stairs, thinking it was a pity that if Sebastian had to arrange a marriage for his brother he didn't do so with pretty little Luisa, who plainly was quite ready to fall in love with him, just as he was with her.

She was halfway through her own part of the *hacienda* when suddenly a thought struck her. She hurried downstairs and out into the courtyard, ignoring the heavy rain as she dashed across to the stables. She had hoped to find Enrico, who was in charge of the horses there, but he had obviously taken shelter somewhere, because the place was deserted. The first thing Jessica noticed as she approached the building Lisa had shown her was that the roof was dipping badly under a weight of water. Once inside she realised that it was also leaking because the floor was damp, but she didn't waste any time worrying about the dampness, hurrying instead across to the cellar door, wrenching it open and anxiously calling Lisa's name. The light was on, and she thought she heard a faint reply, when suddenly almost overhead there was a terrific clap of thunder. She eyed the steps uncertainly. Moisture trickled down the walls, the light was dull and pale, and she felt an increasing aversion to go down, but Lisa might be down there, hurt or frightened. She hesitated, wondering whether to dash back to the house, acknowledging that she should have gone to Señor Alvarez in the first place and told him of her fears. She was just about to go when she heard a sound. Straining her ears, she caught it again. Lisa! She was down there!

'Don't worry, Lisa,' she called out, 'I'm coming down!'

She had almost reached the bottom when she heard a sound, a dull heavy rumbling which she tried to tell herself was thunder, but which instinct told her was something much worse. The only sound she had ever heard to resemble it was avalanches witnessed on television, and there was certainly no snow on the *hacienda*. There was water, though, she reflected nervously, remembering the dilapidated roof, bowing under the weight of water. If that roof collapsed! She daren't allow herself to think about it. Terror clawed painfully at her stomach and she crossed her hands protectively over it, knowing in a blinding moment of realisation that she *did* want Sebastian's child.

Somehow the thought that she might already have conceived it made her feel all the more protective towards Lisa. Half running, half stumbling, she hurried down the steep steps, searching the cavern at the bottom with frantic intensity, until she saw the little girl at the farthest end, her face tear-stained.

'Oh, Lisa!'

'Jessica, I can't get up,' Lisa cried plaintively. 'I fell and hurt my ankle. I thought I was going to be here for ever!'

'Hush, darling, it's all right,' Jessica comforted her, hurrying over and crouching on the floor beside her. 'Let me look,' she said gently, running her fingers over the little girl's leg and ankle-bone. She thought it was more sprained than broken, but she couldn't let Lisa risk putting any weight on it. She would have to carry her out.

'Put your arms round my neck,' she instructed, 'and hold on tight. It might hurt a little bit, but just think of how quickly we're going to be back in the house. You gave us all a nasty fright, you know,' she went on, talking quietly as she tried to make Lisa as comfortable as she could. 'Tio Sebastian is coming back from Seville to help us look for you.'

'But you found me,' Lisa protested drowsily, gasping as Jessica tried to lift her. Dear God, what if she had banged her head when she fell? She could have concussion—anything! Should she leave her and go and get help?

'Don't let Tio send me to school, will you?' Lisa begged tearfully.

'Is that why you came down here, so you wouldn't have to go to school?'

Lisa shook her head. 'I just wanted to think,' she said simply, and they both winced as they heard a loud rumbling overhead.

'Only thunder,' Jessica said firmly. She glanced upwards and stared in horror at the crack appearing in the arched ceiling. Dirt and rubble trickled down, spattering on to the floor, the light bulb swinging wildly before the cavern was suddenly plunged into darkness. With the light gone Jessica's ears became attuned to sounds she had not heard before—the steady trickling of moisture on the walls, the ominous rumblings from above them, and the slowly increasing dribble of debris through the now invisible crack in the ceiling.

She couldn't possibly leave Lisa now, Jessica acknowledged. In fact neither of them could stay where they were for a moment longer than they had to.

'We've got to move,' she told the little girl, relieved when Lisa answered in a matter-of-fact if somewhat breathless voice,

'Yes, otherwise the roof might fall in on us, mightn't it?'

'Well, just hold on tight,' Jessica cautioned her.

Surely the best thing to do would be to feel her way along the wall. That way they were more likely to avoid any cave-in. It was a painfully laborious task inching her way along the wall, trying her best not to jar Lisa's ankle. She had no idea how far they had gone when they both heard the sudden crack above, and it was only blind instinct that sent her stumbling for the stairs, her head bent over Lisa's as they were showered with debris and the water that cascaded through the hole in the ceiling.

She could have cried with relief when she felt the first step; she had been terrified that they were going to be trapped by the falling ceiling. Her body was trembling with tiredness and relief when they finally reached the top stair. She fumbled for the catch and pushed, but the door refused to open. She tried again, forcing her whole weight behind it, and still it refused to move.

'Something must have blocked it,' Lisa murmured apprehensively. 'What are we going to do?'

'We're going to sit here and wait for someone to come and unblock it,' Jessica told her, trying to appear calm.

'But no one knows we're here.'

It was all too dreadfully true. What could she say? Taking a deep breath, Jessica lied, 'Oh yes, they do—I told Jorge I thought you might be here, but I didn't say anything before, because I didn't think you'd want me to tell anyone else about your secret place.'

'Now four of us know,' Lisa replied drowsily. 'You, me, Tio Sebastian and Tio Jorge.'

Yes, Sebastian knew, but did he care enough about either of them to think of looking here? Eventually someone was bound to notice that the roof had caved in, but they might not realise that they had been trapped in the cellar.

Dreadful pictures flashed through her mind, stories of walled-up nuns and petrified skeletons tormenting her until she wanted to scream and beat on the door until it gave way, but if she did that it would only upset Lisa. She would perhaps never know whether she had been carrying Sebastian's child, and he would have lost another bride, although this time ... She sighed and shivered as the cold sliced through to her bones.

Lisa's teeth were chattering; the little girl was only wearing a flimsy dress and Jessica pulled off her own knitted jacket, draping it round her shoulders and pulling her into the warmth of her own body.

Time dragged by. Jessica wasn't wearing a watch, and the only sounds to break the silence were their own voices and the ominous cracking sounds as more of the ceiling gave way.

Lisa started to cry. 'We'll be trapped in here for ever,' she sobbed. 'We'll never get out!'

'Of course we will. Look, I'll tell you a story, shall I?'

She did her best, inventing impossible characters and situations, but she only had a tiny portion of Lisa's concentration.

'Stop!' she insisted at one point. 'Jessica, I thought I heard something.'

Her heartbeat almost drowning out her ability to say anything else, Jessica listened. There were sounds ... faint, but clearly discernible from those of the falling ceiling.

'We must shout,' Lisa urged, 'so that they know we're here.'

'No, we'll tap on the door instead,' Jessica told her, terrified that if they shouted the reverberations might be enough to bring down what was left of the ceiling.

She tapped, and there was no response, and no matter how much she strained her ears she could hear nothing from the other side of the door. Perhaps they had simply imagined those sounds after all, perhaps there wasn't anyone there—or even worse, perhaps someone had been and gone.

'We must keep tapping,' she told Lisa doggedly, not wanting the little girl to lose heart.

Her wrist was aching with the effort of supporting Lisa and trying to tap on the door at the same time, when at last she heard a faint but unmistakable response. Just to be sure she tapped again—Morse code learned when she was a girl and only dimly remembered, the same definite pattern of sounds coming back to her.

Tears of relief poured down her face. Her chest

felt tight with pain, and she could scarcely think for relief.

The sounds outside the door became louder and took on definite patterns; at the same time more of the roof came crashing down, bricks and rubble falling sharply on to the steps. It was a race between life and death, Jessica thought, shivering at the knowledge, and they were the prize.

A piece of brick fell on her foot, but she scarcely felt any pain. She was so cold her body was practically numb.

'How long to you think it will be?' Lisa asked huskily. 'I'm so cold, Jessica!'

'Not long now,' she comforted her. There was a splintering sound above them, followed by a high-pitched whine. In the darkness Jessica could see nothing, but she could feel a faint dust settling on her face. They must be cutting through the door. A tiny glimmer of light appeared, followed by a small hole.

'Jessica?' It was Sebastian's voice, crisp and sharp. 'Jessica, where are you?'

'We're here,' she told him tiredly, hugging Lisa. 'At the top of the steps.'

'Listen carefully, then. The roof has collapsed and the door is jammed. We're going to cut the top half away, but whatever you do, don't move from where you are. We think there's been some subsidence underneath and the shift of your weight might cause the steps to collapse.'

'Lisa's hurt her ankle,' she told him, 'but I think it's only sprained.'

There were sounds of further activity beyond the door. The thin beam of light grew and at last she could see Lisa's face. She could also see how precarious their position was. Where the cellar had been there was simply a mound of rubble, and she shuddered to think of their fate had they been trapped beneath it. Several of the lower steps were already cracked, and even as she watched the cracks deepened and spread. At last the buzzing of the saw ceased, and light flooded their prison. She looked up, joy and love flooding her eyes as she saw Sebastian looking down at them.

'Take Lisa first,' she told him, lifting the little girl. His face was smudged with dirt, his hair ruffled and untidy, a curiously bleak expression in his eyes.

'Sebastian, hurry, the whole thing's going to go at any minute!' she heard Jorge call behind him, and she realised that Sebastian was alone in the crumbling shell of the building.

She also realised that she couldn't scramble over the half door without some help and that she would have to stay here alone while he carried Lisa to safety. He seemed to hesitate as though he guessed her fear, but she forced a smile, and lifted Lisa towards him.

His arms closed round her and he turned. Watching his back disappear into the darkness was the most terrifying and lonely feeling Jessica had ever experienced. When he disappeared she wanted to claw and tear at the wood in panic, but no matter how much she stretched she couldn't get over the wooden barrier. Behind her she heard a dull crack, and gasped in horror as half the steps suddenly disappeared, leaving her clinging to the door.

'Jessica, Jessica, it's all right, I've got you!' Strong arms clamped round her body, lifting her upwards, as she clung unashamedly to their warm strength.

It was only as he lifted her over the door that Jessica realised the appalling risks Sebastian had run. The building was completely demolished, a yawning chasm gaped beneath them. As Sebastian carried her to safety she heard a dull rumble, and glanced over his shoulder just in time to see the ground sliding away, taking the remnants of the building with it.

'It's the rain,' Jorge muttered as Sebastian reached him. Señor Alvarez was with him, holding Lisa, and both men were soaked to the skin, their faces anxious and drawn. Jessica hadn't even realised it was still raining until that moment, and she felt she had never enjoyed anything quite as much as the rain against her skin, and the cold breeze blowing down from the Sierras. 'It eroded away the ground beneath and the sheer weight of the building caused it to collapse.'

'If Sebastian hadn't remembered Lisa's "secret place" we might never have found you,' Señor Alvarez said gravely as they hurried towards the house. 'It is a blessing that he reached you in time.'

It was indeed, Jessica reflected numbly, shivering with the cold that seemed to reach into her bones, despite the warmth of Sebastian's arms.

In the house Tia Sofia was waiting, fear etched deeply into her face until she saw the two burdens Sebastian and Jorge were carrying.

'Lisa has hurt her ankle,' Jorge told her quickly. 'Doctor . . .'

'I shall telephone him now . . . but first we must get them upstairs and out of those wet things. Tia, you help Lisa, I . . .'

Lisa murmured a protest and begged feverishly for her aunt Jessica. 'Go with Lisa, Tia Sofia,' Sebastian said quietly. 'I can help Jessica.'

Jessica wanted to protest, to tell him that she was too weak now to endure the touch of his hands on her body without betraying her love—a love he did not want. She knew that now. She had seen rejection in his eyes when he turned away from her by the cellar door when she had looked at him with her heart in hers.

He took her to a room she had never seen before, richly furnished in peaches and greens.

'You will want to be alone,' he told her almost curtly. 'This was my mother's room, it is part of the suite she shared with my father. I once said that when I married my wife would always share my bed, but there are times . . .' He paused by the door. 'I am sorry about the child. I did not intend that it should happen,' and then he was depositing her on the bed, ignoring the dark smudges she was making on the silk coverlet.

The child? Did he mean . . .? But . . .

He disappeared into the bathroom, re-emerging several seconds later with a sponge and towel.

'Tia Sofia told me,' he said quietly. 'She was concerned for you and wanted me to know.'

'She may be mistaken,' Jessica told him, as a terrible pain tore at her heart. He didn't want her and he didn't want their child.

'Perhaps.' He didn't sound convinced. 'Come,

let me sponge your skin, and then I will leave you in peace. You will feel better directly.'

She would never feel better again, Jessica thought numbly as he sponged away the dirt and dust, treating her as though she were a child of Lisa's age. The warmth of the room was making her feel sleepy, soothing away the intense cold that had gripped her in the cellar.

Sebastian finished his self-imposed task and reached for the towel, and Jessica looked at him. His face seemed almost austere, and for the first time she could see the ascetic in him. 'You had a lucky escape.' He said it almost broodingly, and Jessica wondered bitterly if he had hoped that she wouldn't.

'It was lucky for us that you knew about Lisa's special place,' she told him.

His mouth tightened and he seemed about to say something, but instead he simply dried her body, then pushed back the covers. As he lifted her and slid her beneath the sheets, Jessica had a wild longing to reach up to him and beg him to stay with her, to take her in his arms and heal her aching body with the beneficence of his. But what was the point? He didn't want her; he didn't want their child. He probably wished he had never married her.

She was almost asleep when the doctor came, accompanied to her disappointment by Tia Sofia and not Sebastian. He examined her thoroughly, smiled at her and told her that she was a very brave young lady and that she had had a lucky escape.

'It is fortunate that your pregnancy is so little advanced,' he added calmly, 'otherwise . . .'

So it was true. She was carrying Sebastian's child. Tears stung her eyes and she longed for things to be different, for him to want their child as much as she did herself.

She thought later that she must have been given something to help her sleep, because she was suddenly aware of feeling oddly lightheaded, with a longing to close her eyes. When she opened them again it was morning, and the sun was dancing on the ceiling of her bedroom.

Her bedroom! She felt like a small child banished for a sin it didn't know it had committed. Why had Sebastian put her in this room? Perhaps because he could no longer endure her presence in his room, in his bed. Perhaps the fact that she carried his child reminded him too much of the past, of Manuela who he had loved as he would never love her, but he had not kept faith with Manuela. He was denying their child. It was a strangely cowardly act for so brave a man. He hadn't hesitated to risk his own life to save both hers and Lisa's.

The day dragged. She was to stay in bed for several days, Tia Sofia told her when she came to see her. Lisa's ankle was merely sprained and she too was confined to bed. Jorge and Luisa wanted to come and see her.

'And Sebastian?' Jessica asked, dry-mouthed.

'He has had to go to Seville on business,' Sofia told her, avoiding her eyes. 'He will come and see you when he comes back.' There was pity in her eyes. 'Do not distress yourself, Jessica. Think of the child you carry and let that give you hope.'

Jessica was alone when the door opened later in the afternoon and Pilar came in. As always she was dressed impeccably and expensively, her face and nails fit to grace a *Vogue* cover.

'Ah, you are awake—that is excellent,' she purred with one of the coy smiles that Jessica dreaded. 'We can have a little talk.'

'What about?' Jessica asked wearily.

'Why, Sebastian, of course, and your folly in believing you could possibly hold him. He only married you out of pity and compunction because he thought he had wronged you. You must know that?'

She did, of course, but she realised that Maria didn't like Pilar saying so. 'And now you carry his child and you believe, foolishly, that it will give you the key to his heart. It won't. His heart . . .'

'Belongs to your sister. Yes, I know,' Jessica agreed tiredly. 'But I am his wife, Pilar, and I am to have his child.'

'His wife, yet you have separate rooms,' Pilar pointed out maliciously. 'His child . . . Yes, but men can easily have children, you cannot hope to keep him because of that. You would do better to leave now, before he asks you to do so. It must be obvious to you that he doesn't want you; that your marriage was a mistake from the start. Sebastian doesn't want you—if he did why would he move you in here?' she asked scornfully. 'He is a deeply passionate and sensual man, not a man who would give his wife her own bedroom unless he was trying to tell her something. I shall leave you now,' she finished softly, sweeping towards the door, 'but think about what I have said and soon, I am sure, you will realise that I speak the truth.'

She was gone before Jessica could retaliate, leaving her with the sickening knowledge that what she had said was probably the truth. Sebastian didn't want her, and if she had any pride, any backbone, she would leave, just as soon as she was able to!

CHAPTER TEN

'JESSICA, how are you feeling now? Tia Sofia says that you are well enough to receive visitors, but that I am not to tire you out.'

Jessica smiled at Jorge. 'How is Lisa?' she asked. 'I haven't seen her yet.'

'Recuperating faster than you. Dr Bartolo told Sebastian that if you hadn't shielded her from the cold with your coat she might well have been much worse. She has a weak chest,' he explained, 'something she inherited from her mother, and if she had got badly cold it would be aggravated. On the other hand, our good doctor is very concerned about you. He says you are too pale and drawn. You do look pale.'

'I'm just a little tired. How is everyone else, Señor Alvarez and Luisa?'

'Very well, but soon their visit ends. Señor Alvarez has invited me to visit them in Argentina,' Jorge said carelessly. 'Of course, it all depends on whether Sebastian will let me go.'

'Have you told him how you feel about Luisa?' Jessica asked him.

Jorge shook his head. 'I've never known him so unapproachable,' he admitted. 'I just don't know what's got into him.'

She did, Jessica reflected. He was feeling the strain of being tied to a marriage he didn't want. Pilar was right; it would be best if she left.

Jorge was just confiding in her how much he

wanted to go to Argentina, when the door opened and Sebastian walked in. Jessica's first thought was that he looked drained and tired; her second that he was furiously, bitterly angry.

'Er . . . I'll come back and chat to you later,' Jorge muttered to her, obviously also seeing the anger in his brother's eyes.

'What was he doing here?' Sebastian demanded angrily, when Jorge had gone. 'You are supposed to be resting!'

'He came to talk to me.'

'Just to talk?' His mouth twisted aggressively. 'Did he have to sit on your bed simply to talk to you?' Jessica couldn't understand his mood. He seemed bitterly antagonistic towards Jorge, for some unknown reason. 'And what was he talking about?'

'He was telling me that Señor Alvarez had invited him to visit Argentina, and how much he wanted to go. I suspect he thought I might be able to plead his cause with you,' Jessica added with wry self-mockery.

'Dr Bartolo tells me that you are not recovering as fast as he had hoped,' he told her with an abrupt change of front. 'He believes a change of scene might be beneficial for you. Perhaps a visit to your family.'

Jessica felt as though all the breath were being squeezed out of her lungs. It was true, he did want to get rid of her.

She turned away so that he wouldn't see the pain in her eyes. '*Por Dios,*' *he* muttered savagely, 'did you not think to tell someone where you were going? Did it not occur to you that no one knew where you were? If I hadn't thought on the long drive back from Seville of the *pequeña*'s secret place, both of you could have died there!'

'Much you would have cared!' Jessica flung at him bitterly. 'Your own child, and you talk about sending her away to some convent—and not even to one of those close enough to her to soften the blow! You tell Pilar, who you must know hates her, even though she is her sister's child. Well, that isn't going to happen to my baby! Poor Lisa, she doesn't even know she is your child, but everyone else does; how can you keep the truth from her for ever? Haven't you thought of her pain and disillusionment when she discovers the truth, possibly at a time when it can do her the most harm?'

'Lisa—my child?' He frowned down at her, making her feel conscious of her flushed cheeks and undoubtedly tousled hair. 'What are you talking about?' he grated. 'Lisa is not my child!'

'I know that's the polite fiction you would want to preserve, but I've been told differently. She's Manuela's child, conceived during the time of your betrothal.'

'Who told you this?'

Jessica trembled under the look of biting anger he gave her. 'I . . .'

'No matter . . . You believed it, whoever told you. You think I would actually dishonour the girl I was to have married? A virgin?'

There was so much horror in his voice that Jessica felt acute jealousy of Manuela.

'I am not talking about dishonour, Sebastian,' she said tiredly. 'You loved her and she loved you. What could be more natural . . .'

'*Dios*, you talk as though you were reading a

fairy-tale!' he snapped at her. 'And what you say contains about as much truth. Manuela did have a child out of wedlock and that child is Lisa, but she is not my child.' He saw her expression and smiled bitterly. 'You don't believe me? I assure you it is quite true, although no one knows the truth apart from myself and Pilar. Perhaps I had best tell you the whole and then there will be no more of these hysterical accusations about my lack of feelings towards my "child".

'Manuela's family and mine had always been close friends, through several generations. The idea of a marriage between us was first mooted when we were quite small, as is our custom, and both of us grew up knowing we were destined to marry, although we were more like brother and sister. The year Manuela was eighteen we were to marry. When she was seventeen we were formally betrothed; it was then that Manuela's father confided to me that he had been seriously worried by her suddenly changed behaviour. There were wild moods, fits of tears, terrible emotional storms that blew up out of nothing. It was decided that she would go to South America to spend some time with relatives over there. Her father felt that the change would do her good. We parted as the friends we were. If our relationship was not all that I could have hoped for from marriage, it was pleasant and undemanding. I would be free to make a life for myself as long as I was discreet. There would be children.' He broke off when he saw Jessica's expression.

'There is no need for your pity,' he told her

brusquely. 'It is an accepted code of behaviour that harms no one. While Manuela was away I prepared for our wedding. She was to return two weeks before our wedding day. I have since learned from Pilar that her father feared if she returned any sooner her bouts of hysteria might overcome her. Pilar was already married at this time and had no idea how serious Manuela's condition had become.

'She had been away eight months, but I barely recognised her when she returned. I met her at the airport, and she was swathed in black garments, her face haggard and pale. She refused to see me when I called at the house. "Wedding nerves", her mother told me.

'A week before our marriage was due to take place I received a phone call from the hospital in Seville. Manuela had been involved in a car accident and was asking for me. They gave me no hint of whether she was injured or how badly, and it was only when I got there that they told me she was not likely to live. They also told me that she was seven months pregnant, and knowing of our betrothal they had imagined that the child was mine and had called me to ask my permission to try to save its life even though they couldn't save Manuela's.

'Of course I telephoned her parents, but they refused to come to the hospital, so great was their shame. How on earth they had expected her condition to go unnoticed at the ceremony I do not know, but it seems they believed by some miracle that once we were married, everything would be all right.

'I didn't know what to do, and then, briefly,

Manuela regained consciousness. She told me her lover had been someone she had met in Argentina, someone she loved in a way that she could never love me. She knew she was going to die and begged my forgiveness, urging me to try to save the life of her child and look after it. I learned later from . . . connections in South America that her lover had also been married, something he had obviously neglected to tell her, and in some ways I wonder if it was not kinder that she should have her brief moment of happiness and then oblivion before it was destroyed by the realisation that she had been deceived.

'I stayed with her until the end. She died just after Lisa was born, and I'll never forget the look on her face when she opened her eyes and saw her child. I vowed then that I would bring Lisa up as though she had been our child. I suppose it is inevitable that people should think she was mine.'

'I'm so sorry,' Jessica managed in a husky whisper. 'I should never . . . You must have loved Manuela dreadfully,' she added.

'Loved her?' He looked at her incredulously. 'As a brother, yes, but as a lover—no. One selfish part of me even rejoices that we did not marry. With the benefit of hindsight I can see that there was a weakness in her—not her fault, poor child, but the result of too much marrying among cousins, too much thinning of the blood. Her hysteria, and bouts of temper . . . But I am tiring you, and Dr Bartolo says that you are to rest.'

Jessica wanted to tell him that she wasn't tired. She wanted to beg him to stay, but she knew she wouldn't. Not once during their conversation had

he said anything about their marriage, and she
wondered if he was regretting it as much Pilar
had said.

Pilar had led her to believe that he still loved
Manuela, she had lied about Lisa, while
according to Sebastian . . . Was Pilar too tainted
with her sister's weakness, was that perhaps why,
in spite of the obvious suitability of it, he had not
married her? She wanted him, Jessica knew that,
and she would stop at nothing to get him, she
acknowledged with a sudden flash of insight. Her
possessiveness was almost maniacal.

Two days passed and Dr Bartolo pronounced
that Jessica was well enough to get up. Sebastian
as always was scrupulously polite when he saw
her, which seemed to be more and more
infrequently. When they did talk, it was about
the factory, the designs—polite, distant conversation that tore at her heart, leaving it bruised and
aching. She couldn't stay any longer, she
admitted one afternoon after he had gone to
inspect the vines, and she was alone in the house,
Lisa and Tia Sofia were out visiting, and Jorge
had taken Señor Alvarez and Luisa on a
sightseeing expedition.

Only that lunchtime Sebastian had mentioned
in conversation that he had been making enquiries
about a flight to England for her. His aunt had
looked surprised when he mentioned that she
might go for a visit, and Jessica had tried to hide
the hurt in her eyes that he was so anxious to get
rid of her.

And he never even mentioned their child. Dr
Bartolo had confirmed that she was indeed

pregnant, but Sebastian had simply compressed his mouth and looked grimly distant when, falteringly, she told him that her condition was confirmed.

Perhaps now was the time to leave, she thought miserably, before the decision was forced on her. Oh, she knew Sebastian would disguise it in the guise of sending her home for a 'holiday', but they both knew that she would not be coming back. There was simply no point.

Many of her things were still in Sebastian's room, and now would be a good time to retrieve them. She was busily engaged in removing clothes from cupboards and they were on the bed in neat piles when the door was suddenly flung open. She straightened, her heart pounding, half longing and half fearing to see Sebastian. Only it wasn't Sebastian, it was Pilar, her face contorted with a rage that made fear curl unpleasantly along Jessica's spine.

'You here!' she hissed malevolently. 'I thought I told you that Sebastian didn't want you, but then the maid tells me you are in his room!'

Jessica was just about to tell her that she was simply removing her clothes when a sudden spurt of anger—and the memory of what Sebastian had told her—moved her to say lightly, 'I am his wife, Pilar. I have a perfect right to share his room, if I want to.'

'He doesn't want you,' Pilar spat positively. 'Jesu Maria, you must know that! Sebastian is a man above all else, he would not deny himself your bed and body as he has been doing these last weeks if he desired you!'

Jessica knew that it was true, but something

compelled her to stand her ground and say calmly, 'If Sebastian has been denying himself, it is for my sake, and the sake of our child,' she added softly. 'Sebastian knows that I have . . .'

'You are to have his child?'

The bitter hatred in Pilar's eyes appalled Jessica, who realised how unwise she had been to fan the flames of the other woman's resentment. Far better to have simply told the truth. Now she was alone in the room with what she was convinced was a badly deranged woman, who was advancing on her like a panther on its prey, scarlet-tipped fingers curled into talons, as though they would like to tear into her flesh and destroy the life growing within it.

'All these years I have waited for him to turn to me,' Pilar said softly, 'all these years of waiting and watching, knowing he must eventually marry for the sake of his name, and then, just when I think he will be mine, you come along . . . Well, he will be mine,' she snapped venomously. 'Manuela thought she could take him from me, and was punished for it, and I shall not let you and the brat you carry come between me and what is rightfully mine!'

She was mad—she had to be, Jessica thought shakily as she stared at the wild eyes and twisted features. But she was also dangerous, and Jessica could almost feel those fingers on her throat, gripping it, depriving her of breath.

She backed into the corner, realising too late that it was the wrong thing to do. Pilar was stalking her like a cat with its prey, a rictus smile twisting the full lips. She lunged, her hands reaching for Jessica's throat, her wildly exultant laughter filling the room.

The door was suddenly flung open and Sebastian was standing there, his jacket thrown carelessly over one shoulder, his shirt unbuttoned at the neck, tiredness lying in the shadows and hollows of his face. His expression changed as he took in the scene, alertness replacing his earlier exhaustion.

'Pilar-*Dios*, what are you about?' He gripped her arms, dragging her away from Jessica and opening the door, as he called to someone outside.

Dr Bartolo came hurrying in, his expression one of shock as he looked at Pilar and saw the murderous intent in her eyes.

'Allow me to deal with this, my friend,' he said sorrowfully to Sebastian. 'I have been afraid for a long time that . . .' He broke off as Jessica felt herself succumbing to the eddying whirls of blackness trying to suck her down.

'I'm all right,' Jessica managed to assure him. 'Just a little faint. I . . .'

'She wanted to take you from me, Sebastian!' Pilar cried bitterly. 'I told her you were mine. I . . .'

'Pilar, you must come with me,' Dr Bartolo said firmly. 'She needs specialised treatment,' he murmured in an aside to Sebastian. 'Her behaviour has troubled me for a long time, but there is a clinic I know of where they are used to cases of this kind. She has allowed her feelings for you to become obsessive.'

Pilar allowed herself to be led out of the room, and Jessica fought off the attack of faintness that had threatened her. Her legs felt weak and shaky, but when Sebastian moved towards her she fended him off, her expression unknowingly one of sharp horror.

'I am sorry about that,' he said flatly. He had his back to her, and walked across the door leading out into the courtyard. 'I should have warned you about Pilar, but she had seemed so much improved . . . She has already suffered two breakdowns; on each occasion she convinced herself that she was deeply in love with the victim of her obsession. I am sorry that you had to be involved.'

He turned round, his eyes going to the neat pile of clothes, his expression changing, darkening. 'What is this?'

'My clothes,' Jessica told him quietly. 'I was just getting them when Pilar came in. I suppose finding me here in your room was the last straw.'

'If you wish your clothes moved from my room to yours one of the maids can do it,' he told her brusquely. 'There is no need for you . . .'

'To invade your privacy?' Jessica suggested shakily. 'You needn't worry about it happening again. I'm removing my clothes, because I'm also removing myself from your life. I'm going home.'

'No!' The denial was grittily abrasive. '*Por Dios*,' Sebastian suddenly added hoarsely, crossing the room and taking her roughly in his arms. 'I can endure no more—I will not permit you to go! You are carrying my child, and I will not allow you to go.'

'But you wanted me to go,' Jessica reminded him shakily, wondering if he could feel the unsteady thud of her heart, and the quick race of her pulse. His arms felt like a haven—heaven itself, and she never wanted to leave them. She could see the faint beginnings of a beard growing along his jaw, and wanted to touch it. He smelled of the outdoors and fresh sweat, and the combination was unbearably erotic to her heightened senses.

'Because I feared something like this would happen.'

Within the circle of his arms, she raised her hand to push her hair back off her forehead, the brief gesture emphasising the gentle thrust of her breasts. Sebastian's eyes flared hotly as he studied the soft mounds, then with a savage imprecation he drew her against the hard pulsating length of him, letting her feel his arousal, his mouth moving blindly over her skin, touching and tasting, until he buried it hotly in hers, kissing her with an intensity that sapped her willpower and made her cling helplessly to him, offering herself up to whatever it was he wanted from her.

'I won't let you leave me,' he muttered throatily against her skin. 'You are mine, Jessica, and mine alone. *Dios*, the torment I have suffered seeing you smile at my brother, my aunt—anyone but me! You cannot know how I have longed to see you look at me with love, how I have hungered for you to want me as I want you—not simply for the pleasure our bodies find in one another, but with your heart and soul!'

She was unbearably moved, unable to deny the conviction in his voice, the emotion in his eyes as they searched her face as though willing a response.

'You love me?' Jessica asked uncertainly, still not fully able to accept.

'Do you doubt it?' He smoothed her hair back off her forehead, and she could feel the heated shudder of his body as she touched him. 'I wanted you from the first,' he told her softly. 'I hated you at the same time because of what you were. Or what I thought you were.'

'I thought you despised me,' Jessica told him. 'You were so cold, so distant.'

'Because I daren't let myself be anything else. All the time I was giving myself reasons why I shouldn't, all I wanted to do was to take you in my arms and make you admit that no man could give you the pleasure I could. I hated Jorge because he had been your lover, and when you threatened to stay in Seville and see him. I couldn't understand why he had stopped wanting you. I thought if he saw you again, he would do . . .'

'And so you concocted that tale about needing a designer to save him from me,' Jessica supplied dryly.

Sebastian smiled grimly. 'Nearly right, only it was because I wanted to keep you away from him and with me,' he supplemented. 'And then he arrived and my whole world was turned upside down. You weren't the girl he had met, you were someone else; someone about whom I knew nothing. Someone who might have a lover or a boy-friend in the background whose claims on you I couldn't destroy. And then Jorge gave me the perfect weapon. People were talking about us, he told me. He was concerned for you. I knew my aunt and Pilar intended to come and see you. I must admit I hadn't quite intended that we should be discovered as we were . . . some things cannot be controlled,' he added with a wry mockery that brought vivid colour to her skin, 'and you were so sweetly responsive I forgot why I had come to your room and remembered only how much I wanted you ... loved you,' he amended softly, 'because by then I did, although I was loath to admit it even to myself.'

'But when you married me you were so distant I thought you hated me!'

He cupped her face and looked at her sombrely. 'Why didn't you tell me you were a virgin? Was it to punish me, to make me suffer?'

Jessica didn't understand what he meant.

'I tried to,' she told him huskily, 'in the car on the way back to the *hacienda*, but you told me how relieved you were that I didn't need "initiating" and after that I just couldn't ...'

'And so instead you make me suffer a thousand torments, hating myself for what I have done to you. It was bad enough when I simply thought I was forcing you into a marriage you didn't want. There was desire between us and I hoped that in time it might grow to something else. When I discovered that not only had I robbed you of your freedom, but that I had also taken from you the right to give your body and sweet innocence to the lover of your choice, I hated and despised myself ...'

'You were so cold,' Jessica whispered, 'so distant, and so hateful.'

'Because it was the only way I could stop myself from taking you in my arms and making love to you again and again,' Sebastian told her whimsically. 'I wanted you so much, I had to erect a barrier between us for your sake. I wanted to get down on my knees and beg your forgiveness, kiss every inch of your beautiful, precious body and promise you that never again would it know pain, but to do so would be to inflict my desire and love on you again, and I told myself that was something I would never do.

'We both know how long my resolve lasted,' he added wryly, adding with a frankness that half shocked her, 'Your sweet cries of pleasure on that second occasion have haunted my nights like a siren song ever since.'

'You made me sleep on my own,' Jessica accused, still not daring to believe that it was true and that he loved her.

He smothered a groan. 'My sweet love, it was torture, but I had no alternative. I had promised myself that I would set you free, that it was wrong of me to hold you to our marriage. I couldn't forgive myself for taking your innocence when you didn't love me, and when I discovered you were to have my child . . .'

'You were so cold towards me I thought you didn't want it,' Jessica interrupted bleakly. 'Then Pilar came and told me that you wanted me to leave, and . . .'

'And you already believed that I had turned my back on my daughter,' he finished for her. 'Oh, Jessica, I can't tell you what it meant to me to think you carried my child! I longed fiercely to keep you here with me, but I couldn't do it. I couldn't hold you on so fragile a thread. I'm a proud man, as you have so often said, and my pride would not allow me to constrain my wife to stay with me only for the sake of our child.'

'But if she loved you . . .'

He cupped her chin, his eyes dark with emotion. 'If she loved me—if you loved me,' he corrected huskily, 'I would never let her go. When I saw that building and knew you were in it . . . If you had died then life would have had no meaning for me,' he told her simply.

'You risked your life for us,' Jessica said softly. 'I . . .'

'Do you think I would have let anyone else near you?' he demanded with a ferocity that surprised her. 'When everything a man holds of value in his life is in danger of course he trusts no one but himself to remove that danger. When you told me to take Lisa, even though I knew you were right, you'll never know what it cost me to go, leaving you there, possibly facing death.'

'And you'll never know how I felt, seeing you disappear,' Jessica told him softly, 'wanting you so badly . . . and then you were so cold, putting me in that bedroom when all I wanted was the warmth of your arms, your . . .'

'My . . .?' he questioned teasingly. 'Go on, *querida*, you are just about to get to the interesting bit, I think?'

'Your . . . body against mine,' Jessica admitted hesitantly, laughing at her own shyness. 'Oh, Sebastian,' she sighed ecstatically, 'I fell in love with you almost straight away, despite all those dreadful things you said to me!'

She frowned as Sebastian suddenly released her, picking up the piles of clothes from the bed and depositing them on a chair.

'What are you doing?' she asked anxiously. 'Sebastian . . .'

'I thought you wanted to be in my arms,' he

reminded her with a slow smile, 'to feel my body against yours? Is that not right, *querida*?'

'Oh, but . . .' She tried to look scandalised and failed, laughing when he took her in his arms and said wryly,

'What is the matter? Is it not permissible for a man to make love to his wife in the afternoon?'

'I . . .'

He nibbled the delicate cord of her throat, sending tremors of pleasure coursing over her. 'Why else do you think we have the *siesta*, *amada*?' he questioned softly. 'It is for children to rest, and for their *mamás* and *papás* to make love.'

His fingers reached for her zip, pressing her against the taut length of his body, and the sudden urgency of the desire flooding through her made her expel her breath in brief shock.

'I love you,' Sebastian murmured smokily as her dress slid to the floor.

As he lifted her and carried her towards their bed Jessica wondered hazily if that first Rosalinda had known this heady, enveloping pleasure; this depth and intensity of love and need for her proud knight. Possibly she had, she thought lazily as Sebastian drew her against him, his fingers playing lightly against her spine, his mouth teasing her skin. Certainly if he was anything like his present-day descendant, she must have done!

BY THE SAME AUTHOR

STRONGER THAN YEARNING
– With nothing in common but their hatred for the Deveril family, both Jenna Stevens and James Allingham needed to buy the Old Hall in recompense. Allingham was a determined opponent, but Jenny refused to allow him to stand in the way of her plans.
£3.99

POWER PLAY – Pepper Minesse has paid dearly for her success. For ten years her thirst for revenge has fuelled her ambition and made her rich. But now the four men who had raped her as a teenager must pay too – their futures for her shocking past.
£3.99

W●RLDWIDE

BY THE SAME AUTHOR

Love's Choices - A sensitive and moving story of a young girl's passionate journey into womanhood. Removed from her sheltered convent life, Hope Stanford quickly realised she was no match for the ruthless Comte Alexei Serivace, but in the sensual warmth of the Caribbean, would she finally offer a total surrender to this dangerous man?
£3.99

Silver - When her teenage love turns to hate, Geraldine Frances vows to even the score. After arranging her own "death" she embarks on a dramatic transformation, emerging as Silver, a beautiful and mysterious woman few men would be able to resist. With a new face and a new identity, she is now ready to destroy the man responsible for her tragic past.
£3.99

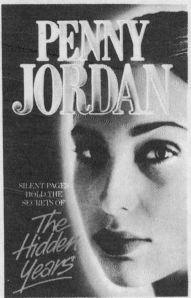

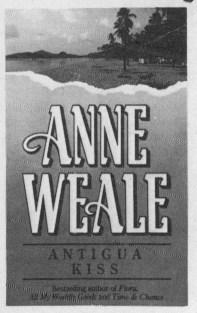

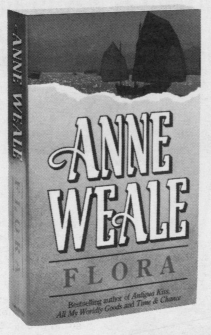